THE PLUNDERERS

[See p. 82.

TEN THOUSAND GAMBLERS' HEARTS ALMOST STOPPED WHEN
THE TICKER DID

THE PLUNDERERS

A NOVEL

BY
EDWIN LEFEVRE

Short Story Index Reprint Series

BOOKS FOR LIBRARIES PRESS
FREEPORT, NEW YORK

First Published 1916
Reprinted 1971

INTERNATIONAL STANDARD BOOK NUMBER:
0-8369-3804-6

LIBRARY OF CONGRESS CATALOG CARD NUMBER:
75-152945

PRINTED IN THE UNITED STATES OF AMERICA

CONTENTS

THE PLUNDERERS

THE PLUNDERERS

I

THE PEARLS OF THE PRINCESS PATRICIA

I

ON the day before Christmas a man of middle age, middle height, and middle weight, smooth-shaven, dressed in black and wearing black gloves, walked into the business office of the New York *Herald*. He approached the first "Advertisements" window, looked at the clerk a moment, opened his mouth, and said several words—at least, so the clerk judged from the motion of the man's lips.

"I didn't hear that, Cap," said the clerk, Ralph Carroll.

The stranger thereupon made another effort.

"You'll have to come again," Carroll told him, kindly, at the same time leaning over the counter and presenting his left ear to the voiceless talker. He heard:

"How much to print this ad under Male Help Wanted, in big type, so it will make about two inches?"

THE PLUNDERERS

He handed a slip to the clerk, which the clerk read, counting the words from sheer force of habit:

WANTED—A Man With St. Vitus's Dance and an Introspective Turn of Mind. High Wages to Right Party. Apply Saturday Morning, Room 888, St. Iago Building.

"Four-sixty-four," said the clerk.

The man raised his eyebrows inquiringly.

"Four dollars and sixty-four cents," repeated Carroll.

The man took out a wallet and tried to pull out a bank-note, but could not because of his gloved hands. He took off the right glove, fished out one five-dollar bill and gave it to the clerk, who handed him back thirty-six cents. As the man took the change the clerk distinctly noticed that he had a big ivory-colored scar which ran from the knuckles to the wrist and disappeared under the cuff. He remembered it by reason of the freak ad and the man's voice.

The advertisement appeared in the *Herald* on the next day. Being Christmas, the one day of non-reading in America, few people saw it. Nevertheless, at nine on Saturday morning, ten men with spasmodically twitching necks or limbs waited for the advertiser to open the door of Room 888, on which they saw in gilt letters:

ACME VIBRATOR COMPANY

W. W. LOVELL, Manager

The elevator man was heard to tell an inquirer, "Here's Lovell!" And presently the voiceless man, dressed as usual in black, with black gloves, stepped from the elevator, nodded to the waiting men in the hall, and opened the door of 888. At first they thought he was a mute, but realized later that he was merely saving his bronchial tubes, just as asking men to come Saturday forenoon—pay-day and pay-hours—would save effort by bringing only men without employment.

Lovell and the afflicted entered. The outer office had half a dozen chairs, and a table, on which were some medical magazines. Lovell scrutinized the ten applicants keenly, and finally beckoned to a tall, well-built chap with a blond mustache, whose unfortunate ailment was not so extreme as the others, to follow him into the inner office. The man did so. There were a desk, three chairs, a table, and a dozen polished-oak boxes that looked as though they might contain vibrators. Lovell closed the door, sat down at the desk, motioned to the blond man to approach, and whispered:

"What's your name?"

"Lewis J. Wright."

"Age?"

"Thirty-six."

"Working?"

"Not steadily."

"Profession?"

"Cabinet-maker."

"Family?"

"No."

"Do you object to traveling?"

"No; like it."

"We pay sixty dollars a week, all traveling and living expenses. Will you go to London, England?"

"To do what?"

"Nothing!"

"What?"

"Nothing!" again whispered the manager, very earnestly. He seemed anxious to convince Mr. Wright of his good intentions. "Nothing at all! Sixty a week and expenses!"

"I don't understand," said Mr. Lewis J. Wright, with an uneasy smile. His excitement aggravated the malady and his neck jerked and twitched almost constantly.

"I want a man with St. Vitus's dance."

"That's me," said L. J. Wright, and proved it.

"And with an introspective turn of mind. Understand?"

"Not quite," confessed the cabinet-maker.

"A man who likes to think about himself."

"I guess I can fill the bill all right," asserted L. J. Wright, confidently. Sixty a week, all expenses, and a trip to London began to look very attractive.

"Then you're engaged." The manager nodded.

"I don't know yet what I'm to do," ventured Wright.

"Nothing, I tell you."

"Well, I'll do it, then!" And L. J. Wright smiled tentatively; but the manager of the Acme Vibrator Company looked at him seriously—almost reprovingly—and whispered so hoarsely that Wright felt like going after cough-lozenges for him:

"Listen, Wright. You will go to London with a letter to Dr. Cephas W. Atterbury, 23, Abbey Road, St. John's Wood, N. W. Every day you will sit down in a comfortable chair in the doctor's anteroom, where the patients wait, from nine to eleven

THE PEARLS OF PATRICIA

A.M. and five to seven P.M. You will think of your St. Vitus's dance. For doing this you will get sixty dollars a week from us and your hotel bill will be paid by the doctor. You may not have to sail for a month, but your salary begins on Monday. Come here every Saturday and get twenty-five dollars on account. When you sail you will get all that's owing to you besides four weeks' salary in advance, and a round-trip ticket, first-class."

"But if I get stranded in London—"

"How can you, with three or four hundred dollars in your pocket, a return-trip ticket, and no need to spend except for clothes, which are very cheap there? Come next Saturday, but leave your name and address in case we need you. Can we depend on you?" He looked searchingly into the grayish-blue eyes of Lewis J. Wright, and seemed comforted when Lewis J. Wright answered:

"Yes. I'll go on a minute's notice." He wrote his name and address on a slip, gave it to the manager, and went out. Lovell followed him to the outer office and, beckoning to the afflicted nine to draw near, whispered:

"I've hired a man, but I shall need more soon. Write your names and addresses and leave them here. Don't come unless I send for you," and he distributed printed blanks on which each applicant wrote out his name, address, and answers to the questions:

1—Do you object to traveling alone?
2—Do you object to sitting in comfortable chairs?
3—Do you object to people making remarks about you?
4—Do you object to minding your own business or earning your wages?

5

One of the applicants spoke:

"Mr. Lovell, I'd like to know—"

Lovell, however, cut him short with a hoarse but peremptory "Don't talk! Can't answer!" pointed to his throat, and disappeared in the inner office, the door of which he closed.

Whereupon the disappointed applicants, expressing their feelings in a series of heartrending jerks, twitches, tremors, and grimaces, trooped out into the hall. There they cross-examined Wright and arrived at the conclusion that they were to be used as living advertisements for the Acme Vibrator. Doctors were employed to boom it and the company supplied dummies or "property" patients.

II

To the same clerk in the *Herald* office, a fortnight later, came the same man in black, and whispered something. The clerk recognized him, leaned over, and asked, pleasantly:

"What is it this time?" He had a good memory. He afterward remembered thinking that the hoarseness was chronic.

"How much for one inch in Help Wanted, Male?"

"Pica caps?"

The man nodded eagerly, half a dozen times.

"Two dollars and thirty-two cents."

The stranger, in trying to take the exact amount from his pocket, dropped a dime on the floor and had much difficulty in picking it up by reason of his black gloves. This naturally made the clerk remember about the scar, which the man evidently desired to conceal. Carroll, the clerk, alert-minded and imaginative—as are all American Celts—caught a glimpse of the scar between the end of the glove and the beginning of the cuff.

On the next day, the unemployed males of New York read this in the *Herald:*

WANTED—A Brave Man. Wages One Hundred Dollars a Day. No Questions Answered. Apply Room 888, St. Iago Building.

There are many brave men in New York. When W. W. Lovell stepped from the elevator at the eighth floor he had almost to force his way through a crowd of men of all kinds—brutes and dreamers; sturdy animals, and boys with romance in their eyes; fierce-visaged, roughly dressed men, and fashionably attired chaps, with high-bred, impassive faces; young men seeking adventure and old men seeking bread. Lovell was darting keen glances at the men. He let his gaze linger on a man neither short nor tall, of about forty, who suggested determination rather than reckless courage. He was shabby with the shabbiness of a man who not only has worn the clothes a long time, but has slept in them. Lovell approached him and whispered:

"Come about *Herald* ad?"

"Yes." Others drew near and listened.

"Are you really brave?" He looked anxiously into the man's face. The man, at the question and at the grins of his fellow-applicants, turned a brick-red.

"Try me!" he answered, defiantly.

"Before all these men?" There was a challenge in the hoarse whisper.

"If you want to," answered the man, with quick anger. He clenched his fists and braced his body, as for a shock.

"Come in!" and W. W. Lovell opened the door of 888.

"I'm braver than that guy!" interjected a youth, extremely broad-shouldered and thick-necked.

Mr. Lovell looked at him coldly, steadily, inquisitively, as though he would read the man's soul. He stared fully a minute and a half before the thick-set youngster dropped his gaze, whereupon Mr. Lovell pushed in the man he had picked out, followed him, and slammed the door in the faces of the others. They tried the door-knob in vain. It was a spring lock.

Mr. Lovell sat down at his desk, motioned to the man to draw near, and said, sternly:

"No questions answered!"

"I'll ask none."

Lovell gazed at him intently. He nodded to himself with satisfaction, and proceeded, in a painful whisper:

"Your name is W. W. Lowry."

The man hesitated. Lovell frowned and, leaning forward, said:

"One hundred dollars a day!"

"My name," said the man, determinedly, "is now W. W. Lowry."

"Do you know anything about travelers' checks used by the American Express Company?"

"Yes."

"Ever used any yourself?"

"No."

"Ever in Paris?"

8

"Yes."

"When?"

"When I was—er—years ago."

"How many years?"

"Ten; no—eleven!" The man's face twitched. Remembrance was evidently not pleasant.

"I'll pay you one thousand dollars for eight days' work in Paris."

"I'll take it."

"Listen carefully."

"Go ahead." The man looked alert.

"You will get a first-class ticket from New York to Paris and return, and hotel coupons for ten days in the Hotel Beraud, in Paris. You will leave, in all probability, on February first, arrive on the eighth. On the ninth you will go to the American Express office and cash some of your checks. They will serve to identify you. Do it again on February tenth. At exactly eleven minutes past eleven on the eleventh you will whisper to the mail clerk: 'It is eleven-eleven, to-day the eleventh. Give me the eleven letters for W. W. Lowry.' If you do not receive eleven letters, don't take any, but return the next day at precisely the same hour, and say exactly the same words. What was it I said you should say to the correspondence clerk?"

"It is eleven-eleven, to-day the eleventh. Give me the eleven letters for W. W. Lowry," repeated the man.

"Right! When you get the eleven letters you will bring them unopened to me—here. Now go to Mrs. Brady's boarding-house, 299 East Seventy-third Street; tell her you are Mr. Lowry. Your room and board are paid for. Make it a point to be at the house every day at eleven in the morning until after luncheon and at six P.M. You must not go out evenings under any circumstances. I'll allow you eleven dollars a week for tobacco and will bring you some clothes. Come back Wednesday at eleven-thirty. Here's this week's eleven dollars. That will be all."

"That's all right, my friend; but—" began the man.

Lovell frowned and interrupted sharply:

"No questions answered."

"I wasn't going to ask; I was going to remark that you would have to show me that one thousand dollars for the week's work."

"Next Wednesday I'll take you to the American Express Company. I'll give you one thousand dollars and you will buy the checks yourself and sign them. I'll keep them until sailing-day and I'll give them to you on the steamer. Forging," he went on with a sneer, "is signing another man's name with intent to defraud. You will sign your own name—your own signature—on travelers' checks that you yourself have paid for. See? A thousand dollars for asking for eleven letters and bringing them to me, unopened, is good graft, friend. If you make good I'll keep you busy."

"You are on!" said W. W. Lowry.

"No drinking. Above all things, no talking! I may be crazy, my friend; but what would you be if you gave up a job worth a thousand dollars a week and all expenses paid? Remember our motto: No questions answered!"

"Damned good rule!" agreed W. W. Lowry, with conviction.

"Look out for reporters and for men who say they are reporters!" warned W. W. Lovell. "When you go out, close the door quickly behind you and hang this sign on the door-knob. I don't want to see anybody."

W. W. Lowry obeyed. The sign said:

POSITION FILLED

III

A particularly beautiful limousine stopped before the door of Welch, Boon & Shaw, the renowned jewelers, on Fifth Avenue. There alighted from it, on this cold but bright January day, a tall, well-built man, erect, square-shouldered, head held high. He wore a fur-lined overcoat with a beautiful mink collar, and a mink cap. He was one of those blond-mustached, ruddy-complexioned, daily-cold-plunge British officers you sometimes see in Ottawa. He walked quickly into the shop and spoke to the first clerk he saw.

"Where's the proprietor?"

"Who?"

"The proprietor of the shop!" He spoke with a pronounced English accent. His eyes were gray and cold. They looked a trifle close together, but that may have been from the frown—said frown impressing even a casual observer as a chronic affair. His appearance, even without the frown, was aristocratic.

"Do you wish," said the clerk, politely, "to see Mr. Boon or Mr. Shaw?"

"I wish to see the man who owns this shop; the—ah—boss, I think you call it here."

"Well, Mr. Boon—" began the clerk, about to explain.

"I don't care if it's Mr. Loon or Mr. Coon. Be quick, please!" he said, peremptorily.

The clerk, now resenting the stranger's words, tone, manner, attitude, nationality, and ancestry, turned to a floor-walker person and called:

"Mr. Smith, this—ahem—gentleman wishes to see one of the firm."

Mr. Smith came forward, smiling suavely.

"You wish to see one of the firm, sir?" He bowed in advance.

"Yes. That's the third time I've said what I wish. I have no time to lose and not much patience, either!" He twitched his neck and twisted his head as though his collar were too tight. It was a habit, and it became more pronounced with his annoyance. All the clerks noticed it.

Mr. Smith bit his lip and said, very politely: "Yes, sir. It happens that none of them is in at present. If you will tell me what you wish to see them about I may suggest—"

The fur-coated man turned on his heel, his face dark red with annoyance, and started to leave the shop.

"Good-by, old Jerk-Neck!" muttered the offended clerk.

Mr. Boon entered at that very moment.

"Here's Mr. Boon, our senior partner," said Mr. Smith, with an irritation in his voice that he could not conceal, and that now gave Mr. Boon his cue.

THE PEARLS OF PATRICIA

"You wish to see me?" Mr. Boon asked it very coldly, ready to say no.

"You have an annoying set of clerks here," said the fur-coated stranger. "I wished to see one of the firm and—"

"You see him now," interrupted Mr. Boon, letting the words drop out with an effect of broken icicles. "I am Mr. Boon."

"My good man, I came after some pearl necklaces and a few rings, and trinkets. Do make haste! I am Colonel Lowther."

"Indeed! Well, what if you are Colonel Lowther?"

In Mr. Boon's eyes was a look that made all the clerks in the store busy themselves with their own affairs. Explosions scatter dangerous fragments that may injure lookers-on. The fur-coated Englishman stared at the sizzling jeweler in amazement.

"Damme!" he sputtered. "Do you mean to say— Oh—I see! Yes! I am the secretary of the Duke of Connaught. The jewels are for his Royal Highness."

The change was instantaneous and magical. They all understood now, and forgave. There wasn't a clerk in the store who did not stare with unchecked interest at the fur-coated member of the royal party, concerning which the newspapers were printing columns and columns.

The man opened his coat, took a card from a Russia-leather case, which he gave to Mr. Boon.

"Colonel the Honorable H. C. Lowther, K.C.B.," it read, "Private Secretary to H. R. H. the Duke of Connaught."

"Colonel Lowther," said Mr. Boon, in a voice from which all the icicles had melted and turned into warm honey, "I regret exceedingly that you have

13

had to wait. Had I known you were here, or if you had only mentioned who you were—"

"Exactly so. Yes! And now I'll have a few words with you in private, Boon."

The colonel could not know that Mr. Boon was not a misterless Bond Street tradesman, but a millionaire expert in gems and human vanity. So Boon forgave the omission of "Mr." and magnanimously said, "This way, Colonel Lowther, please!"

In the office Mr. Boon opened a box of his good cigars—and they were very good, indeed—and held it toward the colonel, who took one with his gloved hands, lit it at the flame of the match which Mr. Boon himself held for him, and puffed away, with never a "Thank you."

Again Mr. Boon was magnanimous.

Colonel Lowther wiggled his neck as if his collar were uncomfortably tight, and then shot his head forward with a motion that made the chin go up six inches—a nervous affliction that Mr. Boon politely ignored by looking exaggeratedly attentive.

"His Royal Highness wishes to leave some remembrances to gentlemen he has met, you know—chairmen of committees and presidents of clubs, and others who have been very nice to him. At home he would have given them snuff-boxes or cigarette-cases, with his arms on them; but there won't be time to engrave them, so he will give scarf-pins." He paused, puffed at his cigar, and cleared his neck of the constricting collar.

"I understand," Mr. Boon assured him, deferentially.

"And the duchess will give rings and—ah—lorgnette-chains—trinkets—ah—you know. Everybody in New York has been so kind to the party. 'Pon my honor, Boon, I really think Americans are keener for royalty than the British. I do! What?"

"Blood," observed Mr. Boon, with the impressive sententiousness of a man inventing a proverb, "is thicker than water!"

"Eh? What? Oh! I see! Yes! Quite so!"

"Our people," pursued the encouraged Mr. Boon, "have always thought a great deal of the English— er—British royal family."

"Oh, indeed! Now, Boon, I didn't think you showed great affection for George III! What?"

Mr. Boon blushed to think of Bunker Hill. His daughter was a D. A. R., too! He hastened to change the subject.

"You mentioned," he said, as though he were reading aloud from one of the sacred books, "some pearl necklaces. At least, I think you did." He put on the tradesman's listening look in advance. It is the look that courtiers assume when they listen to his Majesty excitedly telling how once, on a hunting-trip, he almost dressed himself.

"Oh yes! The pearls are for the Princess Patricia. A necklace to cost not over ten thousand. You see, the duke is not one of your Pittsburg millionaires. He's not what you'd call rich, in America!" He smiled, democratically, as a man always does when he is pleased with his own wit. Mr. Boon smiled uncertainly.

"You can't, of course," he said, regretfully, "do much with ten thousand dollars."

"Not dollars—pounds! Perhaps we may go up to fifteen thousand; but his Highness would prefer to keep at about ten thousand pounds. That's fifty thousand dollars."

"I am sure we can please his Highness," said Mr. Boon, with impressive confidence. There fleeted across his mind the vision of the tremendous value of the advertisement which the royal patronage would give him. The papers were full of the doings of the distinguished visitors. He himself on his way to the office had been guilty of the pardonable curiosity which the lower classes call rubber-necking; and he had even discussed—in common with 89,999,-999 fellow-Americans—the personal pulchritude of the royal ladies. Usually democracy is enabled to apologize to itself for its undemocratic interest in feminine royalty by saying, "She isn't at all good-looking." That excuse, however, did not serve in this instance. The Princess Patricia was the most popular girl in New York—with the classes because she was the princess, and with the masses because she was so pretty! And to think of selling pearls to her!

He closed his eyes and ecstatically read what the papers would print about the sale! He heard himself saying to Mrs. Carmpick, of Pittsburg: "This necklace is handsomer than the one we sold to Princess Patricia!" He heard the rattle in the throats of Johnson & Pierce, of J. Storrs' Sons, of the sixteen partners of Goffony's, dying from apoplexy superinduced by envy, or from starvation following the loss of all the swell customers!

"Ah, you realize, of course, Boon, that his Royal Highness's patronage is worth many thousands to your firm. What?"

The colonel's eyes, Mr. Boon thought, were cold

and greedy, as befitted a common grafter. Mr. Boon resented this, having himself been caught red-handed getting something for nothing. If he had to pay a commission—

"We appreciate the honor, of course, Colonel Lowther," he said, deferentially — and non-committally.

"Quite so! You ought to, considering how the newspapers will mention your shop."

"I may suggest, Colonel Lowther, that our firm's reputation—"

"I know its reputation. That's why I am here" —the colonel's voice seemed colder than a Canadian cold spell—"but it is no better than your competitors'—Goffony, Johnson & Pierce, or J. Storrs' Sons. I figured that the duke's patronage should be worth thousands to Welch, Boon & Shaw; so you must make me a special price."

"We have but one—"

"I've heard all that, Boon," the colonel interrupted, angrily. "If you are going to talk like a bally ass I'll waste no more time here. Bring in the pearls. I can't take over a half-hour to this."

Mr. Boon's hard sense and knowledge of advertising values triumphed over his injured dignity. He excused himself, and presently returned with a tray full of pearl necklaces.

"I say, Boon, on second thought, you must not reduce your prices. It's a bad principle."

"Yes, it is," agreed Boon, cordially.

"Therefore, my good fellow, name me one price— the lowest possible after considering how much the duke's patronage is worth to your house. The very lowest! Put it in plain figures on new price-tags.

The duke is accustomed to the prices across the pond, you know; so don't frighten him. Now that one?"

He picked up at once the most beautiful necklace —and also the most valuable, though by no means the most showy. Mr. Boon's respect jumped. He looked at the colonel, whose neck and head were twitching and twisting violently.

"This one—" he began. The colonel interrupted him:

"Now, Boon, think carefully—the very lowest price," he said, sternly. "If you name a really reasonable figure I'll pledge you my word to recommend its purchase and not visit the other shops. Take your time!"

Thus placed on the rack, Mr. Boon figured and cut and restored and reduced again until he was angry at the torturer and at the opportunity for a glorious advertisement. Finally he said, vindictively:

"This I'll sell for sixty-five thousand dollars!" Immediately he regretted it. Perhaps he was overestimating the advertising value of the Princess Patricia's beautiful neck to exhibit his pearls on. The price was exactly thirty-five thousand dollars less than he had expected to get for it during the next steel boom.

"Oh, come now, I say," remonstrated Colonel Lowther, impatiently. "That's thirteen thousand pounds. It's too much, you know."

"Colonel Lowther," said Boon, pale but determined, "I am losing considerable money on this, which I am charging to advertising account and may never get back. If the price is not satisfactory, I'm sorry; and I can only suggest that you'd better go to the other firms you've mentioned. They are all," he finished quietly, "very good firms."

Colonel Lowther, who had not taken his keen eyes off the jeweler's face during the speech, appeared impressed by Mr. Boon's earnestness. His neck jerked spasmodically half a dozen times before he said:

"I believe you. I'll take it. But first mark it— in pounds; thirteen thousand pounds." And he looked on, eagle-eyed, while Mr. Boon himself wrote out a new price-tag. Evidently he would take no chances with sleight-of-hand substitutions. "Put it here," he said, "beside me."

It made Mr. Boon say, half angry, half amused: "We won't change it for an imitation string. We are really a reputable firm, Colonel Lowther."

"Oh! Ah! Really, I—ah!" stammered the colonel, "I wasn't thinking of such a thing!" He looked so absurdly guilty, however, that Mr. Boon forgave him. "I think you'd better show me others—ah!— cheaper, you know, in case the duke should not wish to go above ten thousand pounds. Say, that one— and this!—and this!"

He had selected the three next best; but Boon figured very closely and in all instances named a price below cost: fifty-seven thousand five hundred dollars, fifty thousand dollars, and forty-five thousand dollars.

"Put them here also with the first one," said Colonel Lowther.

"Don't you wish us to put them in boxes?" asked Mr. Boon.

"Ah—ah!—I say, bring the boxes in and I'll put them in. We'll do it more quickly," he finished, lamely.

There flashed across Mr. Boon's mind the possibility of crookedness. Colonel Lowther did not trust them—perhaps because he hoped to avert suspicions by that same attitude of distrust! Mr. Boon determined to watch closely. He asked a clerk to bring some cases for the necklaces.

"You fix them, Boon," said Colonel Lowther, who was watching the jeweler's hands as children watch the hands of a prestidigitator.

It actually eased Boon's mind to be taken for a crook. He arranged the necklaces, each in its own Russia-leather case, and then gratefully helped Colonel Lowther to select two dozen scarf-pins, amounting in value to eighteen thousand dollars, a score of rings worth in all a little over twenty-five thousand dollars, and a few lorgnette-chains and other trinkets. Once all these were duly price-tagged, packed, and placed beside the necklaces, Colonel Lowther, after a series of mild cervical convulsions, said, calmly:

"Now, Boon, you and I must settle a personal matter. You know, of course, the royal party never pays cash."

"Then," said the impetuous Mr. Boon, "the deal is off!"

"Silly ass! The royal family of England always pays. You know very well that the jewels bought by King George for gifts for his coronation guests have not been paid for yet. It's all a matter of red tape. The money is as safe as the Bank of England! Any banker here would be glad to guarantee the account—only that would never do, of course. Now you know I can't take any commission. I've made you give me the lowest prices for the duke, haven't I? What?"

"Yes, you have; and therefore I can't—"

"If I were a bally Russian I'd have made you name a price twice the usual figure and I'd have taken the difference as a commission. It's what you Americans call graft, I believe. What?"

"Of course," said Boon, coldly, disgusted with the venal aristocracy, "we'd never have done such a—"

"Tut, tut! It's done everywhere; but not to me!" Colonel Lowther said, so sternly that Mr. Boon considered himself accused of unnamed crimes. He resented this, but, being unable to fix the exact accusation, contented himself with remarking, diplomatically:

"Of course not! But at the same time—"

"Yes, yes," rudely broke in the colonel, with a silencing wave of his gloved hand. "Now I can myself pay you in cash for whatever the duke buys —say, up to twenty thousand or twenty-five thousand pounds. For advancing this money, which will not be paid to me for months, I ask you to allow me a half-year's interest. That," finished Colonel Lowther, impressively, "is banking. What?"

"At what rate?"

"Oh, eight or ten per cent."

"Impossible!"

"Then, Mr. Welch, Boon, or whatever your name is, I wish you a very good morning!"

"But we'll allow you interest at the rate of six per cent. a year."

"But I myself have to pay five for the use—ah!— that is—er—" floundered the Englishman. Mr. Boon perceived instantly that the colonel borrowed the money from Canadian bankers at five per cent. and got ten per cent. It was not a bad scheme for high-class aristocratic graft! Even a jeweler could philosophize about wilful self-delusion, the point of view, custom, and so on. "Make it seven per cent. What?"

Mr. Boon could not help admiring the persistency of the Englishman in coating his graft-pills with the sugar of legitimacy. Doubtless the colonel had really convinced himself this was not graft!

"Very well," said Mr. Boon, with a smile. "I'll take three and a half per cent. off for cash."

"But we agreed on seven!" remonstrated the Englishman.

"Well, three and a half per cent. of the whole is the same as six months at seven per cent."

"Oh!" The colonel began to figure in his mind. His cervical contortions, twitchings, and jerkings were painful to behold. Mr. Boon thought it was a mild form of St. Vitus's dance. It would enable him to recognize the colonel in a crowd of ten thousand.

"Quite so! Yes—three and a half per cent. of the total bill. It will be at least twenty thousand pounds—that's one hundred thousand dollars. Not half bad! What?"

"Do you mean your commission will be one hundred thousand dollars? I'm delighted to hear it!" Mr. Boon was so pleased that he jested. He would play up the royal patronage to the limit.

"Oh no! I meant the total amount, you know," corrected the colonel, earnestly. He saw that Boon was smiling, and gradually it dawned on him that the jeweler was an American humorist. "Oh! Ah! Yes! Very funny! Quite so! I wish it were! How many millions would the bill have to be for the cash discount to be twenty thousand pounds? What?

Right-O! Well, now bring the pearls and the other things to the motor. I shall show them to his Royal Highness at once. I can let you know in a half-hour which he will keep." And he rose.

"Ah!—er—Colonel, you know we don't like to—ah!—there's over two hundred thousand dollars' worth of jewels, worth four hundred thousand dollars in any other place in New York; and if anything happened—"

"Nothing will happen," said the colonel, with assurance.

"And then, it will take a long time to prepare the memorandum of—"

"Why do you need a memorandum?" inquired the colonel, coldly. He looked as if he began to suspect that Mr. Boon distrusted a member of the suite of his Royal Highness, Prince Arthur William Patrick Albert, K.G., K.T., K.P., P.C., G.M.B., G.3. S.I., G.C.M.G., G.C.I.E., G.C.V.O., Duke of Connaught and Strathearn, Earl of Sussex, Prince of Coburg and Gotha, Governor-General of Canada, and potential customer of the world-renowned firm of Welch, Boon & Shaw.

Reading the emotions on the colonel's face and not desiring to offend, but at the same time determined not to deliver two hundred thousand dollars' worth of goods to a stranger, who might be the duke's secretary, but might not be a reliable man financially, for all that, Mr. Boon groped for an excuse. But Colonel Lowther pursued, frigidly:

"Why should you need a memorandum if you yourself will bring the jewels? Did you think I was a bally clerk to sell your jewels for you? You do the talking—and don't change the prices!"

So profoundly relieved as not to resent the last insult, Mr. Boon smiled pleasantly and said, "I must take a man to carry them."

"Take a regiment if you wish; but there's room for only three in the motor," said the Englishman, his neck twitching and twisting and jerking quite violently. Anger seemed to aggravate his nervous malady. Wherefore Mr. Boon hastily gathered up the packages, put them into a jeweler's strong valise, and followed the colonel, accompanied by Terry Donnelly, the store's private policeman, who carried the precious satchel in one hand, and in the other—in his overcoat pocket—an automatic pistol of the latest model.

One of the clerks must have told of the affair, for there was an eager crowd on the sidewalk. They had heard that the Duke of Connaught's secretary was in the store, buying diamonds. By the time it had passed seven mouths it was the duke himself. Mr. Boon heard: "There he comes!" and, "Is the princess with him?" and, "Which is the duke?" And he had pleasant visions of free reading-notices and renewed popularity among the ultra-fashionable. One of the traffic squad was trying to make the crowd move on—in vain.

The colonel good-naturedly forced his way through the mob to the motor, followed by the jeweler and the store policeman, who saw on the door of the limousine the letters "W. R." And both of them concluded that this stood for the well-known initials of the duke's host.

A short woman, with red hair and a self-assertive bust, stared boldly at the colonel and said, "He don't look like his pictures."

THE PEARLS OF PATRICIA

"Say, are you the duke?" asked a messenger-boy.

However, the colonel merely said "Home!" and entered the motor, followed by Mr. Boon and T. Donnelly. The store footman closed the door as if it were made of priceless cut-glass. The traffic policeman touched his cap and the motor went up the Avenue.

The colonel picked up a newspaper from the seat and turned to Mr. Boon.

"See!" he said, "our pictures. Your reporters are—ah!—very enterprising and clever. But the photographers are worse!" He laughed and went on: "The pictures don't look like me, d'ye think?"

"I recognize the coat and the fur cap," laughed Mr. Boon.

"Oh, do you?" said the colonel, seriously. He looked at it and said: "But it might be my other fur cap, you know. What?" He looked challengingly at the jeweler.

"It might be," admitted Mr. Boon, diplomatically confessing his error.

"Quite so!" said the owner of the fur cap, triumphantly.

Mr. Boon, finding himself nearer the house of the duke's host, began to feel more confident of putting through the epoch-making deal. It is not often that a New York jeweler sells pearls to an uncle of the King of England, to be used by the king's most beautiful cousin! He would have the princess's photograph in his window. It should show the famous necklace!

The motor took its place last in the long string of automobiles and carriages that were creeping toward

3

the door of the house which his Royal Highness was honoring.

"Democracy meekly leaving its card at the house of royalty," laughed the colonel, pointing to the twoscore vehicles ahead of theirs.

"Americans paying their respects to an Englishman who is honored even in his own country," said Mr. Boon.

"Oh, now, I say, Boon, that's uncommonly neat, you know. What? But perhaps we'd better get out and walk; otherwise it may be a half-hour before—"

A footman in livery came up to their motor, touched his hat with a respect that entitled him to a bank president's wages, and said to the colonel:

"I beg pardon, sir, but 'is Royal 'ighness 'as gone to Mr. Walton's, sir, at number 899 Fifth Avenue. I was hinstructed to tell you to go there, sir."

"Tell the chauffeur where to go," said the colonel, briefly.

"Yes, sir—very good, sir." The man touched his hat and told the chauffeur.

Their motor pulled out of the line and turned to the west.

"Mr. Walton was at Eton with the duke," explained the colonel to Mr. Boon.

"J. G. Walton?" asked Mr. Boon.

"Yes."

"I didn't know he was educated in England," said Mr. Boon in a tone that implied he knew Mr. Walton well.

"Didn't you?" said the colonel, more sharply than the occasion warranted.

"But then, we never discussed the subject," apologized the jeweler.

"Do you know the house?"

"Yes. I've been in it several times. I understood Mr. Walton was in Florida and had rented his residence for the winter."

"I don't know a bally thing about his private affairs," said the colonel, coldly; "but I do know the duke intended to visit him, and I've been told to go there."

It occurred to the store detective that if the Englishman was rude to Mr. Boon it was altogether likely the duke treated his private secretary as a servant. It gave the detective pleasure to imagine this, for whenever the colonel had looked at Mr. Donnelly it was with the casual indifference with which men look at chairs or cobblestones. This made T. Donnelly feel that he was not alive, and he disliked the aristocratic undertaker.

The motor turned into Fifth Avenue, sped northward, and halted before a house. Mr. Boon recognized Mr. Walton's residence.

The colonel alighted quickly and said "Come with me!" in the tone foreigners use to menials, and didn't even turn his head to see if he was followed, but walked up to the door and rang the bell.

A man in livery opened the door.

"I am Colonel Lowther!"

"Yes, sir. His Royal Highness said you were to wait in the drawing-room unless there was somebody with you; in which case you were to be taken to him, sir."

"Come on!" said the colonel to Mr. Boon and the private policeman. The footman preceded them to a door at the back of the foyer hall, opened it, drew back heavy portières, and announced, solemnly:

"Colonel Lowther!"

The colonel entered. So did Mr. Boon and Donnelly. A man stood gazing out of a window. His back was toward them. For the first time Mr. Boon —so he said later—felt that something was wrong. Yet he made no effort to protect himself.

"Your Highness, here are the pearls."

The duke turned round. He had a kindly face, had white hair and mustaches.

"Let me have them!" said his Royal Highness, in the husky whisper of a man suffering from acute laryngitis or partial paralysis of the vocal cords.

"I know that voice!" shouted Donnelly, and the jeweler knew he might fear the worst; but, before they could put their hands in their pockets for their revolvers, strong fingers took strangle-holds on their throats, a spray of ammonia had been squirted into their nostrils and eyes, and they were helpless. In a jiffy their wrists were handcuffed behind their backs, their feet were fastened with leg-irons, their mouths pried open with a bowie-knife blade that made them cease struggling. Pear-gags were inserted into their mouths. Donnelly squirmed and carried on like a frightened child—but at the same time kept unfrightened eyes on the duke. Not so Boon, who was as pale as ivory.

The duke turned his back on his captives and put on a black cloth mask, but the watchful Donnelly noticed that he put into his pocket what looked like false mustaches. He also donned a pair of black gloves, but not before the policeman had seen a long, white scar, beginning at the knuckles and disappearing up the wrist into the cuff. Donnelly recalled having heard or read a description of a professional crook that tallied with what he had seen. It would make the work of capture easier.

The masked duke picked up the precious valise and said, "Take them to the others."

The four men who had nearly strangled the jeweler and the policeman were dressed in overalls and jumpers, had on black masks, and wore gloves. They carried the helpless victims into what seemed to be the servants' dining-room.

Propped up in high-backed chairs, Mr. Jesse L. Boon, of Welch, Boon & Shaw, saw Mr. Wilfred Gaylord, president of Goffony's, Mr. Percival Pierce, of Johnson & Pierce, Mr. J. Sumner Storrs, of J. Storrs' Sons, and five of their clerks. Beside Mr. Pierce was an empty chair. Mr. Boon was placed on it. The detective was dumped on one near Goffony's clerk.

"Tie 'em in couples," whispered the duke. Each man was tied to the back of his chair—and the chairs themselves were tied back to back.

"That," explained the colonel, "will prevent you from hurting yourselves by toppling over in regrettable efforts to reach the door. We wish no harm to befall you. What?"

The masked men in overalls left the room like perfectly trained servants.

"You are a damned fool!" whispered the duke, angrily.

"Why?" amiably asked the Englishman.

"The only people that don't talk are those that can't."

"I know—but murder will out! Never knew it to

fail. We have—ah!—you might say—ah!—borrowed a few trinkets from these gentlemen. They may get them back, possibly; but you can't ever bring back the breath of life if you decapitate them. What?"

"I tell you I will not leave them here to blab!" hissed the duke; and Boon could not help thinking of the anger of a rattlesnake with laryngitis. "A slight nick in the jugular and they'll bleed away painlessly. Just before the end they will begin to dream. By ——, I'll do it! Right now!"

The duke pulled out a barber's razor, opened it, and approached Boon.

Something about his manner told the jeweler that this creature was about to cut their throats as much for the pleasure of it as because of the supposed safety. It was confirmed when the masked fiend wheezed, malignantly:

"It's sterilized!"

Mr. Boon was suddenly conscious of an extreme cold, as if he had been thrown naked into an ice-cave. On Pierce's face, grown gray, the sweat stood in a microscopic dew. Gaylord's florid face was livid and tense; J. Sumner Storrs had closed his eyes and seemed asleep, but the breath whistled unpleasantly through his nostrils.

"Stop!" said the colonel so sharply that the duke turned like a flash—to look into the barrel of a blue-steel automatic.

"Drop the razor, old chap! I can't let you kill the beggars in cold blood. Upon my soul, I can't, you know!" His head was jerking and twisting at a furious rate, but the revolver was as steady as a rock.

THE PEARLS OF PATRICIA

"It's our only chance. It won't hurt them. They won't feel it any more than a feather—it's so sharp," whispered the black-masked devil.

"Drop it, I say!" said the colonel, peremptorily. They heard a gritting of teeth from behind the mask as the duke closed the razor and dropped it on the floor. Still covering his accomplice, the colonel put his foot on the weapon. "Thanks, old chap!" he said, pleasantly. At that very moment he could have capitalized the gratitude of the ten prisoners at many thousands.

"Fool!" came in a husky whisper.

"Oh, now! I say!"

"What's the difference between twenty years in the pen and twenty seconds in the electric chair? I myself prefer the chair. But I'd rather cut their throats and keep out of danger. I tell you, it's tempting Providence to leave these men—"

"Is it as much as twenty years, old fellow?" queried the colonel, obviously perturbed.

The duke nodded.

"I say, gentlemen, I don't want to stay twenty years indoors, you know. Really, it's not a pleasant thought. What? If I give you your lives you must not take away my liberty. So I will go out now and leave you here with my friend, unless you promise not to tell the police anything that will serve as a clue and yourselves do nothing to harm us. If you will act like gentlemen I'll undertake to prevent my friend here from severing your respective jugulars. Nod for 'Yes' and shake your heads for 'No.' Promise not to talk?"

Ten heads nodded vehemently.

"Come, old chap; you must take their words.

Gentlemen, you will be released this evening without
fail. We must have time to leave New York.
Avoid the reporters as you would the plague. It
would not be wise to publish the facts! Think of
it—the heads of the great firms! In parting from
you, gentlemen, I wish to thank you in behalf of
the Plunder Recovery Syndicate, to the success of
whose operations you have in this instance so gen-
erously contributed. Gratitude surely is not in-
compatible with business methods. Gentleman,
again I say, Thank you kindly, and—why not?—
au revoir!"

And that was the last the captives saw of the man
who, on behalf of the Plunder Recovery Syndicate,
had reduced the holdings of pearls and trinkets of
New York's most famous jewelers by a trifle over
one million dollars' worth.

It was nearly closing-time—midnight—that night
when two men entered P. T. Ayres's corner drug-
store. One of them wore a fur overcoat and a silk
hat. The other was dressed in black, had a mourn-
ing-band about his hat, and wore black gloves. He
carried a bag on which the sleepy lady cashier saw
the "L" and the cabin tags of a transatlantic line.
The man in black said to her:

"May this gentleman telephone for me, miss?
My throat is in pretty bad shape, and I don't want
to use it."

It was in bad shape, indeed. She could hardly
hear him.

"But, I say, dear chap—" remonstrated the fur-
coated man, whose collar was so tight that he
wiggled his head violently as if in search of comfort.

"This is as good a place as any," whispered the

man in black, impatiently. "Call 'em up! I say, miss, have you got any slippery elm or some kind of troches good for laryngitis?"

She remembered afterward that when she said she would call the proprietor he kept her from it by engaging her in conversation, which likewise prevented her from trying to hear what his companion was saying.

The fur-coated man had called up Spring 3100, which is police headquarters.

"Are you there? I say, are you there? Yes, I know this is not London. You know Mr. Pierce and Mr. Storrs and Mr. Boon and Mr. Gaylord? Well, tell your men they are in a residence on Fifth Avenue, in the servants' dining-room. It's Colonel Walton's house. Right-O! That's not your business. Go to the devil!" He came out of the booth with an angry face. "Confound their impudence! Where is my friend?"

"He's gone," said the cashier. "Here—come back and pay for that call; five cents!"

The telephone clerk at police headquarters promptly told the news of the whereabouts of the missing jewelers—for whom the star men had been searching six hours diligently and secretly — and then tried, through the telephone Central, to get in touch with the pay station from which the "tip" had come, but couldn't, as they would not answer. The reason Ayres's drug-store wouldn't answer was that the Englishman in his ignorance had disarranged the connection without betraying that fact. The detectives said it showed a technical knowledge of telephones and their construction.

The news was kept from the newspapers, in the

first place, because the jewelers requested it of the Police Department; and, secondly, because it was deemed wise by the sleuths to fight mystery with mystery. As a matter of fact, the detectives were confident of apprehending the miscreants shortly—for had they not left a trail as broad as Fifth Avenue?

The jewelers went back on their words to the colonel, who saved their lives. From their descriptions and the information given by Ayres and the fair cashier, they knew the husky-voiced man with the scar on the back of his hand must be Whispering Willie, a clever all-round crook. The Englishman, they thought, was an amateur. The police communicated with the *Ruritania* by wireless, and asked the purser if among the passengers were a man of middle height, smooth-shaven, about forty years of age, with paralyzed vocal cords that made him talk as if he had acute laryngitis, and a tall, well-built, blue-eyed, blond Englishman with a nervous affliction of the neck like a mild form of St. Vitus's dance. Within twenty-four hours the purser had sent the reply: "St. Vitus here, under name of Lewis J. Wright. No trace of Laryngitis."

So headquarters cabled to Scotland Yard to hold the tall blond afflicted with St. Vitus's dance, who was thought to have sailed under the name of Lewis J. Wright, until the detective sergeant and one of the jeweler's clerks could arrive with extradition papers. And that's how Mr. L. J. Wright was arrested in Liverpool, less on account of New York's request than by reason of the absurd yarn he told. There was no such Dr. Cephas W. Atterbury as Wright declared he was going to see. The letter of introduction to the doctor, moreover, was a blank sheet of paper. The New York police learned about W. W. Lovell in this way and knew they were on the right trail.

Ten days later there was arrested in Paris, at the office of the American Express Company, a man answering the description of Whispering Willie, who had presented some checks signed by W. W. Lowry. The Paris police reported that W. W. Lowry was probably one of a band, because the scar on his hand vanished when washed with alcohol. And his voice grew normal when questioned by the prefect of police. He told an absurd story of having been hired at the rate of one thousand dollars a week to ask in a whisper for eleven letters at the American Express Company's office on February 11th, at 11.11 A.M., and declared that when his employer bade him good-by on the steamer he painted a scar on the back of his hand and told him always to wear black gloves. The employer answered the description of Whispering Willie and also of W. W. Lovell. The police found that the whisperer's trail led a second time to the *Herald* office. The clerk, Carroll, remembered the mysterious advertiser very well indeed. Messrs. Reese & Silliman, real-estate agents, told the police they had rented Colonel Walton's house for the winter to a Mr. J. C. Atkinson, an Englishman who had given as references a firm of international bankers on whom his letter of credit for five thousand pounds was drawn. The bankers knew nothing about him personally or socially. Mr. Atkinson had drawn the entire five thousand pounds. He had occupied the house two months, paid his rent promptly, and had given a satisfactory deposit against possible damage happening to any of the furniture.

The police had lost four weeks of valuable time in following clues that merely led back to the St. Iago Building and to the man with the paralyzed vocal cords and the scar on the back of his hand, calling himself W. W. Lovell, who was probably William W. Long, *alias* William W. Longworth, *alias* W. W. Latshay, *alias* Whispering Willie. The Englishman was not known to any member of the New York police force, but fortunately he had a nervous affliction which would betray him without recourse to the third degree.

Exactly one month after the departure of the real Duke of Connaught from New York Messrs. Jesse L. Boon, Percival Pierce, J. Sumner Storrs, and Wilfred Gaylord each received a copy of the following letter, typewritten on note-paper of the Ritz-Carlton:

Having disposed of the pearls of the Princess Patricia at a price only eight per cent. below that at which you offered them to H. R. H. the Duke of Connaught, we beg to suggest that it is a waste of money for you to encourage the detectives and downright dishonesty for the detectives to encourage you. You have caused to be arrested unfortunate men suffering from chorea in Liverpool, Bremen, Genoa, Buenos Ayres, and Panama, as well as Mr. W. W. Lowry in Paris and W. W. Longman in the City of Mexico. For the last eleven months Whispering Willie has been in the Missouri State Penitentiary, where he is Number 317. Our Colonel Lowther has not St. Vitus's dance, is not an Englishman, and has not left New York! The Duke of Connaught, otherwise W. W. Lovell, of the Acme Vibrator Company, has a fine, strong barytone voice, has no scar on the back of his right hand, is too young to have gray hair, and his nose is not what it was when he was known as Mr. Lovell. We needed time to move about unwatched in New York, hence the elaborate false clues. We always plan our deals carefully and we are uniformly successful. We may inform you, in self-defense, that we operate only on the rich enemies of society. Pearls and diamonds have ruined as many women as drink has ruined men or Wall Street has destroyed souls! We regard them as plunder to be recovered. You may be interested to know that we propose to induce one of our most famous high financiers to contribute a couple of millions to our surplus this month. At the proper time we shall supply the name and the particulars, in order that you may compare notes with the other patrons of

Yours truly,

THE PLUNDERERS.

The jewelers were inclined to regard the letter as a jest in very bad taste perpetrated by one of their number. But all denied it, and the communication was turned over to the police. The detective sergeant who was in charge of the case also thought the letter was a joke—until Mr. Boon told him he didn't see anything funny in the loss of a million dollars' worth of gems and a score of false arrests. He wondered, like the rest, whether there really was a syndicate, and presently found himself waiting for the news of the second exploit. "He fooled *me*," Boon confided to Donnelly. But what he really meant was that the man who impersonated the private secretary of the Duke of Connaught could fool anybody.

II

THE PANIC OF THE LION

I

A MAN walked into the office of Richards & Tuttle, bankers and brokers, members of the New York Stock Exchange. All he could see was a ground-glass partition, with little windows only a trifle larger than peepholes, over which he read, "DELIVERIES," "COMPARISONS," "TELEGRAMS," and "CASHIER." If you had business to transact you knew at which window to knock. If you had not you should not disturb the unseen clerks by asking questions that took valuable time to answer. It was a typical, non-communicative, non-confiding Wall Street office.

The man approached the "CASHIER" window because it was open. He was tall and well built, with unmyopic eyes that looked through tortoise-shell-rimmed glasses. The brim of his high hat, the cut of his coat, the hang of his trousers, the hue of his necktie and the gray, waxed, needle-pointed mustaches proclaimed him unmistakably Parisian.

"I wish to see Mr. Richards," he said, in a nasal voice, so like the twang of a stage Yankee that the cashier frowned and twisted his neck to see if some

38

down-easter were not hiding behind the Frenchman.

"You what?" asked the cashier, and looked watchful.

"I wish to see," repeated the stranger, with a formal precision meant to be rebuking, "Mr. George B. Richards, senior member, I believe, of this firm."

The cashier, with a frown that belied the courtesy of his words, said:

"Would you be kind enough to tell me the nature of your business, sir?"

Gourley, the cashier, insanely hated book agents, and his one pleasure in life consisted of violently ejecting them from the office. When a man clearly established his innocence Gourley never forgave him for cheating him out of the kicking.

The stranger said, very slowly:

"The nature of my business with Mr. Richards is private, personal, and urgent!"

The stranger might be a customer, and customers make brokers rich and give wages to cashiers.

"Mr. Richards is very busy just now, sir, with an important conference. It would be a favor if you could let me have your name."

"He doesn't know me and he has never heard my name."

"Would any one else do?"

The stranger shook his head. Then:

"Say to Mr. Richards that a gentleman from Paris wishes to give to him—personally—ten letters of introduction, one card of same, and one life secret." The man's gaze was fixed frowningly on Gourley.

"Ten letters of introduction, one card of same, and

one life secret!" repeated Gourley, dazedly. "Here, Otto. Hold the fort. I'll go myself."

The cashier's place was promptly occupied by a moon-faced Teuton. Presently Gourley, whose misanthropy had in this instance merely made an office-boy of him, returned to the window and said, in the insolent tones of a puglistic *agent provocateur:*

"He says to send in the letters of introduction."

"My friend," said the stranger, so impressively that the cashier was made uneasy, "are you sure Mr. Richards said that?"

"Well—ah—he said," stammered Gourley, "to ask you—er—would you please send in the letters. He will read them, and as soon as possible he will—ah—see you."

"H'm!" muttered the stranger, skeptically. Then, as a man rids himself of angry thoughts, he shook his head and, without another word, went out.

"Ha! I knew it all along," said Gourley, triumphantly, to his assistant, Otto. "It beats the Dutch what schemes these damned book agents get up to see people during business hours. But I called his bluff that time!"

Less than ten minutes later the French-looking man with the down-east voice opened the door, tapped at the cashier's window, and told Gourley, sternly:

"Here are the ten letters and the one card. They are very important! I'll be obliged, sir, if you will yourself give them into Mr. Richards's own hands. The life secret I, of course, will impart to him myself. Make haste, please. I have only five business days and three hours left."

Gourley laid the letters on Mr. Richards's desk and

said, in the accusing tone old employees use when they are in the wrong: "Here are the letters of introduction from the book agent I spoke to you about. He acts damned impudent to me, but I didn't want to make any mistake."

Richards, a man of fifty, fastidiously dressed, but relieved from even the implication of foppishness by a look in his eyes at once shrewd and humorous, said, with a smile, "Well, he certainly has enough letters to be anything, even a rich man."

"Funny letters of introduction," said the cashier— "all sealed and—" His jaw dropped. That made him cease talking.

Mr. Richards had taken from the first envelope not a letter, but a ten-thousand-dollar gold certificate!

The cashier closed his mouth with a click. "What the—!" he muttered.

"Next!" said George B. Richards, cheerfully. He opened envelope number two and pulled out another ten-thousand-dollar bill. One after another he opened the letters until he had laid in a neat pile on his desk ten ten-thousand-dollar notes.

"The letters of introduction are from the Treasury Department," said Richards, laughing. "Now let us see whom the card is from."

"I don't care whom the card is from. I know the man is crazy," said Gourley, in the defiant tone of one who expects not logic, but contradiction. "It is as plain as the nose on your face."

"Maybe they are counterfeit," teased Richards; he knew they were not.

The cashier snatched one from the desk, looked at the vignette of Jackson, and examined the back. "It's good," he said, gloomily.

THE PLUNDERERS

Richards opened the eleventh envelope and took out a card.

"From Amos Kidder, of the *Evening Planet*," he told Gourley, and read aloud:

DEAR GEORGE,—The bearer, Mr. James B. Robison, of Paris, France, a friend of Smiley, our correspondent there, asked me to recommend some highly intelligent stock-brokers. I, of course, at once thought of you. Deal with him as you do with

Yours,

AMOS F. KIDDER.

"Maybe it's a set of those French books that are awful until you've signed the contract and Volume I. comes, and they are not awful at all. Those fellows," said the cashier, indignantly, "will do anything to get your money."

"You forget I've got his," suggested Richards.

"That's a new one on me, I admit," said the cashier; "but I'll bet a ten-spot—"

"I'll have no gambling in this office! Send in Mr. Robison; and if Kidder should happen in, tell him I'd like to see him."

The waxed-mustached man, preceded by Otto, the moon-faced clerk, entered the private office of Mr. George B. Richards, who rose and smiled pleasantly even as his keen eyes quickly inventoried Mr. Robison.

"Mr. Richards?" twanged the stranger. That Yankee voice issuing from between those unmistakably French mustaches made Richards start; and yet the vague atmosphere of disquietude and suspicion that the ten letters of introduction had created seemed to be dispelled by the man's Yankee twang. It was so genuinely down - east that it humanized

THE PANIC OF THE LION

Mr. Robison and made his eccentricity less eccentric. Also, the eyes gleamed not with the fire of insanity, but with a great earnestness.

"Yes. And this is Mr. Robison?"

"Yes, sir!" Mr. Robison bowed very low, like a man who has lived abroad many years.

"Won't you be seated, sir?"

"Thank you, sir." There was another bow of gratitude, and Mr. Robison sat down by Richards's flat-topped desk.

"What can we do for you, Mr. Robison?" asked Richards, amiably polite. His course of action would be determined by the stranger's own words.

"You can help me if you will." Mr. Robison spoke very earnestly, after the manner of strong, self-reliant men when they ask for favors.

"We shall be glad to if you will tell me how."

"By being patient. That's how."

Richards laughed uncertainly. Mr. Robison held up a hand as if to check unseemly merriment and said, very seriously:

"I have lived alone too long to be politic or diplomatic or evasive. I wish to ask you a question."

"Ask ahead," said Richards, with an encouraging recklessness.

"Tell me, Mr. Richards—what is the most difficult thing in the world?"

Mr. Robison was looking intently at the broker's face, as if he particularly desired to detect any change in expression. This intentness disconcerted Richards, who had at first intended to answer jocularly. He now said, distinctly apologetic:

"There are so many very difficult things!"

"Yes, there are—a great many indeed. But of

43

all things, which is by far the most difficult?" His eyes held Richards's.

"I shall have to think a little before I can answer that question."

"Take all the time you wish!" and Mr. Robison leaned back in his chair, his attitude somehow suggesting a Gibraltar-like ability to withstand a three years' siege.

It made Richards do much thinking very quickly: Here was a man who was not crazy; who had lying on the desk a hundred thousand dollars in cash to which he had not even casually referred; who probably intended to do business that would prove a source of profit to the firm of Richards & Tuttle. He might be a crank or a crook, but against either contingency the firm could and would protect itself. It was just as well to humor this man until he proved himself unworthy of humoring. The problem of the moment, therefore, became how to raise the siege politely.

"I suppose," began Richards, trying to look philosophical, "that telling the truth always and everywhere is about as difficult a thing as—"

"It isn't a question," interrupted Robison, with a polite regret, "of as difficult a thing as any, but of the most difficult of all!"

"I am afraid I'll have to ask you to tell me what you consider the most difficult thing in the world."

Brokers have to earn their money in more complicated ways than by shouting "Sold!" or "Take it!" on the floor of the Stock Exchange. They have to listen to potential customers.

"The most difficult thing in the world, Mr. George B. Richards, is for a man to give money—

in cash—to a woman who is not his wife or his mistress or a blood-relation or a pauper!"

"That *is* difficult!" acquiesced the broker.

"It is what I have to do. That is why I am here."

"You mean you wish us to give this money—"

"No—no! How can you, pray, give money to a lady any better than I?"

"I wondered," said Richards, patiently. He was beginning to fear that Robison might be one of those mysterious people out of whom no money is to be made.

"Would you mind hearing my story?" Mr. Robison looked at Richards pleadingly.

"Not at all," politely lied the broker.

"There is a lady in New York—to be explicit, an old sweetheart—" Mr. Robison paused, bit his lip, looked away, bit his lip again and cleared his throat loudly. He did all these things so untheatrically that they thrilled the keen-eyed Wall Street man. Presently Mr. Robison went on in that Yankee nasal voice of his that somehow sounded like the extreme antithesis of sentiment: "The only woman I ever loved! I have never married! She did—unfortunately; and now, this girl, this woman, accustomed to every comfort and every refinement, has to earn her own living! She has five children and she is earning her living!" He rose and walked up and down the office like a caged wild animal. Then he sat down again and said, determinedly, "Of course I simply have to do something for her!"

"I appreciate your position," said Richards, tenderly. He was a very good stock-broker.

"Thank you. You cannot imagine what she was to me! I came to America to find her. I have found her. I wish to give her money or securities that will insure a comfortable income, and I have to do it circuitously. I'd give half a million to anybody who killed her damned husband! Yes, I would!" He looked at Richards with a wild hope in his eyes. He calmed himself with an obvious effort and proceeded: "Knowing her as I do, and because of—of certain circumstances of our early affair, I know she will never accept any help directly from me. Last night I was calling on her. Other friends of hers were present, among them a man who called himself a lawyer. His name is W. Bailey Jackson. Know him?"

"No, I don't. I think I've heard of him, though." Richards lied from sheer force of professional habit.

"Well, I led the conversation round to Wall Street and incidentally said I didn't know which was easier for a man, to be a fool or to make money in the stock-market. I, myself, I hastened to add, had always found folly extremely easy—but successful stock speculation infinitely easier. That, I may remark to you in passing, sir, is gospel truth."

"You are right," agreed Richards, heartily. It did not behoove a stock-broker to point out the difficulty of making money in Wall Street. Moreover, Mr. Robison showed so quiet a confidence that Richards had lightning flashes of memory, and recollected every story he had ever heard about queer characters who had taken millions out of the Street.

"This Mr. W. Bailey Jackson jeered and sneered, however, until I said I would bet him fifty dollars to fifty cents that I could double a sum of money in the Street in one week, in a reputable broker's

office, operating on the New York Stock Exchange
in a reputable and active stock—no bucket-shop, no
mining-stock, and no pool manipulation. But I
made this point: The trick was so easy that it was
not interesting. I didn't wish to do it to make
money, but if Mrs.—if my friend would accept the
profits, I would prove that I knew what I was talking about; and, besides, would keep the children in
candy for a month. And, of course, everybody
laughed and urged her to consent—especially the
Jackson person. In the end she gave in, doubtless
thinking I'd win a few dollars—if I won at all.
Also my offer was accepted in the presence and by
the advice of men and women who could stop Mrs.
Grundy's mouth."

"Very clever!" said Richards, with the enthusiasm
of a man who sees commissions coming his way.

"It was love that made me so ingenious," explained
Mr. Robison, very simply. "I've got her written
acceptance in my pocket as well as that damned
W. Bailey Jackson's bet, duly witnessed by the two
gossipiest women there. And in this envelope you
will find instructions for your guidance in case of
my sudden death. So I now wish to double the
money."

He looked inquiringly at Richards, who thereupon
felt the pangs of disappointment. Neither crank nor
crook, decided the broker, but simply *Suckerius
Americanus; genus D. F.*

Mr. Robison evidently was going to ask Richards
& Tuttle to take the one hundred thousand dollars
and double it for him, which meant that Mr. Richards
would have to inform Mr. Robison that the firm
was not in the miracle business; and that would

make Mr. Robison go away mad. Total—no commissions!

"Well," Richards said, just a trifle coldly, "did you come to us to ask us to double your money for you?"

"No, indeed," answered Robison; "I came here to do it."

"When?"

"In one week—or, rather, in five days and two hours."

"How are you going to do it?" The broker's curiosity was not feigned.

"I propose to study the Menagerie."

Richards said nothing, but looked "Lunatic!"

"That way inevitably suggests the combinations to you." Mr. Robison nodded to himself.

Richards, to be on the safe side, did likewise and muttered, absently, "That's so!"

"Do you care to come with me?" asked Mr. Robison, with a politeness that betrayed effort.

"Thank you, no. I am very busy, and—"

"And you didn't cut me short!" said Robison, his voice ringing with remorse. "I'll come in to-morrow morning. Good afternoon—and please forgive my theft of your time, Mr. Richards."

"One moment. Do you wish this money—"

"I'll get the receipt to-morrow. I am going to see Kidder now. I didn't mean to take up so much of your time." And before the banker could stop him Mr. James B. Robison was out of the inner office and out of the outer office and out of the building and out of the financial district.

Shortly afterward Amos F. Kidder, financial editor of the *Evening Planet*, went into Richards's office. He was thirty-five years old, a trifle under six feet, had

THE PANIC OF THE LION

light-brown hair and the eyes of a man who is a cynic by force of experience and an optimist by reason of a perfect liver—the kind of man who is fooled by strangers never and by intimate friends always. If what he had seen of Wall Street gave him a low opinion of men's motives he had the defect of steadfast loyalty. Having imagination and a profound respect for statistics, he wrote what might be called skilful articles on finance.

"Your friend Robison was here to-day. What do you know about him?" asked Richards. He would not take a stranger's account, but he did not relish losing an account he already had.

Kidder took a letter from his pocket, gave it to the stock-broker, and said:

"Smiley gave him a letter to me and in addition sent me that one by mail."

Richards read:

THE NEW YORK PLANET, 5 RUE DE PROVENCE.

PARIS, February 18, 1912.

DEAR KIDDER,—I've given a letter of introduction to a Mr. James B. Robison, who comes originally from some manufacturing town in Massachusetts, like Lynn or Lowell—I've forgotten which. He is well liked by the colony here and, I am told, has been kind to poor art students and other self-deluded compatriots. He is queer; is suspected of being rich—which he must be because he never borrows, lives well, and says moneymaking is too easy to merit discussion when men can discuss the eternal feminine or the revival of cosmetics. His trip to New York is prompted, he tells me, by the receipt of a letter from an old flame of his whom he warned against marrying her present husband. She would not listen to Robison, accused him in choice Bostonian of being a short sport, and now after long years she writes him, asking for forgiveness, being at last convinced that her husband is all that Robison said—and then some. He is off to try to find her; she is somewhere in New

York. Put him in touch with some private detective who won't rob him too ruthlessly.

I don't think he'll want to borrow money, as I know he is taking a letter of credit on Towne, Ripley & Co. for fifty thousand pounds; and they told me at his bankers'—Madison & Co.—that he owns slathers of gilt-edged bonds and that they cash the coupons for him. They also tell me he carries more cash about him than is prudent. You might suggest to him that the New York banks are safe enough. You'll find him a character—odd but charitable. Knowing your fondness for fiction in real life I commend Mr. Robison to you. Regards to the boys. Why don't you make a million and come over to spend it in the company of   Yours as ever,

LURTON P. SMILEY.

Richards handed the letter back. "He came here with ten ten-thousand-dollar gold certificates."

"Yes; he got 'em from Towne, Ripley & Co. I went with him. They had instructions to pay any amount he might call for, and they did. He asked for large bills."

"He got 'em!" said Richards, greatly relieved at seeing no necessity why he should refuse Robison's account.

"What's he going to do?" asked Kidder.

"I don't know. He told me he had found his old sweetheart and that he is going to give her all he makes in Wall Street. He expects to double the one hundred thousand dollars in a week."

"For Heaven's sake, George, find out his secret! Half a million will do for me," laughed Kidder.

"He gave me an envelope," said Richards, taking it from his desk. On it was written:

PROPERTY OF JAMES B. ROBISON

To BE OPENED BY RICHARDS & TUTTLE
IN CASE OF SUDDEN DEATH

THE PANIC OF THE LION

"What do you think?" asked Richards.

"You really mean do I advise you to open it, don't you?" asked Kidder.

"Not exactly; but—"

"Of course," said the newspaper man, "it does not say it is *not* to be opened in case of *living*. That is sufficient excuse—that and your curiosity."

"I don't like to open it," said Richards, doubtfully.

"Don't!"

"Still, I'd like to know what's inside."

"Then open it."

"I don't think I have a right to."

"Don't, then!"

"Oh, shut up! I won't open it! I don't know whether to take the account. You don't know anything about this man—"

"You broker fellows make me tired—posing as careful business men. All Robison has to do is to go to any of your branch offices or anybody's branch office, say his name is W. Jones and that he keeps a cigar-store in Hackensack or Flatbush, and your branch manager will never let him get away. And afore-mentioned manager will swear, if you should be so mean as to ask who W. Jones is, that he and W. J. went to school together—known him for years!"

"After all," said Richards, a trifle defiantly, "there is no reason why I shouldn't do business for Robison that you know of?"

"Not that I know of—but if he buncoes you out of a big wad don't blame me."

"He is welcome to anything he can make out of us," smiled Richards, grimly, and Kidder laughed so heartily that the broker looked pleased with himself and his witticism. He rang for the cashier, gave him the one hundred thousand dollars, and had the amount credited to James B. Robison, address unknown.

II

After leaving the office of Richards & Tuttle Mr. James B. Robison went to the Subway station at Wall Street, rode up-town as far as Forty-second Street, walked to Sixth Avenue, took a surface car, jumped off at Forty-eighth, walked to Forty-ninth, waited there for the next car, and, being certain he was not shadowed, rode on to Fifty-sixth Street. He got off, walked north on the avenue and, half-way up the block, paused at the entrance of the employment agency of "*Jno. Sniffens, Established 1858.*" On the big slate by the door he read that there was wanted a coachman—careful driver; elderly man preferred.

He walked up-stairs one flight and accosted the agent.

"Good morning, Sniffens."

"Good morning, Mr. Maynard," answered Sniffens, son of the original Jno., very obsequiously.

"Are they here?"

"Yes, sir."

"How many?"

"Seven."

"I've seen fifty-six so far—haven't I?"

"No, sir," contradicted Sniffens with the air of a man who will tell the truth even if death should result. "Fifty-five. You forget you saw the Swede twice."

"That is true, Sniffens. You are an honest man!

Here!" And he gave ten dollars to the agent. "Send in the men."

He sat down in the inner office and Sniffens went out, presently to return with an elderly man.

"This is Wilkinson—worked twenty-nine years—"

"Sorry. Won't do. Here, my man! Take this two-dollar bill for your trouble. Next!"

Much the same thing happened with the next four applicants. The fifth man, however, made Robison listen patiently while Sniffens finished his elaborately biographical introduction. The man's name was Thomas Gray; age fifty-eight; worked twelve years for General James Morris and fourteen for Stuyvesant R. Morris. Very careful. Excellent references. Morris family went abroad to live. Gray had not done anything for five years, but was willing and anxious to work.

Robison, who had been studying Gray keenly, said sharply, and not at all nasally:

"Height and weight?"

"Five foot eleven and a half inches; one hundred and seventy pounds, sir."

"Deaf?"

"No, sir."

"No?"

"No, sir; but I don't hear as well as I did."

"Can you hear this?" And Robison whispered, "Constantinople!"

"Beg pardon, sir!" Gray looked at Mr. Robison's face intently, but Robison shook his head and said:

"No fair looking! That isn't hearing, but lip-reading. Close your eyes and listen!" And he whispered, "Bab-el-Mandeb!" No one could have heard him three feet away and Gray was across the room. Robison raised his voice and said, "Did you hear that?"

There showed in Gray's blue eyes a pathetic struggle between telling the truth and getting the job.

"I—I only heard a faint murmur, sir."

"Try again. Listen!" Mr. Robison moved his lips soundlessly and asked, "What did I say, Gray?"

The old man drew in a deep breath. It was not so much the money, for the Morris family gave him a pension; but he wished to feel that he was not yet useless, that he was still worth his keep. However, he shook his head and said, determinedly:

"I heard nothing."

"Open your eyes! You get the job, Gray," said Mr. Robison. "Come here!"

As Gray approached his new employer Sniffens left the room.

"You are not to tell any one for whom you are working, or where, or why, or for how long, or for what wages. There will be no night work. Are you very careful?"

"Yes, sir."

"You'll have to take some children to school every day—poor children to a public school in the morning. You are not to ask their names. Do what you are told, no matter how queer it seems to you, so long as you are not asked to break the law of the land or the rules of the road."

"Very good, sir."

"I shall send people to ask you questions, and I warn you that I'm going to put you to various tests. I want a man who is honest enough to trust with valuables, wise enough to mind his own business, and faithful enough to do what his employer tells him."

"Yes, sir."

"Until you prove you are the man I want you will be paid by the day—five dollars. You will feed yourself and sleep home. I supply the livery and a second man. If after one month's trial you are found satisfactory you will get your wages by the month. It's big wages, but I want an honest man!" He looked at Gray sternly.

"Yes, sir. I'm careful and honest, sir. I think you will find that to be true, sir."

"I trust so. The stable is on Thirty-first Street, near Avenue B. Here is the number." He gave a card to Gray. "Be there at eight sharp. You will drive a coupé; quiet horse; New York City."

"Yes, sir. I'll be there, sir."

"Here's five dollars for you. You don't have to pay any fee to Sniffens. I've paid him."

"Thank you, sir. Good day, sir."

At seven-thirty the next morning Gray was at the stable. It was not a very good-looking place. He rang the bell, feeling vaguely uncomfortable. No one answered. He rang a second and a third time, and still there was no answer. He listened, his ear close to the door. He heard the muffled sound of a horse pounding in a well-littered stall.

At eight o'clock—Gray heard a clock within chime the hour—the door opened. Gray entered. A man was hitching up a dark bay horse to a coupé. Mr. Robison was sitting in a sumptuous green-plush arm-chair in the carriage-room. Behind him, on a mahogany table, was a small valise, opened.

"Good morning, Gray," said Robison.

"Good morning, Mr. Maynard," said Gray, respectfully.

Robison took a clean white-linen handkerchief from his pocket and said:

"See that brick over there?" He pointed to a common red brick on a little shelf near the street door.

"Yes, sir."

"Well, wrap it up in this handkerchief—here on this table. No—don't dust it. Just as it is!" He watched Gray's face keenly. The old man's countenance remained English and impassive.

"Put it in the valise."

"Yes, sir."

"In yonder box you'll find some tenpenny nails. Fetch three and wrap them up in the sheet of paper you'll find in the valise. Then lay them on top of the brick."

Gray did as he was bid. If he thought his employer was crazy he did not look it.

Robison then took from his pocket a sealed envelope, threw it into the valise, and closed the valise.

"You will find your livery in the dressing-room— door to your left. Put it on. Then drive so as to be before 197 West Thirty-eighth Street at exactly nine minutes after nine. Compare your watch with that clock. Wait there—Thirty-eighth Street— until a footman in dark-green livery comes out alone. If he asks you, 'James, did Ben win?' you will say to him, 'The answer is inside. Take it!' You will then return to this stable, fasten the horse to that chain, put on your street clothes, go home, and return to-morrow at eight sharp. But—" He paused.

"Yes, sir."

"Pay attention, Gray! If, instead of the servant alone, the servant comes out of 197 West Thirty-eighth Street accompanied by a gentleman who gets in, you will drive him to my office."

"Where, sir?"

"This is my office—here. You will drive back here quickly and disregard everything your passenger may say or whatever orders he may give you. You understand? These are your orders that I now give you. They are not to be changed under any circumstances, no matter what happens. Have you understood?"

"Yes, sir. I'll follow orders, Mr. Maynard."

"See that you do." And Mr. Robison walked out of the stable.

At nine-nine sharp Gray stood in front of 197 West Thirty-eighth Street. At nine-fifteen a footman in dark-green livery came out of the house. He was followed by Mr. Robison himself. The man opened the door of the carriage and Gray's employer got in.

"Will you go to the office, sir?" asked the footman. Gray heard him.

"No! Metropolitan Museum!" answered their master, distinctly.

"Metropolitan Museum!" said the footman to the coachman.

Gray was torn by doubt, anger, and fear. Should he drive to the Metropolitan or back to the stable?

He decided to go back to the stable. If he were discharged he would not regret losing so unsatisfactory a job. If, on the other hand, driving back should prove to be the right thing he would greatly strengthen his position.

5

He arrived at the stable, fastened the horse to the chain, and went to change his clothes. He heard Mr. Robison tap on the glass of the door and saw him beckon to him and then heard him shout, "Open the door!" But Gray went to the dressing-room and changed his clothes. As soon as he was done the second man came in, showed him two envelopes, and said:

"You win! You get the ten dollars! I get the five-spot. That's how he pays. You obeyed orders. You are the first man that's succeeded in holding the job over one day. The Lord only knows what test Mr. Maynard will prepare for you to-morrow! It may be the children's lunch stunt or the runaway lunatic. Run out! Mr. Maynard won't like you to be here when he comes in. You can go out into the street by that door without going through the carriage-room."

Gray put the ten dollars in his pocket and walked out. "Rum go, that!" he muttered. It was indeed. He nodded his head with a sad sort of triumph to show that though he had not solved the mystery he had at all events grasped the situation and was, moreover, ten dollars to the good.

III

It was after the opening of the stock-market and most of the early orders had been executed. The rush had given place to the calm efficiency of a well-organized broker's office. Mr. Robison walked into the Customers' Room, approached Gilbert Witherspoon, a valued customer, touched his hat-brim with two fingers in the French military fashion, and said:

"Please, where's Mr. Richards?" His nasal twang and his Parisian appearance produced the usual impression of striking incongruity upon all men within hearing distance. Everybody frankly listened.

"That's his private office," answered Witherspoon, non-committally, pointing his finger at a door.

"Thank you very much!" said Robison and bowed. Then he knocked, heard a peremptory "Come in!" and disappeared within.

Witherspoon, who cultivated a reputation as a wit—there is a buffoon in every stock-broker's office —shrugged his shoulders Frenchily, and, in a nasal voice obviously in imitation of Robison, said:

"Another world-beater!"

"You never can tell," retorted Dan McCormack, oracularly. He was fat, always played "mysteries" in the market—traded in those stocks the movements in which were unaccounted for—and he did not like Witherspoon.

Inside Mr. Robison had said *"Bon jour!"* and bowed so very low that Mr. Richards immediately thought of the language of a fashionable bill of fare.

"Wie geht's?" retorted Richards, jocularly. Then, nicely serious, "How are you this morning?"

"Don't I look it?" said Mr. Robison. "I am, of course, perplexed."

"What's the trouble?"

"The usual trouble when I try to beat the stock-market—*embarras de richesses.*"

"It is an embarrassment that most people would welcome."

"Tut! The more elaborate the menu is in a good restaurant the greater your indecision as to which particular dish you will order! Well, I went through

the Menagerie!'' There was a catarrhal despair in
his voice.

"Yes?"

"And I am undecided between four."

Robison looked anxiously at the broker, and
Richards felt such an annoyance as a man might feel
if compelled at the point of a pistol to listen to the
reading of one hundred pages of the city directory.
But he smiled tolerantly, for he had the professional
amiability indispensable to men whose business consists of making money and of consoling clients for
losing money.

"Four what?" he asked.

"Four sure ways."

"Which four?" asked Richards. He managed to
convey both that he was dying to listen and that the
rest of the world did not exist for him.

"The Ant, the Spider, the Beaver, and the Lion.
Out of the nineteen combinations in the Menagerie
I've narrowed my choice to these four. You know
conditions better than I and probably have seen
the Cribbage Board. Have you a choice?" He looked
at Richards so eagerly, and withal so shrewdly and
sanely, that in self-defense the broker said:

"I can't say that I have. Of course I am bullish—"

"Of course. But the question is: Which—in a
week?"

Richards had no idea what was meant by this man
with the sane eyes who said crazy things through
his nose—a man who had one hundred thousand
dollars to his credit with the firm. Perplexed to the
verge of exasperation, Richards was stock-broker
enough—when in doubt, bluff!—to say, with a
frown, "Yes, that's the question: Which—in a

week?" He shook his head as though he were trying to pick out the best for his beloved Robison.

"I never was so puzzled in my life, and I want you to know that I've made money even in Rumanian bonds!"

"I'm afraid I can't help you much."

"What does the I. S. Board say?"

"Mr. Robison, exactly what do you mean by the I. S. Board?"

"What? You don't know the International Syndicate Cribbage Board! Then how in Hades do you pick your combinations?"

"We buy and sell stocks on our judgment of basic conditions or for special reasons."

"Ah, yes—like the public. You base your trades on gas and guess. Well, *I* don't! I'd play the Ant, but I don't see the Granary full in a week. Jay Gould had a perfect mania for it; it was an obsession with him. And yet he seldom won commensurately with his risks. In the Northwest corner he was tied up over a year and lost more than a million. I guess we'll dispense with the Ant, though it looks so safe for the Granger group."

Robison seemed to be thinking aloud rather than asking for advice. But Richards, who was a Wall Street man to his finger-tips, said, gravely, "I think you are right."

Robison nodded, to show he had heard, and went on: "The situation in the Pacific Coast, of course, suggests the Beaver at once. I can see the Dam in Union Pacific; but I don't like to try it so soon after the Rothschilds worked it so openly in Berlin over the Agadir excuse. Too many people who have access to the Menagerie remember it. I realize all this, but," he finished, with profound regret, "it *is* such a cinch!"

"Yes. But—" Richards shook his head in sympathy. He felt that he ought to humor this man; moreover, business was quiet, and this man was saying incomprehensible things that would be repeated by Richards, with sensational success, at luncheons and dinners for weeks.

"Of course, the Spider is the oldest stand-by. Personally I never liked it. In the Governor Flower boom and, indeed, up to the Northern Pacific panic, its popularity was due to John W. Gates. But do you know, Mr. Richards, I have always believed that in the first two Steel and Wire coups and in the Louisville & Nashville affair, Gates hit upon it by accident. Else," pursued Mr. Robison, controversially, "why was he pinched so badly in 1901 and again in 1907? He hit upon it, after he got out of Federal Steel, by accident, I tell you! He was a man of genius and courage, but it was all instinct with him. He was no student, sir—no student!"

"I've always said," observed Mr. George B. Richards, "that Gates was not a student!" He glared, thereby successfully defying contradiction.

"It leaves the Lion!" muttered Robison. "Should I try it? And which Peg?"

"I'd try it!" counseled Richards, who was not only intelligent, but had a sense of humor.

"Would you, really?"

"Yes, I certainly would!" And the broker looked as if he certainly meant it.

"It's the Dutch favorite," said Robison, musingly. "And they are a very clever people. You know

THE PANIC OF THE LION

Van Vollenhoven in his book says that once a year, for thirteen consecutive years, the great Cornelius Roelofs, of Amsterdam, made a million gulden in London by the Lion—the most hopeful pessimist in the history of stock speculation! It comes easy to the phlegmatic Hollanders, but Americans are too nervous to take kindly to it. I once begged the late Addison Cammack to join me in a Lion deal, but he didn't. He was not very well at the time. Anyhow, he was too American."

"Did you know him?"

"Like a book! Dangerous man to follow! Cynicism sounds impressive, but is wind. You don't win in the stock-market with catch phrases, but with combinations."

"Do you use charts?"

"A stock speculator is not a navigator, but all commission-houses should have a chart. With some customers, after you have exhausted every other invitation, you can use the chart to get them trading. But not for us, Mr. George B. Richards. I think you will soon realize that I am in this affair not to lose money, but to make it. I shall, therefore, either buy Dock Island, sell Middle Pacific, buy National Smelting, or sell Consolidated Steel. I'll have a pad of special order-slips made so you will not mistake my orders for those of any one else. You will execute for me no order that is not written and signed by me on such a slip. I'll keep up my margin. We'll operate on a ten-per-cent. basis; and I hereby authorize you to sell me out when my margin is down to six points. That gives you ample safety. It is really unnecessary, as I never lose; but I always protect the broker. The sudden death by heart disease of Baron Lespinasse in 1883 sent into bankruptcy the great firms of La Croissade et Cie. and Mayer, Dreyfus et Cie., of Paris, Verbrugghe Frères, of Brussels, and about a dozen smaller houses. Mine, to be sure, is a trifling operation, designed to supply a modest income to an old flame. But I may—who knows?—decide to take a few millions back with me. And your firm, Mr. Richards, will be my principal brokers."

Mr. Robison said this so impressively, so much as though he had made the firm of Richards & Tuttle rich beyond the dreams of avarice, that George B. found it easy to look grateful as he said, "Thank you, Mr. Robison." It would be worth while watching this mysterious man, to see, first, if he made money; and if he did, how!

"I'll write it here and now. If my margins are down to six points at any time close me out, for I shall have been mistaken, which is a sign I've gone crazy; or I shall be dead, in which case protect yourself!"

Mr. Robison wrote out the instructions, signed them, and gave them to Mr. Richards. He must have noticed a look of uncertainty or dissatisfaction on the broker's face, for he said:

"I have no desire to pose before you as an unfailing winner, though I assure you I seldom lose. It is not brains, but carefulness. If you know nothing about the International Syndicate's information-collecting machinery, why, just take my word for it that there are people in this world who don't work on the hit-or-miss plan. We don't eliminate all possibilities of failure; we merely reduce them to a negligible minimum. We cannot prevent all accidents, but we can and do foresee some of them. This sounds crazy to you, I know—no, don't deny it!—but all I can say is that your natural suspicions don't affect your kindness and courtesy, and I am more grateful than I can say. Of course, my own operations here will be conducted with your approval, in strict accordance with the rules of the New York Stock Exchange."

"Oh, I am sure I haven't doubted your sanity," said the broker, who had been much reassured by Mr. Robison's look of frankness and earnestness as he spoke. "I have merely suspected the depths of my own ignorance."

"Your retort is both kind and clever. I thank you. I shall have to borrow one of your clerks or office‑boys between nine‑forty and ten A. M., to whom I may give my orders to bring to this office, and also ask you to recommend to me some young man who is intelligent but honest, wide awake but deaf to the ticker."

"I beg your pardon?"

"I shall need a young man who can watch certain developments and at the crucial moment will hasten to me without stopping on the way to take advantage in the stock-market of what he has learned while working for me."

"I shall let you have one of my own clerks. He'll do as he is told."

"That is not always to be taken as praise—but I thank you. There will be some telegrams come for me. Will you kindly see that they are held? Good morning!" And he left the room.

An hour later cablegrams and telegrams by the dozen began to come in for Robison, care Richards

& Tuttle. But Robison did not return to the office until after the close of the stock-market.

"Any messages?" he asked Richards.

"Not over a hundred!" answered the broker, smilingly. He felt less suspicious after the telegrams began to arrive; they were tools he understood.

"I used the Triple Three," explained Robison, opening telegram after telegram; the cables he seemed to leave for the last. The telegrams were, as Richards later ascertained, from San Francisco, Seattle, Tacoma, Los Angeles, Salt Lake City, Vancouver, and other points west of the Rockies. Each contained but one word, but always the word ended in "less," such, for example, as Headless, Toothless, Tailless, Nerveless. All were signed in the same way, to wit: Three-Three-Three.

"No Beaver! I'm just as glad," Robison mused aloud and took up the cablegrams. They were from London, Paris, Berlin, Frankfort, and Amsterdam. They were in code, but he seemed to have the key by heart. The very last one made him thoughtful.

He handed the cablegram absently to Richards and said, "The Lion after all—and artificial at that!" He seemed to be lost in thought, oblivious of his whereabouts, as Richards read:

ROBISON, care RICHTUT:
Mogulgar wind Lloyd Vast Nigger Shaw twice home urban sweet Edward.

"Code, hey?"

"Lion! Oh! Code, did you say? No. Code is too risky. Plain reading! Of course I have more practice than you. Give it to one of your office-boys to decipher. If he succeeds give him fifty dollars and charge it to my account. But what I can't tell is the politics of it. Is it collusion, philanthropy, or fear? Is it wise? After all, the unusual is not necessarily dangerous. I shall double my money within four days and you will make the commissions in a perfectly simple, legitimate way; and you will think I am a pretty sane lunatic; and you will respect me for having such sources of information; and if I can induce Mrs. Le—my friend to take it, I'll make a million for her in a month, and you will get the benefits accruing from having the market named after you—a Richards & Tuttle market, the papers will call it. Thank you very much for your kindness. I'll be down to-morrow before the opening. Good day, sir!"

And Mr. Robison left the office with a calm, confident look in his face. Richards gazed after him, a look of perplexity on his own face. Presently he shook his head. It meant that he gave up efforts to solve the puzzle, but that he would wait until commissions began.

IV

From Richards & Tuttle's office Robison went to the nearest Western Union office and gave a letter to the manager.

"Send this at once! City editor, *Evening World*, Park Row. No answer. How much?"

The manager told him. Robison paid him and then went to the Postal-Telegraph office and sent a message to the city editor, *Evening Journal*. Inside

of each envelope was a letter. Both read alike, as
follows:

DEAR SIR,—Three years ago one of your reporters did me a
good turn. In return I promised to tip him off if ever I came
across a big piece of news. He saved me from being wrongly
sent to state prison. Things looked pretty black for me, though
I was not guilty. I've forgotten his name. He looked to be
twenty-eight or thirty years old, about five foot ten, not very
heavy-built, smooth-shaven, dark-brown hair, and wore eye-
glasses. He had on a dark-blue serge suit and was always
smoking cigarettes. It happened on Chambers Street, not far
from the Irving Bank. Ask him if he remembers my promise
to pay him back for being good to me. Here is where I do it.
Mr. W. H. Garrettson, the banker and promoter, is going to
be kidnapped. The plans are all made. He will be held for
one hundred million dollars ransom, and no harm will come
to him, because he will be sure to pay.

Don't warn the police of this, because the other papers would
get it and you would lose your scoop. You can warn Garrettson
if you wish, but it will be useless, as in that event we should
wait until vigilance relaxes, as it will surely do. Please do not
think this is a crazy yarn! Don't print anything now. Simply
be ready, with photographs of Garrettson, his home, art-gallery,
bank, list of his promotions, and corporations controlled by him,
and so on. Keep this letter for reference, and just before you
throw it into the waste-basket remember this: It costs you
nothing; it commits you to nothing, involves no expense;
there is no concealed dynamite and no fool joke. Remember
my writing and my signature, and wait for the tip I shall send
you if I possibly can, so that you alone publish the news.

GRATEFUL FRIEND.

The city editors thought it was a crank's letter and
threw it away, but each made a mental note—in
case! Also they did not "tip off" anybody. They
afterward stated that they said nothing to Garrettson, because if they acted on every freak missive
they received half the city would not sleep. They

thus were ready for the kidnapping of the great Garrettson.

At nine-forty-five on Tuesday morning Mr. James B. Robison, accompanied by an office-boy and an order-pad on which was printed "From J. B. R., for Richards & Tuttle," went to the Broad Street entrance of the New York Stock Exchange. His gaze was fixed steadily on the Subtreasury, or so it seemed to the office-boy. At nine-fifty-two he exclaimed:

"There he is!"

The office-boy, Sweeney, looking in the same direction, saw nothing but hurrying pedestrians and a carriage or two. Robison seemed so disappointed that the office-boy out of kindness asked, sympathetically, "Who, sir?"

"Nobody!" answered Mr. Robison, shortly. "Go back to the office and tell Mr. Richards to send me the clerk he promised me—the clerk with the ticker deafness, tell him. I'll wait here."

The boy left and presently returned with one of the bookkeepers.

"Here is Mr. Manley," the office-boy told Mr. Robison.

"Thank you. Here is something for you, my boy. Go back to the office."

The office-boy put the five-dollar bill in his pocket, said "Thank you" in a voice celestial, and hurried away before the crazy Frenchman with the Cape Cod voice discovered the size of the tip. To Manley, the clerk, Mr. Robison said:

"Look across the street—W. H. Garrettson & Co. You can see Mr. Garrettson by the window. See him?"

"Yes, sir."

"Well, just you stay here and watch him; and if you see him do anything unusual or if anything happens in Garrettson's office that you think strange, run to our office and let me know. I'll be waiting for you. Don't be afraid to say so if you think something unusual is going on, because I tell you now that Mr. Garrettson never does anything unusual."

"Yes, sir."

"Now what would you call unusual?"

"What would you?"

"If a bareheaded man came out of the office, stood at the head of the steps and threw an egg into the middle of the street, I'd call it unusual."

"So would I."

"Especially if I went up to the smashed egg and found the insides were of ink. It might be red ink or black."

"That would be queer!"

"Exactly. You watch. Go to lunch at twelve-thirty and be back at one. Remember! Watch closely, and if anything unusual happens look carefully and then come and tell me. Here's ten dollars for you."

"Thank you, sir."

"It's only a beginning," smiled Mr. Robison, promisingly.

Manley, the clerk, put the money in his pocket and began to think he might be able to buy the motorboat next spring if this business kept up.

Between what Sweeney, the office-boy, suspected aloud and what Manley, the clerk, confirmed the office force of Richards & Tuttle discussed Mr. Robison with the zest of the deciding baseball game.

THE PANIC OF THE LION

Richards had confided to his intimates some of his experiences, and Amos Kidder, the *Evening Planet* man, was as interested in the mystery as if he had not been the man who first let loose the flood of surmise by introducing Robison to the brokers.

Nothing happened on Tuesday more exciting than keeping tally on the telegrams and cables received by Mr. Robison, which amounted to thirty-seven in all. The object of so much conjecture—and hero of the office-boy's improvised dime novel—spent the day in an arm-chair looking at the blackboard, making elaborate calculations that convinced other customers he must be a "chart fiend." At three o'clock sharp he went home.

He stopped long enough to send by messenger-boy a letter to the city editor of the *Evening World* and another to the city editor of the *Evening Journal*. They bore the same message and said:

Refer to my letter of yesterday. To-night W. H. Garrettson goes to the opera to see "The Jewels of the Madonna." He will leave the Metropolitan in his automobile. In it will be his wife, his daughter, and his friend, Harry Willett. And he will not arrive at his house—Lexington Avenue and Thirty-eighth Street. Somewhere between the Opera House and his residence he will vanish! It will be the most mysterious kidnapping on record. Follow the Garrettson motor and have your reporters watch carefully.

GRATEFUL FRIEND.

Whatever the city editors may have intended to do in the matter is of no consequence, because at seven o'clock messages were received as follows:

Kidnapping of W. H. G. postponed. Will keep you posted.
GRATEFUL FRIEND.

THE PLUNDERERS

V

At nine-forty-five on Wednesday morning Mr. James B. Robison entered the office of Richards & Tuttle, sought the senior partner, and said:

"I shall both buy and sell Con. Steel—or possibly sell first and buy later. The order clerk knows about my printed slips. The orders will go to you first. If at any time you are worried about margin, remember to tell me at once, because, as you know, I have not yet used half of my letter of credit; and, besides, the cables are working. I'd like to see Amos Kidder."

"He's in his office."

"Would you mind having some one telephone to him? Thank you."

Mr. Robison promptly left the office, followed by his faithful attendant Sweeney, the office-boy. They took their stand just north of the Broad Street entrance of the Stock Exchange.

It was not long before Amos Kidder, of the *Evening Planet*, who had received the message, found Mr. Robison in the act of gazing unblinkingly toward the Subtreasury.

"Good morning, Mr. Robison."

Mr. Robison started as if he had been rudely awakened out of a profound reverie.

"Oh! Kidder! How d'ye do? Ah, yes! Ah—I'd like you to dine with me and a few friends—interesting people. You will—don't be offended!—you will learn why all newspaper articles on the stock-market arouse mirth among the people who pull the wires. What do you say?"

"I say," replied Kidder, with a good-natured smile,

"just this: When and where?" His smile ceased. Mr. Robison had turned his back on his friend. Kidder heard a nasal mumble and made out:

"Here in eight minutes."

"What do you mean?"

"I shall learn if the Lion ate the man or if it's a case of another day."

"Mr. Robison, I don't understand—"

"I beg your pardon. I was thinking of the old man who was seen in a front seat at the circus every day. They asked him what he found so interesting, and he said that some day the lion would eat the man and he wanted to be a spectator. Well, one day he was sick. That day the lion ate the lion-tamer. Well, I am here waiting to see Garrettson come out of the cage."

"Garrettson?"

"The great W. H. Garrettson! I am planning a campaign in Con. Steel. Garrettson's health is important. I must consider the state of his liver as carefully as the condition of the iron trade, because it is not only a question of the dividend rate, but of the price per share—not alone an investment, but a speculation. You can't lose all your mills and furnaces in one minute and you can't destroy all your customers overnight; but Garrettson can die in a second!"

"Of course that contingency has been provided for. His firm would undoubtedly be on the job."

"So would the undertaker. As a matter of fact everything to-day depends upon the character of Garrettson's life. Have you ever stopped to think of how much depends upon the character of his death?"

THE PLUNDERERS

"All deaths are alike. You talk like a novelist unaware of the resources of a firm like Garrettson's."

"And you talk like a plain ass or a bank president, my boy. Is there no difference to the stock-market between the death of Garrettson by pneumonia and his death by lynching at the hands of a thousand indignant fellow-citizens? Stop and think."

"Oh, well, that will never happen."

"I cannot swear that it will, but you cannot guarantee that it never will. Stranger things have come to pass. By Jingo! it's three minutes to ten! Would it not be curious if something had happened?"

"How do you mean?"

"I have studied the great Garrettson and his habits, that I may, in my operations in Con. Steel, know on what to bank and against what to guard. He leaves his Lexington Avenue house every morning at nine and arrives at his office not later than nine-fifty. He is like the clock. All his life he has come down-town in his coupé, driven by a coachman who has been in his employ thirty years. In this age of novelties that old-fashioned coupé suggests a stability and solid respectability comparable to *Founded 1732!* on a firm's letter-head. However, just as the wireless has introduced a new element into maritime life, so has the automobile changed the character of street traffic. Do you remember the case of James M. Barrier, the famous sculptor, smashed in his taxicab on his way to his studio? You remember the insurance advertisements, and how he carried a two-hundred-and-seventeen-thousand-dollar accident policy? Well, it's ten o'clock. In one minute, if Garrettson is not here, I shall sell short one thousand shares of Con. Steel. For each delay of one minute, one thousand shares."

Robison looked impressive, but the newspaper man was unimpressed.

"You'll have the pleasure of covering when he arrives as usual. Your operation is of the kind that sounds wise."

"How much do I stand to lose by covering, say, in a few minutes? A fraction! How much do I stand to gain if something has happened? Five or ten points! It's a fifty-to-one shot. I'll take it every time. Here, boy, rush this to the office and hurry back. Tell Mr. Richards I shall need another boy besides you, for a few minutes only."

Young Sweeney hurried away with Robison's order to sell one thousand shares of Con. Steel "at the market."

"There are men who will risk money on the shadow cast by a human hair," observed Kidder, pleasantly. "In assuming that disaster has overtaken Garrettson—"

"I assume nothing. I know that something unusual has happened! What the nature of it is I know not—nor whether it is capitalizable, sight unseen. Here, boy!" Sweeney had returned with a colleague and Robison sent the new boy back with an order to sell two thousand shares of Steel. Watch in hand, Robison stood staring unblinkingly toward the north. Kidder also looked up Nassau Street, expecting and—such, alas, is human nature!—hoping to see Garrettson's familiar coupé.

"Here, boy!" And Robison sent off another selling-order. He kept this up until he had put out a short line of ten thousand shares.

At ten-fifteen he said to Kidder:

"Let us go over to Garrettson's office. His non-arrival is news, Kidder."

"He may have stopped on the way to do some shopping—"

"Well, that's a story! Any deviation from the normal is, even though it may not be tragedy. The delay may mean—"

"Nothing whatever," finished Kidder, a trifle exultingly. "There comes Garrettson's carriage. I guess you'd better cover!"

And the *Planet* man laughed.

"Kidder, you'll never be rich! Of course I shall not cover until I know the reason for the delay. Make haste! I ought to take a good look at his face. I want to see how he looks and notice how he walks up the steps to the office. One glimpse of Harriman getting off the train once put a cool quarter of a million in my pocket."

"Stocks went up when he died. People sold them thinking—"

"When you know a man is dying and you know that the rabble doesn't know it, you don't always sell stocks short, Kidder," anticipated Robison, with a gentle smile.

"Hello!" said Kidder, and ran forward.

Robison followed. The coupé had stopped before the door of the banking firm's offices. The herculean private policeman in gray had hastened to open the door of the chief's carriage and had staggered back as if horrified by what he had seen.

"Murdered!" thought the newspaper man in a flash. "What a story!"

THE PANIC OF THE LION

The policeman turned an alarmed face toward the coachman and asked:

"Where's Mr. Garrettson?"

"What!" Lyman, the coachman, who had been in Garrettson's employ thirty-odd years, turned livid. He stared blankly at the big man in the gray uniform.

"He isn't here!" said Allcock, the policeman. Kidder and Robison heard him.

The coachman looked into the coupé.

"Good God!" he muttered.

"Are you sure he was inside?" asked Allcock.

"Sure? Of course! There's the newspapers. Look at the cigar-ashes on the floor."

"Did you see him get in?" persisted the policeman.

"Of course I saw him! I heard him call to the footman, who was going back to the house without leaving the newspapers."

"And you didn't stop anywhere?"

"No. I was delayed a little at Twelfth Street and Fourth Avenue, and again—"

"Are you sure he didn't jump off?"

"What would he be jumping off for?" queried the old coachman, irritably. "And wouldn't I have heard the door slam? I can't account for it! My God! Where's Mr. Garrettson? Where is he? Where is he?" He repeated himself like one distraught.

"Could he have jumped out without your knowing it?" queried Kidder.

"Shut up, Jim. That's a reporter!" the policeman warned the coachman. "Wait here and I'll tell Mr. Jenkins."

The private policeman rushed into the bank, and

rushed out, followed by William P. Jenkins, junior partner of W. H. Garrettson & Company.

"What is all this about?" Mr. Jenkins, who had been speaking in a sharp voice to the coachman, caught sight of Kidder. Nothing concerning Mr. Garrettson's whereabouts could be discussed by or before newspaper men.

"Come with me, James," Mr. Jenkins said, peremptorily, to the old coachman.

"Get on the job!" whispered Robison to Kidder. "Don't be bluffed. You've got enough to raise the dickens if printed. It's the scoop of a lifetime!"

Amos Kidder nodded eagerly. He had ceased to think of Robison's eccentricities and was occupied with the disappearance of the great financier. He followed Jenkins and the coachman into the office, but all efforts to listen to their colloquy were in vain. He could see perturbation plainly printed on the face of Mr. Jenkins, for all that Garrettson's junior partner was one of the master bluffers of Wall Street and a consummate artist at poker. The newspaper man was, moreover, fortunate enough to overhear Mr. Jenkins's private secretary say:

"Mrs. Garrettson says Mr. Garrettson left the house about nine-twenty in the carriage, as usual. The butler saw him get in; the footman helped him into the cab. She wanted to know what had happened. I said, 'Nothing that I know of.'"

Jenkins nodded approval of the typical financier's evasion and hastened back to the private office, where the cross-examination of the coachman—a man above suspicion—was carried on by the other partners.

THE PANIC OF THE LION

Amos Kidder had heard enough. He rushed out and, accompanied by the patient Robison, telephoned to his office this bulletin:

W. H. Garrettson left his residence in Lexington Avenue near Thirty-eighth Street this morning as usual in his coupé, driven by James Lyman, his coachman. Lyman, who has been in the employ of the family from boyhood, declares positively that Mr. Garrettson got in as usual. He was smoking one of his famous $2.17 cigars and had all the daily newspapers. These and cigar-ashes were all that could be seen in the coupé when it reached the Wills Building, at Broad and Wall streets, where the offices of W. H. Garrettson & Company are. His partners are unable to say where the multimillionaire promoter is to be found. Mrs. Garrettson is equally positive that Mr. Garrettson left the house as usual. The butler saw him get in. Nobody saw him get out. What makes this remarkable is that Mr. Garrettson is punctuality itself and not once in forty years has he failed to reach his office before ten o'clock. His disappearance from the coupé is not thought to be a joke; but, on the other hand, there is no reason to apprehend a tragedy. "It is mysterious—that's all," remarked a prominent Wall Street man; "and mysteries are not always profitable in the stock-market!"

"How long," inquired Robison, as Kidder came out of the telephone-booth, "will it be before the *Evening Planet*, with your account of the non-arrival of Garrettson, is out on the street?"

"Well," said Kidder, looking a trifle important, "if it had been any one else who telephoned a story of that importance time would be wasted in verifying it, but my story ought to be out in five minutes!"

"As quickly as that?"

"Well, maybe seven minutes—but that," said Kidder, impressively, "would be slow work for the *Evening Planet!*"

79

"Amazing!" murmured Robison, in a congratulatory tone. "And did you make it clear that there was no explanation for the non-arrival of—"

"I said it had not been explained as yet. A man isn't kidnapped in broad daylight in the city of New York—taken out of his own cab and carried away. If conscious, he would have shouted to the coachman; if unconscious, he would have attracted attention. It can't be done!"

"No, it can't," agreed Robison. "Nevertheless, it has been done."

"How could—"

"Kidder, the taxicab has introduced a new and easily utilizable possibility into criminal affairs, against which the police cannot yet protect the public. I can see one, two, three, five, ten, fourteen different ways in which Mr. Garrettson could have been abducted from his own carriage, put into a taxi, and carried away. Suppose there are six taxis. Three are in front to prevent the coachman from passing them. The coachman is also compelled to regulate his speed according as they desire. Then put one taxi on each side and one behind. These taxis not only escort the cab; they pocket it and keep out help. At one of the many halts the cab door is opened and Garrettson induced to enter one of the side taxis while the coachman is occupied taking care of his horses because one of the taxis in front threatens to back, which will crush the prancing beasts. Do you suppose the coachman, especially if he is elderly and somewhat deaf, as all old people are, could hear a cry for help with six taxis making all the noise they can, muffler cutouts going, or backfiring, or—"

"Do you think that is—"

"I think nothing! I cited it as one of fourteen—indeed, twenty—possible ways," said Robison, quietly.

"It's funny—I mean it is a curious coincidence that on the one day you had sold Steel short—"

"My young friend," interrupted Robison, gravely, "I sold after Garrettson was late! Wisdom is always accused of unfairness. A man whose mind enables him to win steadily at cards is invariably suspected of marking them. I had planned to buy Con. Steel provided Garrettson's health, state of mind, and trade conditions satisfied me! Instead I sold a little because of his delay. Why, man, we did that in London once—Cecil Rhodes and I—when Barney Barnato, at the height of the Kaffir craze, suddenly decided—"

"Wait till I get a piece of paper," said Amos Kidder. He saw a big story. But Robison said:

"I'll tell you all you wish to know—if you promise not to use names—in Richards's office later, when Garrettson's disappearance is officially admitted. You should hang round Garrettson's office. Don't lose sight of it for one minute! Your office will keep in touch—"

"Yes; they are sending three men down to work under me."

"Keep me posted, will you? I am going to Richards's office and watch the market."

Kidder nodded and hurried to the Wills Building. Robison went to the office of his brokers, stopping previously at a telephone pay-station to telephone to the city editors of the *Evening World* and the *Evening Journal*. This was his message:

THE PLUNDERERS

The *Evening Planet* is getting out an extra about the disappearance of W. H. Garrettson. Send your men to Garrettson's office and also his residence. Hurry!

The *Evening Planet* story was on the street before Robison returned to Richards & Tuttle's office, and five minutes later *World* and *Journal* extras were selling in the financial district. Curiously enough, both papers used the same scare-head, and that fact had a great deal to do with the acceptance of the story by many people. The heading was:

HELD FOR RANSOM!!

And each stated it had information that W. H. Garrettson had been kidnapped and was held for one hundred million dollars ransom. The Wall Street news agencies sent out the news on the tickers. One of them subtly finished:

Those who know Mr. Garrettson state that the two things the greatest financier of our times cannot do are: first, take advice; and second, be coerced. A man who has compelled a President of the United States to come to him for advice, and who has flatly told a reigning monarch, No! is not going to do as he is told by any band of crooks! The worst is, therefore, to be feared!

VI

For one brief dazed moment the stock-market hesitated! Then suddenly the ticker stopped, as it did in the old days whenever a member's demise was announced. The ticker's silence, with its suggestion of death, did in truth strangle bull hopes. Ten thousand gamblers' hearts almost stopped when the ticker did. Then the storm burst, increasing in violence as corroboration came from newspaper extras, from the Wall Street news agencies and the news tickers, from brokers and bankers who had rushed to the offices of W. H. Garrettson & Company and had rushed out again to sell stocks. And for one fatal moment the great house of W. H. Garrettson & Company was guilty of the capital crime—in high finance—of indecision.

The stock-market at times suggests a reservoir—the selling-power is liquefied fear. Like water, all it asks is one tiny crevice—a beginning!—and it will itself complete the havoc.

Inside support—that is, buying by Garrettson's firm—would have been the only effective denial of the alarming rumors. Therefore, in the brief instant that saw absolutely no "support" forthcoming the flood of selling-orders raged down upon the stock-market, carrying with it big margins and little margins and minus margins, fortunes and hopes and reputations.

The price of Con. Steel declined faster and faster as the volume of selling-orders grew larger. It was the snowball rolling down the hillside. From sixty-eight it went to sixty-seven; to sixty-six; to sixty-five by fractions. Then it broke whole points at a time—to sixty; to fifty-five! In fifteen frightful, unforgetable minutes the capital stock of the Consolidated Steel Corporation shrank in value fifteen million dollars—one million a minute! A psychological statistician would have figured that this million a minute was the tribute of the moneyed world to the great Garrettson's reputation for financial invulnerability; it was the cost of the blow to his prestige, the result of his partners' inefficiency during the one crucial moment of the firm's existence. The partners would have understood death and could have provided against it, stock-marketwise. It is likely that they even might have capitalized their senior partner's demise had it come from typhoid, tuberculosis, or taxicab. But the disappearance of the great Garrettson, the fatal incertitude, the black ignorance, the fearing and the hoping, paralyzed the faculties of the junior partners of Wall Street's mighty firm. And the costliness of their indecision was raised into the millions by the fact that, just as Jenkins, Johnson, and Lane, the junior partners, agreed that Garrettson, though absent, was well, and were about to take steps to check the gamblers' panic, the telephone summoned Jenkins.

"Hello! Is this Mr. Jenkins? Good. This is Dr. Pierson. Come at once to Mr. Garrettson, Hotel Cressline, Suite D. No, not B—D! Say nothing to the family! Hurry!" And the speaker rang off.

His face livid with apprehension, visibly tortured by the still unrelieved uncertainty, Jenkins turned to Walter Johnson, the youngest and—Wall Street said —the cleverest of Garrettson's partners, and repeated the message.

"Was it Dr. Pierson's voice?" asked Johnson.

"I don't know—yes; I think it was. He said, 'This is Dr. Pierson,' and I didn't suspect—yes; I think it was." After a second's pause, "I know it was Pierson!"

"Then, for Heaven's sake—" began Lane.

"Your knowledge of Pierson's voice, Jenkins, is vitiated by your obvious wish. Call up Dr. Pierson's office, of course!" said Johnson.

"Meantime we are losing precious time—"

Johnson had already gone to the desk telephone and asked for Dr. Pierson's office. To his partner he said, the receiver at his ear:

"We have all eternity before us to solve the problem if—" The emphasis on the conditional particle indicated so clearly his meaning that there was no need to say it. "You need not go on a wild-goose chase, and we hoping and expecting and uncertain if— Hello! Dr. Pierson's office? This is Mr. Johnson, of W. H. Garrettson & Company. Is the doctor there? Out? Where did he go? Speak out— I am Mr. Garrettson's partner. Hotel Cressline, Suite D? Thank you." Johnson turned and said: "Dr. Pierson was summoned by telephone to the Cressline, Suite D, to attend Mr. Garrettson. Hurry call! I'll get the hotel and ask—"

"And meantime," said Jenkins, excitedly, "he might be dying or dead; and we—"

"Yes! Go! I'll arrange to have a telephone-line kept for our exclusive use. Hurry!"

Jenkins rushed madly from the office and Johnson took up the telephone once more.

"Give me the Hotel Cressline!" And presently, "Hello! Cressline? This is W. H. Garrettson & Company. Yes—Mr. Johnson, Mr. Garrettson's partner. Is Mr. Gar— . . . Yes—yes—I want to talk to him. . . . Why not? Is it our Mr. Garrettson . . . Here! Hold your horses! You will tell me!—or, by Heaven, I'll . . . Hello!—Hello! Damn 'em!"

"What did they say, Walter?" asked Mr. Lane, partner and brother-in-law of Garrettson.

"He said I could go to hell!" growled Johnson,

his face brick-red from anger; people did not talk that way to the partners of the great Garrettson. "He said a Mr. Garrettson, accompanied by a heavily veiled lady, took Suite D this morning at nine-forty-five, and left orders not to be interrupted under any circumstances—no cards sent up, no telephone connection made, no messages of any kind delivered!"

The two partners looked at each other gravely. In their eyes was something like a cross between a challenge and an entreaty, as though each expected the other to say he did not expect a terrible final chapter. In the veiled woman each feared what was worse than mere death—scandal! Of course, much would be suppressed, as had been done in the case of Winthrop Kyle or of Burton Willett, to whom death had come suddenly and under dubious circumstances.

"William is not that kind!" said Lane, loyally. "He has never—"

"I know that, of course. I don't believe it. I don't! I don't!" repeated Walter Johnson, vehemently.

"Neither do I," agreed Lane. "But—" He looked furtively at Walter Johnson.

Johnson nodded, and said, "Yes, that's the devil of it!" He lost himself in thoughts of how to suppress the scandal; for these men loved Garrettson, admired his abilities, gloried in his might, and reverenced his greatness. They would rather see the firm lose millions than have posthumous mud flung upon the historic figure of W. H. Garrettson.

That was the explanation of why the ordinary precautions for staving off a panic were not taken

by the partners. That was why they denied themselves to everybody who brought no news of Mr.
W. H. Garrettson; and such was the discipline of
the office that no word was brought to the pale-
faced partners in the inner office about the big break
in stocks or of the newspaper extras.

It was the fatal mistake. By the time Walter
Johnson, by accident or force of habit, or possibly
subconsciously, moved by the telepathic message of
the ticker, approached the little instrument the
slump in stocks had taken on the proportions of a
panic.

"Great Scott! Fifty-eight for steel!"

"No!" incredulously shouted Lane.

"It 'll never do!"

"Yes, but—"

Walter Johnson, forgetting that Mr. Garrettson
was a man who liked to do things in his own way,
rushed out of the private office and began to give
out buying-orders to the better-known of the Garrettson brokers—they kept some of these for the
effect of obvious "Garrettson buying." It was all
the firm could do to check the decline. No matter
what had happened, the house of Garrettson must
not lie about it! Silence, yes; untruth, never!
And yet silence might be taken as corroboration of
the awful stories. He could not say that the great
Garrettson was alive and could not say he was dead.
He must not mention Hotel Cressline. A trying
situation! To the news-agency men, who would
put out the news on the Street, from whom also the
daily papers would get it, he said, very calmly and
impressively:

"I know of no reason why anybody should sell

Consolidated Steel. The iron trade is in excellent shape; the company is doing the biggest business in its history at reasonable but remunerative prices, and we consider the stock a good investment. We deprecate these violent speculative movements. They are designed to frighten timid holders. I advise every man who owns Consolidated Steel stock to hold on to it."

"But about Mr. Gar—"

"Not another word!" he said, firmly, with a smile that was a masterpiece of will-power.

The newspaper men translated it: "Not a word about W. H. Garrettson!" And in the Stock Exchange a similar construction was put upon the message. What was wanted was to know whether the great Garrettson was dead or not—the kidnapping was by now accepted as a fact!—and if so what would be done with the enormous Garrettson holdings of Steel. Wherefore the traders sold more of the same stock—short—and the bona-fide holders could develop no conviction strong enough as to the wisdom of holding on, so long as the price continued to go down.

Jenkins arrived at the Cressline in time to find Dr. Pierson engaged in a fight with the office force, who would not show Suite D to him or send up any message. But Jenkins, who in his youth had been a book agent, succeeded in inducing the management to break open the door after repeated knocking brought no response from within.

They found nobody in Suite D. Mr. Garrettson had vanished! But they found on the bureau a long lavender automobile veil.

Jenkins and Dr. Pierson stared at each other in

perplexity. At length Jenkins, red and uncomfortable, said to Dr. Pierson:

"I came up as soon as I got your telephone message; and—"

"I never telephoned you!" interrupted Dr. Pierson.

"Why, you said—"

"I didn't say it. I came up here because I got a message from the hotel—or so the voice said—to see Mr. Garrettson, who had been taken suddenly ill in Suite D. His companion, a young lady, was with him."

"Damn!" said Jenkins, with an uneasy look. He bethought him of the office, hastened to the telephone and told Walter Johnson all about the fake messages and Dr. Pierson's story.

"That was to throw us off the scent. Con. Steel has broken ten points, and—"

"It's a bear raid then!"

"Yes. But have the bears got W. H. Garrettson? If so, where? Hurry down!"

Meantime in the office of Richards & Tuttle Mr. Robison was carefully following the course of the stock-market. The lower Steel went the higher Robison rose in the estimation of the firm, the customers and the office-boys.

In one of the interludes between the slumps George B. Richards asked in a voice which one might say sweated respect:

"What do you think now, Mr. Robison?"

The office had been doing a great business and the big room with the quotation-board that took one side was crowded with customers. These customers, with eyes that shone greedily, drew near and frankly listened to the colloquy. They were all happy because they were all short of Steel, and they were all short of Steel because a mysterious stranger had scented a strange mystery ten minutes ahead of Wall Street.

"Yes?" said Mr. Robison, absently.

"What do you think now?"

"What do I think now?" repeated Mr. Robison, mechanically.

"Yes, sir," said George B. Richards, in the tone of voice of an office-boy about to ask for a day off. Robison stared unseeingly at the broker. Then, with a little start, he said so distinctly that every listening customer heard very plainly:

"I have not changed my opinion. When I do I'll let you know."

"It looks to me," persisted Richards, fishing for information, "that they can't keep on going down forever."

"No—not forever," assented Mr. Robison, calmly.

"Maybe the bottom is not far off."

"Maybe not."

"If a man bought now he might do well."

"Then buy 'em."

"Still, until we know just what is back of this break it isn't safe to go long."

"In that case," said Mr. Robison, with a polite nod of the head, "don't buy 'em."

Richards did not persist, and with an effort subdued the desire to say "Thank you!" in a most sarcastic tone of voice. The disappointed customers drifted away. To be told when to begin making money is great, but any experienced stock speculator will tell you that it is even more important to be told when to stop making it. The tale of the Untaken Profit is the jeremiad of the ticker-fiend.

Con. Steel was down to fifty-five and beginning to show "resiliency," as financial writers used to say, when an office-boy rushed to Mr. Robison's side. The lad's face shone with pride at being the bearer of money-making news to the most distinguished of the firm's customers, whose paper profits at that moment were about one hundred thousand dollars.

"Mr. Robison!" he said in the distinct, low voice of one who is accustomed to repeating confidential messages in a crowded room. The other customers, who were still hopeful of getting the tip when to cover, looked at the boy's lips and listened strainingly to catch his whispered words.

"Speak up, my boy. I am a little hard of hearing," said Mr. Robison through his nose, with a pleasant smile.

The customers, to a man, blessed the catarrh that caused the deafness which would give them the tip they all expected.

"The photographer says the pictures came out very fine indeed."

The looking and listening customers, to a man, murmured, "Stung again!"

"Wait a minute my lad. Here!" and he gave the office-boy a five-dollar bill and a small envelope.

"Thank you very much, sir," said the boy. He put the five dollars in his pocket, beamed gratefully on Mr. Robison, gazed pityingly at the customers, and looked at the envelope. It said, "Mr. Richards."

He gave the envelope to Mr. Richards, who had retreated into the private office. The broker opened it. It contained one of Robison's slips, on which was written:

Buy twenty thousand Con. Steel at the market.

J. B. ROBISON.

Richards rushed the order to the Board Room. It helped to steady the price. Presently Mr. Richards approached Robison and sat in the empty place beside him. Feeling that they were not wanted, two polite customers moved away, ostensibly not to hear; but they tried to listen just the same.

"Your order is executed, Mr. Robison." Mr. Richards whispered it out of a corner of his mouth without turning his head, all the time looking meditatively at the quotation-board.

"Got the whole twenty?"

"Yes."

"Good!"

"Do you think—" began the broker in a voice that would make flint turn to putty.

"I do!" cut in Robison. "I do, indeed! There is no telling what has happened. The sharpness of the break was intensified by two facts." He had unconsciously raised his voice.

A startled look fastened itself on the seventeen faces of the seventeen customers who were short of Steel. The seventeen owners of the faces drew nearer to Mr. Robison, who, apparently unaware of having any other listener than Mr. George B. Richards, went on, nasally but amiably:

"By two things: First, the mystery. What has become of Mr. W. H. Garrettson? Second: If the great Garrettson has disappeared it must be because of a worse-than-death. Many things can be worse than death, in the stock-market—failure, for in-stance."

"Oh, but that's out of the question."

"Yes, it is! So is the disappearance of W. H. Garrettson, one of the best-known men in America, in broad daylight, in a crowded and very efficiently policed city thoroughfare."

"Yes; but a failure—"

"When the Baring Brothers failed Englishmen the world over wouldn't believe it. They couldn't fail, you know!"

"Do you think—"

"No, I do not. I was merely objecting to the habit of loose assertions so characteristic of Wall Street. I told you to what two things I ascribed the sharpness of the break. Mystery is the greatest of all bull cards, as you all know. It may also be made to work on the bear side. Now it isn't likely that anything serious has happened to Mr. W. H. Garrettson. There would be no sense in murdering him—not even by a stock speculator; but, even if he is dead, the break in the Garrettson specialties has by now discounted that sad contingency. There-fore I should say prices ought to be touching bottom; and what ought to be generally is, in the stock-market. I fancy we'll hear, one way or another, very soon now. If the news is good the price of Steel will rebound smartly. If it is bad we'll at least know what to look to, and with the elimination of the mystery there should be a cessation of the selling. There will follow a rush to cover and then— There you are! I believe it's begun already. Fifty-nine; and a half; sixty; sixty-two! Get 'em back!"

The seventeen shorts in the room rushed to give

their orders to cover and gloomily watched the massacre of the bears as melodramatized in figures on the quotation-board.

Sixty-three! Sixty-five! Sixty-seven! Higher than it had been before the newspaper extras came out! Big blocks were changing hands. W. H. Garrettson & Co. were buying the stock aggressively, even recklessly now. Somebody must pay—and it wouldn't be the firm.

Amos Kidder rushed into the office. "He's found!" he yelled, excitedly, addressing Mr. Robison.

"Where was he?" asked Mr. Robison, very calmly.

"At home—damn 'im!"

"Why that, my boy?"

"He won't talk—says he was in his library all the time."

"We know better than that. Don't we, Kidder?" said Robison, with a smile.

"Yes; but you don't have to print the official statement as though it were the truth, and I have. How can I say he lied when I can't prove that he wasn't in his library? If I knew the whole truth—"

"The whole truth?" echoed Mr. Robison, with the shade of a smile.

"Don't you know it?" Amos Kidder shot this at Mr. Robison suspiciously.

"Don't make me laugh, Kidder! Nobody knows the whole truth about anything. Take dinner with me to-morrow night—will you?"

"Yes." There was a smoldering defiance—it wasn't suspicion exactly—in the newspaper man's voice and eyes.

"Good for you! Mr. Richards, please sell my Steel."

"Now that Garrettson is—"

"Yes, now—at the market, carefully. Have I doubled my money in a week?"

"Yes."

"I told you I would."

"An accident is not a fair test of—"

"An accident is not a fair test of anything, because there is no such thing in the stock-market as an accident! The sooner you let that fact seep in the better it will be for the bank account of your children. I must be going up-town now. Good night, gentlemen."

VII

As early as practicable the next day, after the interest had been figured out to the ultimate penny, Mr. James Burnett Robison was informed by Mr. George B. Richards that he had to his credit the sum of $268,537.71 with the firm.

"I've won my bet!" murmured Mr. Robison, staring absently at the broker.

"You have indeed, Mr. Robison." Richards spoke deferentially.

"H'm! I hope I can induce Ethel to— Mr. Richards, I'll thank you to sign this paper. There is a notary public up-stairs."

This was the document:

To whom it may concern:

This is to certify that on July 18, 1912, Mr. James B. Robison opened an account with the firm of Richards & Tuttle, bankers and brokers, members of the New York Stock Exchange, by depositing with them the sum of $100,000. On July 23d he closed this account, which showed a net profit of $168,537.71.

A copy of the itemized statement, showing purchases and sales of stocks and prices paid and received, will be given to any one upon an order from Mr. James B. Robison.

For RICHARDS & TUTTLE:
GEORGE B. RICHARDS.

When Mr. George B. Richards had signed this certificate Mr. Robison said, amiably:

"If you wish I'll give you, in return, a letter testifying to the pleasure it has given me to trade in an office where they let customers more than double their money in one week."

"Thank you. I hope you are not going to withdraw your account."

"And I hope you will send and get me a hundred thousand dollars in new, clean hundred-dollar bills to give to the beneficiary of my wager. I told you it was easy to make money in Wall Street. You wouldn't have given me a certificate of sanity a week ago. What?"

"Oh yes, I would. But if you don't think my curiosity impertinent—"

"All curiosity in a stock-broker is a sign of intelligence; and intelligence, my dear Mr. George B. Richards, is never impertinent." Mr. Robison smiled with such amiable sincerity that Richards felt flattered enough to blush.

"Thank you. But there is one thing I don't understand—" The broker paused; he was about to inquire into the personal affairs of a profitable customer. He did not wish commissions to stop.

Mr. Robison bowed his head acquiescingly and, as though it were his turn to speak, said:

"It is always wise for a man to have a number of things he doesn't understand. It affords occupation during idle moments, gives the mind healthy exercise, and, indeed, maintains a salutary interest in life. Humanity loves knowledge, but is fascinated by mystery. Is life interesting to you? Yes. Why? Because it is so important and you know so little about it. Is death interesting to you? Yes. Why? Because of death you know only the first letter of the first word of the first line of the first chapter of a big, black book—Mystery!"

"Yes," murmured the dazed broker.

Robison continued, cheerfully: "My dear Mr. Richards, by all means don't understand! I'll drop in later in the day for the hundred thousand dollars. Meanwhile pray continue to be mystified and unhappy, but interested, and believe me your sincere friend and well-wisher, James Burnett Robison."

With these words the man who looked like a Paris dude and talked like an actor with the voice of a down-east farmer, whose speech suggested insanity but whose deeds yielded him twenty-five thousand dollars a day, walked out of the office of his brokers.

A few hours later he received ten bundles of hundred-dollar bills, which he carelessly stuffed into his coat pocket, and then asked for a check for his balance. When George B. Richards regretfully complied and lachrymosely hoped Mr. Robison would reconsider his decision to close the account, Mr. Robison answered, very impressively:

"My dear Mr. Richards, if you were Rockefeller, would you work in a glue-factory for the pleasure of it? I don't need money and I hate the marketplace. If ever I decide that humanity needs more money than I personally possess I'll come back and take it out of Wall Street through Richards & Tuttle, at one-eighth of one per cent. commission and the state tax. Good day, sir!" And he left, Mr. Richards remembered just afterward and wondered, without shaking hands.

VIII

Amos Kidder dined with Mr. Robison that evening at Mr. Robison's hotel, the Regina.

"Americans," explained the host, "always flock to the newest hotel on the theory that material progress is infallible and that the latest thing is necessarily the best thing. But cooking is not sanitary plumbing; it is an art! I am here not because of the journalistic, Sunday-special character of the filtered air and automatic temperature adjusters of this hotel, but because I discovered it had the best chef of all New York here. The food," he finished, with an air of overpraising, "is almost as good as in my own house. Have you any favorite dishes or doctor's diet to follow?"

"No, thank Heaven! I'll eat and drink whatever you'll order," replied the newspaper man.

"Thank you, Kidder—thank you!" said Mr. Robison, with an air of such profound gratitude that Kidder forgot to laugh. "I was hoping you would leave it to me to order the dinner; in fact, it is ordered. Thank you!" And he beckoned to the *maître d'hôtel*, who immediately hastened to the table and covered his face with a mask of extreme respectfulness. "You may begin to serve the dinner, Antoine," said Robison, simply.

"Dewey at Manila!" thought Kidder, impressed in spite of himself. His Wall Street work and his

THE PANIC OF THE LION

friendship with millionaires had accustomed him to all sorts of extravagances, but he admitted to himself he had never eaten so unconsciously well in his life. Emboldened by the dinner and the heart-warming wine, and his own growing affection for the curious man who said remarkable things through his nose and did remarkable things in a remarkably matter-of-fact way, Kidder was inspired to say over the coffee:

"I'd like to ask you two questions—just two."

"That's one more than Carlyle, who said that man had but one question to ask man, to wit: 'Can I kill thee or canst thou kill me?'"

"O king, live forever!" said Kidder, saluting.

"Thanks. Shoot ahead."

"Did you know what was going to happen or were you really betting on the chance that Garrettson's absence meant something serious?" Kidder was looking at Robison with a steady gaze.

"There is, my dear boy, no such thing as chance. Irreligious people have invented chance to fill in a hiatus otherwise unbridgable. Right, my boy!" And Robison nodded.

"Your talks with Richards were mighty mysterious," said Kidder, with an accusing tone of voice he could not quite control.

"So is the internal economy of a bug mysterious."

"And your talk about the Lion eating the man and the International Cribbage Board—"

"But not exactly criminal, eh?"

"No; but—"

"Kidder, my rhetorical eccentricities are of no consequence. Suppose you call it a harmless desire to give to myself the importance of the inexplicable, or even an intent to confuse impressions by making the mind of the broker dwell more on the mysteriousness of the customer than on the possible meaning of that customer's trading. Do you wish me to tell you that I have a system for beating the ticker game? Because I sha'n't! But that I go about my business scientifically you yourself have seen. At least you are witness that I have won."

"Yes; but—"

"What's the second question?"

"There isn't a second if you won't answer the first," said Kidder, with the forced amiability of the foiled.

"I have answered it. What you really wish is a detective story. Suppose we imagine. The only real people are those that live in our minds. Now let us wonder what happened to Garrettson and why he will not tell. Here is an incident that precipitated a slump which had the semblance of a panic—short-lived though it was—that caused mental anguish to his friends, relatives, and associates; and yet that great genius of finance, Wall Street's demigod, says nothing."

"He says he was in his library."

"We know he lies. That makes it more serious. Why does he lie? What compels so powerful and courageous a man as the great Garrettson to lie?"

"I don't know."

"You ought to; there is only one thing."

"Do you mean fear of a petticoat scandal?"

"No; because Garrettson does not fear that. Being highly intelligent, he protects himself against all possibility of scandal. No. It is something else. It's fear!"

"Of the alleged kidnappers?"

"No. He doesn't fear men. But he might fear—" He paused.

"What?" eagerly asked the newspaper man.

"Ridicule!"

Kidder aimed what he fondly hoped was a piercing glance at Mr. Robison. He discovered nothing. Mr. Robison had a far-away look in his philosophical eyes.

"It's too much for me," finally confessed Kidder, hoping that the frankness of his admission might induce Mr. Robison to speak on.

Robison smiled forgivingly, and said:

"You have what I may call the usual type of mind. You look at usual things in the usual way. And yet the application of well-known principles to well-known people seems to benumb your usual mind most unusually. Now what do you gather from the Garrettson episode?"

"Nothing, unless it is that you made a lot of money by what seems to be a most unusual succession of coincidences."

"Your voice," said Robison, with a sort of sedate amusement, "exudes suggestions of the penitentiary. The idea of law and order has become an instinct. The lawful is usual. The unusual, therefore, is unlawful. It puts the blessed era of scientific anarchy as far off as the old maids' millennium—or as the abolition of stupidity among bankers and—"

"And newspaper men—what?" Kidder prompted, pleasantly. "Don't mind me. I enjoy it."

"Kidder, you are a nice chap! That's why I asked your Paris man for a letter of introduction to the financial editor of his newspaper. It gave me what

I as a stranger needed in Wall Street. It was easy to get. It is an American failing to give such letters promiscuously, because we are an irresponsible people. I have, I suppose, voiced a suspicion of yours about me?"

"I did not have it. I have it now, however."

"If we talk about poor me any longer you'll be asking for my aliases and my Bertillon measurements. Now let's get to Garrettson. We know he left his house in his carriage at his usual hour and that he did not arrive at his office. We have the evidence of his coachman—a man above suspicion—of the newspapers, and of the cigar-ashes. We know, for you heard Jenkins call up the house, that Mr. Garrettson was not at home. We know that his disappearance must have been connected with alarming circumstances or his partners would not have been so badly upset as to allow that reputation-shattering slump in the Garrettson shares—led, I am thankful to say, by Consolidated Steel. We know that Jenkins rushed up-town to the Cressline Hotel and found Dr. Pierson, but no Garrettson there, as had been tipped off, thereby increasing the mystery or suggesting that a bear clique was at work and was taking advantage of the obvious possibilities of the situation. Merely out of curiosity I found out that the hotel people had rented Suite D to a man calling himself W. H. Garrettson, who was accompanied by a veiled woman. It wasn't Garrettson, though."

"How do you know?"

"It was clearly a ruse—having a woman. Don't you see it? The gossip that would—"

"Very ingenious; but—"

THE PANIC OF THE LION

"At all events, Garrettson got back. We suspect he scolded his partners, and we know he gave out a statement to the reporters that was, to say the least, disingenuous. We know that, had it been any one but Garrettson, Wall Street would have seen stock-market strategy in his highly inconvenient disappearance."

"Yes, yes; but—"

"Friend Kidder, let us evolve an explanation that explains. Let us form a syndicate of intelligent men!" He made a motion with his hand as if waving away the necessity of further elucidation.

"Friend Robison," said Kidder, jocularly mimicking the older man's manner, "you are one of those unusual men whose speeches are better than his silences. *Continuez, s'il vous plaît.*"

"Intelligent men, deprecating alike violence and the immoderate accumulation of wealth by others. To reduce such wealth would be their object."

"A band of robbers?"

"No; an aggregation of philosophers."

"None the less crooks."

"No; since they would take from crooks, annexing only that class of wealth which is called tainted! They would take plunder from the plunderers, themselves pardonable plunderers. That would give to the syndicate a confidence in itself and a faith in its righteousness that would make success easy. How would they go about making Wall Street contribute to the fund? Now they must have seen that Garrettson's life was a bull factor, and his death a bear card. But they had old-fashioned, unphilosophical scruples against murder. Moreover, the sensational disappearance of Garrettson would serve even better than his death. Problem: How to kidnap Garrettson? Or, better still: How to make Garrettson kidnap himself? Simplicity itself!"

"It I am Dr. Watson to your Sherlock Holmes, consider me gazing on you with admiration. And so—"

"The time would be when the Street was full of people long of Con. Steel and the newspapers full of articles showing the greatness of W. H. Garrettson. If I, who merely desired to trade in a few thousand shares, studied Garrettson's habits, think of the syndicate playing for millions! They learn about his daily carriage trip to his office. The rest is obvious, even to you—isn't it?" Mr. Robison gazed benignantly at his guest.

"No; it isn't obvious to me—or to any one else," retorted Kidder, sharply.

"You still think I am Delphic or a crook? My dear Kidder, how can you ask me to insult your intelligence by filling in the obvious gaps in an obvious way?"

"Insult ahead."

"Very well. Mr. Garrettson is sane in everything except in the matter of collecting MSS. At five minutes to nine a man goes to his house—an impressive stranger, well-dressed, cold-eyed, with the aristocratic attitude toward servants that sees in them merely pieces of furniture. He tells the footman in a dehumanized voice that he must see Mr. Garrettson. The footman tells the butler. The butler comes out. The stranger says to the butler: 'I am leaving for Europe this morning. Tell Mr. Garrettson he will see me at once or not at all. Give him this paper and show him this sheet. Make haste!' The dazed butler gives Mr. Garrettson the paper, which is apparently the first page of the *Knickerbocker History of New York.* The memorandum informs Mr. Garrettson: 'I have, in their entirety, the MSS. of this history, Cooper's "Spy," Poe's "Goldbug," three love-letters of George Washington to Mrs. Glendenning, and no less than sixteen signed letters of Thomas Lynch, the one signer of the Declaration of Independence whose autograph is really rare.' Of course Mr. Garrettson would see the stranger!

"The sheet supposed to be the first page of Irving's *Knickerbocker History* is a forgery, so well done as to writing, paper, and ink as to make Garrettson's mouth water for the rest. He has the stranger taken into the library and shows him various rare MSS., the history of which the stranger knows, thereby growing in Garrettson's estimation, particularly since Garrettson does not know how carefully the stranger has prepared himself for this same self-chosen test. But the man is a lunatic, for he wishes Garrettson to give him fifty thousand dollars and five fifteenth-century enamels for the MSS., sight unseen. They argue and haggle and fight. Time thus passes. While Garrettson and the lunatic are quarreling, the Garrettson coupé and the coachman are waiting outside as usual.

"As nine o'clock strikes, which the coachman hears as usual and is the usual signal for Garrettson's appearance, the coachman sees a man running from round the corner, pursued by a well-dressed woman with a horsewhip; also six urchins yelling, 'Give it to him, Liz!' This attracts the coachman's attention. The man stops just across the street from the Garrettson house and the woman lashes him. Of course the coachman has turned his head away from his master's house on the left to the horse-whipping on the right. Suddenly he hears the door of the coupé slam—a rebuking sort of slam! He turns round, gathers up the reins and prepares to start. He doesn't have to be told where to go. It's always the office. While he was looking at the horsewhipping Mr. Garrettson has come out of the house and entered the waiting carriage, as he has done every day for thirty years.

"Out of the corner of his eye the coachman sees the footman returning to the house—a bareheaded footman in the dark-green Garrettson livery, a bundle of newspapers in his hands. The footman stops short and turns round. He is smooth-shaved, as all footmen are. The coachman hears him say, 'Beg pardon—here they are, sir!' and sees the footman hand papers to Mr. Garrettson inside; for who should be inside but Mr. W. H. Garrettson? The footman returns to the house and the coachman drives away, sure that his master is within. His customary route has been studied and it is easy to cause delays, so as to make the carriage arrive at the office fifteen minutes late. No Garrettson! Why? Because he was in the library! The footman was an accomplice. The syndicate has in readiness an exact replica of the Garrettson carriage, of the horse, and even of the coachman; and when Garrettson and his cranky visitor do come out, Garrettson sees his carriage waiting for him, gets in, and is driven away — but not to his office! And there you are."

THE PANIC OF THE LION

"Do you really think that is what happened?"

"It is what a gang of intelligent men would do."

"It is very fine—only it cannot happen."

"Why not?"

"The coachman would never swallow such a fool trick as that."

"If you knew the history of our old New York families you would recall the episode of Mrs. Robert Nye, whose old coachman, English and stiff-necked, one day drove the empty victoria round Central Park, thinking he carried his mistress, because the lap-robe had been placed in the carriage by the footman before the old lady had gotten in—and usually the old lady got in first and the lap-robe followed."

"But he said he saw Garrettson get in," objected Kidder; "and the cigar - ashes were there on the floor!"

"The ashes were thrown in by the footman for the very purpose of making Argus-eyed reporters make a point of it. That and the crumpled newspapers clinched it, so that the coachman thought he remembered seeing Garrettson get in. It is what psychologists call an illusion of memory."

"Oh, well—"

"Oh, well, it merely means that progressive people keep posted. Here, let me read you what Henry Rutgers Marshall, an American psychologist, better known to the learned bodies of Europe than to benighted compatriots like you, has to say about this. I copied it:

"Few of our memories are in any measure fully accurate as records; and under certain conditions, which arise more frequently than most of us realize, the characteristics of the memory-experience may appear in connection with images, or series of images, which are not revivals of any actual past events. In such cases the man who has such a memory-experience, automatically following his usual mode of thought, accepts it as the revival record of an actual occurrence in his past life. When we are convinced that this is not the case we say that he has suffered from an 'illusion of memory.'

"The term 'illusion of memory' thus appears to be something of a misnomer. What we are really dealing with is a real memory-experience, but one by which we are led to make a false judgment—and this because the judgment, which in this special case is false, is almost invariably fully justified.

"A man of unquestioned probity is thus often led to make statements in regard to his experience in the past that have not the least foundation in fact."

"But, when Garrettson came out of his house do you mean to say he wouldn't notice a different coachman?" Kidder looked incredulous in advance of the answer.

"He wouldn't be looking for a different coachman and, therefore, he wouldn't find one. The imitation was close enough to show nothing unusual, nothing different. A lifelong habit never develops introspective misgivings. No, my boy; Garrettson never noticed. Of course the coachman drove to some place or other and left the great financier a prisoner in the cab."

"How?"

"By making the door of the coupé impossible to open from the inside, so that Garrettson was compelled finally to climb out of the window, a matter of some difficulty to a man of his years and weight. The rest you know."

"I don't."

"I don't, either, if you use that tone of voice. But I imagine that, since there was nothing illegal or violent thus far, the syndicate continued to be intelligent. For instance, they might have made it impossible for Garrettson to escape from the carriage-room of the private stable whither he was taken, carriage and all, except by going through a lot of cobwebs and coal-dust and stable litter. As he emerged from the coal-chute a photographer could take pictures of him—no hero of a thrilling escape from desperate criminals, but just a plain chump, full of dirt and soot and mud and manure, hatless, grimy, and unscathed! A quickly developed photographic plate, a print, and a line or two would, of course, make him keep the entire affair mum on the eve of the most gigantic of his promotions—the Intercontinental Railway Consolidation. Indeed, Garrettson can use the break in prices and the recovery of the market to increase his prestige by pointing out how important not only his life is, but, indeed, his physical presence."

"But the syndicate—"

"It might have been short a hundred thousand shares of the Garrettson stocks, on which it made an average profit of eight or ten points. Well, my friend Kidder, we'll just about have time to see the last act of Bohême. Come on!"

Amos Kidder, torn by conflicting emotions, grateful for an epoch-making dinner, interested as never before by his host's conversation, talked a great deal about it, but it was only months afterward that he finally knew.

One day he received three photographs. One showed the great Garrettson in the act of emerging from a coal-hole. His clothes were a sight and his face was much more! Another showed Garrettson dusting himself of cobwebs and wisps of stable litter. The photographs explained why Garrettson had not told the reporters where he had spent that fateful forenoon—and why he had not tried to learn to whom he was indebted for his misadventure. Accompanying the photographs was this letter:

Sir,—We send you herewith photographs of the great Mogul of Wall Street in the act of leaving the house whither he was taken on a certain morning. The house number was removed so he could not identify the house. We are sure you can reconstruct the story of the famous forenoon by what you know and by what you can guess. This syndicate of ours was formed to reduce the tainted wealth of our compatriots, and is still operating successfully. If we ever send you a telegram in code, read it by taking the first two letters of each word — except only the first word, which is always the abbreviation of a name. We take the trouble to tell you this because your paper was of great use to us, as we intended it should be, and because we expect to use you again very shortly. You might compare notes with Mr. Boon, the jeweler. Once more thanking you for your benevolence, we remain,

Respectfully,

THE PLUNDER RECOVERY SYNDICATE.

Kidder showed this letter to Richards. "Let us see," said Richards, "whether we can now read the cablegram that Robison left with the office-boys, with a reward for the successful translator."

He rang the bell, sent for the message, and applied the test; it worked!

"Mogulgar must stand for Garrettson, the great Mogul of Wall Street," said Richards. He was one of those men who always are glad to discover the obvious.

" Yes. ' Will vanish tw(o) hours Wed.' Well, he certainly did. It proves it really was planned.

But I am not sure this was a bona-fide cablegram. Possibly Robison himself faked it."

"Why don't you find out?" suggested the broker.

"I will," said Kidder, and he did. He learned that neither the telegraph nor the cable companies had any record of the deluge of messages received by Robison in the brokers' office.

"They were fakes, probably to carry out the appearance of reality," said Richards, with a Sherlock Holmes nod of explanation.

"Yes, yes," acquiesced Kidder, impatiently; "but what astonishes me is the syndicate's moderation. I wonder what they'll do next."

"I wonder," echoed the broker, who really was wondering whether the market was going up or down.

Kidder, however, went up-town and saw Jesse L. Boon. He told Boon all he knew and much that he suspected, and Boon in return admitted that Welch, Boon & Shaw "had lost a few pieces"—but not for publication. Such things are bound to happen, and are charged to profit and loss. Kidder knew better, but all that he could do was to pray that he might again cross the trail of the plunder-recoverer who had called himself Robison.

III

AS PROOFS OF HOLY WRIT

I

THE bell of the telephone on the desk of the alert city editor of the New York *Planet* rang twice. The alert city editor did not instantly answer it. He was reading a love-letter not meant for his eyes. It had been sent in with his mail by mistake. The bell rang again.

"Yes?" he said, angrily. "Who? Oh, hello, Bill!" There was a pause. Then: "Shall we? Why, friend, he's already started. Thanks awfully! Sure thing!"

He swung round and cast a roaming glance about the big room. It was Sunday, the sacred day when nothing happened.

"Parkhurst!" he called.

Parkhurst, one of the *Planet's* star men, sauntered over to the desk. He had planned to do other things with his time this nice Sunday afternoon. Monday-morning stories are not apt to be exciting. Therefore he limped pathetically in anticipation of the excuse he proposed to make to get off. He was Williams's chum.

"Jimmy," said the city editor, with his habitual

air of giving assignments as though they were decorations awarded for distinguished services, "I just had Bill Stewart, of the Hotel Brabant, on the telephone. He says there is a man there who has seven million dollars in gold-dust in the engine-room of the hotel. Klondike mine-owner. Does not believe in banks, I guess. Takes mighty big stocking to hold the cash—"

"Do you want *me* to write the story?" interrupted Parkhurst, coldly. It was his way of showing his city editor his place.

"Coal-Oil Johnny up to date! Don't fall for any press agent—"

Parkhurst forgot the excuse he was going to make. His limp vanished. The story promised well. He hastened to the Brabant and saw the room clerk, Stewart, who had tipped off the city editor.

"Yes; he is in," said Stewart. "But if you think it is another case of Coal-Oil Johnny you've got another guess coming. Not that he is a tightwad; he is liberal enough with his nuggets, the bell-hops say. But he is no fool. And yet—think of it!— he takes into Seattle with him from Nome eight or ten millions of gold-dust! There he hires a special train to bring him and his gold-dust to New York. He arrives at the Grand Central in the early morning. They hustle round and find seven trucks to carry the boxes of gold-dust for him. He follows in a taxicab. He comes straight to this hotel—"

Stewart here swelled up his chest. It made the reporter say, amiably:

"It was considered a good hotel once; but news travels slowly in the frozen North."

"He comes up here, registers, and then expects

me to let him take the whole fifteen tons of gold up to his room. What do you know about that? Well, then he wanted to hire a whole floor so as to distribute the weight. But you know it is a highly concentrated weight. No floor would stand it. Gold is the heaviest thing there is."

"It is," agreed Parkhurst, hastily. "It is, dear friend. That's why I never carry more than a couple of tooth-fillings with me, and—"

"Let me tell you," cut in Stewart, full of his story. "So, being Sunday and no banks open, we arranged for him to keep the gold-dust down-stairs in the engine-room. And it is there now, a hundred and fifty boxes, worth, he says, about eight million—"

"Lead me to it before you hand in your bill," entreated the reporter.

"There are eight Old Sleuths, with sixteen automatic pistols, on the job of keeping hungry newspaper men from the nice little paper-weights, Jimmy," said Stewart. "I am so kind to Mr. Jerningham myself that I think he will remember me in one of those wills you fellows are always writing about— don't you know? How a fabulous fortune is left to the polite hotel clerk who was so nice to the stranger in the spring of eighteen seventy-four?"

"What's the full name?" asked the reporter.

"There it is!" and Stewart pointed to the autograph in the hotel register.

"Alfred Jerningham. Nome and New York. Suite G."

There followed the names of the eight bullion guards and his two personal servants.

"Looks like a school-boy's writing."

"He is about forty," said the clerk.

"Then it means he probably stopped writing for publication when he was about fourteen. That is the immature chirography of a man who is more at home with a pick than with a pen. And, furthermore—"

"Here he comes," interjected Stewart. "I'll introduce you."

J. Willoughby Parkhurst, the reporter, was startled by the change in Stewart's face. It had taken on the ingratiating soul-sweetness of one who enjoys your story with all his faculties—the complete surrender of self, soul, and hopes of heaven. The clerk exuded gratitude from every pore.

"Gosh!" exclaimed J. Willoughby Parkhurst in amazement, and turned quickly to see who it was that had made Stewart's greed-stricken face turn itself into a moving-picture film of all the delights.

A man was approaching—a man of about the reporter's height, square-shouldered, smooth-shaved, strong-chinned, with an outdoor complexion, and the clear, clean, steady eyes of a man without a liver. There was a metallic glint to the gray-blue of the iris that made the eyes a trifle hard. The lips were not only compressed, but you guessed that the compression was habitual. Even a private detective could have told that this man had made up his mind to do one thing, and therefore he would do it. There was no doubt of it.

"Oh, Mr. Jerningham!" The name issued like a stream of saccharin out of the eddying smiles on Stewart's face.

"The expectation of twenty millions of gold, at least, on that face!" thought Parkhurst, more impressed by the smile than by the cause thereof.

"Here is that nugget I promised you." And Mr. Jerningham dropped four-and-three-quarter pounds troy of gold into the clerk's coy hand. "It is the largest I ever found in six years' mining on the Klondike."

The reporter later told the city editor—he did not print this—that Stewart, as he got the nugget, showed plainly on his face his disappointment that Jerningham had not come from the South-African diamond-fields. A carbon crystal weighing four pounds and three-quarters—that would have been worth a real smile! But the clerk said, gratefully:

"It's very good of you. Thank you ever so much! I'd like to introduce to you my friend, Mr. Parkhurst."

"Glad to make your acquaintance, sir. Parker, did you say?"

The Klondiker spoke coldly. It made the reporter say, subtly antagonistic:

"Parkhurst!"

"Any relation to—"

"Haven't a relation in the world."

"Shake again, friend," said Jerningham, warmly. "I am in the same boat myself!"

They shook hands again.

"Do you want to be very nice?" asked Jerningham, almost eagerly, of the reporter.

"It is my invariable custom to be that," Parkhurst assured him, gravely.

"Dine with me to-night." Jerningham looked expectant.

"I have an engagement with my friend the bishop," said the reporter, who hated clergymen for obvious reasons. "But—let me see!" Parkhurst closed his eyes the better to see how he could break his engagement. "I'll send regrets to the bishop and dine with you with pleasure."

"Mr. Parkhurst is on the *Planet*," put in Stewart. It was the way he said it!

"Ah, yes," said Jerningham, vaguely.

"In fact, Mr. Jerningham," said Parkhurst, "I was sent to interview you."

"Huh?" ejaculated the Klondiker, blankly. It was plain he was virgin soil.

"All to myself!" thought J. Willoughby, with a mental smack of the lips. Then he began, in that congratulatory tone of voice with which practised interviewers corkscrew admissions out of their victims: "We heard about your trip from Seattle, and about your—er—baggage. Would you mind telling me a little more about it? We could"—with a honeyed grin at Stewart—"sit down in a nice little corner of the café and have a nice little chat."

"I don't mind—if you don't," said Jerningham, with one of those diffidently eager smiles of people who are doing you a favor and do not know it.

The reporter led the way to the café, selected a small table in the farthest corner, beckoned to a waiter, pointed to a chair, and nodded toward the Alaskan Monte Cristo.

"Thank you!" said Jerningham, with real gratitude, and sat down. Then he looked at his watch, saw that it was only four o'clock, and said to the waiter, "A cup of tea, please."

"Huh?" It was all J. Willoughby could rise to. A miner and tea? What about the free champagne for the hundreds? A tea-drinker would not scatter walnut-sized diamonds along the Great White Way.

"I got used to it. My pal was English. We found it preferable to whisky in the Klondike." Mr. Jerningham made no effort to disguise the apologetic tone.

"I'll have the same," cleverly said J. Willoughby. Then, to clinch it, "Of course you know that in the exclusive clubs to-day men drink more tea than liquor!"

"It's the proper thing—eh?" said Jerningham, with a sort of head-waiter deference that made the reporter stare in surprise. "I am glad you told me that."

"Oh yes. It is no longer good form to get load—er—intoxicated. It's one of the few good things we've got from England—tea-drinking," the reporter said. "And, Mr. Jerningham, to get back to our subject, just how did you happen to go to the Klondike?"

"It began in New York," said Jerningham, and drew his lips together. It was clearly not a pleasant memory.

"It did?" You could tell that J. Willoughby was grateful. "Well, well! And—" He frowned as though a date had escaped him. He really suggested time to the miner, for Jerningham volunteered:

"When I was twelve years old."

"That's about twenty years ago," ventured the reporter in the affirmative tone of voice that inevitably elicits contradiction and the exact figures from the victim.

"Thirty-two years ago, sir."

"Well, well! And— How did you say it began?"

The reporter put his hand to his ear to show that his hardness of hearing had prevented him from getting Jerningham's previous answer to the same question.

"My father!" Mr. Jerningham nodded twice, to show that those two words told the whole story.

"Ah, yes! And then?" The reporter looked as if instant death would follow the non-receipt of information; and Jerningham, as though against a life-long determination to be silent, spoke—and frowned as he spoke:

"My father! He was a coachman in the employ of old David Soulett, who was the son of Walter and the father of Richard and David the third, and of Madge, who married the Duke of Peterborough. Old David Soulett—the second, he was—was my father's employer. My father was English. He came to New York when he was eighteen. He went straight into the Souletts' stable, became head coachman, and lived with the family for fifty years. They pensioned him off. I grew up with the boys—called one another by our first names. Do you get that?— by our first names!"

Jerningham compressed his lips tightly and nodded. His eyes filled with reminiscence—sweet, yet sad.

"You did, eh?" said the reporter.

If J. Willoughby had been addicted to slang he would have used the same wondering tone of voice and would have exclaimed, "What do you know about that!"

"And that is why I went to the Klondike!"

There are times when a man's voice and attitude show that he is speaking in italics. This was one of the times. Having said all there was to be said, he turned to the tea with a gesture of such determination that Parkhurst leaned over, half expecting to see a dozen starving grizzly-bears jump out of the cup. Then the thought came to the watchful reporter that the grim-shut lips merely expressed that some memory was bitter. He asked, very sympathetically, "Did they send you away?"

"They did not send me away. They did nothing! They were! That's all. It was enough."

"Yes, of course!" The reporter agreed with Jerningham absolutely. "But I don't quite see the exact reason, as you might say."

"They were!" explained Jerningham as one might talk to a child. "They were Souletts, rich by inheritance, in the best society. They had everything I did not have. So I went to the Klondike."

"Yes?"

"Is it not clear?"

"No!" said the reporter, grateful for the chance to use the plain negative.

"They were in the Four Hundred. They were gentlemen. They were good-looking, pleasant-mannered, kindly-hearted fellow-Christians. But if they had not been the sons of David Soulett, and if David had not been the son of Walter, and Walter the son of the first David, they wouldn't have been in the Four Hundred, or in the Four Thousand even. Policemen at the corners used to touch their hats to them as they drove by and seemed really glad to get a pleasant smile in return. You felt the cops would never have dreamt of taking a Soulett to the station-house—always to the Soulett mansion. New-Yorkers used to point to it—the Soulett mansion—with an air of pride, as though they owned it! Clerks in shops would send for the proprietor if one of the Souletts walked in, and later they would brag how they said to David Soulett, they said; and he said, said he—and so on. And why? Why, I ask you?"

"Why?" repeated the reporter, hypnotically.

"Because an ignorant old cuss couldn't read or write and had to go to digging graves in Trinity churchyard for a living. It was old David's proud boast that he put away one thousand six hundred and thirty-two people, including the very best there were in literature, art, science, theology, commerce, and finance, besides nineteen murderers, thirty-eight pet slaves, and one dog of his own. A very snob among grave-diggers, laying the foundation for the non-snobbishness of his great-grandchildren! Digging graves, you see, turned his mind to soil. The only thing that didn't burn up or evaporate or shrink was soil. Genius for real estate they call his madness to-day. But it was an obsession. He bought a farm in what is now the swell shopping district; and another where the Hotel Regina is; and another beginning where the Vandeventer houses are. The old lunatic's mad purchases are now worth one hundred and fifty million dollars; and he himself is an ancestor, with fake portraits showing an intellectual-looking country squire. Grave-digger—that's what! But the money really began with him and the near-gentleman with Walter, who knew the best families because his father buried them one after another. By the time the real-estate market got to going in earnest David was born—of course a gentleman! What did it? Unearned money!"

"Yes. But what's digging graves got to do with your going to the Klondike?"

"Everything. It gave me the secret of it—the unearned part. Don't you see?"

"No."

"My dear sir, I loved the company of the Soulett boys and I enjoyed the society of their equals. So I naturally desired to become their equal. To become a gentleman I had to become rich. But the money must not be earned; so I couldn't make it in trade—which, moreover, was too slow. The careers of butcher, plumber, and liquor-dealer, that might have made me rich quickly, were closed to me by the social disqualifications they carry. And the careers of Jim Sands and Bill Train in Wall Street were too malodorous; besides which, you can't make very much money on the Stock Exchange without treading on influential social toes. Hence the Klondike. Do you see now?"

"I'm beginning to."

"Well?"

"Do you mean," said the reporter, to get it straight, "that you went to the Klondike to make money so as to climb—I mean, so as to go into society?"

"Exactly so! Yes, sir! And I tell you, Mr. Parker—"

"Park-*hurst!*" said J. Willoughby, with a frown of injured vanity.

"Mr. Parkhurst, a man has to have some strong motive to enable him to conquer success. In all my wanderings for twenty-five years, prospecting in Montana, Wyoming, Utah, Colorado, the Southwest, Nevada, California, Oregon, and Washington, and finally all over Alaska, I had but one object in mind, one purpose. It sustained me. It gave me courage when others despaired; it kept me marching onward when others fell by the wayside and died or became sheep-ranchers. I had no thought for amusement, none for pleasure, none for love. I simply kept up my search. It was the search for happiness that the old knights used to go out on. It was a search, Mr. Parker-hurst, for the yellow admission ticket to the Four Hundred!"

"Have you found it?" J. Willoughby could not help it.

"Let me tell you," pursued Jerningham, ignoring the question. "I used to read the society columns of the New York papers whenever I felt myself growing discouraged; and that always revived me. Up in the Klondike I had saved fifteen hundred dollars and I paid one thousand dollars in gold-dust for a six-months-old copy of a society paper which had an account of Mrs. Masters's ball. To me, 'among those present' meant more than a list of gilt-edge bonds. I've got it yet."

He paused to take from his pocket-book a tattered clipping and showed it to the newspaper man with a mixture of pride and tenderness and solicitude lest it be harmed, as a father shows the only extant photograph of the most wonderful baby in captivity.

"I thought my name would fit in very nicely between the Janeways and the Jesups. It was a good investment, that one thousand dollars, for I felt I had to get a gait on, and that very same day I went on that prospecting trip to the Endicott Mountains which changed my luck for me. Everything came my way then—I mean, in mining. I am getting six hundred thousand dollars a year out of my claims; and that is because I believe fifty thousand dollars a month enough for a bachelor. More would be—er—sort of ostentatious. Don't you think so?"

"Yes, indeed," agreed J. Willoughby Parkhurst, with a shudder.

"When I marry I'll make it one hundred and twenty-five thousand dollars a month."

"I agree with you," said Parkhurst—"because, really, two cannot live as cheaply as one." He thrilled when he thought how he would play up that promised income in his story.

"That's what I say," Jerningham said, gratefully. "Of course there's the seven millions and a half of gold-dust I have brought with me. It's down-stairs." His grim mouth became more determinedly grim than ever. This man was the kind that gets what he wants, with or without money. He will not climb, thought Parkhurst; he will vault into society. He asked Jerningham:

"Have you really got that much down-stairs? I mean," he hastily corrected himself, "have you no fear of the danger of going about with that much loose change?"

"No. It's guarded by men who are getting big pay for being honest. You can buy honesty—if you treat it as a luxury and pay for it as such. Each box weighs one hundred and fifty pounds, for convenience in handling. Would you like to see the stuff?" He could not hide a boyish eagerness—not at all offensive—to impress his new friend. J. Willoughby Parkhurst forgave him in advance, and to prove it said, heartily:

"Very much indeed!"

"Very well. Please come with me." And he led the way to the engine-room. They went down two flights. At the door of the engine-room they met the engineer, who bowed with an obsequiousness that indicated sincere gratitude and renewed hope—as of a man who has received a handsome gratuity and is expecting another.

In the middle of the concrete floor of the engine-room, piled up in an amazingly small mound of boxes, was the gold.

"Each box has about fifty thousand dollars in dust," explained Jerningham, with what one might have called a matter-of-fact pride. "Would you like to open one?"

"I don't want to put you to any trouble—not for worlds; but I do want to see the inside of one like anything."

"No trouble. I say, Mr. Wilkinson," to the hotel engineer, who had followed them, a deferential smile fastened to his face, "could you get me a hammer and chisel and a screw-driver?"

"Certainly, Mr. Jerningham," said the engineer, with obvious pride at being part of an extraordinary adventure. He reappeared presently with the tools and a burly assistant. They pried off the steel hoop and cracked off the sealing-wax from over the heads of the screws that held the lid in place. They then unscrewed the cover—and there before their wide-gaping eyes was a boxful of yellow Yukon gold.

Jerningham smilingly looked at J. Willoughby Parkhurst and waved his hand toward the treasure—a gesture that said Help yourself!—only it said it humorously. And so the reporter smiled indulgently and plunged his hand in it.

"How heavy!" he exclaimed, involuntarily. He had meant to be witty, as penniless people always are in the presence of great wealth to show that they are not impressed.

"It will be light enough to blow away here," said Jerningham so seriously that nobody smiled—indeed, everybody hoped for a blast in the direction of his own pocket. But Jerningham merely said: "Thank you. Will you screw it on again?" And the engineer did. Jerningham did not stay to see the re-screwing finished. He took Parkhurst's arm and walked out. The reporter told him:

"I can't help thinking it was imprudent. The detectives now know they can open the boxes and—"

"It isn't likely that all eight will be dishonest at the same minute. That's why I got eight instead of four. But, even if they all wanted to, how much could they get away with? With the contents of one of the boxes, fifty thousand dollars? Well, that isn't much. I can't afford to let that gold be a bother to me. I brought it along so that it could be my servant—not for me to be its slave."

"I've heard others make that selfsame remark," said J. Willoughby, cheerfully, "but they never struck off the aureate shackles!"

"My friend, it's not in striking off shackles; that is always difficult. The secret is in not letting them become shackles!" said Jerningham, grimly. "A man does not confidently expect during twenty-five years to strike it rich some day without very carefully thinking of what he is going to do with the gold after he gets it."

II

The story, as James Willoughby Parkhurst wrote it, and even as the *Planet* printed it, was a masterpiece. It was far more interesting than a fake. The truth often may be stranger than fiction, but it is seldom so exciting. With the generous desire to repay Jerningham's hospitality with kindness, to say nothing of an eye for the picturesque, the reporter made his victim an Admirable Crichton. Parkhurst's Jerningham was very distinguished-looking, which every woman knows is better for a man than being handsome. He not only was "probably the richest man in the world," but a fine linguist—indeed, a philologist. You saw Jerningham digging in his gravel-bank by day—spadeful after spadeful of clear gold-dust—and at nights reading Aristophanes in the original by the flickering and malodorous light of seal-fat lamps.

On the same day that Jerningham learned that his own wealth was practically inexhaustible, and decided to limit his income in order that gold might not be demonetized, he—the philologist in him—discovered also amazing analogies between certain Eskimo and Aleutian words and their equivalents in Tibetan. This and a monograph on "Totemism in the Light of Its Undoubted Babylonian Origin," he would read in London before the Royal Society. Of Jerningham's ancestry the article said that the erudite Crœsus was "of the Long Island Jerninghams."

At three separate and distinct places in the article, each time differently worded, but the intention and purpose thereof being the same, the writer said that for generosity, lavish extravagance, capacity for spending, and deep-rooted belief that there was no difference between gold coins and stage money, the learned Klondiker was a combination of Monte

Cristo, Boni de Castellane, Coal-Oil Johnny, and Alcibiades—only more so. But his feverish efforts were all in vain—he only grew richer! If he decided to give a million to a newsboy who was polite, that same moment he would be sure to get a cablegram from one of his superintendents that the vein had widened to three miles and the assays jumped to three hundred thousand dollars a ton.

Parkhurst finished by saying that Jerningham had no use for women. In divers countries world-famous sirens had sung to him—in vain. He was the kind that registered zero, even though plunged to the chin in Vesuvian lava. So the dear things might as well save time, breath, and muscular exertion; he would have none of them, no matter what their age, color of hair, temperament, accomplishments, or even faces might be. He was arrow-proof and Cupid had given up trying. Still, there must be One—somewhere!

When J. Willoughby Parkhurst went to the Hotel Brabant on Monday morning in the hope of a second-day story, he was not sure how Jerningham would take his masterpiece. He was going so early in the hope of shunting off the head-line artists of the afternoon papers, for all that he had begged Stewart to fix it so that nobody got to Jerningham before the *Planet* man turned up.

As he entered the lobby he saw in a corner lounge five reporters from the yellows, three photographers from same, a professor from the Afternoon Three-Center, and a "psychological portraitist," feminine and fat, but dressed with unusual care and even piquancy, from a magazine. He saw Jerningham's finish—not!

AS PROOFS OF HOLY WRIT

The competitors were too busy talking to see J. Willoughby Parkhurst, author of the day's sensation, walk up to the desk and greet Stewart affectionately. They did not see J. W. P. turn sharply, approach a well-built, square-shouldered man, with an outdoor complexion, who had just emerged from the elevator, and shake hands warmly.

After one and a half seconds of dialogue, consisting of "Good morning!" and "Good morning!" J. Willoughby cleverly realized that Mr. Alfred Jerningham could not possibly have read the article. On general principles he took the Klondiker to one end of the corridor, out of sight of the other reporters.

"I am very anxious to make arrangements to store my gold in some bank's vaults. I don't know any bank—that is, I have no account in any; and I wondered if I needed to be introduced."

Jerningham looked anxiously at Parkhurst.

"Of course!" said J. Willoughby, and immediately looked alarmed. "Of course! They are very particular—very! The good ones, you know. A man's bank is like a man's club—it can give him a social standing or it can prove he hasn't any." He looked at his Klondike friend with a frown of anxiety.

"I never thought of that side of it. But I can see there is much in what you say. I should like to put the gold in the VanTwiller Trust Company."

"Fine! I think I can help you. I'll call up our Wall Street man and he will make the trust company take it—unless he thinks there is another still better. Let's go to your room and telephone from there; and we'll tell Stewart to tell the telephone operator not to bother us—what?"

J. Willoughby intended that Jerningham should

be the sole and exclusive property of the *Planet*. From Jerningham's sumptuous room he called up the office, ordered a corps of photographers to the battlefield to take pictures of sundry loads of gold on trucks on their way to the great vaults, escorted by the *Planet's* special commissioner in one of the armored automobiles which the *Planet* supplied to its bright young men.

Then he called up Amos F. Kidder, the *Planet's* financial editor; and Kidder, who, of course, knew the president of the VanTwiller Trust Company, Mr. Ashton Welles, hustled thitherward and made all arrangements, including the securing of the trucks owned by Tommy O'Loughlin, who did all the gold-trucking for W. H. Garrettson & Company, Wolff, Herzog & Company, and other gold-shipping banking firms. Photographers were duly stationed at the various points by which the aureate procession would pass.

Mr. J. Willoughby Parkhurst had the boxes of gold-dust taken out by the ash-and-cinder exit, caused his fellow-reporters to be "tipped off" by hall-boys that the gold would be taken away at twelve-thirty sharp to the Metropolitan National Bank vaults, and then took Jerningham in the *Planet's* automobile and followed the trucks.

In Wall Street Parkhurst introduced Jerningham to the waiting Kidder, and Kidder introduced Jerningham to the waiting Mr. Welles. The gold was carried down to the vaults. Jerningham separated twenty boxes from the heap.

"I'd like to have these cashed," he said, with that delightful humor of all very rich men. And everybody within hearing laughed, as everybody always laughs at the so-delightful humor of all very rich men. There was not a clerk in the trust company who did not repeat the historic remark at home that night.

Word of what was happening went about, and soon the great little narrow street was blocked by people who wished to see six or eight millions go into a place where there were one hundred and fifty. But there was this difference—the one hundred and fifty already there would stay there; but a handful or two of the six or eight might be distributed among those present by the latest Coal-Oil Johnny from the Klondike. The hope of a stray nugget or two kept two thousand busy people about the doors of the VanTwiller Trust Company nearly two hours.

As for Jerningham, the trust company was to send the twenty boxes of gold-dust to the Assay Office and credit Mr. Jerningham's account with the proceeds of the sale thereof. Two days later Mr. Alfred Jerningham had to his credit in the Van-Twiller Trust Company $1,115,675.28; and in the vaults boxes containing, as per his most conservative estimates, gold-dust valued at six millions and a half. And everybody knew it—the *Planet* saw to that. Great potentialities in that golden fame of Jerningham's—what?

III

The *Planet's* official version of the Jerningham affair, and the flood of sensational literature turned loose on the community by the other papers, made the Klondiker's name as familiar to New-Yorkers as a certain breakfast-food advertisement.

THE PLUNDERERS

His daily mail was enormous, especially after the newspapers said that he was looking for a house in which to entertain. "The richest bachelor in the world," he was called, and the real-estate agents acted accordingly. So did no end of unattached females of dubious age, but of not at all dubious intentions. Also it became known that he needed a social secretary to guide him in two things—the two things being whom to invite and how to spend six hundred thousand dollars a year in entertaining those who were invited by the social adviser.

The applications came by the dozen—in the strictest confidence. If somebody had said this aloud in the hearing of society, society would have laughed scornfully. A gentleman was always a gentleman, and could never, never be secretary to a parvenu! But, for all that, there were scores of well-born men who appeared willing enough—don't you know?—to help spend the six hundred thousand a year. Or else some historic names were forged by dastards. The *Planet's* society editor, who would never allow herself to be called editress, proved invaluable as a living Who's Who, and demonstrated her worth to her paper by making connections that would further her work; for she was much sought by people who wished introductions to Mr. Jerningham. They would trade with her—items for letters.

It helped all concerned that not only Parkhurst, but the rest of the kind-hearted space-grabbers, informed the world that the possessor of the income of six hundred thousand a year was a fount of erudition, and withal a man of the world, with exquisite manners—invulnerable to the optical artillery of the fairest sirens on earth. And always the six hundred thousand dollars a year to spend, so that the beastly stuff would not accumulate and choke up the passages of the palace he proposed to build! That was how Francis Wolfe came to be introduced to Mr. Jerningham by J. Willoughby Parkhurst, and how the position was delicately offered to him, and how F. Wolfe delicately accepted.

A fine-looking, well-built young fellow, this Frank —dark-eyed, black-haired, with a wonderfully clean pink but virile complexion that made him physically very attractive. In those Broadway restaurants that have become institutions Francis Wolfe was himself an institution. His debts were discussed as freely as the cost of gasoline. And yet the chorus contingent and their lady friends, consisting of the most beautiful women in all the world, not only preferred, but publicly and on the slightest provocation proclaimed their preference for, Frank Wolfe penniless to almost any one else—short of millions. But if Frank Wolfe was the chorus-girls' pet, Mr. Francis Wolfe was the only brother of Mrs. John Burt and Mrs. Sydney Walsingham, and favorite nephew of old Mrs. Stimson. And everybody knew what that meant!

J. Willoughby Parkhurst left them alone, even if he was a reporter.

"If you do not mind talking business," said Jerningham, with a deprecatory smile.

"Not at all," eagerly said young Wolfe, who was consumed by curiosity to listen to the golden statistics. "In fact," he added, with a burst of boyish candor, "I'd be glad to have you."

"You are a nice boy!" said Jerningham, so gratefully and non-familiarly that Frank could not find fault with him.

"I need a friend," continued Jerningham. "I know friendship cannot be bought. It grows—but there must be a seed. It may be that after you know me better you will give me your friendship. That is for the future. I also need a man! A man whom I can trust! A man, young Mr. Francis Wolfe," he said, with a sternness that impressed young Mr. Francis Wolfe, "who will not laugh at me!"

Frank was not an intellectual giant, but neither was he an utter ass. He said, very seriously, "Go on!"

"I am willing to pay such a man twenty-five thousand a year—" He paused and almost frowned.

"Go on!" again said young Mr. Wolfe, looking the Klondiker straight in the eyes.

"Twenty-five thousand dollars—to begin with!"

"Yes?" said young Mr. Wolfe, quite calmly.

"The duties of such a man—and keep in mind I mean a man when I say a man!—entail nothing whatever of a menial or dishonorable character; nothing to which a gentleman could possibly object. But it would necessitate a certain spirit of good-will toward me. I am not only willing, but even anxious, to pay twenty-five thousand dollars a year, and all traveling expenses, to a clean-minded young man who, for all his wild-oat sowing, is a gentleman and will learn to like me enough not to laugh at me when I intrust him with the secret desire of my heart."

Before Frank's thoughts could crystallize into the definite suspicion that Jerningham wanted to be

helped to climb socially, Jerningham went on so
coldly that again young Wolfe was impressed:

"You will admit, Mr. Wolfe, that a man who has
prospected all over North America from the Rio
Grande to the Arctic Circle, and who has, unfortunately, been compelled"—he rose, went to his bureau,
brought out two revolvers of a rather old-fashioned
kind—"compelled against his will to draw first"—
he showed the young man about a dozen notches
in the handle of one of them—"one who fears no
man and no government and no blackmailer; who
owns the richest placer mines in the world—is not
apt to be an emotional ass!" There was a pause.
But Jerningham continued before young Wolfe could
speak: "Neither is he a damned fool—what?"

Mr. Francis Wolfe felt he had to say something,
so he said, "I shouldn't think so."

He felt that Jerningham was not a man to trifle
with—a tough customer in a rough-and-tumble fight;
a man who had taken life in preserving his own;
altogether a man, a character, who would make an
admirable topic of conversation with both men and
women—therefore a man to be interested in.

"Do you know Mr. Ashton Welles?" asked Jerningham, almost sharply.

"Not intimately."

"Do you know Mrs. Ashton Welles?"

"Same answer."

"Ever dine at their house?"

Frank thought a moment. He had dined at so
many people's houses. "No," he answered, finally.

"Could you?"

"How do you mean?"

"Are your relations with Welles such, or could

they be cultivated so, as to make him invite you—
not me—you!—to dine at his house?"

"Look here, Mr. Jerningham," and young Mr.
Wolfe's face flushed, "a fellow doesn't do some
things for money; and this is one—"

"I know it! Not for money. For friendship,
yes! That's why—you understand now, don't you?"
He looked so earnestly at young Wolfe that Frank
absolved him of wrong-doing.

"No, I don't!" said the young man.

"Did you ever know Randolph Deering, who used
to be president of the VanTwiller Trust Company?"

"Do you mean Mrs. Welles's father?"

"Yes."

"I don't recall speaking to him more than to say
'How do you do?' I don't remember when or how
I met him."

"Do you know Mrs. Deering, Mrs. Welles's
mother?"

"No."

"Do you know anybody who does?"

"I suppose I do."

"Anybody who would give you a letter of introduction?"

"I don't know. If my aunt or my sisters know
her it would be easy. But, of course, I should have
to know first why I should want to meet her."

"Of course. Did you ever hear anything about
Mrs. Welles's sister, Naida Deering?"

"Didn't know she had a sister."

"Then, of course, you never saw her."

Francis Wolfe thought a long time. His mind
did not work very quickly at any time. At length he
said: "I don't think there could have been a sister,

for I never heard of her having any; indeed, I distinctly remember hearing that she was an only child. Maybe she was a cousin or—er—something of the sort."

"No; Naida was a sister; a good deal older and— But we are drifting away from business. Will you accept my proposition to be my—er—adviser in certain matters on which I think you are qualified to give advice, and accept twenty-five thousand dollars a year?"

"Do you mind if I speak frankly?"

"Certainly not. Speak ahead."

"Are you offering me this—er—salary when, of course, I know I am not worth a da—a cent in business; I mean, isn't it really in exchange for what I may be able to do for you in a—a social way? You know what I mean."

"No, sir!" said Jerningham, decisively. "Not for an instant! I do not, dear Mr. Wolfe, give an infinitesimal damn for what is called society."

"But I thought Jimmy Parkhurst told me—"

"I cannot help what Jimmy Parkhurst told you; but I tell you that I like interesting people, and I don't care who or what they are socially. I hate bores—whether they are hod-carriers or dukes. If I can meet people who will instruct me when I want to learn, or amuse me when I want to laugh, I'm satisfied. And I can always meet that kind without anybody's help. You know how it is." Then he spoke perhaps thirty words in a foreign language that Frank thought must be Hungarian. "You remember your Latin, of course. That's from Petronius."

"I thought so!" said Frank Wolfe, the pet of the

chorus-girls, laughing to himself. Remember his Latin! He? Haw!

"It is from his 'Cena Trimalchionis.' The *arbiter elegantiarum* knew what social climbers might be expected to do, though I neither boast of my money nor do I eat with my knife. The Latin of the 'Cena' is difficult—too slangy, full of the *sermo plebeius*."

"Yes, it is," agreed Frank, so gravely that it was all he could do to keep from laughing at himself. This Klondiker was not only a gun-fighter and richer than Crœsus, but also a highbrow! Could you beat it?

"Will you accept my offer? Will you try to be my friend?"

"Suppose I find I can't?"

"I'll be sorry. The money is nothing. The inability to make a friend will be my real loss."

"Well, we might try six months." He looked inquiringly at Jerningham. "I don't exactly know what you wish me to do."

"Become my friend! You yourself said some things cannot be done for money by a gentleman; but there is nothing—so long as it is not dishonorable—that a gentleman may not do for a friend. Shall I explain a little more?" He looked anxiously at young Mr. Wolfe.

"Yes—do," said Frank. It occurred to him that this singular man was in reality proceeding with a curious delicacy.

"Just as soon as you feel you know me I will ask you to help me. Mrs. Deering is now abroad. Mrs. Welles may be of help to us. Mr. Wolfe, now that I am not so poor as I was, I want to find Naida Deering, the only woman I ever loved—and, God help me, the only woman I still love!"

Jerningham rose hastily and walked up and down the room, his face persistently turned away from Wolfe. He walked to a window and stared at the sky a long time. Finally he turned to the young man, who was watching him, and said, with profound conviction:

"*Amare et sapere vix deo conceditur!*"

Young Mr. Wolfe at first felt like saying, "Yes, indeed!" which would, as a matter of fact, have been a very pat retort. But he weakened and said, "What is that quotation from?"

"Publilius Syrus. Mr. Wolfe, I must find her. And of course I can't employ a private detective. You understand?"

"Yes. That is true," said Frank.

"In her youth something happened." Young Mr. Wolfe sat up straight. Here at last was something really vital! Jerningham proceeded: "She was a high-strung girl—pure as gold. Her very innocence made her indiscreet. There was no scandal—no, indeed! But she disappeared. And now, when I have more than enough money for the two of us, I wish to find her. If I don't—of what possible good are my millions? Tell me that!"

Jerningham glared so angrily at young Mr. Wolfe that young Mr. Wolfe felt a slight spasm of concern. The Klondiker had a metallic gray eye that at times menaced like cold steel.

"Excuse me!" said Jerningham, contritely. "My dear boy, do you know what it is to go chasing over the landscape for years and years in the hope of striking it some day so as to be able to go back to your native city and marry the one woman in all the world—particularly when she was one whom her parents, not understanding her nature, practically disowned? In all my prospecting what I wanted was to find Naida's mine—gold by the ton— so I could buy back her place in society!"

There was such determination in Jerningham's voice and look that young Wolfe felt a thrill of admiration and, with it, a distinct masculine liking.

"That's a great story!" he said. "I never heard of your—er—Miss Naida. She never married, I suppose?"

"I don't know! I don't know! She promised to wait for me. The Deerings used to live in Jersey; and living in Jersey when I was a kid wasn't what it is to-day. They were not prominent in society. Of course the Deerings kept it quiet. I think Mrs. Welles may know where her sister is—the sister who is never mentioned by her own flesh and blood! Mrs. Deering, of course, does; but she is abroad somewhere. I must find Naida, I tell you—and—"

Jerningham was silent, but Wolfe saw that he was breathing quickly, as though he had been running. Frank never read anything except the afternoon papers, love-letters, and the more romantic of the best-sellers. He now very laboriously constructed a romance of Jerningham's life that became so thrilling it took away his own breath. It made him feel very kindly toward the new Jerningham—everybody feels kindly toward his own creations; and so he said, in a burst of enthusiasm:

"By George! I'll help you!"

And thus was begun the pact between the two men.

AS PROOFS OF HOLY WRIT

On the very next morning Mr. Jerningham, instead of going to Wall Street as was his custom, went instead to Mrs. Charlton Morris's Agency for Trained Nurses.

An empress—no less—sat at a desk. She was not, however, one of those empresses who change the destiny of nations by their beauty. She had merely an arrogance more than royal.

"I should like to see Mrs. Charlton Morris," said Jerningham, briskly.

"I am Mrs. Morris," she said.

You at once perceived that she was even more than imperial. She was a woman of forty, dark, slender, with shell-rimmed, round lenses that gave her that look between a Chinese philosopher and an ancient owl, which those tortoise-shell goggles always do. You also obtained the impression that a completely successful operation had removed Mrs. Morris's sense of humor.

"I should like, if you please—" began Jerningham; but Mrs. Morris interrupted with an effect as of thrusting an icicle into the interior mechanism of a clock.

"I beg your pardon, but we must know with whom we are dealing. What is the name, please?"

"I prefer not to give you mine yet."

"Oh no, sir; I must know."

"Suppose I had given you a false one, how would you have been the wiser?"

"Oh, but also you must give me the name of your doctor."

"He sent me here."

"And who is he, sir?"

From her voice and her look you gathered that she was in charge of a hospital and was obtaining indispensable clinical data.

"Madam," said Jerningham, very coldly indeed, "you talk like the census man. Would you also like to know my age, sex, and color?"

"We never," retorted Mrs. Morris, imperturbably, "do business with strangers."

"Do you want me to get a letter from the President of the United States? I know him pretty well. Or from my bankers? They are known even in Brooklyn."

"We are here to supply trained nurses to people whose physicians we know."

A trained nurse must have unfailing good humor —it is part of her professional requirements. But a purveyor of trained nurses may permit herself much dignity, as though her mission in life consisted of fitting nurses to cases—the best nurse for the worst case.

"My doctor," said Jerningham, "is Dr. Jewett."

It was the name of a very great surgeon.

"Ah, yes. Surgical case! Yes! I have Miss Sennett and Miss Audrey. Dr. Jewett knows them very well."

"Kindly wait a second! I must see them myself. And it is not a surgical case. It is no case at all— yet. Show me the girls!"

"Sir, this is not an intelligence-office; but—"

"I know there is no intelligence in this office. This is merely the anteroom of a hospital and you are the superintendent. By rights you ought to be on the faculty. I am perfectly willing to pay for any loss of time or trouble to which you and the young ladies may be put."

"Must she be young?" asked Mrs. Morris.

Her voice was at least thirty degrees below zero, for all that there was no devilishness about Mr. Jerningham. He said:

"Yes; and good-looking — not a girl in her teens, but a young woman. I should say, without meaning to be personal, about your age, Mrs. Morris."

It was plain that Mrs. Morris had almost superhuman control over her facial muscles—she did not beam on him!

"I understand," she said, in a quite human voice. This man was, after all, neither rude nor blind. "A woman—"

"About thirty—or a little less," said Jerningham. He looked at Mrs. Morris's face and nodded confirmatively.

"Exactly," said Mrs. Morris, genially. First impressions are so apt to be unfair!

"I'll be more than satisfied with one of your age and good loo — and — er — appearance" — here the Morris smile irrepressibly made its début—"and also tactful. It is an unusual case. It will necessitate going to Europe."

"With the patient?"

"For the patient," said Jerningham, and waited.

"If you will tell me a little bit more about the case—" said Mrs. Morris, encouragingly. She had just taken a good look at the pearl in the scarf of this delightful judge of ages—at the lowest estimation, five thousand dollars!

"My— I— We have reason to believe that a—

friend is ill in London. Kidneys. We wish her to take care of herself. She is a woman of fifty-odd. We want a nurse, refined, well-bred, good-looking, and competent—like yourself; so that she could be a companion and at home among wealthy people. You know what I mean." He paused.

"Perfectly, sir!" said Mrs. Morris, veraciously. Did she not know Mrs. Morris?

"It would be nice to find such a nurse—and, if possible, also one to whom the fact that she is going to visit England, and possibly other countries, may be a sort of compensation for her sudden departure from New York. Of course she will be paid all her traveling and living expenses—first-class all through —and her regular honorarium. I believe it is thirty-five dollars a week. As I am leaving New York myself soon, I'll pay in advance, and will leave instructions with my bankers to honor any of your drafts, Mrs. Morris. It will be a good opportunity for the young lady to know London—and you know how attractive it is—and Paris!"

"Yes, indeed," acquiesced Mrs. Morris, suddenly looking like Baedeker.

"The young lady—I am sorry you could not go in her place! Yes, I am!—will live at the same hotel with the patient and become acquainted with her— and advise her to see a physician regularly—a specialist in kidney diseases. We think her only daughter ought to be with her. But you can't say anything to either of them, because if the mother doesn't think she is ill the daughter cannot know it, either. We only suspect it is Bright's. You can't afford to wait until you have to go to bed with Bright's—can you?"

"No, indeed!" gravely agreed Mrs. Morris, special-ist.

"So now you know what sort of a girl I wish—one who will be there if the trouble should take a sudden turn for the worse; one who will induce the old lady to consult a physician. Do I have to give a pre-liminary fee?"

"Not at all. Call this afternoon at four and I'll try to have one of my best nurses here. She is—well, quite young; in fact"—with what might be called a desiccated archness—"she is a little younger than I and quite pretty. I call her handsome!"

Some women are so sure of their own position that they do not fear competition.

"Thank you! I'll be here at four, sharp." And Mr. Jerningham went away without having given his name to Mrs. Morris.

At four o'clock Mr. Jerningham called at Mrs. Charlton Morris's agency and had an interview with Miss Kathryn Keogh. Mrs. Morris gave them the use of her own little private office; Jerningham very impressively waited for Miss Keogh to sit down and then did so himself.

He threw at Miss Keogh one of those inventorying looks that women find so difficult to appear uncon-scious of, probably because they know their own weak points.

Miss Keogh was beautiful—and when an Irish girl is beautiful she is beautiful in so many ways! She had the wonderful complexion of her race and a mouth carved out of heaven's prize strawberry. Her eyes were an incredibly deep blue when they were not an incredibly deep pansy-purple, and they were abysses of velvet. In the darkness, without seeing them—just by remembering them—you loved those eyes. In the light, when you could see them, you simply worshiped! Her throat was one of those paradoxical affairs, soft and hard, which made you think at one and the same time of marble and rose-leaves—Solomon's tower of ivory, crowned by the glory of golden-brown hair, so fine that you thought of clouds of it!

If you looked at her eyes you suspected, and if you looked at her throat you were certain that you, a respectable married man, had in you the makings of a criminal—the crime being bigamy. Also you would have sworn to her only too cheerfully that she was the only girl you had ever loved. With one look, remember!

Jerningham looked at her with a cold, impersonally appreciative eye, as he might have scrutinized a clock that was both beautiful and costly.

Miss Keogh understood it perfectly. It piqued her, accustomed as she was to instant adoration. Yet it was not entirely displeasing. This man knew as a connoisseur knows—with his head. That he had not permitted the silly heart to disturb the critical faculties was less flattering, of course. It deferred the inevitable triumph and thus would make it sweeter.

"Has Mrs. Morris told you what I should like you to do?" Jerningham's voice was coldly emotionless, and his gray eyes showed frosty lights.

"She has told me what you doubtless told her. But I must confess I am not very clear in my own mind," answered Miss Keogh.

Her voice was what you would have expected an artistic Providence to give her. It complemented the lips. If you closed your eyes and heard the voice you saw her eyes and felt the heavenly strawberries on your own lips!

Jerningham had not taken his cold eyes off her. He asked as if she were anybody—a woman of forty, for example, "Will you listen to me carefully?"

"Oh yes!"

"I provide transportation, first-class, to London. I pay you thirty-five dollars a week for your services and allow ten dollars a day for hotel expenses, and so on. At the end of the case your contingent fee will depend upon your success. We don't want to skimp—but we are not throwing away money. It may be one hundred or five hundred dollars. But forget all about it."

"I have—in advance," said the marvel, calmly.

Jerningham looked at her steadily. She looked back unflinchingly and yet not at all defiantly as a lesser person would.

"If you accept my offer you will go when in London to Thornton's Hotel—an old-fashioned but very select hotel—where you will find a nice room reserved for you; I will cable for it. It will cost you a guinea a day—for the room and table board. You will thus have five dollars a day for cabs and incidentals. In that hotel lives Mrs. Margaret Deering, an elderly American widow, who looks healthy enough. We fear she is not so strong as she looks, and don't want her to be alone. But she will not take hints. I wish you to make friends with her, so that if she should become ill enough to need attention you may see that she gets proper care and induce her to cable to her only daughter." He stopped and looked at Miss Keogh inquiringly, as if to convince himself that Miss Keogh had understood.

"What," said Miss Keogh, calmly, "is the rest of it?" Her eyes were very dark. They always seemed to deepen in color when she frowned. She always frowned when she concentrated—all women do, notwithstanding their dread of wrinkles.

Jerningham stared at her. Then he said, "The lady is not insane."

"Nervous?"

"Not yet!"

"Ah!" Miss Keogh nodded her head. Her color had risen somewhat.

"Is there anything in what I have said so far that makes you unwilling to take this case?" asked Jerningham.

"Nothing—so far," she said, looking steadily into his cold, gray eyes. She was, of course, Irish.

"Very well. You can save her family much worriment by suggesting to Mrs. Deering that she ought to have a trained nurse in constant attendance."

"By the name of Keogh?" interjected the most wonderful.

"No. You are supposed to be a young lady with an income of your own. You might explain that you took up trained nursing to help your only brother, a physician."

"Very well. And—"

"After you meet Mrs. Deering you might make judicious remarks about her health."

"For example—"

"Well, at breakfast you say: 'You didn't sleep well last night, did you?' If she says no, you can immediately suggest a physician. If she says she did, you say: 'Well, there is something wrong with you! Did you ever have your kidneys examined?' A simple remark in the proper tone of voice sometimes does it—like, 'Whatever in the world is the matter with you, dear Mrs. Deering?' You understand?"

"If you mean that I must suggest to her that she is ailing—"

"Precisely. The idea is not to frighten her to death, my dear young woman with the beautiful but suspicious eyes, but simply to induce her to send for her only daughter, so that afterward the two will not be separated. And the old lady, I may say for the benefit of your still suspicious eyes, is not very rich, though the daughter is. So your imagination need not invent any devilish plot. I think you can accomplish your work in six weeks. For every day under the six weeks you will receive five pounds. That's twenty-five dollars a day. That is intended, Miss Keogh, to make you hurry. But you must be tactful."

"Make it a fixed sum. You look like a clever man."

She looked at him challengingly. He stared back, and gradually a look of admiration came into his eyes. He said, with a smile of appreciation:

"You win! You are certainly the most wonderful girl in the world! I'll make it one thousand dollars, win, lose, or draw. But the quicker the cablegram—"

"—grams," she corrected—"plural. For greater effect at this end!"

"—grams!" he echoed. "And now you must come with me to the bank to get your letter of credit and some English money. I'll pay in advance."

He rose. Miss Keogh motioned to him to sit down again. He did so and looked at her alertly. It might have disconcerted some girls—but not the only absolutely perfect one. Not at all!

"There remains something," she said.

"What?" he queried, sharply.

"You forgot it!" she told him, with one of those utterly maddening smiles of forgiveness with which beautiful women rivet the fetters and make one grateful.

"What? What?" he asked, impatiently.

"Why?" she answered. "That is what! Why?"

Her beautiful head nodded twice with a birdlike gracefulness. Her eyes were very bright—and very dark! Her cheeks were flushed. Her ripe lips, slightly parted, were overpoweringly tempting.

Jerningham stood up again and stared fixedly at her as though he would read miles and miles beyond her wonderful eyes—into the very depths of her soul! He approached her and held out both his hands. After a scarcely perceptible hesitation she placed hers in his. He shook them with profound gravity; then bowed and raised her right to his lips—and kissed it twice. Still holding her hands in his, he said to her, earnestly:

"My dear child, you are the most wonderful woman in all the world. You are simply the last word in utter perfection. I am a millionaire, but not a crook. I am forty, but still strong. I have never been in love with a woman; but I now know I could be. If you ever wish to marry for the ease and comfort that great wealth gives, or if you ever feel like using your wonderful gifts to make a man who has both money and brains become an important personage in the world—just say the word. There is nothing—nothing, do you hear?—that we could not do together, you and I. My name is—" He paused and looked at her as if to make sure again.

"Yes?" she said, in her most heavenly voice. She released her hands, but her eyes never left his.

"Jerningham."

"The Klondike millionaire who—"

"The same!"

"Ah!" said Miss Keogh, calmly, but her flower-like cheeks were azalea-pink, and her eyes were full of light. She had read the *Planet's* articles. She did not remember how many million dollars Jerningham was supposed to have; but she did remember how the fairest of the fair had tried—and failed!

"Remember—any time, with or without notice. My offer is open until you accept it or definitely refuse it. Perhaps I never could make you love me; but I know I could love you if I let myself go."

"You have not answered me," said Miss Keogh.

"Ask again," he smiled.

"Why?" There was no smile in her eyes.

It made him serious. He answered:

"For friendship."

"To a woman?"

"To a man."

"Again I ask, Why?"

There was a pause. Then he said:

"Mrs. Ashton Welles is the only daughter of Mrs. Deering."

"And—"

"She is twenty-two."

"And—"

"Her husband is fifty-two. That's all!"

"Is it?"

"So far as I am concerned, it is—really!"

"Is Mr. Ashton Welles your friend?"

"No. But he is no enemy, either."

"No? But you have a friend, a Mr. Wolfe—a Mr. Francis Wolfe?" She knew it from a newspaper item.

But Mr. Jerningham jumped up from his seat. "Marry me, dear girl! Marry me, I beg of you! You are the only woman in the world! You are the most beautiful ever created and, beyond all question, the cleverest. You are a genius! Why isn't all mankind on its knees worshiping? Will you marry me? Wait! Don't speak. I know what your answer will be."

"You do?" She smiled inscrutably.

Imagine the Sphinx—if the Sphinx were Irish and very beautiful—with those eyes and those lips! Guess? You couldn't guess where your soul was—or whose!

"Yes, I do," answered Jerningham, confidently. "I will write it on a piece of paper and prove it. But first tell me this: Will you take Mrs. Deering's case?"

She looked at him, and said, "Yes."

"Very well." He wrote something on one of his cards, doubled it so she could not see what he had written, and gave it to her, saying, "Now answer me: Will you marry me?"

She looked at him a long time. He met her gaze squarely. Presently she said, very seriously:

"Not yet!"

"Look in the card," he said, also very seriously.

She did. It said: *Not yet!*

AS PROOFS OF HOLY WRIT

A vague alarm came into her purple-blue eyes. She was on the point of speaking, but he held up his hand, and said, earnestly:

"Please don't say it. We'll meet in London. You will enjoy the Continent later on. Now let us go and get your letter of credit, and see whether you like the stateroom that I ordered reserved." They did.

On the next day Jerningham's limousine took Miss Keogh and her hand-luggage to the steamer. Jerningham was there to see her off. She had invited a dozen of her friends to do the same, and they were there—all of them women and most of them frankly envious, for her stateroom was full of beautiful flowers and baskets of wonderful fruit—quite as if she already were a millionaire!

As she said good-by to Jerningham there was in her eyes a look of intelligent, almost cold-blooded, gratitude which seemed to embrace Mr. Jerningham's kindness, his thoughtfulness, and his bank account.

"I wish you a very pleasant voyage!" he said. "Think over my offer. When you get to London will you mail these letters for me? Remember, you are to cable if you need anything, money or advice —or a husband. And cable at once if Mrs. Deering cables. Good-by! *Bon voyage!*"

When Miss Keogh came to open the package of letters she found in it thirty-three, stamped with British stamps, on stationery of Thornton's Hotel! They were addressed in a woman's handwriting to various business houses, some of which she recognized as manufacturers of medical goods and agents of mineral waters of the kind used by people who suffer from kidney diseases. It made her think that if—between the deluge of medical prospectuses and Miss Keogh's efforts—Mrs. Deering did not cable for her only daughter it would be a wonder! Jerningham was neglecting nothing to succeed.

V

Frank Wolfe's first task in his new and now famous job consisted of helping Jerningham buy two automobiles. Then, when the weather permitted, they toured Westchester County and Long Island.

Usually they took along some of Frank's men friends. It was pleasant work—at the rate of twenty-five thousand dollars a year.

Jerningham did not again refer to his love-affair, and Frank could not very well allude to it; but it was perfectly plain to the young man that within a very short time their friendship would be sufficiently strong to justify Mr. Jerningham in asking Frank to help actively in the search of the vanished Naida Deering.

One day Mr. Jerningham waited in vain for young Mr. Wolfe. They had planned to go to Mount Kisco to look at a farm that was offered for sale, Mr. Jerningham having developed the usual millionaire's desire to own an estate. At one o'clock the telephone-bell rang. Jerningham answered in person. He heard a feminine voice say that Mr. Wolfe regretted that a severe indisposition had prevented him from going as usual to Mr. Jerningham's rooms, but he hoped to be sufficiently recovered to have that pleasure on the next day.

Jerningham merely said, "Say I hope it is nothing serious—and ask him, please, whether there is anything I can do."

Silence. Then: "He says, 'No—thanks!' It is nothing very serious."

"Tell him not to come down until he has entirely recovered and to take good care of himself. Good-by!"

If Mr. Jerningham heard the tinkling music of an irrepressible giggle at the other end of the wire he did not show it. His face was serious as he found an address in the telephone-directory. He called up the Brown Lecture Bureau and made an appointment to see Captain Brown, the manager, at 3 P.M. At that hour, to the minute, he was ushered into the private offices of the world-famous manager of the lecture bureau.

"Captain Brown?"

"Yes, sir. What can I do for you?"

"I should like to know what lecturers you have available at the moment," said Jerningham.

The Klondiker did not look like the chairman of a church entertainment committee or like a village philanthropist. So Captain Brown asked:

"Where is the—er— Is it a club?"

"No. It is myself. Here in New York."

"Well, we provide speakers and lecturers, not exactly entertainers, to—"

"I know all that. I wish to know whom you could send me to entertain me. Let me see! Is Commander Finsen, the explorer, here now?"

"Yes."

"And his terms?"

"It depends upon where it is."

THE PLUNDERERS

Evidently Jerningham did not think Captain Brown realized what was wanted, for he said, earnestly:

"Captain Brown, get this clearly fixed in your mind, if you please: I am anxious to hear some of your lecturers by myself alone, in my own apartments. I wish men who have done things—men who are, above all things, brave and resourceful. I don't want decadent poets, but explorers, gentlemen adventurers, humanists, or scientists, who have a knack of imparting their knowledge in such a way as to interest men who are neither old nor scientific. I am perfectly willing to pay your usual rate. What's the odds if one of your clients spends an evening with me or whether he spends it in Norwalk, Connecticut, or Boundbrook, New Jersey? Do you get me?"

"Oh, perfectly. I might suggest—"

Here the genial manager ceased speaking to smile, grateful that so unusual a man as Jerningham should condescend to listen. It was a habit—this thankful smiling—that came from having dealt with geniuses for thirty years. Then Captain Brown permitted himself to suggest a dozen or more men who had very interesting stories to tell. Jerningham asked him to make a memorandum of the men and their specialties, and agreed to call on Captain Brown when he needed entertainment. After Captain Brown had given him the names and prices, Jerningham gave his own name and address.

Captain Brown looked grieved. He read the newspapers. He might have asked double the fees from the Alaskan Monte Cristo!

On the next day, when Mr. Francis Wolfe showed

up with never a trace of anything but good health on his pleasing face, Jerningham invited him to spend the next evening in the apartments and hear Finsen tell how he had discovered the tribe of Antarctic giants, the shortest of whom was seven feet three inches; and how he had captured alive thirty-three white bears. He asked Frank to invite five friends who might be interested, first, in dining with Jerningham and Commander Finsen, and then in hearing Finsen spin his yarn.

Frank gladly undertook to find the audience.

So they had a very nice little dinner, with just enough to drink and no killjoys in activity. And later, in Jerningham's little sitting-room at the hotel, they heard the great Dane, who was a prosaic viking with iron muscles and pale-blue eyes that made you uncomfortable for reasons unknown, tell them all about his remarkable voyage of discovery and his hunts—no end of things that he could tell them, but could not tell a mixed audience: perfectly amazing details, of which Frank and his friends talked for weeks.

Then there was a little midnight supper, at which they all told stories that left no unpleasant after-effects.

One day after luncheon Jerningham, who had been in a particularly jovial mood, suddenly became very serious. He aimed at Frank one of those searching looks that seemed to go to the young man's soul. Then he said:

"My boy, I'd like to say something to you."

"Say it."

"I shall probably hurt your feelings, so you must be prepared to keep your temper well in hand."

"You ought to know me better than that by now, Jerningham," retorted Frank. He had grown not only to like, but even to admire, this strange miner.

"Wolfe," said Jerningham, slowly, "you are one of those unfortunate chaps who are cruelly handicapped by perennial youth. It is doubtless a pleasing thing to feel at fifty as you did at twenty. Nevertheless, it is bad business. It is all very nice to shun responsibility, but it makes you careless; and you can't expect to saddle consequences on your guardian after you are twenty-one. A boy of forty can't be trusted to take care of his own property."

"I can take care of mine," laughed Frank, "without any trouble." His property was about minus thirty thousand.

"Your property now—yes. But suppose you had a million or two left you—or even more? Do you know what would happen to those millions, and do you know what would happen to you?"

"I know—but I won't tell."

"Will you let me tell you?" asked Jerningham, so earnestly that Frank almost stopped smiling.

"I'll hear you to the bitter end."

"The millions would go from your pocket into the pockets of—well, you know whose pockets! And your life would go into the Big Beyond by the W. W. route."

"I bite. What's W. W.?"

"Wine and woman. You would last perhaps five years. You would die a dipsomaniac at thirty or thereabout. The chief folly of fighting booze when you are rich is that it renders wealth utterly futile."

"How?"

"Well, you can get just as drunk on ten dollars a

day as you can on one thousand dollars—with this difference, that in the one case you would have to get drunk on whisky by yourself and in the other you might get drunk on vintage champagne in the company of paid parasites. The morning after is the same in both cases: you don't remember any more of the ten-dollar jag than of the thousand-dollar orgy! When a drunkard sets out to squander a million all he really does is to carry a sign on his back with letters a mile high—the sign reading, 'I am a d——d fool!'"

Frank took it good-naturedly because he liked Jerningham and because he was not a millionaire. It really would be asinine to be a millionaire and try to drink all there was; so he said, amiably:

"Having downed the Demon Rum, then what?"

"I'll put it up to you this way: I have no family and I may never marry. I certainly won't if I don't find my first and only sweetheart. Suppose I felt like leaving you some of my money? You are a nice boy, but you also have been a D. F., and you must admit that no man likes to see his friend trying to beat all D. F. records. Don't get mad and don't look indignant! I want to make a proposition to you: I'll agree to deposit to your account in a trust company one hundred dollars a day for every day you don't touch a drop! I don't want to reform you. I merely want to train you—in case! There will be some times when you will forfeit that. It will amount to paying one hundred dollars for a Martini. It will become a luxury."

"Too expensive for me!" said Frank, seriously.

"And, my boy, it is more than being on the water-wagon—it's being able to stay on! Booze is so

foolish! I want to give you some business matters—
for you to handle for me."

"You know what I know about business—"

"Can't you do as you are told? Don't you know
enough to look clever and say, 'Sign here!' in a
frozen voice?"

"Oh yes. But—"

"I know you will miss your evenings at first.
But I'll tell you what to do. I am no killjoy. Well,
you spend as many evenings as you wish with me.
Invite as many friends as you please—sex no bar.
Will you?"

"Jerningham, you are a nice chap. I'll do it. But
you must not think of that one hundred dollars—"

"Tut-tut! Can't you understand that I want to
do it—that I love to see your bank account grow?
Run along now. I want to read Lucretius."

From that day Francis Wolfe became Jerningham's inseparable companion. Every night they
went to the theater together or else they spent the
evening in Jerningham's rooms, listening to celebri-
ties. Their evenings soon became famous. Indeed,
people began to talk about Frank Wolfe's reform.
Even his fairest and frailest friends, knowing that
Frank forfeited one hundred dollars a day by falling
off the water-wagon, kept him firmly on the seat—
and borrowed the hundred. In due time the miracle
reached the ears of Frank's sisters and of his aunt,
Mrs. Stimson. They had a talk with Frank. They
were first amazed, then delighted, when they saw
Frank and when they heard about Jerningham's intention of making him his heir.

Thus it came about that, out of gratitude for the
man who was making a man of their brother, Mrs.

John Burt and Mrs. Sydney Walsingham accepted Mr. Jerningham's invitation and attended one of the lectures at the Klondiker's apartments. The little supper that followed was a great success. Mr. Jerningham talked little, but extremely well—as when he said to Mrs. Jack in a low voice that he loved Frank Wolfe and some day everybody would be sure of it!

"I am merely training him. But don't think I am asking the impossible. I wish him to know enough to hold on to what I'll leave him."

Of course after that Mr. Jerningham was not only in society, but even in a fair way of becoming a fad. Gerald Lanier, the short-story writer, said that Jerningham was society's gold cure and had climbed into the inner circles on a ladder made of tightly corked wine-bottles; in fact, he wrote what his non-literary friends called a skit—and Frank's friends a knock—entitled: "How to Capitalize Intemperance." But that did not hinder Jerningham from receiving invitations from families with thirsty younger sons.

VI

One morning Jerningham, who had seemed preoccupied, said to Frank:

"I wonder if I can ask you—" He paused and looked doubtfully at Frank.

"What?"

"A favor."

"Of course. Why, you can even touch me if you want to."

"I wonder if your—if Mrs. Burt would invite Mrs. Ashton Welles to dinner?"

"I guess so. I'll ask her."

"That way you could meet Mrs. Welles, and—"

"You mean," said Frank, trying to look like Sherlock Holmes, "I could ask her about your—about her sister?"

Jerningham jumped to his feet in consternation.

"Great Scott, no! No!" he shouted.

"Why, I thought—"

"You can't ask her that until you know her so well that you can take a friend's liberty. Promise me you won't ask her until I myself tell you that you may! Promise!"

There was in his eyes a look of such intensity that young Wolfe was startled.

"Of course I'll promise."

"You must make friends with her first. She must learn to like you—"

Francis Wolfe smiled a trifle fatuously. It was merely boyish. A little more, however, would have made the smile ungentlemanly. Jerningham continued, very earnestly:

"Listen, lad. She will have to do more than merely like you—she will have to trust you. And the only way to make a young and pretty woman trust a young and not unattractive man is by having that man never, never, never fail in respect of her. He may be in love with her, or he may only pretend to be in love with her; but he must act as if he regarded her with such awe that he dare not make direct love to her. Do you get it?"

"Yes. But—"

"There is no but. She must first like you, which is not difficult; and then she must trust you as a

true friend, which is, to say the least, a slower matter. Be a brother to her. Do you think you like
me well enough to do this for me now?"

Jerningham looked at young Wolfe steadily—a
man's look.

Frank said: "I'll do it gladly. And my sisters—"

"They must never know about—about Naida!"
interrupted Jerningham, hastily.

"Of course not. But they will do anything for
me—and for you, too!"

That is the true story of how it came about that
Mrs. Ashton Welles was taken up by the Jack
Burts; and how she met Francis Wolfe; and how
Mrs. Stimson invited Mr. and Mrs. Ashton Welles
to one of her old-fashioned and tiresome but famous
and very formal dinners; and how Frank again took
in Mrs. Welles. Thereafter they met often. At
some of these dinners they met Jerningham.

The Klondiker paid his court to Mr. Welles.
Indeed, he seemed to have for the president of the
VanTwiller Trust Company an admiration that
closely resembled the worship of a matinée girl for
an actress like Maude Adams. It was an innocent
sort of worship, but, nevertheless, not displeasing.
In men it sometimes makes the worshiped feel pater-
nally toward the worshiper.

Jerningham developed a habit of going every day
to the trust company; and he made it a point always
to see Ashton Welles, if only to shake hands. One
morning he told Mr. Welles he desired advice about
an investment. Jerningham, it must be remembered,
had on deposit with the trust company over a million
dollars, and there were six or seven millions in gold-
dust in the company's vault.

THE PLUNDERERS

"Mr. Welles, I—I," said the Klondiker, so earnestly that he stammered—"I should like to buy some VanTwiller Trust Company stock, to have and to hold as long as you are president."

There was in Jerningham's eyes a look of that admiration that best expresses itself in absolute confidence in the infallibility of a very great man. Welles was a very cold man; but flattery has rays that will thaw icebergs.

Welles nearly blushed and smiled one of his politely deprecating smiles—as if he were apologizing for smiling—and said:

"Why, Mr. Jerningham, I'll confess to you that I myself think well of that stock. I guess we'll keep on paying dividends."

Jerningham smiled delightedly—the king had jested! Then he said:

"I'll buy as much as I can, but I don't want to put up the price on myself. Who can give me pointers on how to pick up the stock quietly? Do you think I should see Mr. Barrows or Mr. Stewardson?"

He looked so anxiously at Mr. Welles that Mr. Welles said, kindly:

"Oh, see Stewardson. I'll speak to him, if you wish."

"Thank you! Thank you, Mr. Welles," said Jerningham, so gratefully that Welles felt like a philanthropist as he rang the bell to summon the second vice-president.

"Mr. Stewardson, Mr. Jerningham wants to buy some of our stock. I want you to help him in any way possible."

"Delighted, I'm sure!" said the vice-president,

very cordially. He was paid to be cordial to customers.

"If I had my way I'd be the largest individual stockholder," said Jerningham, looking at Welles almost adoringly.

"I hope you will," said Welles, pleasantly. "Mr. Stewardson will help you."

Jerningham and Welles shook hands. Then Jerningham and Stewardson left to go to the vice-president's private office.

VII

The remarkable Miss Keogh was one of those remarkable people who are really remarkable. Within three weeks came a cablegram from her to Mr. Jerningham to the effect that a letter had been sent by Mrs. Deering to her daughter—the first. Mrs. Deering had begun to doubt her own health. Then came cablegrams from her to Mrs. Welles; and in a few days, before Ashton Welles could think of a valid excuse for not letting his wife go to England, Mrs. Welles told him to engage passage for her on the *Ruritania*.

It was very unfortunate that he could not accompany her; but the annual meeting was only three weeks away, and the minority, never strong enough to do real damage, always was devilish enough to be very disagreeable to the clique in control. Ashton Welles, after the extremely stupid fashion of all strong men, had always kept the absolute control of the company's affairs in his own hands. It was the one thing he refused to share with his subordinates. He was a czar in his office. He was, in reality, the trust company—or he so believed and so he made others believe. His vice-presidents were merely highly paid office-boys, according to the gossip of the Street, which was not so far out of the way in this particular instance.

Ten minutes after Mrs. Ashton Welles engaged Suite D on the *Ruritania*, due to sail on the following day, Jerningham said to Mr. Francis Wolfe:

"My boy, I should like you to go to London on business for me—and for yourself. You've got to represent me in a deal with the Arctic Venture Corporation. You will have my power of attorney and you will sign the deed for one of my properties, as soon as they have deposited two hundred and fifty thousand pounds to my credit in Parr's Bank. And also you will call on the prettiest girl in the world—the prettiest, do you hear?—who unfortunately is also the brightest and cleverest. Her name—" He paused and looked at Francis Wolfe meditatively, almost hesitatingly.

"Go on!" implored Francis Wolfe.

"Her name is Kathryn Keogh and she is stopping at Thornton's Hotel. She will help you find Naida. Miss Keogh is a friend of Mrs. Deering."

"She is Irish—eh?" asked Frank.

"Mrs. Deering?"

"No; the peach—the—Miss Keogh?"

"She is of the Waterford Keoghs, famous for their eyes and their complexions. But business first. You are not to fall in love with Miss Keogh until after my two hundred and fifty thousand pounds are safe in bank. I'd go myself, but I have a still bigger deal on here in New York. I've taken the liberty to engage a stateroom on the *Ruritania*, sailing to-morrow, and a letter of credit has been ordered for five thousand dollars. Have I taken too much for granted?"

"No; but you know perfectly well that I don't know a thing about business, and I'd be afraid—"

"My solicitors in London will call on you when they are ready for you. I shall give you a memorandum for your own conduct; you will find there instructions in detail—just as though you were a ten year-old boy; but that is really for your own protection, and I don't mean to imply that your mind is ten years old—"

"No feelings hurt," said Frank, who in reality was much relieved to learn that the chances of his making a mistake had been intelligently minimized.

"I'm glad you take it that way. Now we'll go down-town to Towne, Ripley & Co. and give them your signature for the letter of credit; from there we'll go to the British Consulate and have my own signature on my power of attorney certified to by the consul, and then you can skip up-town and say good-by to your friends."

Frank left Jerningham at the consulate and went home to pack up and arrange for his more pressing adieus. Jerningham went into a public telephone-booth and called up the offices of *Society Folk*. When they answered he asked to speak with the editor.

"Well?" presently came in a sharp voice.

"This is Mr.—er—a friend."

"Anonymous! All right. What do you want?"

"To give you a piece of news."

"We verify everything and take your word for

absolutely nothing. I tell you this to save your telling me a lie."

"That's all right. You'll find it true enough. I—"

"One minute. Where is that pencil? All right! Now the name of the woman?"

"How do you know I want to—"

"All you fellows always do. What's her name?"

"Mrs. Ashton Welles."

"The wife of the president of the VanTwiller — "

"Correct!" said Jerningham.

"Now the name of the man?"

"Francis Wolfe," answered Jerningham, unhesitatingly.

"The chorus-girls' pet?" asked the voice.

"The same!"

"Has it happened yet? Or do you merely fear it? Or is it a case of hoping?"

"I don't know what you are driving at."

"Then you don't read *Society Folk*."

"Well, I don't—regularly. All I know is that Frank has been very assiduous in his attentions lately. He's shaken the Great White Way and hasn't been in a lobster-palace in two months. He and Mrs. Ashton Welles are sailing on the *Ruritania* to-morrow."

"Under what name?"

"Their own."

"Thank you, kind friend. Thank you!"

"Why do you say that?"

"Because we can now use names. Does Mr. Welles also go?"

"Of course not!"

"Excuse me for asking such a silly question.

What other crime has he committed besides being old?—I mean Mr. Welles."

"Stupidity is worse than criminal."

"Aye, aye, sir!"

"When does your paper come out?"

"Day after to-morrow. Much obliged. You are a friend in need. Don't ring off yet. Listen! You are also a dirty, low-lived, sneaking, cowardly dog, and a general, all-round, unrelieved, monumental—"

It was the one way the editor had of showing that he was better than his anonymous contributor.

Jerningham, of course, went on board the *Ruritania* to see Frank off. Ashton Welles was also there to say good-by to his young and beautiful wife. It was their first separation, and Welles did not like it. He seemed to feel her absence in advance; it was really that, as the hour drew near, he realized more vividly how lonely she would leave him! They have a saying in Spain that a man may grow accustomed to bearing sorrow, but that nobody can get used to that happiness which comes merely to disappear immediately after. A cigar manufacturer from Havana had once quoted this to Ashton Welles, and Ashton Welles was impressed less by the saying than by the fact that the Spaniard was so serious about it. But now he remembered it.

He was very uncomfortable and this discomfort made his mental machinery act queerly; it seemed to tint his thoughts with strange, unusual hues that made them almost morbid. He would have felt contempt for his own weakness had he not been so full of half-angry regret at being left alone in New York—this man who never had possessed an intimate friend; who not even as a boy had a chum!

THE PLUNDERERS

Of course it was only a coincidence that young Mr. Francis Wolfe was to be young Mrs. Ashton Welles's fellow-passenger; and it was also a coincidence that Mr. Wolfe's stateroom was just across the passageway from Mrs. Welles's suite. Indeed, neither of the young people had picked out the cabins—but there they were. And there, in Ashton Welles's mind, was another unformulated unpleasantness.

Frank's sisters were so proud Frank was going to put through an important business deal that they showed it. But if they were glad that Mrs. Welles was also going they did not show it. They recalled Frank's desire to meet the pretty young matron whose husband was thirty years older, and they were rather ostentatiously polite to her. Ashton Welles, in his disturbed state of mind, somehow felt that the attitude of Mrs. John Burt and Mrs. Sydney Walsingham was one of blame-fixing; but he could not definitely understand why there should be any blame to fix! He dismissed his semi-suspicions with the thought that women had petty minds. His wife was very pretty and Wolfe's sisters were not as young as they used to be. And youth is a terrible thing— to lose! It is hard to forgive youth for being, after one is past—well, say, past a certain age. And to prove that he himself had nothing to fear—absolutely nothing—he even smiled and said to young Mr. Wolfe:

"I feel certain, of course, that if Mrs. Welles should need anything—"

It was the season of the year when east-bound liners carried few passengers. The young people were bound to be thrown together a great deal.

"Of course, Mr. Welles. Only too delighted, I'm sure!" said Frank, very eagerly.

He was a fine-looking chap, with that wonderfully clean, healthy pink complexion which suggests a clean and healthy mind. His eyes were full of that eager, boyish light that makes the possessors thereof so nice to pet, small-childwise.

Ashton Welles received an impression of Frank Wolfe's face that was photographic in its details.

The floating hotel moved off slowly. Ashton Welles, on the pier, watched the fluttering handkerchief of his wife out of sight. He had the remembrance of her beautiful young face framed in Siberian sable to cheer him. She certainly looked heavenly. She had cried at leaving him. She had waved away at him vehemently, and there was the unpleasant suggestion that always attends such leave-takings—that the parting was forever. A frail thing—human life! A little speck of vitality on the boundless waste of grim, gray waters! And she seemed so sorry to go away from him! And she waved and waved, as if she, also, feared she might never see him again! And Francis Wolfe stood beside her, very close to her, and waved also—to Jerningham, who stood beside Ashton Welles.

Ashton Welles accepted Jerningham's invitation and rode to his office in the Klondiker's sumptuous motor in the Klondiker's company. Ashton Welles looked at the flower-holder. Instead of the white azaleas he saw two white handkerchiefs waved by two young people.

"You are very friendly with young Wolfe?" said Ashton Welles, carelessly inquisitive—merely to make talk, you know. All rich old men who marry young women have ostrich habits. They put an end to danger by closing their eyes to the obvious. That is why they always discover nothing.

"Rather—yes. I think he is a fine chap—one of those clean-cut Americans of the present generation that European women find so perfectly fascinating."

Ashton Welles instantly frowned—and instantly ceased to frown.

"Yes," he said, and grimaced, thinking it looked like a smile. "What business is taking him to London? I thought he was a young man of—er—elegant leisure."

"He was that until very recently; but he has turned over a new leaf. He has forsworn his old and, I suppose, rather disreputable companions. I find him rather serious."

"What has changed him?" Ashton Welles was foolish enough to be brave enough to ask. When a question can have two answers—one of them disagreeable—it is folly to ask it.

" I don't know," answered Jerningham, as if puzzled. "He has acted a little queerly and secretive-like; but it is, I admit, a queerness that other young men would do well to imitate, for it has made him cease drinking, and cease—er—you know. I rather suspect it is his sister, Mrs. Burt. He is very fond of her. A man will do things for a good woman that he won't for his best man friend, or for his own sake. You saw him. There is no viciousness or dissipation in that face. Damned handsome chap, I call him!"

"H'm!" winced the glacial Ashton Welles. He could not help it.

There came upon him a strange mood, almost of

numbness, that made him silent against his will. He answered by nods—the nods of a man who does not hear—to Jerningham's chatter. He gathered in some way that the Alaskan Monte Cristo was talking of buying VanTwiller Trust Company stock, and that he would ask Stewardson how much he could borrow on the stock.

"Yes—do!" said Ashton Welles as the motor stopped in front of the imposing entrance of the trust company's marble building.

They stepped out; Welles excused himself almost brusquely and went into his own private office to think all the thoughts that a millionaire of fifty-two thinks when he thinks that he married at fifty a girl thirty years his junior, with cheeks like flower petals and eyes like skies, who is going to spend the best part of a week on a steamer in the company of a man who is much worse than handsome—young!

Mr. Jerningham, who did not seem to have noticed the near-rudeness of Mr. Ashton Welles, promptly sought the second vice-president and asked how much the company would lend on its own stock.

"It is against the law for us to lend money on our own stock," said the vice-president, who did not add that this provision had prevented many an inside clique from eating its pie and having it too.

"Will the banks loan money on V.T. stock?" asked Jerningham. He had already bought three thousand shares at an average of four hundred dollars a share.

"Well, I guess so."

"On a time loan?"

"No trouble in borrowing three hundred dollars a share, I should say."

"That is not much," objected Jerningham.

"No, it isn't. But— May I ask you a question?"

"Two if you wish," said Jerningham, with one of his likable smiles.

"Why should you need to borrow a trifle, with all the millions in gold you have down-stairs? Or are they only gold bricks you've got in your boxes?"

This was, of course, meant in jest; but Stewardson thought in a flash the trust company did not know for a positive fact that Jerningham's iron-bound and wax-sealed boxes had real gold-dust in them.

"Let me tell you something, Mr. Stewardson," said Jerningham, with that curious earnestness people assume when they discuss matters they do not really understand — "let me tell you this: The time is coming—and coming within a few months!— when good, hard gold is going to command a premium just as it practically did during the Bryan free-silver scare in 1896. I am going to save mine. I want to have it in readiness to take advantage of—"

"But present conditions are utterly different—"

"They are always different—and yet the panics come! You thought that after 1896 there would never again be any need for clearing-house certificates; and yet, in 1907—"

"They were unnecessary—" began Stewardson, hotly.

He had been left out of all conferences among the powers at that trying time, and naturally disapproved their actions.

"But they happened, just the same! I know myself. If I cash in now I'll buy something with the money. I don't want to buy now. No, sir! If I should happen to need a million or two I prefer to borrow it for a few weeks until my next shipment comes in. There will be two millions coming in about the middle of next month. I've sent word to get out as big an output as possible. See? You bet your boots Wall Street is not going to get either my cash or my mines, as they did Colonel Cannon's. You know he was 'the Mexican copper king' one day and 'that jackass from Chihuahua' the next! See?"

The vice-president looked at him and said "I see!" in a very flattering tone of voice; but in his inmost mind he was thinking that such a thing was precisely what doubtless would happen to Mr. Alfred Jerningham, late of Nome. It is always the extremely suspicious, too-smart-for-you-by-heck! farmer who buys the biggest gold brick.

"They'll find out I'll never let them change my name into 'that blankety-blank-blank from Alaska!'" And Jerningham put on that look of devilish astuteness that buyers of stocks always put on when they buy at top prices.

He left the vice-president of the VanTwiller Trust Company and called on the vice-presidents of several other trust companies and banks, and found out that he could borrow more than three hundred dollars a share on his V.T. stock. And he did—then and there. He impressed the genial philanthropists on whom he called as being a child of Nature—a great big boy playing at being a financier. There was in consequence much smacking of financial lips. It was morsels like this naïve and honest Alaskan miner with the millions that helped to reconcile men to living the Wall Street life.

THE PLUNDERERS

VIII

On the day after the *Ruritania* sailed Ashton Welles, whose first wifeless evening at home had not been pleasant, found on his desk a marked copy of *Society Folk*. These were the four marked paragraphs:

The man who first said there was no fool like an old fool had in mind that form of folly which consists of the purchase of a beautiful girl by a man who endeavors to span a difference of thirty years in age by means of a bridge of solid gold. It is unnatural, unwholesome, and even immoral. The sordid romances of high life that begin in a Fifth Avenue jewelry-shop are apt to end in a Reno divorce-mill. Why shouldn't they? A girl who marries once for money is always ready to marry again for more money—or for more love—for she always wants more than the desiccated ass who first bought her can give her. A girl of twenty who is famous for her good looks is always a beautiful young woman, no matter what else she may be. But a man close to sixty, whether he is the head of a big trust company or a poet, is nothing but an old man. Speaking of remarkable coincidences, is it not odd that both Fool and Financier should begin with an F? And Frailty, too, whose other name is Woman?

If there are some things that gold cannot do it is perfectly wonderful how many things love can do! It bridges all chasms with kisses, and solves all riddles—with glances. It even defies the high cost of living and makes men think themselves demigods. It has been known to make champagne drunkards swear off long before they are bankrupt. It even now depopulates the lobster-palaces. It turns dining-room navigators into fearless vikings, braving the wild Atlantic and its midwinter gales in order to be by their lady-loves. It may even reform Tammany leaders—for we know it can transform young asses into handsome Lancelots.

Among the passengers on the *Ruritania*, sailing for Liverpool at this unfashionable season of the year, were Mrs. Ashton

Welles, who has the gorgeous Suite D all to herself, and young Mr. Francis Wolfe, who is content with the more modest stateroom across the way. Frank's friends are always singing his praises these days. He never looks at a chorus-girl save from the middle of the house, and has not taken anything stronger than Vichy in long weeks. If we were not averse to advertising male beauty shows we would remark that young Wolfe is the handsomest bachelor who ever sidestepped matrimony.

It takes more than money to keep the Wolfe from the door—eh? What?

The Ashton Welles who finished reading the beastly paragraphs of *Society Folk* was not the same Ashton Welles who began them. He was no longer an efficient financier, but a man benumbed, whose brain had turned to plaster of Paris. His mind at once lost all elasticity, all power to functionate. And, since he could not think, he could not act. That wonderful world, which financially successful people create for themselves with so much pride, tumbled about his ears. Out of the chaos made by a few printed words, only one thing was certain—he suffered!

Men are always wounded in a vital spot when they are wounded by jealousy, and Ashton Welles was particularly vulnerable because he lived in only two places—his office and his home. He did not have other houses of refuge to which his soul could retreat—like music or literature or art—in case of need. He had been so busy winning success that he had not had time for anything else. He had worked for the aggrandizement of the personal fortune of Ashton Welles. When circumstances and that reputation for luck, shrewdness, and caution, which is in itself a golden sagacity, finally placed him, still a

young man, at the head of the VanTwiller Trust
Company, David Soulett, one of the directors, re-
marked: "Welles has married the company; but
we don't yet know whether he is to be the company's
husband or whether the company is to be his wife!"
And a fellow-director, who had been in profitable
deals with Welles, retorted, "Well, I call it an ideal
match!"

Welles brought to the company what it needed
and the presidency brought to Welles many oppor-
tunities—none of which he neglected. He saw the
deposits increase tenfold—and his own fortune
twentyfold. What might not have been politic in
an individual playing a lone hand was altogether
admirable in the head of a financial institution—his
cold-bloodedness, for example, and the dehumanized
attitude toward life habitually assumed by the
principal cog-wheel in that intricate aggregation of
cog-wheels known as a modern trust company. Being an excellent money-lender, he was an uninter-
esting human being. You lose much when you win
money—for gold is hard and cold, and the enjoyment
of life calls for softness and warmth. It is the appalling revenge capital takes on its self-called masters.

As he approached his fiftieth year Welles began to
find that his isolation might be splendid, but that it
was also damnably uncomfortable. Did you know
that in certain millionaire households, where everything always runs very smoothly, the master gets to
long for a burnt steak or the spilling of soup by the
very competent servant? Welles, accustomed to the
wonderfully comfortable life of a very rich bachelor
in New York, desired a home where everything need

not be so comfortable. And as his fortune became a matter of several millions it began—as swollen fortunes always do, also in revenge!—to take on the aspect of a monument, something to admire during the monument-builder's lifetime and to endure impressively afterward! With the desire of permanence came the dream of all capitalists that makes them dynasts of gold—an heir to extend the boundaries of the family fortune! It was inevitable that Ashton Welles should grow to believe that, though the trust company's deposits were in other people's names, they really belonged to Ashton Welles, because they were merely the marble blocks of the Welles monument. The name of Welles must never cease to be identified with the work of Ashton the First!

Wherefore the need of an heir became almost an obsession with him, and with it came a quite human dissatisfaction with hotels and clubs, and trained nurses in times of illness. When a capitalist realizes clearly that, apart from his money-lending capacity, he has absolutely no power to bring tears to human eyes, he grows jealous of his own money. He wishes to be feared, though penniless, just as he would be loved, though a pauper. All these desires combined to force Ashton Welles into a decision. He had kept up a desultory sort of friendship with Mrs. Deering, the widow of his predecessor in the presidency of the trust company, and Anne Deering was the girl he knew best of all—though he really did not know her at all.

The Deerings had not been fortunate in their investments; in fact, the Deering holdings of Van-Twiller stock had been benevolently assimilated at one-fifth of their value by Ashton Welles himself during one of those panics that make reckless persons cease being reckless ever after. It was not very difficult for Anne Deering to be made to feel that she could save her mother's life and assure ease and comfort for herself forever by marrying Mr. Ashton Welles, who at fifty was one of those men whom old friends invariably classify as well-preserved. To be just, he was really distinguished-looking and had a sort of uniform urbanity that made him at least unobjectionable.

He was also very rich. She married him. She learned to like him. He grew to love her!

She was a doll—beautiful and utterly useless; but it was this very uselessness that made Ashton Welles worship her. This financier, who in his office was not only a skilful bargain-driver, but preached and practised the religion of efficiency, in his home plunged into an orgy of utterly juvenile love-making. He reveled in his wooing, which he had to do after his marriage. He did not merely desire to have a wife—he must have a wife of an extreme femininity; she must be one of those womanly women who exist only in the imaginations of men of a tyrannical cast of mind. His life having been for years exclusively a money-making life, he became very selfish. And he continued to find his greatest pleasure in pleasing himself—only that he now best pleased himself by being a boy sweetheart; by achieving his puppy love at fifty and deeming it marvelously rejuvenating and therefore altogether admirable.

Very well! Now imagine that man, living for two years amid those pitifully evanescent illusions so cherished by middle-aged men of money who marry very young women of looks—imagine that man suddenly informed that he is no longer to be anything but an old man! And not only old, but deserted! Imagine that selfsame man brought face to face with the invincible opponent of all old men—youth!

To Ashton Welles, sitting in his office, surrounded by glittering millions, there came the deadly chill of age—doubly cold from being surrounded by gold. In the twinkling of an eye all young men suddenly became redoubtable warriors, love-conquerors, irresistible as a force of nature—and as heartless! He was beaten by the universal victor—Time!

He stared fixedly at a photograph of his wife in an elaborately chased silver frame, but he did not see her. He saw ruins, as of a conflagration—the smoking débris of a destroyed home; and heaps of ashes—ashes everywhere! And in the rising puffs of smoke he saw faces of men—of young men—of very handsome young men!

Stewardson, the vice-president, walked in—the door was open, as usual. He saw his chief's face and was shocked into a quite human feeling of consternation.

"Great heavens, Mr. Welles, what is the matter?"

"Nothing!" said Ashton Welles. He suddenly felt an overwhelming impulse to hide his face from the sight of his fellow-men. He thought his forehead must show in black letters—*Fool!* and—and—and ten thousand terrible legends that changed with each beat of his heart, and told what he had been and what had happened; and—yes—what was bound to happen!

"Nothing! Nothing!" he repeated, fiercely.

"Nothing, I tell you!" He was certain all the world knew his disgrace.

"Shall I call a doctor?"

"No! No!" he snarled. Call in the entire world and gloat at his discomfiture? He glanced at the vice-president. The impolitic alarm on Stewardson's face exasperated him. "What do you want? Damn it, what do you want?" It was almost a shriek.

"I wanted to consult with you about that Consolidated Cushion Tire bond issue—"

"Yes, yes! Well?"

"Have you decided whether to—"

" Yes! I mean — no! I mean — Wait! Ask Witter. I dictated a memorandum to him, I think. Yes, I did!"

He was making desperate efforts to speak calmly; but he stopped, because Stewardson, a dastard of thirty-two, suddenly grew to resemble young Mr. Francis Wolfe! Stewardson saw the gleam in Ashton Welles's eyes and felt that the president must have hated him all his life!

"I'll get it from Witter," he said, and hastily left the room.

Welles stared wide-eyed at the open door for perhaps a full minute; always he saw ruins—smoke and ashes—ashes everywhere! And then he started up and squared his shoulders. He rang for an office-boy and said to him, "Tell Mr. Witter I've gone for the day"—Witter was his private secretary — and left the office.

He could not bear even to think of going home, for he now had no home! Therefore he went to Central Park and walked aimlessly about until his unaccustomed muscles compelled him to sit down. There he sat, thinking! After three hours he had grown sufficiently calm to believe himself when he called himself a fool for being jealous. Having convinced himself of his folly, he clutched eagerly at every opportunity to close his own ears to the whisperings of his own doubts. At length he went to his house, dressed as usual, and went to the Cosmopolitan Club to dine.

IX

A few minutes after Ashton Welles left his office, stabbed to the soul by the poisoned paragraphs of *Society Folk*, Jerningham sought Stewardson and told him he had decided to send some more gold-dust to the Assay Office. His own attendant, a young man, dark-haired and blue-eyed, who properly answered to the name of Sheehan, accompanied him. Stewardson, whose nerves had not recovered from the shock of Mr. Welles's behavior, decided that he, also, would go to the vaults.

"I want ten boxes sent to the Assay Office," said Jerningham.

"Certainly, sir," said the superintendent of the vaults, very obsequiously. To show how eager he was to please, he asked, "Any particular boxes, Mr. Jerningham?"

Immediately a half-formulated suspicion fleeted across the mind of the second vice-president of the VanTwiller Trust Company. How did they know what those boxes contained? How did they know that all of them were full of Yukon gold? How did they know anything about this man or about his treasure—his alleged treasure?

Almost immediately afterward, however, he reproached himself. Why, the man had deposited over a million — the proceeds of twenty of the boxes!

"Oh, take any ten," said Jerningham—"the first ten. They are the easiest to take out."

"The last ten!" said Stewardson, hastily, obeying an impulse that came upon him like a flash of lightning.

Jerningham turned and asked: "Why the last ten? They are away back, and—"

"I have my reasons," smiled Stewardson—the smile of a man who knows something funny about you, but does not wish to tell it—not quite yet. It is the most exasperating smile known.

Jerningham looked at him a moment. Then he said, coldly: "Why not pick them out haphazard— one here and another there, as if you were sampling a mine and wanted to make sure they hadn't salted it on you?" He turned to the men and said, "Pick out ten at random, no two from the same place; and be sure they are not full of stable litter!"

Stewardson flushed, and whispered apologetically to the superintendent, "The more the boys work, the more grateful he will be."

"Oh, he is very generous, anyhow," said Sullivan, the superintendent, watching his helper and Sheehan pick out the ten boxes at random.

Stewardson accompanied Jerningham up-stairs and then excused himself long enough to say to a confidential clerk: "Follow Mr. Jerningham and his ten boxes of gold-dust, and find out what he does, how much he gets, and every detail of interest. Don't let him see you."

The clerk found out and later reported to the vice-president that the ten boxes all contained Alaskan gold-dust, and that their value was $531,687, the boxes averaging a little better than fifty thousand dollars each. Stewardson then had the remaining boxes counted. There were one hundred and twenty-one left. They were worth over six million dollars. Jerningham ought to have the gold-dust coined and then deposit the proceeds in the trust company. The company would allow him two and a half per cent.—or maybe three per cent.—on the six millions. That would be one hundred and eighty thousand dollars a year. The company could then loan the entire six millions, not having to bother with keeping a reserve like the national banks, and, the way the money-market was, the money could be loaned at five per cent. That would be three hundred thousand dollars a year.

Men properly must end in dust; but dust, when gold, should end in eagles. He would speak to Jerningham about it—one hundred and eighty thousand dollars a year that Jerningham was not making—which was silly! And one hundred and twenty thousand a year the company was not making—which was a tragedy!

Ashton Welles sent word to the office on the following morning that he would not be down until late, if at all. He did not send word that he had decided to consult his lawyer about the *Society Folk* article. He had received eight marked copies, addressed to him at his house in different hand-writings, and he did not know that on his desk at the office there were a dozen more. Friends always tell you about anonymous attacks anonymously. They wait for them.

Jerningham seemed disappointed when he learned, at ten-thirty, that Mr. Welles might not come to the office at all. Stewardson came upon him looking disgruntled. That did not deter the vice-president from broaching the subject nearest his heart. "I'd like to ask you one question, Mr. Jerningham. Of course I know you must have a reason—a very good reason, too—"

"If the reason is good I'll confess," said Jerningham, pleasantly.

"Well, I'd like to know what your reason is for not sending all your gold to the Assay Office?"

"My reason is that I want to make a lot of money later by not sending the gold to the Assay Office now. Remember my very words!"

"But how are you going to do it?" Stewardson could not help asking, because he was so puzzled that his sense of humor was paralyzed.

"By having the gold—that's how."

"That's all right! But why don't you change it into coin? That way you can have it at a moment's notice."

"My dear chap, do you know how many hours it will take the Assay Office, after I take my dust in there, to give me a check for the proceeds? I get ninety per cent. of the value at once. If I cash this gold now I'll spend it. I know it! I never could resist the temptation to spend—it is my one weakness. And if I spent it what would I have to show for the hardships of thirty years?"

"But why don't you deposit it with us? We'll

allow you two and a half per cent. Or if you make it a time deposit we can do better than that by you. You know you can always get gold for it if you ask us for it."

"I can, can I?" laughed Jerningham, with a sort of good-natured mockery. "How about 1907 and your old clearing-house certificates—eh? What?"

Stewardson was nettled. So he permitted himself the supreme, all-conquering argument of business:

"But you are losing one hundred and eighty thousand dollars a year by leaving your gold uncoined and undeposited."

"I won't lose a year's interest, because it isn't going to take a year for the big panic to come."

Stewardson laughed—a kindly laugh. "For pity's sake, don't wait for that! Panics have a habit of not coming if expected. Just now everybody is bluer than indigo. You'd think the United States was on its last legs. Invest at once, and don't wait for the bargains at the funeral that may never come."

"How sound is this institution?" Jerningham looked Stewardson full in the face.

The vice-president answered, smilingly, "Oh, I guess we'll weather the storm."

"Then I'll buy more stock. Mr. Welles advised me to buy all I could get hold of. A wonderful man—"

"Yes, indeed," acquiesced Stewardson, solemnly.

"Wonderful! Great judgment!" pursued Jerningham, with a sort of boyish enthusiasm that made Stewardson think his superior had designs on the Klondike gold in the vaults. "He is so clear-cut— and never, never loses his head! To tell you the truth," and Jerningham lowered his voice, "I used to think he was an icicle—the sort of man nothing can disturb; but, for all his calmness and imperturbability, he has a great warm heart and a great big brain!"

Stewardson had never before heard anybody accuse the president of the VanTwiller Trust Company of having any heart at all. Why had Welles taken the pains to pose before the Klondike miner as a philanthropist? And why had the imperturbable Ashton Welles been so perturbed the day before?

"Ablest man in this country!" said Stewardson, his mind wrapped in the folds of his unformulated mysteries and his own half-asked questions.

"So I'll get a little more of the stock," said Jerningham.

"Go ahead! You can't go wrong," Stewardson assured him; "in fact, you ought to send some of your gold to the Assay Office and—"

"What will you lend me on my gold—on the six millions I've got down-stairs?" asked Jerningham, with a frown. He looked intently at the vice-president with his cold, gray eyes, and Stewardson somehow fancied he saw a challenge in them; but he was an old bird at the game. He laughed and said, jovially:

"Not a penny!"

"I know it. It shows you how incompetent all these financial institutions are. You think you are doing your duty by being suspicious—what? Well, you don't unless you are intelligently suspicious. Never mind; you are only the vice-president. I'll buy the stock just the same." And Jerningham laughed, exaggeratedly forgiving, and went away.

AS PROOFS OF HOLY WRIT

Later in the day, when Stewardson thought he might sell his own holdings of VanTwiller Trust stock to Jerningham and trust to luck to pick it up again here and there at a lower figure, he called up a firm of brokers who made a specialty of dealing in bank and trust-company stocks. He was surprised to learn that V.T. stock was scarce and thirty points higher. The vice-president called up specialists and heard the same story—the floating supply had been quietly bought.

"By whom?" he asked Earhart.

"You know very well!" retorted the last broker, in an aggrieved tone of voice.

"I do not!" Stewardson assured him.

"Well, it all goes into your office."

"Mine?"

"Yes—yours! And it's paid by your checks. The name signed is Alfred Jerningham. Are you going to cut a melon? Just whisper!"

"Oh!" and Stewardson laughed. "What a suspicious man you are, Dave!"

In the alarmingly inexplicable frame of mind in which Ashton Welles was Stewardson did not feel like speaking to his superior about Jerningham's investment. There was no reason why the Klondiker should not buy all the VanTwiller Trust Company stock he could pay for; but a day or two afterward the vice-president learned that Jerningham had secured control, by purchase outright or by option, at prices ranging from three hundred and ninety-five to five hundred dollars a share, of twenty-two thousand shares. That was important for two reasons: In the first place it was more than Jerningham could pay for even if he sold all his gold-dust; and, secondly, such a block in unfriendly hands might work injury to the controlling clique. He decided to see the president; but he was told that Mr. Ashton Welles was engaged at that moment.

Jerningham was talking to him. They had exchanged greetings with much cordiality.

"Have you heard from Mrs. Welles?" asked the Alaskan.

"She hasn't arrived yet—"

"I know it. But I received a wireless from young Wolfe—"

"What did he say?" asked Ashton Welles before he knew it.

Jerningham looked mildly surprised. He answered:

"It was a funny message. He asked me to go to his room and get his trunks, and send all his belongings to London, as he had decided to stay there indefinitely."

"Yes?" It was all Welles could say.

"So I wired back, 'Are you crazy?'"

"Did he answer that?"

"Yes." Jerningham paused. Then he laughed.

"What did he answer?" queried Welles.

"Oh, he is crazy, all right. He answered, 'Yes—with joy! Please send trunks to Thornton's Hotel—'"

"What?" Ashton Welles rose to his feet, his face livid. It was the London hotel where Mrs. Deering lived, the hotel to which Mrs. Welles was going!

"What's the matter?" asked Jerningham, in amazement.

"N-nothing!" said Ashton Welles, huskily. He gulped twice. Then, having spent thirty-five years in Wall Street making money, he explained, "I've got a terrible toothache!" And he put his hand to his left cheek.

"I'm sorry!" said Jerningham so sympathetically that Welles, for all his distress—and nothing is so inherently selfish as suffering—felt a kindly feeling toward the man from Alaska. "Could I ask your advice about a business matter?"

"Certainly!"

Ashton Welles tried to smile. It was ghastly, but Jerningham did not remark it. He said, placidly:

"I've bought quite a little bunch of VanTwiller stock because you are its president, Mr. Welles. On my honor, that is my only reason. I've paid good prices, too; but you are worth it—to me!" And Jerningham beamed adoringly on the efficient president of the VanTwiller Trust Company.

Ashton Welles said, "Thank you!" and even tried to feel grateful to this queer character from the frozen North who was so naïve in his admiration— and envied him for not having a young wife who had sailed on the same steamer with an exceedingly attractive young man.

"I guess I'm all right in my purchase—what?"

"Oh yes!" said Welles. He was thinking of the *Ruritania*. It did not even occur to him that this Monte Cristo might be worth while to pluck.

"Thank you. I hope I didn't bother you. Good morning, Mr. Welles."

"Good morning, Mr. Jerningham. Er—come in any time you think I can be of service to you."

As Jerningham was leaving the president's office he almost bumped into the vice-president.

"You've bought quite a lot of our stock," said

Stewardson, full of his errand. His voice had an accusing ring.

"Yes. I was just speaking to Mr. Welles about it."

"And what did he say?"

"Ask him!" teased Jerningham, with a smile, and went away.

Stewardson felt it his duty to do exactly as Jerningham had mockingly suggested. It was an abnormal situation. That being the case, there was no regular provision—no indicated chapter and verse—for meeting it. The principal function of a chief in business is to supply answers to puzzled subordinates.

Ashton Welles was sitting back in his swivel chair. He was staring fixedly at a hook on the picture-molding that had been left there after the picture was taken away. He was thinking that if he employed private detectives in London he would have to hire them by cable. There are suspicions a man cannot help having and yet cannot set down in plain black and white. He cannot hint when he writes, for written instructions must always be explicit and categorical. That is why no love-letter of which the real meaning is to be read "between the lines" is ever satisfactory to the recipient.

Ashton Welles turned his head and, still frowning, asked Stewardson, sharply:

"Well, what is it?"

"It's about Jerningham. You know he has been buying our stock. But I thought you ought to know—"

He wished to .tell the president what a big block the Alaskan had already secured. But the president, from force of habit, perhaps, or possibly by reason of the irritation of his nerves, assumed the usual financial attitude of omniscience:

"I know all about it," he said. "Anything else you wish to say to me?"

"No, sir!" answered Stewardson, who felt rebuffed and now would not have turned in an alarm of fire if he had seen the place beginning to burn. He was, after all, human.

You cannot, in your lust for absolute power, make your subordinates into sublimated office-boys or decorative figureheads without paying the price some time. Stewardson was justified in assuming that Mr. Welles was worried about business—it was perfectly obvious; and it was a natural suspicion, also, that said deal must threaten destruction to the company since Ashton Welles was so eager to have poor Jerningham buy so much VanTwiller stock. Therefore Stewardson and his intimate friends, in order to be on the safe side, very promptly sold out their own holdings—to poor misguided Jerningham's brokers.

Of course other people who did not wish Welles well heard about it, and the whisper ran about the Street, getting blacker and blacker as it ran, until everybody knew something had happened—everybody except the directors of the VanTwiller Trust Company. And when the transfer-books closed for the annual meeting of the stockholders it was found that Mr. Alfred Jerningham owned, by purchase or option, and had irrevocable proxies on, a little more than twenty-eight thousand shares of the stock. This, together with the twelve thousand shares owned jointly by Patrick T. Behan and Oliver

Judson, the street-railroad magnates, and the blocks
controlled by the Garvin brothers, Tammany con-
tractors, and Mayer & Shanberg, F. R. Chisolm,
John Matson & Company, and others of the Behan-
Judson clique, which once tried to secure control
of the company and were foiled by Ashton Welles,
made a combination that was bound to win at the
annual election.

Jerningham ceased going to the VanTwiller Trust
Company because Ashton Welles had sailed for
London on the receipt of a cablegram that read:

Leaving for Continent. Mother and I cannot return before
three months. Will write soon.

ANNE.

Instead of calling on his friend Stewardson,
Jerningham preferred to spend hours and hours con-
versing with Patrick T. Behan, "the most dangerous man in Wall Street!"—and the slickest. But on
the day before the election Jerningham did call on
Stewardson and offered to sell his holdings of Van-
Twiller stock at six hundred dollars a share.

"Why, I thought you—" began the vice-president.

"I know you did. I wanted you to. But six
hundred dollars is only twenty-five dollars a share
more than Behan, and Judson, and Garvin, and the
rest of those pirates have offered me. I've decided
not to be a stockholder of the trust company; so
just get your friends together and tell them if they
want to retain the control they can give you a
check for me—six hundred dollars a share on twenty-
eight thousand, one hundred and twenty-three shares.
Put it down—twenty-eight thousand, one hundred
and twenty-three shares. Good day!"

"Wait! I want to say—"

"Don't say it! Write it! I'm still at the Brabant," said Jerningham, coldly. "I advise you to get at Mr. Welles on the steamer by wireless. Good day!"

"But, I—" shouted Stewardson.

Jerningham paid no attention to him and walked away.

Later in the day negotiations were resumed. In the end Jerningham accepted a little less; but the deal yielded him a net profit of about two million dollars. He insisted upon being paid in gold coin. This convinced Stewardson and the other victims that Jerningham was out of his mind; but there is no law that enables officers of a trust company to imprison a gold maniac or to take away his gold, particularly when his lawyers stand very high in the profession.

Five minutes after getting the gold coin in his possession—and drawing every cent of it—Jerningham told Stewardson he would leave the dust in the VanTwiller vaults. That reassured Stewardson, who otherwise might have suspected Jerningham of various crimes. He then sent two cablegrams to London. One was to

KATHRYN KEOGH,
  Thornton's Hotel, London.

Your services are no longer needed. Go ahead and have a nice time! Thanks awfully!   JERNINGHAM.

The other was to Francis Wolfe—same address. It read:

You ought to marry Kathryn Keogh. Never mind anything else. I am disappearing for good. God bless you both, my children! Letter follows.   JERNINGHAM.

THE PLUNDERERS

Francis Wolfe showed his cablegram to Miss Keogh and Miss Keogh did not show hers to Francis Wolfe.

A week later Frank asked Miss Keogh to read a letter he had received from Jerningham, and to tell him what to do.

This was the letter.

DEAR BOY,—We needed a million or two out of Ashton Welles, and the only way we could see of getting it was by selling to him what he already had—to wit, the control of the VanTwiller Trust Company. From previous operations the syndicate I have the honor to represent had accumulated enough cash to render this operation feasible; but Welles watched the trades in VanTwiller stock so closely that we could not have bought a thousand shares without blocking our own game. So we planned our operations very carefully, as we always do. And because I like you I will tell you how we went about it—that you may profit by our example.

First, I had to become instantly and sensationally known as the possessor of vast wealth. The mere deposit of a million or two in a bank would not do it. We must have the cash and a stupendous cash-making property—hence the mines in the Klondike. Purely mythical mines, dear lad! We sent to Alaska, bought $1,686,000 of gold-dust, put it in boxes, and put a lot of lead in other boxes—now in the VanT. vaults!—thereby increasing our less than two million into more than eight—and nobody hurt thereby! Then the shipment to Seattle, so that every step could be verified—and the special bullion train to New York; and the eccentric miner—myself—with his gold—no myth about the gold—what? in a New York hotel; and of course the reporters were only too willing to help and to magnify our gold-dust.

The *Planet's* articles were our letters of introduction to the trust company and to Wall Street. Could not have done better —could we? But how to catch Welles off his guard? By breaking it down, of course. Best way? By rousing jealousy. That's where you come in. Mrs. Welles must go to England with you on the same steamer. How? By winning your friendship and rousing your romantic interest in an unhappy love-affair—that would, moreover, explain my interest in Mrs. Welles. Of course there never was any Naida Deering for me to be interested in!

But you had to meet Welles's wife. How? By means of your sisters. How did I make friends of them? By reforming you and making you my heir.

How did I make Mrs. Welles take the same steamer that you did? By having her mother cable for her. How did I do that? Ask Miss Keogh.

I admit that much of what we were compelled to do was not gentlemanly; but, after all, our only crime is the crime of having been business men—buying something at four dollars and selling it at five or six dollars.

Take my advice, dear boy, and stay on the water-wagon! If you marry Miss Keogh I think you can show this letter to A. Welles and ask him to give you a nice position in the trust company.

I am sorry I cannot see you again; but believe me, dear boy, that we are very grateful for your efficient assistance. We would send you a check—only we need it in our business. Tell Jimmy Parkhurst to tell you and Amos F. Kidder all about it.

Yours truly,
THE PLUNDER RECOVERY SYNDICATE,
Per ALFRED JERNINGHAM.

But it was a long time before Frank Wolfe returned to New York—without Miss Keogh, who flatly refused to marry him. Jerningham had disappeared, leaving absolutely no trail. Parkhurst introduced Frank Wolfe to Fiske, but all that came of it was that Fiske added a few fresh notes to his collection.

IV

CHEAP AT A MILLION

I

TOM MERRIWETHER, only son and heir of E. H. Merriwether, finished the grape-fruit and took up the last of that morning's mail. He had acquired the feminine habit of reading letters at the table from his father, who had the wasteful American vice of time-saving.

He read the card, frowned, glanced at his father, and seemed to be on the point of speaking; but he changed his mind, laughed, and tore the card into bits.

The day was Monday, and this was what the card said:

If Mr. Thomas Thorne Merriwether will go to 777 Fifth Avenue any forenoon this week and answer just one little question about his past life he will hear something to his advantage.

Idle men who live in New York are always busy. Tom had many things to think about; but all of them were about the present or the future. His past caused him neither uneasiness nor remorse.

On the following Monday young Mr. Merriwether received, among other invitations, this:

CHEAP AT A MILLION

If Tom Merriwether will call at 777 Fifth Avenue any forenoon this week and answer one question he will do that which
is both kindly—and wise!

It was in the same handwriting, on the same kind
of card, and in the same kind of ink as the first.
Now Tom had the Merriwether imagination. His
father exercised it in building railroads into waterless
deserts whereon he clearly saw a myriad men labor,
love, and multiply, thereby insuring freight and passengers to the same railroads. The son had to
invent his romances in New York.

Ordinarily the second invitation would have given
him something to busy himself with; but it happened
that he was at that moment planning to do a heart-
breaking thing without breaking any heart. Billy
Larremore, the veteran whose devotion to polo was
responsible for so many of the team's victories in
the past, was not aware that age had bade him cease
playing. It would break his loyal heart not to play
in the forthcoming international match. Tom Merriwether had been delegated to break the news.

Thinking about it made him forget all about the
letter until the following Monday, when he received
the third invitation:

Merriwether,—Come to 777 Fifth Avenue Tuesday morning at ten-thirty without fail and answer the question.

He crumpled the card and was about to throw it
away when he changed his mind. Perhaps it would
be wise to give it to a detective agency. But what
could he say he feared? Then he decided it was
probably a joke. Somebody wished to put him in
the ridiculous position of ringing the bell of 777,

showing the card—and being told to get out. It was to be regretted that this would seem funny to some of his perennially juvenile intimates at the Rivulet Club.

An hour later, as he walked down the Avenue, he looked curiously at 777. It was one of those new-comer houses erected by speculative builders to sell furnished to out-of-town would-be climbers or to local stock-market bankers who, being Hebrews, were too sensible to wish to climb, but were not sensible enough not to wish to live on Fifth Avenue.

Tom resolved to ask Raymond Silliman, who played at being in the real-estate business, to find out who lived at 777. Meantime he did a little shopping—wedding-presents—and went to luncheon at his club. He had not quite finished his coffee when he was summoned to the telephone.

"Hello! Mr. Merriwether?" said a woman's voice —clear, sweet, and vibrant, but unknown. "This is Miss Hervey—the nurse—Dr. Leighton's trained nurse. They asked me to tell you about your father. Don't be alarmed!"

"Go on!" commanded young Merriwether, sharply.

"It is nothing serious—really! But if you could come home it probably— Yes, doctor! I am coming!" And the conversation ceased abruptly.

Tom instantly left the club. He took the solitary taxicab that stood in front of the club. He afterward recalled the fact that there was only one where usually there were half a dozen.

"Eight-sixty-nine Fifth Avenue. Go up Madison to Sixtieth and then turn into the Avenue. Hurry!"

"Very good, sir," said the chauffeur.

CHEAP AT A MILLION

The taxicab dashed madly up Madison and up Fifth Avenue, and finally stopped—not before the Merriwether home, but in front of Number 777. Before he could ask the chauffeur what he meant by it both doors of the cab opened at once and two men sandwiched between them Mr. Thomas Thorne Merriwether. The one on the west, or Central Park, side threateningly held in his hand a business-like javelin—not at all the kind that silly people hang on the walls in their childish attempts at decorative barbarity. The man who half entered the taxi-cab from the east, or sidewalk, side held in his left hand a beer-schooner full of a colorless liquid that smoked, and in his right something completely but loosely covered by a white-linen handkerchief.

"Please listen, Mr. Merriwether!" said the man with the glass. "Do nothing! Don't even move! Hear me first!"

"Is my father—"

"I am glad to say he is well and happy, and working in his office down-town. The message that brought you here was a subterfuge. Your father is as usual. We arranged it so you had to take this particular taxicab. Don't stir, please!"

"What does all this mean?" asked Tom, impatiently.

"I am about to have the honor of telling you," answered the man.

He had no hat and wore clerical garments. His clean-shaved face was pale—almost sallow—and young Merriwether noticed that his forehead was very high. His dark-brown eyes were full of the earnestness of all zealots, which makes you dislike to enter into an argument—first, because of the futility of arguing with a zealot; and, second, because said zealot probably knows a million times more about the subject than you and can outargue you without trouble. So Tom simply listened with an alertness that would not overlook any chance to strike back.

"This glass contains fuming sulphuric acid. It will sear the face and destroy the eyesight with much rapidity and completeness. Also"—here he shook off the handkerchief from his right hand and showed a revolver—"this is the very latest in automatics; marvelously efficient; dumdum bullets; stop an elephant! I am about to solicit a great favor."

Tom Merriwether looked into the earnest, pleading eyes. Then he glanced on the other side, at the bull-necked husky with the business-like spear. Then he turned to the clerical garb.

"I see I am in the hands of my friends!" said Tom, pleasantly.

"The doctor was right," said the man with the glass, as if to himself.

"Come! Come!" said young Mr. Merriwether. "How much am I to give? You know, I never carry much cash with me."

"We, dear Mr. Merriwether," said the pale-faced man in an amazingly deferential voice, "propose to be the donors. If you will kindly permit us we shall give you what is more costly than rubies."

"Yes?" Tom's voice was perhaps less skeptical than sarcastic.

"Yes, sir. Would you be kind enough to accept our invitation—the fourth, dear Mr. Merriwether—to join us at 777 Fifth Avenue—right here, sir—and answer one question? Please listen carefully to what I am saying: You don't have to go. Moreover, if you should go you don't have to answer any question. We would not, for worlds, compel you. But, for your own sake, for the sake of your father's peace of mind and of the Merriwether fortune, for the sake of your happiness in this world and in the next; for all that all the Merriwethers hold most dear—come with me and, if you are very wise, answer the question that will be asked you by the wisest man in all the world."

"He must be a regular Solomon—" began Tom, but the man held up the glass and went on, very earnestly:

"Listen, please! If you decide to accept our invitation I shall spill this acid in the street and I shall give you this revolver. I repeat, you do not have to answer the question. You will not be harmed or molested. I pledge you my word. Will you, in return, give me yours to follow me at once into 777, and that you will not shoot unless you sincerely think you are in danger?"

Tom Merriwether looked at the pale-faced man a moment. He was willing to take his chances with that face. Also, he could not otherwise find the solution of this puzzling affair. Therefore he said:

"Yes. I give you my word."

Instantly the pale-faced man with the high forehead laid the revolver on the seat beside young Mr. Merriwether and withdrew from the cab. Tom saw him spill the fuming acid into the gutter. The burly javelin-man took himself off. The temptation to use the butt of the revolver on the clerical-garbed man with the earnest eyes came to Tom, but he saw in a flash that if he should do such a thing he would be compelled in self-defense to tell a story utterly unbelievable.

Moreover, the pale-faced man was a slender little chap of middle age and no match for big Tom Merriwether. So, assuring himself that the revolver was in truth loaded and that it worked, he put it in his pocket, kept his grasp on it there, and got out of the taxicab. His one impelling motive now was curiosity. Afraid? With the pistol and his muscles and his youth, on Fifth Avenue, at two-thirty in the afternoon?

The pale-faced man, the empty glass in one hand, walked toward the door of 777 without so much as turning his head. Tom followed.

The door was opened by a man in livery who took Mr. Merriwether's hat and cane. Tom saw in the furnishings of the house — complete with that curious unhuman completeness of a modern hotel—the kind of furnishings that interior decorators usually sell to first-generation rich on their arrival at Fifth Avenue residenceship. The furniture had every qualification possessed by furniture in order not to suggest a home to live in. Wherefore Tom, whose mind always worked quickly, reasoned to himself:

"Rented for the occasion to the man who has made me come to him."

Also Tom noticed four men-servants, all of them well built and all of them owning faces that somehow were not servant faces. The revolver, which had seemed amply sufficient outside, seemed less so within the house. Supposing he killed one—or even two—the other two would down him in an affray. He tightened his grip on the revolver and planned and rehearsed a shooting affair in which four men in livery were disabled with four shots. A great pity E. H. Merriwether was such a very rich man—a great pity for his son Tom.

At a door, on the center panel of which was a monogram in black, red, and gold the last of the footmen knocked gently. The door was thereupon opened from within.

"Mr. Thomas Thorne Merriwether, 7–7–77!" announced the intelligent-looking footman, with a very pronounced English accent.

Mr. Thomas Thorne Merriwether entered. It was a *nouveau-riche* library. The Circassian-walnut bookcases and center-table were over-elaborately carved, and the hangings of rich red velvet were over-elaborately embroidered. The bronzes on the over-elaborate mantel looked as though they had been placed there by somebody who was coming back in a minute to take them away again.

Altogether the apartment suggested a salesroom, and there was a note of incongruity in a golden-oak filing-cabinet of the Grand Rapids school.

At one end of the room in an arm-chair, with his back to a terrible stained-glass window, sat a man of about forty. He had a calm, remarkably steady gaze, with a sort of leisureliness about it that made you think of a drawling voice. Also, an assurance— a self-consciousness of knowledge—that was compelling. His chin was firm and there was a suggestion of power and of control over power that reminded Tom of a very competent engineer in charge of a fifty-thousand-horse-power machine.

"Kindly be seated, sir," said the man in a tone that subtly suggested weariness.

THE PLUNDERERS

Tom sat down and looked curiously at the man, who went on:

"Sir, I have a question to ask you. If you see fit to answer, be good enough to answer it spontaneously and in good faith. Do not, I beg you, in turn, ask me questions—such as, for example, why I wish to know what I ask. If you decide not to answer you will leave this house unharmed, accompanied by our profound regret that you should be so unintelligent at your life's crisis." The man looked at Tom with a meditative expression, then nodded to himself almost sorrowfully.

Tom, though young, was a Merriwether. He said, politely, "Let me hear the question, sir."

He himself was thinking in questions: What can the question be? Who is this man? What is the game? What will be the end of it all?

"One question, sir," repeated the stranger.

"I am listening, sir," Tom assured him, with a quiet, but quite impressive, earnestness.

"*Where did you spend your vacation at the end of your Freshman year?*"

Tom was so surprised, and even disappointed, that he hesitated. Then he answered:

"In Oleander Point, Long Island, in the cottage of Dr. Charles W. Bonner, who was tutoring me. I had a couple of conditions and I stayed until the third of September!"

"Thank you! Thank you! That is all—unless, Mr. Merriwether, you wish to do me and yourself three very great favors. Three!"

He looked at Tom with a sort of intelligent curiosity, as of a chemist conducting an experiment.

CHEAP AT A MILLION

"Let's hear what they are," said young Mr. Merriwether, calmly.

It was at times like these that he showed whose son he was—alert, his imagination active, his nerves under control, and his courage steady and at par. He had, moreover, made up his mind that he would do some questioning later on.

"First favor: Concentrate your mind on how you used to spend your bright, sunshiny days in Oleander Point and your beautiful moonlight nights. Recall the pleasant people you were friendly with during those happy weeks. Visualize that summer! Make an effort! Think!"

It was a command, and Tom Merriwether found himself thinking of that summer. He closed his eyes. His grip on the revolver in his pocket relaxed. . . . He saw his friends. Some of them he had not seen in years. Others he saw almost daily. And somehow it seemed to him that all the girls were pretty and kindly; and in particular—well, there were in particular three. But the affairs had come to nothing.

He could not have told how long his reverie lasted —the mind traverses long stretches of time, as of space, in seconds.

"Well?" said Tom at length.

"Thank you," said the man, with the matter-of-fact gratitude a man feels toward a servant for some attention.

He took from his pocket a small black-velvet bag, opened it, and spread on the table before Tom Merriwether a dozen pearls, ranging in size from a pea to a filbert. They were all of a beautiful orient.

"I beg you to select one of these. You need not

use it. You may give it to your valet if you wish, or throw it out of the window. Only accept it as a souvenir of our meeting. That, Mr. Merriwether, would be favor number two."

He pointed toward the pearls. Tom picked one— pear-shaped, white, beautiful—and put it in his waistcoat pocket. The man swept the rest into one of the drawers of the long library table.

"I thank you very much," said Tom. He was not sure the pearls were not genuine.

"No; please don't," said the man. There was a pause. Presently he asked, "Do you know anything about pearls, sir?"

"I am no expert," answered Tom.

"Characteristic. You Merriwethers are brave enough to be truthful, and wise enough to be cautious. Have you any opinions?"

"I think they are beautiful," said Tom.

"They are more than 'that. They represent, Mr. Merriwether, the hope of the Kingdom of Heaven. The pearl is the symbol of purity, humility, and innocence. Do you know the legend of the mild maid of God—Saint Margaret of Antioch?"

"No."

"Margaret is from Margarites—Greek for pearl. And the reason why faith— But I beg your pardon. Men who live alone talk too much when they are no longer alone. I beg you to forgive me. Tell me, Mr. Merriwether, did you ever hear of Apollonius of Tyana?"

"Not until this minute," answered Tom.

He felt almost tempted to ask whether the poor man was dead, but refrained because he was honest enough to admit to himself that the question would savor of bravado. Tom was consumed by curiosity as to what would be the end of it all. To think of it—on Fifth Avenue, New York, in broad daylight—all this!

How money was to be made out of him he could not yet see.

"I will show his talisman to you—the Dispeller of Darkness!" The man clapped his hands twice. At the summons a negro walked in. He was dressed in plain black and wore a fez. The man spoke some guttural words and the negro salaamed and left the room. Presently he returned with a silver tray on which were seven gold or gilt candlesticks and candles, and seven gold or gilt small trays or plates, on each of which was a pastil.

He arranged the seven candlesticks in some deliberate design, carefully measuring the distance of each from the other, and of all from a point in the center. He arranged the plates and pastils about the candlesticks. Then he left the room, to return with a lighted taper, with which he lit the seven candles and the seven pastils. Tiny spirals of fragrant smoke rose languidly in the still air.

Again the negro left the room and returned with a small parcel wrapped in a piece of raw silk which he gave to his master. He then went away for good.

The man began to mutter something to himself and very carefully took off the silk cover, revealing a wonderfully carved ivory box. He opened the gold-hinged lid and took out a silver case. He opened that and from it took a gold box elaborately though crudely chased. He opened the gold box and within it, on a little white-velvet pad, was a cross of dull gold curiously engraved. He put the pad, with the cross on it, in the middle of the seven lights. On the arms of the cross and at the intersection Tom saw seven wonderful emeralds remarkable as to size, beautiful as to color.

"Look at it, Mr. Merriwether. It is priceless. The gems alone are worth a king's ransom. If you consider it merely as a piece of ancient art there is no telling what a man like Mr. W. H. Garrettson would not give for it. And as a talisman, with its tried wonder-working powers, there is, of course, not enough money in all the world to pay for it."

Tom stretched his hand toward it.

"Please! Do not touch it, I beg," said the man, in a voice in which the alarm was so evident that Tom drew his hand back as though he had seen a cobra on the table. "Not yet! Not yet!" said the man. "It is the most wonderful object in existence. It is a cross that antedates Christ!"

"Really?"

"It is obviously of a much earlier period than the Messiah. Great scholars have thought it a legend, but here it is before you. It belonged to Apollonius of Tyana, the wonder - worker. Philostratus, who wrote the life of that great man, does not mention this talisman; he dared not! Apollonius, who to this day is not known ever to have died, gave it to a disciple, who gave it to a friend."

Tom looked interested.

"We know who has owned it. It was worn by Arcadius in the fifth century. The Goths took it and Alaric gave it to the daughter of his most trusted captain, who commanded his citadel of Carcassonne. Clovis, a hundred years later, secured it at the sack of Toulouse. We have records of its having been praised by Eligius, the famous jeweler of Dagobert, in the seventh century. It was included in the famous treasures of Charlemagne. It went to Palestine during the first and third crusades—the first time carried by a maid who loved a knight who did not love her. She went as his squire, he not suspecting her sex until they were safely back in France, when he married her. It is a wonderful talisman. The emeralds came from Mount Zabara. They have the power to drive away the evil spirits and also to preserve the chastity of the wearer. Moreover, they give the power to foretell events. Apollonius did—time and again. This is historically true. But alone he, of all the men who have owned it, never had a love-affair; hence his clairvoyance. I have bored you. Forgive me!"

"Not at all. I was interested. It is all so—er—so—"

"Incredible—yes! There is no reason why you should believe it. It is of no consequence whether you think me a lunatic or a charlatan."

He said this with a cold indifference that made Tom look incuriously at the man, whose obvious desire was to excite curiosity. Then the man said, with an earnestness that in spite of himself impressed the heir of the Merriwether railroads:

"Mr. Thomas Thorne Merriwether, classified in our books as 7–7–77, you are the man I need for this job!"

"Indeed?" said Tom, politely.

"Yes, you are." Tom bowed his head and looked resigned. He deliberately intended to look that way. The man went on, "The reason I am so sure is because I know both who and what you are."

"Ah, you know me pretty well, then." Tom could not help the mild sarcasm.

"I have known you, young man, for eighty-five years, perhaps longer." The man spoke calmly.

"Indeed!" said Tom. He was twenty-eight.

"Yes. On top of that cabinet is a book. After the name Thomas Thorne Merriwether you will find 7-7-77. In the cabinet—seventh section, seventh drawer, card Number 77—you will find clinical data, physiological and psychological details, anecdotes, and so on, about you and your father, E. H. Merriwether, and your mother, Josephine Thorne; your grandfathers, Lyman Grant Merriwether and Thomas Conkling Thorne, and of your grandmothers, Malvina Sykes Thorne and Lydia Weston Merriwether. Indeed I know about your great-grandfathers and three of your great-great-grandparents; but the data in their case are of little value save as to Ephraim Merriwether, who in seventeen sixty-three killed in one duel three army officers who laughed at his twisted nose, bitten and disfigured for life by a wolf-cub he had tried to tame. Facts not generally known, but, for all that, facts, young Mr. Thomas Thorne Merriwether, which enable me to say that I have known you these hundred and fifty years—if there is anything in heredity, environment, and education! And now, shall I tell you what favor number three is?"

"If you please," said Tom.

For the first time he felt that the usual suspicions as to a merrymaking game could not be justified in this particular instance. It was much too elaborate for a practical joke. He did not know how the matter would end; but he did not care. In New

York, on Fifth Avenue, on Tuesday afternoon, he was having what, indeed, was an experience!

"I beg that you will listen attentively. You will take the Dispeller of Darkness with you. Do not open the gold box under any circumstances. To-night go to 7 East Seventy-seventh Street so as to be there at eight o'clock sharp. The door will not be locked. Don't ring. Walk in. Go up one flight of stairs to the front room—there is only one. You will stand in the middle of the room, with the talisman resting on the palm of your hand—thus! Do nothing! Say nothing! Wait there! The talisman will be taken from you by a person. Do not try to detain her—this person. After the talisman is taken from you count a hundred—not too fast! At the end of your count leave the room and come back here and tell me whether you have carried out my instructions. Now, young sir, let me say to you that you don't have to do what I am asking you to do. There is no compulsion whatever. There is no crime in contemplation—no attempt is to be made against your life, your fortune, or your morals. I pledge you my word, sir!"

The man looked straight into Tom's eyes. Tom bowed gravely. This man must be crazy—and yet he certainly was not. This interested Tom by perplexing him as he had never been perplexed in his eight-and-twenty years.

"Mr. Merriwether, this will be the most important step of your life. Its bearing on your happiness is vital—also on the success of your great father's vast plans. I give you my personal word that this is so."

There was a pause. Tom had nothing to say. The man went on:

THE PLUNDERERS

"If you care to take reasonable precautions against attack do so. Thus, keep the revolver you now have in your pocket—it is excellent. Try it and make certain. You may write a detailed account of what has happened and leave it with your valet; but mark on it that it is not to be opened unless you fail to return by 10 P.M. Also you may, if you wish, station ten private detectives across the way from 7 East Seventy-seventh Street, and instruct them to go into the house at a single shout from you or at the sound of a shot. Believe me, it is not your life that is in danger, sir!"

"I believe you," said Tom, reassuringly.

"Will you do me favor number three?" The man looked at Tom with a steady, unblinking, earnest—one might even say honest—stare.

Tom considered. His mind worked not only quickly, but Merriwether-fashion. He saw all the possibilities of danger, but he saw the unknown—and the lust of adventure won. He looked the man in the eyes and said, quietly:

"I will."

"Thank you. There is the talisman. Each of the seven emeralds is flawless—the only seven flawless emeralds of that size in existence. Two of them have been in great kings' crowns, and the center stone was in the tiara of seven popes; after which, the Great Green Prophecy having been fulfilled, it came back to its place on the Cross. Apollonius raised people from the dead, according to eyewitnesses. The pagans tried to confute the believers in Christian miracles by bringing forward the miracles of the sage of Tyana—and they did not know that Apollonius wrought marvels by the Sign of the

CHEAP AT A MILLION

Son of Man—the Cross! This cross! I pray that you will be careful with it. Show it to nobody. You have understood your instructions?"

Tom repeated them.

"Precisely! I did not make a mistake, you see. In spite of your father's millions you will be what your destiny wills. Young man, good luck to you!"

The man rose and walked toward the door. Tom Merriwether followed him and was politely bowed out of the room. From there to the street entrance the four athletic footmen, with the over-intelligent faces, took him in tow, one at a time. And it was not until he was out on the Avenue, headed north, walking toward his own house, that Thomas Thorne Merriwether, clean-living miltimillionaire idler, shook himself, as if to scatter the remnants of a dream, felt the butt of the revolver, hefted the silk-wrapped parcel in which was the talisman, and said, aloud, so that a couple of pedestrians turned and smiled sympathetically at the young man, who must be in love, since he talked to himself:

"What in blazes is it all about?"

II

His perplexing experience developed so insistent a curiosity in Tom that he grew irritable even as he walked. That some sort of a game was being worked he had no doubt; but the fact that he could see no object or motive increased his wrath. He discarded all suggestion of violence, though he was bound to admit now that anybody could be kidnapped in New York in broad daylight.

He decided to begin by verifying those allusions

and references that he remembered. He walked down the Avenue to the Public Library and there he read what he could of Apollonius and of Eligius, the marvelous goldsmith who afterward became Saint Eloi. The helpful and polite library assistant at length suggested a visit to Dr. Lentz, the gem expert of Goffony & Company, a man of vast erudition as well as a practical jeweler. Tom promptly betook himself to the famous jewel-shop.

They knew the heir of the seventy-five Merriwether millions, and impressively ushered him into Dr. Lentz's office. Tom shook hands with the fat little man, whose wonderfully shaped head had on it no hair worth speaking of, and handed him the pearl he had picked out from the dozen the man in 777 Fifth Avenue had placed before him. Dr. Lentz looked at it, weighed it in his hand, and, without waiting to be asked any questions, answered what nearly everybody always asked him:

"Persian Gulf. About fifteen grains—perhaps a little more. We sell some like it for about thirty-five hundred dollars."

"Thanks," said Tom, and put the pearl in his pocket.

If it was a joke it was expensive. If not, the other pearls the man had shown, nearly all of which were larger, must have been worth from fifty thousand to a hundred thousand dollars. Such is the power of money that this young man, destined to be one of the richest men in the world and, moreover, one who did not particularly think about money, was nevertheless impressed by the stranger's careless handling of the valuable pearls. He concluded subconsciously that the talisman was even more valuable. He took the package from his coat pocket and gave it to Dr. Lentz.

"Raw silk—Syrian," murmured the gem expert, and undid the covering.

"Ha! Italo-Byzantine. The Raising of Tabitha. No! no!" He glared at young Merriwether, who retreated a step. "Very rare! It's the Raising of Jairus's Daughter. Same workmanship in similar specimen in the Lipsanoteca, Museo Civico, Brescia. If so, not later than fourth century. Very rare! H'm!"

"Is it?" said Tom. "I don't know much about ivories."

"No? Read Molinier! Græven!"

"Thank you. I will, Dr. Lentz."

Dr. Lentz opened the little ivory box and pulled out the silver case.

"Ha! H'm! Not so rare! Asia Minor. Probably eighth century."

"B. C?"

"Certainly not. Key? H'm!"

"Haven't got it here," evaded Tom.

The little savant turned to his secretary and said, "Bring drawer marked forty-four, inner compartment, antique-gem safe."

He was examining the little box, nodding his head, and muttering, "H'm! H'm!" Tom felt the ground slipping away from under the feet of his suspicions even while his perplexity waxed monumental. And with it came the satisfaction of a man convincing himself that he is neither wasting his time nor making himself ridiculous.

The clerk returned with a little drawer in which Tom saw about a hundred and fifty keys.

"Replicas! Originals in museums of world!" explained Lentz. "H'm!" He turned the keys over with a selective forefinger. "It's that one or this one." And he picked out two. "Probably this! Damascus! Eighth century. Byzantine influence still strong. See that? And that? And that? H'm!" He inserted the little key and opened the casket. He saw the gold box within. "Ha! H'm! Thracian! How did you get this? H'm!" He raised his head, looked at Tom fiercely, and then said, coldly, "Mr. Merriwether, this has been stolen from the British Museum!"

It beautifully complicated matters. Tom's heart beat faster with interest.

"Are you sure?" he asked, being a Merriwether.

"Wait! H'm!" He lifted it out and examined the back. "No! No! Thracian! Of the Bisaltæ! Time of Lysimachus! But— Well! Aryan symbolism! Possibly taken to India by one of Alexander's captains—perhaps Lysimachus himself! And— Oh! Oh, early Christians! Oh, early damned fools! See that? Smoothed away to put that— Oh, beasts! Heritics in art! Curious! Do you know the incantation to use before opening?"

"It was in Greek, and—"

"Of course!"

"Yes. He said this had belonged to Apollonius of Tyana."

"How much does he ask?"

"It is not for sale."

"Inside is a pentagram?"

"No; a cross, with seven emeralds as big as that, all flawless."

"There are only two such emeralds in the world

without flaws and we have one of them. The other is owned by the Archbishop of Bogotá, Colombia."

"He said these were flawless and that he has proofs. He says Eligius studied this—"

"Mr. Merriwether, you have on your hands either a very dangerous impostor or else— H'm! He must be an impostor! How much does he want?"

"It is not for sale!"

"H'm! Worse and worse! If I can be of use let me know! They'll fool us all! All! Good day!" And Dr. Lentz walked away, leaving Tom more puzzled than ever, but now determined to go to 7 East Seventy-seventh Street at eight o'clock that night.

He went home and wrote an account of what had happened, placed it in an envelope, sealed the envelope, and gave it to his valet.

"If you don't hear from me by ten o'clock to-night give this to my father; but don't give it to him one minute before ten. And you stay in until you hear from me."

"Very good, sir."

He then went to the club, ordered an early dinner for two, and invited his friend Huntington Andrews to go with him. He did not go into details.

Shortly before eight he stationed Andrews across the way from 7 East Seventy-seventh Street and told him:

"If I am not back here at eight-fifteen come in after me. If you don't find me go to my house and wait until ten. My man has instructions. See my father."

Tom was Merriwether enough to have in readiness not only an extra revolver to give to his friend, but also a heavy cane and an electric torch. Also he drove Huntington to within a hair's-breadth of death by unsatisfied curiosity.

At one minute before eight Mr. Thomas Thorne Merriwether went into the house of mystery, realizing for the first time how often the mystic number seven recurred. The Bible teemed with allusions to the seven stars, the seven seals, the seven-branched candlestick, the seven mortal sins. The Greeks had Seven Wise Men and Seven Sleepers, and the Pythagoreans saw magic in all the heptamerides. And there were seven notes of music and seven primary colors, and seven hills in the Eternal City. Also, it had never before occurred to him that he was born on the seventh day of the seventh month. And now it had its effect.

He tried the door. It opened when he turned the knob. The hall was dark, but he could descry the staircase. He grasped his revolver firmly and entered.

There was a smell of undusted floors and unaired walls. The darkness thickened with each step as he climbed, compelling him to grope. And because he groped there came to him that fear which always comes with uncertainty. It permeated his soul and was intensified, without becoming more concrete, by reason of the ghostly emptiness peculiar to all unoccupied houses. The absence of furniture served merely to fill the corners with shadows that bred uneasiness. People had been there; people no longer were! The house was empty of humanity, but full of other beings—impalpable suspects that made the flesh creep! It was like death—unseen, but felt with the senses of the soul.

CHEAP AT A MILLION

There was no place, decided Tom, so fit to murder people in as an empty house. His adventure now took on an aspect of reckless folly. But though he felt in this ghostly house what might be called the ghost of fear, he also felt the impelling force of an intelligent curiosity. In this young man's soul was a love of adventure, a gambler's philosophy, a reserve force of cold intelligence and warm imagination such as is found in the great explorers, the great chemists, and the great bucaneers of dollars.

That was why in the year of grace 1913 Tom Merriwether stood in the middle of the second-story front room of a house situated in a very good street, only three doors from Fifth Avenue, with his left hand outstretched, and on the open palm of it a cross with a Greek name that meant Dispeller of Darkness —in a darkness that could not be dispelled. His right hand grasped the butt of an automatic .45 loaded with elephant-stopping bullets—but of what avail was that against a knock in the head from behind?

Listening for soft footsteps, he seemed to hear them time and again—and time and again not to hear them! People nowadays, he finally decided, do not want to take other people's lives—only their money. Whereupon he once more grew calm—and intensely curious! He had not one cent of money on his person. He had left it at home intentionally.

Presently he thought he heard sounds—faint musical murmurings in the air about him, low wailings of violins, scarcely more than Æolian harpings, and pipings as of tiny flutes—almost indistinguishable. Then a delicate swish-swish, as of silken garments. Also, there came to him a subtle fragrance that turned first into an odorous sigh and then into a summer breath of sweet peas; and he imagined—he must have imagined—hearing, "I do love you!" ah, so softly!

He smelled now the odor of sweet peas, which stirred sleeping memories without fully awakening them, as all flower odors do by what the psychologists call association. He heard, "I do love you!"—and then the Dispeller of Darkness was taken from his outstretched hand.

He stood there, his muscles tense, braced for a shock, ready for a life struggle, perhaps half a minute before the sound of footsteps retreating in the hall outside recalled to him his instructions. He vehemently desired to follow and see who it was that had taken the Dispeller of Darkness; but he had pledged his word not to. He hesitated.

The odor of sweet peas was flooding him as with waves. And he heard, "I do love you!"—heard it again and again with the inner ear of his soul, the listener of delights. He thrilled at the thought of being loved. It made him incredibly happy. He felt unbelievably young!

Suddenly it occurred to him that he had not counted a hundred as he had promised, though he must have spent more than a minute wool-gathering. He counted a hundred as fast as he could and then hastened from the room. It was plain that Tom Merriwether was already doing incredible things or, at least, failing to do the obvious. Great is the power of suggestion on an imaginative mind!

He flashed his electric torch. He was in a bare room with a dusty hardwood floor, ivory-tinted wainscoting, and a Colonial mantel. The hall was empty.

He walked down the stairs, his steps raising disquieting echoes and creepy creakings.

Mindful of his waiting friend outside, he quickly walked out of the gloom into which he had carried the Dispeller of Darkness of Apollonius of Tyana, the cross of the seven emeralds. Huntington Andrews saw him coming and crossed over to meet him.

"How did you make out, Tom?"

"I'm a damned fool, Huntington; and so are you! And so is everybody!"

"Right-O!" agreed Andrews, who was inveterately amiable and, moreover, loved Tom.

"It's the most diabolical—" Tom paused.

"Yes, it is," agreed Huntington Andrews, so obviously anxious to dispel his friend's ill temper that Tom laughed and said, cheerfully:

"Come on, me brave bucko!" And together they walked to the corner and then down the Avenue to 777.

"Huntington, you wait here; and if I am not back by nine-forty-five go to my house. At ten o'clock have my valet deliver the letter I gave him for my father. You can be of help to the governor if you will."

And Huntington Andrews asked no questions—he was a friend.

Tom rang the bell of 777. The door opened. One of the four over-intelligent-looking footmen stepped to one side respectfully.

"Is your—" began Tom.

"Yes, Mr. Merriwether," answered the man, with a deference such as only royalty elicits.

He then delivered Tom to footman number two, who in turn escorted him as far as number three;

then number four led him to the door of the master's library. The footman knocked, opened the door and announced, with a curious solemnity:

"Mr. Thomas Thorne Merriwether, 7–7–77."

The strange man was there in his arm-chair, his back to the window. The room was lit by candles. The man rose and said, respectfully:

"I thank you, Mr. Merriwether."

"Don't mention it," said Tom, amiably.

The man bowed his head and looked at Tom meditatively. Tom was the first to break the silence.

"May I ask what—" Tom began, but was checked by the other, who held up his right hand with the gesture of a traffic policeman and said, slowly:

"A message in the dark! You carried one to another soul, who waited for it. And that other soul is taking one to you. Some day you will meet her. You will marry her. There is no doubt whatever of that. None! Ask me no questions, Mr. Merriwether. I ask nothing of you—no money, no time, no services, no work, no favors—nothing! Your fate is not in my hands. It never was! You will follow your destiny. It will take you by the hand and lead you to her!"

"That is very nice of destiny."

"My young friend, you are very rich, very powerful. You can do everything. You fear nothing. This is the year nineteen hundred and thirteen. But I tell you this: the woman who will be your wife in this world and throughout eternity has received your message. It was ordained from the beginning. You have not seen her; you have not heard her; you have not touched her. And yet you will know her when you see her and when you hear her and when you feel her. Into the darkness you went. Out of the darkness she will come. Nothing you can do can change it. Improve your hours by thinking of her. Think of the love you have to give her! Think of it constantly! Of your love! Yours! Of hers you cannot guess. The love you will give will make her your mate! Your love! And so, Thomas Thorne Merriwether, think of the One Woman!"

"I think—"

"I know! Amusement, sneers, skepticism, anger —all are one to me. I ask nothing, expect nothing, desire nothing, and fear nothing from you, young sir. A queer experience this—eh? An unexplained and apparently unconcluded little game? A plot foiled by your cleverness—what? A joke? A piece of lunacy? Call it anything you wish. Again I thank you. Good evening, Mr. Merriwether."

And Tom was politely ushered from the room by the strange man and from the house by the four over-intelligent footmen.

III

Next day Tom Merriwether found himself unable to think of anything but the mystery of the fateful Tuesday. He felt baffled. His curiosity had been repulsed at every step. In their definite incomprehensibility all the incidents that he so vividly recalled took on an irritating quality that made him a morose and uncomfortable companion. Huntington Andrews noticed it at luncheon; and so admirable was the quality of his amiability that after the coffee he said:

"Tom, I've got important business to attend to to-day, and if you don't mind I'll be off now. Of course if you think I can help you in any way all you have to do is to tell me what it is."

"Huntington, you are the best friend in the world. I've been thinking—"

Tom paused and stared into vacancy. He was trying to recall whether the man at 777 Fifth Avenue had a criminal look about the eyes. Huntington Andrews rose very quietly and walked away. He knew his friend wished to think—alone.

Lost in his exasperating speculations, Tom finally ceased thinking of the man and began to think of the girl. Was the game to rouse his interest in an unknown, later to be introduced to him? Was the scheme one that involved an adventuress? Why all the claptrap? And why had his thoughts, in spite of himself, dwelt so persistently on love and somebody to love? Why had the springtime— since the night before—come to mean a time for loving? Why had he begun to see, in flashes, tantalizing glimpses of rosy cheeks and bright eyes? Why had he permitted his own mind to be influenced by the strange man's remarks, so that Tom Merriwether was indeed thinking—if he would be honest with himself—of marriage? Was his affinity on her way to him at this very moment, as the man said? He began to hope she was.

He dined at home and was so preoccupied at the table that even his father noticed it.

"What's up, Tom?"

"What? Oh! Nothing, dad! I was just thinking."

"Terrible thing, my boy—thinking at meal-time,"

said E. H. Merriwether, with a self-conscious look of badinage.

"Yes, it is. I'll quit."

"Is it anything about which you need advice— or help, my boy?" said the great little railroad dynast, very carelessly.

His eyes never left his son's face; but when Tom raised his gaze to meet his father's the elder Merriwether showed no interest. Tom knew his father and felt the paternal love that insisted on concealing itself as though it were a weakness.

"No, indeed. There is nothing the matter— really. I was thinking I'd like to do a man's work. I guess you'd better let me go with you on your next tour of inspection."

The face of the czar of the Southwestern & Pacific lighted up.

"Will you?" he said, with an eagerness that made his voice almost tremble.

"Yes."

And that evening E. H. Merriwether delivered a long lecture on railroad strategy and railroad financing to his son, which brought them very close to each other.

On the next day, however, all thoughts of being his great father's successor were subordinated to the feeling that, if Mr. Thomas Thorne Merriwether had to be the successor of a railroad man, he should himself take steps to provide his own successors. Feeling that he was his father's son made him think of paternity. And that made him think of the message he had delivered in the dark and of the message the man had said would some day come to Tom Merriwether. He drew a deep breath and thought he smelled sweet peas. And that somehow made him think of the girl he should marry. Try as he might, he could not quite see her face. He thought he kissed her, and he inhaled the fragrance of sweet peas. Her complexion was beautiful. No more!

On the afternoon of the third day Tom decided that he was wasting too much time in thinking of the possible meaning of his queer experience, and also that it was of little use trying not to think about it. Therefore he would try to put an end to the perplexity.

He went to 777 Fifth Avenue and rang the bell. A footman opened the door and stared at him icily. Tom perceived he was not one of the men whose faces looked too intelligent for footmen.

"I wish to see Mr.—er—your master."

"Does he expect you, sir?" The tone was not as respectful as footmen in Fifth Avenue houses used in speaking to the heir of the Merriwether millions.

"No; but he knows me."

"Who knows you, sir?"

"Your master."

"Could you tell me his name, sir?"

"No; but I can tell you mine."

"He's not at home, sir."

"I'm Mr. Merriwether. Say I wish to speak to him a moment."

"I'm sorry, sir. He's not in."

The footman was so unimpressed by the name of Merriwether that Tom experienced a new sensation, one which made him less sure of his own powers. He took out a card and a bank-note and held them out toward the man.

"I am anxious to see him."

"I'm sorry. I can't take it, sir," said the footman, with such melancholy sincerity that Tom smiled at the torture of the cockney soul.

Then he ceased to smile. The master of this mysterious house had compelled even the footmen to obey him!

"But if you will call again in an hour, sir, I think perhaps, sir—"

"Thank you. Take it anyhow."

He again held out the bank-note. The man saw it was for twenty dollars, and almost turned green.

"I—I d-daresent, sir!" he whimpered, and closed his eyes with the expression of an anchoret resolved not to see the beautiful temptress.

Tom left him, walked across the Avenue to the Park, and sat down on a bench. He settled down to think calmly over the mysterious affair, and looked about him.

The grass in the turf places had taken on a definite green, as though it were May. The trees were not yet in leaf, making the grass-greenness seem a trifle premature, but Tom noticed that the buds on the trees and shrubs were bursting; there were little feathery tips of tender red and pale green—tiny wings about to flutter upward because the sun and the sky beckoned to them to go where it was bright and warm. The sky was of a spotless turquoise, as though the spring cleaning up there had been thorough. The clouds were of silver freshly burnished for the occasion. The air was alive, laden with subtle thrills; it throbbed invisibly, as though the light were life, and life were love. He saw hundreds of sparrows, and they all twittered; and all the twitterings were very, very shrill, and yet very, very musical. And also they twittered in couples that hopped and darted and aerially zigzagged—always together and always twittering!

A policeman stopped and said something to a nurse-maid. The nurse-maid said something to the policeman. He was young and she was pretty. Then the policeman said nothing to the nurse-maid, and the nurse-maid said nothing to the policeman. Then two faces turned red. Then one face nodded yes. Then the other face walked away, swinging a club; and—by all that was marvelous!—swinging the club in time to the tune the sparrows were twittering—in couples—the same tune, as though the club-swinger's soul were whistling it!

Tom smiled uncertainly — he wanted to give money, lots of it, to the policeman and to the nurse-maid; and he knew it was impossible—it was too obviously the intelligent thing to do! So, instead, he drew a deep breath.

Instantly there came to him not the odor of spring and of green things growing, but of sweet peas and summer winds, and changing, evanescent faces, pink-and-white as flowers, with flower-odor associations and eyes full of glints and brightnesses that recalled dewdrops and sunlight and stars. And these glittering points shifted in tune to the twittering of birds and the swinging of Park policemen's clubs.

Love was in the air! Love was making Tom Merriwether impatient, as that love which is the love of loving always makes the mateless man.

He could no longer sit calmly. He could not sit at all. He craved to do something, to do anything, so long as it was motion. Therefore he walked briskly northward. At Ninetieth Street he halted abruptly. He had begun to walk mechanically and he could think of what he did not wish to think. So he shook himself free from the spell and walked back.

An hour had passed. He again rang the bell of 777. The same footman opened the door.

"Is he in?" asked Tom, impatiently.

"Yes, sir—he is, sir. I told him the moment he came in, sir." He looked as uncomfortable as a life-long habit of impassivity permitted.

"What did he say?" asked Tom.

"He said: 'How much did he offer to give you when you said I wasn't at home?' Yes, sir. That's what he asked me."

"And you said?"

"I said it was a yellowback, sir. That's all I could see. I said I wouldn't take it, and he said I might just as well have taken it. Thank you, sir! This way, sir."

The footman led the way to the door in the rear, rapped, and in the sonorous, triumphant voice that a twenty-dollar tip will give to any menial he announced:

"Mr. Merriwether!"

The same man was in the same chair in the same room, with his back to the stained-glass window. Tom recalled all the incidents of his previous visits— recalled every detail. Also the old question: What is the game? Also the new question: Where is she?

The man rose and bowed. It was the bow of a social equal, Tom saw.

"Good morning, Mr. Merriwether. Won't you be seated, sir?" And he motioned him to a chair.

"Thank you."

"How can I serve you?"

"Who is the woman?" said Tom, abruptly.

"Your fate!" answered the man.

"Her name?"

"I cannot tell you."

"Her address?"

"I don't know it."

"What is your game?"

"I have money enough for my whims and time enough to gratify my desire to help you. Eugenics is my hobby. I recognize that I cannot fight against the decree of destiny."

"I am tired of all this humbug."

"I ask nothing of you now. You can go or you can come. You can go to India or to Patagonia—or even farther. You may send detectives and lawyers, or even thugs, to me. You may cease your search for her—if you can!"

"You have roused my curiosity—"

"That is a sign of intelligence."

"I tell you now that I don't believe a word of what you say."

"Free country, young man."

"I've had enough of this nonsense—"

"Though I am always glad to see you, young sir, and would not wound your feelings for worlds"—the man's voice was very polite, but also very cold—"I might be forgiven for observing that I did not ask you to call."

"I'll give you a thousand dollars—"

The man stopped him with a deprecatory wave of the hand.

"One of the pearls I offered you, Mr. Merriwether,

is valued at ten thousand dollars. You did not select that one; but I'll exchange the one you took for it—now if you wish."

"That's all very well, but—" Tom paused, and the man cut in:

"Do you wish to see her from a safe distance? Or do you wish to talk to her without seeing her? Or—"

"To see her and talk to her!"

"Wait!"

The man intently regarded the tip of Tom's left shoe for fully five minutes. Then he raised his head and clapped his hands twice. The black man-servant with the fez appeared.

The man said something in Arabic—at least it sounded so to Tom. The black answered. The man spoke again. The black replied:

The man said what sounded to Tom like, "*Ay adad.*"

The negro answered, "*Al-sabi! Al-sabi wal Saboun.*"

The man waved his hand dismissingly and the negro salaamed and left the room.

After a moment the man turned to Tom and said, with obvious perplexity: "I am not sure it is wise for me to meddle, but perhaps it is written that I am to help you three times. Who knows?"

He stared into Tom's eyes as though he would read a word there—either yes or no. But Tom said, a trifle impatiently:

"Well, sir?"

"Go to the opera to-night. Take seat H 77. No other seat will do."

"H 77—to-night," repeated Thomas Thorne Merriwether.

16

"The opera is 'Madame Butterfly.'"

"Thanks," said Tom, and started for the door. He halted when the man spoke.

"It is the seat back of G 77. None other will do."

"Good day, sir," said Tom, and left the room.

IV

The telephone operator in E. H. Merriwether's office manipulated the plugs in the switchboard and answered in advance:

"Mr. Merriwether's office!"

From the other end of the wire came:

"This is the Rivulet Club. Mr. Waters wishes to speak to Mr. E. H. Merriwether. Personal matter."

"He's engaged just now. Will any one else do?"

"No. Say it is Mr. Waters—about Mr. Tom Merriwether."

People resorted to all manner of tricks and subterfuges to speak to Mr. E. H. Merriwether—deluded people who thought they could get what they wished if only they could speak to Mr. Merriwether himself. They never succeeded. He was too well guarded by highly paid experts who prevented the waste of his precious time. But the telephone operator knew her business. She switched the would-be conversationalist on to the private secretary's line, saying:

"Mr. Waters, Rivulet Club, wishes to speak to Mr. E. H. in regard to Mr. Tom Merriwether."

"I'll talk to him," hastily said the private secretary.

"Hello, Mr. Waters! This is McWayne, Mr. Merriwether's private secretary. Has anything happened to Tom that— Oh! Yes—of course! At once, Mr. Waters."

McWayne then had the operator put Mr. Waters on Mr. E. H.'s wire.

"Who?" said the czar of the Pacific & Southwestern. "Waters? Oh yes. Go ahead!"

And Mr. E. H. Merriwether heard, in a young man's voice:

"Say, Mr. Merriwether, some of the fellows here thought I'd better speak to you about Tom. He's been acting kind of queer; of course I don't mean crazy or—er—alarming; but—don't you know?— unusual. . . . Yes, sir! A little unusual for him, Mr. Merriwether. To-day it was about the opera. Says he's got to get a certain seat, no matter what it costs. Of course it isn't our business. . . . Oh no! he never drinks too much. No; never! We don't think we are called on to follow him to the Metropolitan, where he has just gone; but we thought you ought to know it. Please don't bring us into any—you know we are very fond of Tom; and we were a little worried, he's been so unlike himself lately. We teased him about being in love, and he—er—he seemed to get quite angry. . . . Yes, Mr. Merriwether; we'll keep you posted; and please don't give me away. It was a very delicate matter and— Don't mention it, Mr. Merriwether. We'd all do anything for Tom, sir. Good-by."

E. H. Merriwether, the greatest little cuss in the world, as his admirers called him, hung up the telephone. His face, that impassive gambler's face which never told anything, now showed as plainly as could be that he was wounded in a vital spot.

His son Tom was all this great millionaire had!

His railroad became so much junk and his vast plans just so much waste paper as he thought of Tom. Was the boy going insane? Was it drugs? Was it one of those mysterious maladies that break millionaires' hearts by baffling the greatest physicians of the entire world and being beyond the reach of gold? Or was it a joke? Young Evert Waters was a friend of Tom's; but might not he exaggerate? He rang the bell for his private secretary.

"McWayne, send somebody with brains to the Metropolitan Opera House to find out whether my son Tom has been up there—box-office—and what he is up to. I want to know how he acts. I want to know where the boy goes and what he does, whom he sees and where. Get some specialist on—er"—he could not bring himself to say mental diseases—"on nervous troubles, and make an appointment with him to come to my house to-morrow morning. He will have breakfast with us—say, at eight-thirty. I don't want Tom to know."

He avoided McWayne's eyes.

"Yes, sir," said McWayne.

"Be ready to notify the papers to suppress any and all stories about Tom. I fear nothing and expect nothing, because I know nothing. Drop everything else and attend to these matters at once. I have heard that Tom is acting a little queer. It may be a lie or a joke—or a trick. I want to find out—that's all."

He would learn before he acted decisively. He stared at a pigeonhole in his desk marked T. T. M. There he kept all letters Tom had written him from boarding-school and from college. Presently he raised his head and drew a deep breath. There was no need to worry until he knew. It would be a waste of energy and of time; and, for all his millions, he could not afford the waste. He rang a bell; and when a clerk appeared he said in his calm, emotionless voice:

"I'll see Governor Bolton the moment he comes in."

There was a big battle on between capital and labor. He was in the thick of it. He put Tom out of his mind for the time being. He could do that at will; but he could not put Tom out of his heart—this little chap that people called ruthless.

v

Tom Merriwether went to the box-office at the Metropolitan and said, pleasantly, as men do when they ask for what they know will be given to them:

"I want the seat just back of G 77—orchestra—for to-night. I suppose it will be H 77."

The clerk, who knew the heir of the Merriwether millions, said, "I'll see whether we have it, Mr. Merriwether." He saw. Then he said, with sincere regret: "I'm very sorry. It's gone."

"I must have it," said Tom, determinedly.

"I don't quite see how I can help you, Mr. Merriwether. I can give you another just as—"

"I don't want any other seat. Who bought it?"

"I don't know. It may be a subscription seat, sold months ago."

"It's the double seven on the seventh row that I am concerned about. I want the seat just back of it."

"I'll call up the ticket agencies. There's a bare

chance they may have it." After a few minutes he said, "I'm very sorry, Mr. Merriwether, but I can't get it. They haven't it."

"I'm willing to pay any price for H 77. I'll give you a hundred dollars if you—"

"Mr. Merriwether, I couldn't do it if you offered me a thousand! If I could do it at all I'd be only too glad to do it for you—for nothing," the clerk said, and blushed.

Everybody liked Tom.

The sincerity in the clerk's voice impressed young Mr. Merriwether, who thanked him warmly and withdrew. The baffled feeling that he took away with him from the ticket-window grew in intensity until he was ready to fight.

It was a natural-enough impulse that led him back to 777 Fifth Avenue; but he was not quite sure whether he was angry at the man for telling him to do what was obviously impossible or at himself for determining to find her!

He rang the bell of the house of mystery. The footman that answered was one of the intelligent four; but his face was impassive, as though he had never before seen Tom.

"Your master?" asked Tom, abruptly.

"Your card, please," said the footman, impassively.

Tom gave it to him. The man disappeared, presently to return.

"This way, sir." And at the door in the rear he paused and announced, "Mr. Merriwether!"

The master of the house was in his usual place. He bowed his head gravely and waited.

"I couldn't get the seat," said Tom, with a frown.

"It is written, 'Vain are man's efforts!'"

CHEAP AT A MILLION

"That's all very well, my friend. But the next time—"

"Fate deals with time—not with next time! There is no certainty of any time but one. If you can do nothing I can do nothing. I still say, The seat back of G 77 to-night."

Tom Merriwether looked searchingly into the calm eyes before him. The baffled feeling returned; also, a great curiosity. What would the end be? At length he said, "Good day, sir." He half hoped the man would volunteer some helpful remark.

"Good day, sir," said the man, with cold politeness.

Tom went back to the Opera House and asked for somebody in authority to whom he might talk. They ushered him into Mr. Kirsch's presence. Mr. Kirsch, amiable by birth, temperament, and training, listened to him with much gravity; also, with a concern he tried to conceal, for it was too sad— a bright, clean-living, intensely likable chap like Tom, only heir to the Merriwether millions!

Fearing a scene, he told Tom that he would speak to the ticket-takers in the lobby to be on the look-out for ticket H 77. Then he conferred with the emissary McWayne had sent, who thereupon was able to send in a most alarming report.

The private secretary softened it as much as he could, and even dared to suggest to the chief that it might be a bet; but the little czar of the Pacific & Southwestern, who had never flinched under any strain or stress, grew visibly older as he heard that his son was offering thousands for an opera-seat— for the seat back of the double seven, seventh row. It could mean but one thing!

THE PLUNDERERS

Tom was so fortunate as to be standing beside the ticket-collector at the middle door of the main entrance when the owner of H 77 appeared. He was a fat man with a pink and shiny face, a close-cropped mustache, and huge pearl studs. The fat man was fortunately alone.

"Sir," said Tom, "I should like to speak a moment with you."

The man looked apprehensive. Then he said, "What is it about?"

"For very strong personal reasons I should like to exchange tickets with you. I can give you G 120 —every bit as good—on the other side of the aisle."

"Why should I change?" queried the shiny-faced man, suspiciously.

"To oblige a very nice young lady and myself. Of course, if you prefer to be paid—"

"I don't need money."

"Well, I'll pay you a hundred dollars for your ticket," said Tom, coldly.

The man shook his head from force of habit, in order that Tom might see he was offering too little. Then he said, recklessly:

"It's yours, my friend. I have a pet charity. I'll give your money to it. Where's the hundred?"

Tom took out a small roll of yellow bills, pulled off one, and handed it to the man with the pet charity, who took it, looked at it, nodded, put it in his pocket, gave the coupon to Tom, and then held out his right hand.

"Where is the ticket for G 120 that you'll give me in place of mine?"

Tom gave it to him and walked into the house, not knowing that McWayne's emissary had listened and reported. He sat in H 77 and tried to laugh at his own absurd behavior; but somewhere within him—away in, very deep—something was thrillingly alert, tantalizingly expectant.

The seat before him was empty. It remained empty during the first act. It angered Tom that the climax should be so long in coming. The three seats in front of him remained vacant until just before the curtain went up on the last act. Somebody came in just as the lights were lowered and occupied seat G 77.

Tom sat up and braced himself. He leaned over, vaguely desiring to be near her. Unconscious that he was under a strain he, nevertheless, drew a deep breath.

Instantly there came to him the odor of sweet peas, and with it thoughts of summer, of a beautiful girl, of a soul-mate, of a wife. Love filled his being. He wished to love and be loved. He wished to be somebody's husband, so that he might begin to live the life he was to live until the day of his death!

He leaned back in his chair and again inhaled the fragrance of sweet peas—the odor that must mean kisses in the open; the inarticulate love-making of breezes and blossoms; the multitudinous whispers of midsummer nights heard by love-hungry ears. And then the music! There came the breaking of a heart about to cease beating and the sobbing crash of the brasses in the finale. It was almost more than Tom could bear.

Then the curtain fell and light flooded the house. People streamed out. Tom twisted and turned to see the face of the lady who made him think of the sweet peas, which made him think of love and marriage and children—but she was wrapped to the cheeks in a fur-edged opera-cloak and her head was covered with a black-lace wrap. He could not see her face; and after rivulets of people reached the main stream in the middle aisle he found himself hopelessly separated from her. He tried to jostle his way through. McWayne, his father's private secretary, suddenly happened to be there.

"Hello, Tom!" he said. "What's your rush?"

Tom saw that it was useless to pursue the phantom of sweet peas and dreams of love unless he vaulted over the stalls. McWayne's presence made him realize how his friends would be shocked by such actions.

"No hurry at all," said Tom, who, after all, was a Merriwether. "Just wanted to smoke and to see whether I knew that girl."

"I'll bet she's a pippin!" said McWayne, with a friendly smile. It irritated Tom.

"I don't know any of your friends," said Tom, coldly; "lady friends and pippins, fellows like you call them, I believe."

That was what convinced McWayne that the worst was to be feared about poor Tom, who was so considerate and amiable when normal. Poor Tom! McWayne telephoned to the waiting E. H. Merriwether, whose only reply was to ask the private secretary to arrange to have Dr. Frauenthal, the great specialist, at breakfast in the Merriwether house the next morning, without fail.

It was a common occurrence for Dr. Frauenthal to meet—under false pretenses, as it were—persons whose sanity was suspected by fond relatives who dared not openly acknowledge their suspicions. ·He was a man whose eyes had been compared to psychic corkscrews, with which he brought the patient's secret thoughts to the light of day. Some one said of him that, by inducing a feeling of guilt and detection among the predatory rich, he was able to exact colossal fees from them. He was the man who had made Ordway Blake give up making six millions a year in Wall Street by quitting the game. Mr. Blake was still alive.

Frauenthal was introduced to Tom as a gentleman whose advice "E. H." desired. The men conversed on various topics apparently haphazard; but in reality Tom, without knowing it, was answering test questions. The answers could not conclusively prove insanity, but they would certainly show whether a more thorough examination was necessary.

Mr. Merriwether and Frauenthal left the house together. They entered the waiting brougham. The great little railroad magnate gave the address of the doctor's office to the footman, then turned to Frauenthal and said, calmly:

"Well, what do you think of him?"

His voice was steady and cold; his face imperturbable; his eyes were fixed with intelligent scrutiny on the specialist's, but his fingers tightly clutched a rolled morning newspaper.

Frauenthal turned his clinical stare on E. H. Merriwether, as though the financier were really the patient. He swept the little man's face—the eyes, the mouth, and the poise—and then let his eyes linger on the clenched fingers about the newspaper.

The iron-nerved, glacial-blooded, flint-hearted Merriwether could not control himself after forty-five seconds of this. He flung the newspaper on the floor violently.

"Go ahead!" he said, harshly.

The doctor did not smile outwardly; but you felt that within himself he had found an answer to one of his own unspoken questions about the father of the suspect.

"There are, Mr. E. H. Merriwether," he began, in the measured tones and overcareful enunciation of a lecturer at a clinic, "various forms of—let us say—madness; and your son Tom, a fine young man of twenty-eight, is quite unmistakably suffering from—"

He paused to give the fine young man's emotionless father an opportunity to show human feelings. Frauenthal was always interested in the struggle between the emotional and the physical in his millionaire patients.

"Go on!" said E. H. Merriwether, so very coldly as to irritate.

His eyes never left the alienist's own secret-draggers; but he was drumming on his thigh with the tips of his uncontrollable fingers. Ordinarily his desk would have screened from sight this betrayal of human feeling.

"Your son, sir, is suffering, beyond any question, from the oldest madness of all—love!"

"What?"

"Your son Tom is in love. That is what ails him."

"Are you serious?" Mr. Merriwether was frowning fiercely now.

"You'll think so," retorted Frauenthal, coldly, "when you get my bill."

CHEAP AT A MILLION

"My boy Tom in love?" repeated the czar, blankly.

"Yes."

"With whom?"

"I don't know. I'm a neurologist—not a sooth-sayer."

"Well, suppose he is in love—what of it?"

"Nothing—to me."

"Then what is serious about it?"

"I can't tell you, for its seriousness to you depends on your point of view toward society at large. There are, of course, the obvious disquieting circumstances."

"For instance?"

"He is a fine chap—healthy, bright, honest. What is the reason he has said nothing to you? Is he ashamed or afraid? If he is ashamed it is very serious to both of you. If he is afraid—well, then the seriousness depends on how intelligent a father you have been to him."

"Don't talk like a damned fool! I've been a good father to him; of course—"

"Wait! Wait! First tell me why you do what you ask me not to do?" In the specialist's eyes was a sort of professional curiosity.

"What do you mean?" said E. H. Merriwether, impatiently. It exasperated him to be puzzled.

"Why do you talk like a damned fool?" said Frauenthal.

Nobody ever talked that way to Mr. E. H. Merriwether, overlord of the greatest railroad empire in history. He flushed and was about to retort angrily, but controlled himself in time. The brougham had reached Frauenthal's office. Mr. Merriwether spoke too calmly—you could feel the tense restraint:

"Dr. Frauenthal, I've heard a great deal of your wonderful ability."

He paused. It came hard to him to be ingratiating. This difficulty is the revenge which nature takes on people who acquire the habit of paying money for everything in this world. Such men cannot talk except with a check-book, and the check-book loses the power of speech before happiness—and before death.

"What very difficult thing is it you wish me to do for you?" asked Frauenthal, coldly.

"You are sure Tom is not—" He hesitated.

"Crazy?" prompted the specialist.

"Yes."

"Yes; I'm sure he is not. Therefore he is saner than you who are a money-maker."

Mr. Merriwether let this remark pass. He was anxious to save Tom. This man was uncannily sharp. He said, "And can't you do something, so that Tom will not—"

"I am not God!" interrupted Frauenthal.

"Then, what can I do? What do you suggest might be done?"

"As a neurologist?"

"Yes."

"Nothing."

"Then, as a man of the world—as one who knows human nature? You see, this—this—er—sort of thing is not in my line. What shall I do?" It was a terrible thing for the great Merriwether to confess inefficiency in anything.

"Pray!"

The little magnate flushed. "Dr. Frauenthal," he began, with chilling dignity, "I asked—"

CHEAP AT A MILLION

"And I answered. Have your millions deafened you? Pray! Pray to whatever other god you may have that the lady prove to be neither a prima donna nor a novelist. A temperamental daughter-in-law is really worse than you deserve, for all the money they say you have made. There are check-book gods and stock-ticker gods; and there is also God. I'd pray to Him if I were you. Good day, sir!"

The footman had opened the door, and the great specialist, without another look at the railroad man, got out and walked into his house.

"Where to, sir?" asked the footman.

Mr. Merriwether, however, was vexed to think that in relieving his anxiety over Tom's sanity Frauenthal had replaced it with a dread question— Why had not Tom told his father about her? The boy must be either crazy or in love. If he was not crazy, who in blazes was she? What was she? Why was she? All this angered him. He muttered aloud:

"Hell!"

"Yes, sir—very good, sir," said the footman, from force of habit. Then he trembled; but his master had not heard him. The footman breathed deeply and said, tremulously, "B-beg p-pardon, sir?"

"Nearest Subway station!" said E. H. Merriwether.

He was in a hurry to reach his office, not because he had important business to transact there, but because somehow he always thought best in his own chair before his own desk in his own office. There he was an autocrat, and there he could think autocratically and issue commands that were obeyed. He had much thinking to do—Tom was concerned, his son Tom; and Tom's future. And it was now clear that T. T. Merriwether's future was also the future of E. H. Merriwether!

Why had this thing come on him? Talk about your thunderbolts out of a clear sky—this love-affair was a million times worse! It was mysterious —and it is well known in Wall Street that a mystery is worse than nitroglycerine—infinitely more dangerous.

What was this love-affair? How far had it gone? Just where was the dynamite stored? Who was she? Why did not Tom say something? Why could not Tom have fallen in love safely? Why could he not have married a good girl who would help him and help E. H. Merriwether help both by minding her own business—to wit, a few little male Merriwethers?

It was time Tom became his father's successor-to-be. E. H. Merriwether had loved to do his own work his own way all his life. It was his pleasure. But the work suddenly took on an aspect of far greater importance than the worker. The work was the work of the Merriwethers—not of one Merriwether; not even of the great E. H., but of all the Merriwethers, living and to be.

Tom must be trained not only to be the son of a Merriwether, but to be himself a Merriwether. And therefore E. H. must cease to be a railroad expert toward Tom; he must become Tom's father, the trainer of a successor—flesh and blood the same; the fortune the same.

And, as a sense of impending loss always heightens values, E. H. Merriwether suddenly realized how important to him and to his happiness Tom was. He loved Tom, who was not only his only son, but the only Merriwether. That told everything: He loved Tom.

VI

After his father and Dr. Frauenthal left the house Tom tried to feel that he had finished his breakfast—that is to say, he attempted to read the newspapers. But the printed letters failed to combine themselves into intelligible forms, and even when he read a word here and there his mind did not record it. Obeying an unexplained impulse, he rose.

Then he sat down merely because he had been standing. Then he tried to reason why he was sitting and what sitting there thinking of himself in that particular position meant. But the sky was too blue! It called to him in an azure voice that made him long for the sunshine and the open air, and the rooflessness of outdoors that permits ten million fancies to soar unchecked.

Also, he longed for something; and, though he knew that he longed, he did not know exactly what it was he longed for, because it was not his mind that desired it, but all of him; and all of him did not think with precision. Young men are apt to feel like that in the springtime—also young women. Also widowers and relicts and canaries and heifers and burros—and even bankers!

Therefore Tom swore at that nothing which is always something and gave up trying to make himself think that he wanted to read the morning papers. His nervous system coined a proverb for him: "When in doubt, walk out!" So he walked out of the house and crossed the Avenue.

THE PLUNDERERS

He found himself in Central Park—the remedy which the very rich do not and the very poor cannot use to cure the spring in the blood. And as he walked the soul-fidgets left him, so that after a mile or two he quite cold-bloodedly began to think of his most pressing duties. He went about them systematically.

The first thing he had to do was some shopping; shopping on Fifth Avenue—on Fifth Avenue where the jewelry-shops were; in the jewelry-shops where the wedding-presents were. There! He was off again. Everybody was getting married! What business had people to make people think of wives— yes, wives—plural; lots of wives; all beautiful, all desirable and worthy; all lovely and loving and lovable; and all fit to be rolled into one—Tom's?

It was not polygamy. It was merely composite photography. The one he desired had a little of each of the girls he admired. She was the amorous crazy-quilt that youth is so apt to dazzle itself with in the springtime—a nose from a friend; two lips from a stranger; a complexion from a distant relative; a pair of eyes from the sky; a heart from the heart of the sun—and lo! the wife-to-be!

And so the wedding-presents—a silver service, to be used by two sitting on opposite sides of a table, looking into each other's eyes; a glittering string, to be admired on a wonderful throat—were heavy enough to keep Tom's soul from soaring. And because his feet were on the pavement he soon found himself—of course!—before 777 Fifth Avenue.

Why should be not go to that house? And why should he not ring the bell? Why not? He was just in the mood to meet her!

CHEAP AT A MILLION

His intentions were above suspicion, though marriage is a serious thing; but, really, now was the time for the adventure to appear—even if the adventure turned out to be merely the adventuress.

Therefore, with the inexorable logic of the most illogical state of mind known, he rang the bell and waited with an eagerness—half hope, half curiosity—most unusual among people who, like Tom, early acquire the habit of asking, check-book in hand, for whatever they wish.

The footman who answered was one of the men with the over-intelligent faces.

"I am Mr. Merriwether. I wish to see your master."

Tom's voice rang a trifle more commandingly than the occasion appeared to call for. There was a physiological reason for it. The man hesitated so that Tom wondered; but presently all expression vanished from the non-menial face and the footman said:

"This way, if you please, sir."

He preceded Tom to the door of his master's library. He rapped twice smartly and waited in an attitude of listening. Tom also listened intently; he could not have told why he did it—though it was, of course, inevitable.

Not a sound was heard. The over-intelligent footman's lips moved for all the world as though he were counting, and presently he opened the door and announced:

"Mr. Thomas Thorne Merriwether—7–7–77."

Tom entered. The master of this strange house was seated at the over-elaborate library table, writing. He looked up, but before Tom could speak the man said, coldly:

THE PLUNDERERS

"I cannot do anything for you, sir."

It was so much like a refusal to give alms to a beggar that Tom flushed angrily. He managed to check a sharp retort on the very brink and, instead, began in a mildly ironical tone:

"Of course you know what I—"

"Of course!" interrupted the man, rudely; and he began impatiently to drum on the edge of the table with his penholder. "Do you imagine for a minute that you are the only mateless male in New York looking for his destined bride? And do you really think that the fruitlessness—until now—of your search is a world-tragedy? Because your name happens to be Thomas—which is a descriptive title when applied to marriageable felines of your own sex—do you fancy I am concerned with your affairs? Young man, you are the only son and heir of a very rich man; but there are some things that money cannot buy. Love is one of them."

He frowned at Tom, but something in the young millionaire's face made him relent. He went on, more kindly, more encouragingly:

"My boy, she is seeking you, even as you are seeking her. She is very beautiful! You will meet her at the appointed hour—have no doubt of it. After your perfectly stupid failure at the opera— Wait!" He held up a hand as Tom was about to speak in self-defense. "The very futility of your manœuvers shows that youth, brains, money, persistence, and desire are all powerless to hurry fate. As you, who have never seen her, love her, she loves you, though she has never seen you. She will know you as you will know her; but she is gone!"

"Where?" Tom spoke before he knew it.

CHEAP AT A MILLION

"Be patient! After you meet her you will live with her until death parts you."

He said this, without theatrical emphasis, in a most matter-of-fact way. Tom's suspicions, always present in this house of mystification rather than of mystery, were not made livelier by the man's words; but neither were they allayed by the tone of his voice. He hesitated, and then, adventure whispering, he said:

"To be perfectly frank, I am interested in this—"

"Young man, I told you before that I ask nothing of you—no favor, no money, no service; not even your interest. When I asked you to do a certain thing you did it. I am not particularly grateful. You could not have refused! Possibly you can explain to your own satisfaction your own inexplicable acquiescence; you doubtless have evolved a dozen most ingenious theories to account for your doings and mine. The shortest and easiest explanation is the true one—fate. After you marry you will compare notes with her—and yet you will not understand why I concerned myself with your lives. You will perplex yourselves so unnecessarily; all because of your unwillingness to say, fate! Men hate fate as a hypothesis. It is not flattering to admit that we are but puppets—the strongest of us no stronger than an autumn leaf in the wind. And because you do not see fate you do not believe in it. And, for fear of being considered an ass by a lot of asses, who also do not believe in fate, you will never tell any one your romantic story. And yet, of the scores you call friends, there are only seven men who are happily married. And those seven I helped, as I have helped you and as I shall help those I am ordered to help. Even now the Dispeller of Darkness is out, making one heart send a message in the dark to another heart waiting for it!"

"Do you mean to say you cannot or will not arrange for my meeting the mysterious person you tell me I am going to marry?"

"I mean to say that your coming to this house with such a hope merely means a waste of your time, young sir, and of mine. You will meet your love, but you cannot find her. No man finds happiness by means of a systematic or diligent search. It comes or it does not come—as God wills."

The man rose. Tom also rose and said:

"But at least tell me where this—this alleged fate of mine is."

The man shook his head with a smile that was in the nature of a mild sneer.

"Doubting Thomas! He won't admit it, but he can't deny it! Ah, so wise! So clever in his suspicions! So intelligently skeptical! Ah yes!"

Still nodding in ironical admiration, he approached the filing-cabinet.

"Let me see—you are 7–7–77." He pulled out drawer seven in section seven and took out an envelope from which he drew a lot of papers. He read a typewritten sheet. He replaced the papers, closed the drawer, turned, and stared doubtfully at Tom, muttering half to himself: "I don't know! I don't know!"

"What?" asked Tom.

"Do you really want her? Do you feel that you must meet her soon or die?"

Tom knew he would not die if he did not meet her soon, but as for wanting her, he certainly did. Every cell in his body was on the alert, waiting for her, hoping to see her; and adventure, through a megaphone, was vociferating in the middle of his soul: "Come! Come!" Therefore Tom looked the man straight in the eyes and answered:

"Yes, I do!"

The man hesitated. Then he said:

"Listen! It is for the last time. Do you hear? For the last time! Do you agree?"

He looked sternly at Tom, who thereupon answered, impatiently:

"Yes! Yes!"

"Boston! Hotel Lorraine! Secure Room 77, seventh floor. On Thursday at exactly 7 P.M. be in the southeast corner of the library or reading-room, which is on the left of the hall as you go to the main dining-room. Green arm-chair. Hold your hat between your knees—bottom side upward. Close your eyes. A letter will be dropped into the hat. Then do as you please. Personally I don't think it will help or hinder. But you are young; and perhaps if you wish hard enough it may happen according to your desire. Good day!"

The man turned his back squarely on Tom, leaving to the heir of the Merriwether millions no alternative but to go out dissatisfied, excited, skeptical, hopeful, and determined to go to Boston—danger or no danger, swindle or no swindle.

The mysterious man, too mysterious to be anything but a charlatan, who said he did not wish Tom's money and, for that reason, probably did—this man promised Tom he should meet a girl—a beautiful girl, the girl he would marry. If there was to be no compulsion about it; if they, the man and his accomplices, counted on her charms to capture Tom's heart and hand—why, the sooner she began the attack, the better. Also, it was one of those things that only an ass would talk about, since the telling would put an end to all doubts as to the teller's asininity.

Therefore, without saying a word to anybody, Tom went to Boston, not knowing that McWayne's detectives had orders to follow Tom wherever he went and to report in detail what he was seen to do and what he was heard to say and to whom.

Tom arrived in Boston, went to the Hotel Lorraine, registered, and asked the polite room clerk for Room 77 on the seventh floor. The clerk smiled pleasantly, as he always did whenever a guest-to-be asked for rooms that did not end in thirteen, disappeared to look at the index, and returned.

"I'm sorry, sir, but that room is taken. I can give you—"

"Taken!" said Tom, in such a disappointed tone that the clerk deigned to explain sympathetically:

"Engaged by telegraph."

"Who engaged it?"

Tom asked this so peremptorily that the clerk looked at him icily with raised eyebrows, turned his back on the New-Yorker, made a pretense of once more looking at the index of rooms and guests, and said to him with a cold determination in his voice:

"I made a mistake. I thought we had a vacant room on the eighth floor. I find we have no vacant room anywhere. I'm sorry, sir. Nothing left."

He marked something after Tom's name on the register and turned away. He evidently considered the incident closed.

Tom was too surprised to be angry. Then he recovered himself. His business in Boston was to get a certain room in this hotel. He was a son of his father; so he said, with a quiet determination that disturbed the clerk:

"I must have Room 77 on the seventh floor! The price is of no consequence. I am Mr. Merriwether."

"I told you it was engaged."

"And I told you I must have it. Don't you understand English?"

"Don't you?" said the clerk, trying to disguise his growing uneasiness with a sneer.

This made Tom calm. He said, quietly:

"Will you be good enough to send my card to Mr. Starrett, the owner of this hotel? He knows who I am and who my father is; but if he should have forgotten, say that he is to call up Major Wilkinson, of Pierce, Wilkinson & Company, the bankers, or Mr. Blandy, of the Moontucket National Bank, or anybody who knows where New York is on the map. Good heavens! there must be somebody in Boston who hasn't been asleep for the last twenty years!"

The clerk decided to be polite. The name Merriwether had a familiar sound, but he could not associate it. He said, more politely:

"I am sorry, Mr. Merriwether, but the room you want—and three others with it—have been engaged."

"By whom?"

"You are asking me to break one of our rules."

"Well, can you tell me whether it has been engaged since yesterday?"

"Oh, longer than that!" He disappeared, consulted a book, and came back with the triumphant expression human beings put on when they do not wish to say "I told you so," aloud. "Engaged and paid for since the eighth, Mr. Merriwether. That's nine days ago. So, you see, we can't do what you ask us to. Sorry!"

Wherever he went, Tom thought he was confronted by crude attempts at mystery. To send him to this particular room, 77 on the seventh floor, was merely the same as an effort to impress children by using the magical number seven.

Who had engaged the room? Was it an accomplice or some stranger guiltless of participation in the rather juvenile joke?

Still, Tom was in Boston to do a particular thing; and, though much of the spring restlessness had gone from his veins, there remained the desire to see the affair through to the end, whether the end should be a smile or a mild oath. Therefore, after a pause, Tom said to the clerk:

"Can you give me the room exactly opposite 77 on the seventh floor?"

The clerk hesitated, then said:

"Just a minute, please."

He consulted one of the bookkeepers, from whom he must have learned whose son Tom was. And, though Boston is not New York, money is money, even in Massachusetts; and the heir to fifty or a hundred million dollars is something, whether or not he is somebody.

"Certainly," said the clerk, and handed the key to a young man called, in New York, a bell-boy. The young man now preceded Tom to the seventh floor and ushered the New-Yorker into Room 78.

Tom gave the studious youth a dollar and never noticed that the boy regarded the bill with a mixture of suspicion and alarm, put it gingerly into his pocket, and left the room, closing the door. Tom opened the door. The boy thought it had opened itself and returned to close it. Tom waved him away. The boy hastily retreated. He did not, however, throw away the dollar. He had discovered it was not "phony."

The bell-boy found the room clerk engaged in conversation with two men. He, divining that the talk concerned the generous lunatic, flung at the room clerk that look of exaggerated perplexity which will cause any normal human being inevitably to ask: "What is it?"

The room clerk saw the look and still kept on talking with the men; whereupon the bell-boy walked up to the desk, frowned fiercely, and muttered, "He is in his room!"

"What's that, boy?"

"I said," retorted the studious youth, glacially, "he was in his room—78. He gave me a dollar and left the door open. I tried to close it, but he opened it again—after he gave me the dollar."

The clerk, awe in his face, turned to the men and nodded confirmatively.

"Your man!" he said. "Of course we don't want any fuss—"

"We'll telephone Mr. McWayne, the private secretary. The young fellow isn't violent, you know."

The hotel clerk said the inevitable thing:

"Only son, too—isn't he?"

"Yes. Over a hundred million dollars, I've heard." The detective, induced thereto by the invitation in the clerk's voice, had vouchsafed inside information.

"Too bad!" murmured the clerk, thinking of the hundred million and Tom. "Too damned bad!" he almost whimpered, thinking of the hundred million and himself. To show that he was unimpressed by vast wealth he added, sternly, "No trouble, you understand!"

One of the men whom McWayne had instructed to shadow Tom sat in the lobby just in front of the elevator. The other, with the clerk's permission, went up to the seventh floor and sat down by the floor telephone operator. From there he could keep a ten-dollar-a-day eye on Room 78.

Meantime Tom's impatience had reached such a point that he could not sit still. Through his open door he could see the closed door of Room 77. The thought came to him to see who was in that room. Then it struck him that perhaps the mysterious man in New York had reckoned precisely on rousing the Merriwether curiosity. Perhaps an unpleasant surprise awaited the man who should enter Room 77. Perhaps the room was occupied by some one who had nothing to do with her—and therefore nothing to do with him. Perhaps he should put himself in a ridiculous predicament. Perhaps a million disagreeable things might happen, making it obviously the unwise thing to do to go into Room 77.

All these reflections, however, weighed no more than a shadow with him. The more he thought of why he should not go into Room 77 the more difficult it became to resist the call of adventure. He walked across the hall and knocked sharply on the door. No answer came. He knocked again. A hotel maid approached him.

"I beg your pardon, sir. Are you in the party?"

CHEAP AT A MILLION

"What party?"

"In Room 77."

"No. I am in 78."

"I am very sorry—but it is against the rules of the house, sir."

Tom had nothing to say to the maid; so he closed the door of his own room, conscious that his actions must appear erratic, but not much concerned over it. Presently he went out for a walk and did not go to either of his Boston clubs. This omission was duly noted by the clever Mr. McWayne's star sleuths.

Tom returned to the hotel, feeling almost cured. He realized that he had come on a fool's errand; and yet there was something that told him it was not a fool's errand. It was too elaborate for a practical joke. So long as no motive was apparent the mystery remained a mystery; and no mystery is laughable—at least, not while in the act of mystifying.

So he decided for the tenth time to go through with his part, absurd or not. He walked about the lobby, utterly unconscious that he was a marked man. He could not see that the clerks and the bellboys and the two men from the New York agency followed his movements, not only with the liveliest curiosity, but with deep pity.

All he was doing was to wait more or less impatiently for seven o'clock; but impatience is so natural a feeling, and comes so easily to most human beings, that it always rouses suspicion. Tom did not "act right" to the watchers. Any perfectly sane and intelligent man, accused of being mad, will confirm the accusation if he is watched for five minutes. People who never think and never imagine are never taken for lunatics. That nowadays is about the only compensation for being an ass.

At 6.56 P.M. he walked into the hotel library and found that the green-plush arm-chair in the corner by the window was occupied by an elderly woman. It annoyed him because he desired to sit in that chair at exactly seven o'clock. Absurd or not, the problem became how to get rid of the old woman quickly and without disturbing the peace or alarming the office.

His mind worked logically enough for a man under observation for insanity, and his sense of humor acted as a safety-valve for his inventiveness. He merely drew his chair very close to the startled old lady and opened a magazine. He found a poem and began to read it in the exasperating undertone used by the demons who have the next seats to yours at the opera.

Presently he began to drum on his thigh with the tips of his fingers, and at regular intervals of ten seconds he thumped it with his clenched fist bass-drumwise. Every twenty-five seconds he pulled out his watch, looked at it, exclaimed, "Gracious!"— and blew his nose loudly and determinedly.

Within two and three-quarter minutes the old lady glared at him, rose, looked at the clock, glared again at him to make sure, and left the room. In the hall she stopped and spoke to the young lady who checked hats and coats near the entrance of the main dining-room.

"I had to leave the reading-room. A perfectly horrible person came in! He simply drove me out."

"Yes, madam. He is insane. It is a very sad case."

CHEAP AT A MILLION

"Goodness! What a narrow—"

"Oh, he is quite harmless, madam."

"It's a wonder a first-class hotel, like this claims to be, allows—"

"You are right!" agreed the wise young woman, whose business was to encourage generosity.

The old lady went away, muttering. Thomas Thorne Merriwether sat down in the vacated chair, put his hat between his knees, and waited. The mahogany clock on the mantel presently began to chime the hour and Tom felt a pang of angry disappointment. Nothing had happened—except that he again had made an ass of himself!

A tall, strongly built man at that moment entered the room, looked at Tom, saw the hat held between the knees, and turned away as if the last person in the world he wished to see was young Mr. Merriwether.

Tom saw him stretch his hand toward a panel in the wall. Instantly the room was in darkness. It occurred to Tom that this would be a good way to attack him; but there instantly followed the reflection that it was not a good place in which to do any robbing or murdering.

Therefore young Merriwether sat on quietly. He felt something drop into his hat. A faint odor of sweet peas came to his nostrils—the odor he had associated with his youth until he began to associate it with her, and therefore with love.

This evanescent perfume that made vague memories stir within him—that made him desire to see the woman who was to be his wife—that made him thrill obediently at the call of adventure—made him feel that the mysterious man of 777 Fifth Avenue was not a cheap charlatan.

THE PLUNDERERS

Suddenly the light was turned on again. Tom saw a slip of paper within his hat, fished it out, and, without stopping to see what it was or what it said, rushed from the room into the corridor.

He saw men and women coming and going. He could not tell whether she was among them or whether the man who had entered the library—who probably was the man that put out the light—was among the crowd. But the sleuths and the bell-boy and the coat-girl watched him. What doubt could remain? In their minds there was none.

Tom abandoned the chase. The key to the mystery eluded him, as usual. He was not clever enough to catch the mystery-manipulator in the act, as it were. He looked at the paper. It was an envelope. On it was written in a woman's hand:

For T. M.

He opened the envelope and pulled out a sheet of the hotel note-paper, on which he read, in the same handwriting:

Too late!

He walked to the desk and spoke to the room clerk.

"I must—" he began, but stopped.

"Yes, sir, Mr. Merriwether!" The clerk used the voice and manner of a man saying nice things to a child in order to propitiate its mother.

"About Room 77 on the seventh floor," said Tom.

"We can give it to you now, if you wish. Yes, sir."

"What? Has she— Is it vacant?"

"Given up this very minute. If you'll wait until

we send up and see whether it is ready to be occupied, I'll—"

"I'll take it; but I'd like to go up at once."

He wished to see whether there was any clue left by the previous occupants.

"Certainly. Front!"

Tom followed the bell-boy. The room was empty and undisturbed. He thought he smelled sweet peas and sat down in an arm-chair to think; but the odor, which made her recognizable in his dreams of her, prevented him from thinking as you would expect a healthy young man to think. There was no sharpness of outline in the visions of her seen through the mist of dreams and longings.

He knew there was a girl somewhere whom he would marry. Indeed, he often had wondered what his wife would be like. Every man, when he endeavors to look ahead, thinks that some day he shall have a wife—the mother of his children—the woman whose mere existence will influence his life more than anything else in the world; whose love will make him a different man; whose necessities will give to him an utterly different point of view.

Our lives depend on our point of view; and Tom knew that his point of view would be utterly changed by this girl he had never seen. Would she be the girl the man in 777 Fifth Avenue said she would be? Was she the mysterious person with whom, of course, he was not in love, but with whom he might fall in love—adventuress or not? His love of love had not yet changed into love of somebody; but he was keen to enter into a definite love-affair with a concrete being, and he rather suspected that this affair was being stage-managed for his benefit.

He would forgive everything so long as in the end
something happened—something in which there was
a girl, whether or not she was the girl. What most
irritated him was the indefiniteness of the mystery
so far. The spice of danger; the tragical possibilities; the lure of adventure; the call of the unusual;
the attraction of the unknown and therefore of the
interesting—were no longer quite enough. The
glimpse of a face—of a living face—and a hand to
shake, a waist to clasp and lips to kiss—these things
he now desired.

His irritability over his failure to develop an adventure in Boston grew keener until it became anger.
He would have it out once for all with the mysterious
man at 777 Fifth Avenue.

He went down-stairs, paid his bill, and took the
midnight train for New York.

VII

Some men are so picturesque that they do not
need publicity agents, and so intelligent that
they wish to be let alone by the public prints.
E. H. Merriwether was one. He employed the ablest
experts for his corporations and they got more than
their share of publicity; but for himself—nothing.
Possibly he realized that ungratified curiosity is a
valuable asset; and, of course, he knew that in a
democracy the less a man raises his head above the
level of the mass the better it will be for his comfort.

He took pains to make it plain that he cared only
for his work, because that proved he had no thoughts
for mere money-making; and, since he was not interested in money-making, he could not be primarily

concerned with despoiling the public—which, in turn, clearly proved he was not dangerous. And, of course, the more he kept himself out of the papers the more the papers wanted to see him in their hospitable columns. Everything he did or thought was, therefore, news. Anecdotes about him were so hard to get that the brightest minds in the profession manufactured a few. They had to be very good anecdotes—and they were.

To the metropolitan reporters, however, E. H. Merriwether was known to be mute, dumb, silent, constitutionally incapable of speech, and, besides, devoid of vocal cords. His office was always free from reporters, because they had learned to save themselves time by the simple expedient of writing their interviews with him in their own offices, after this fashion:

Mr. Merriwether refused to discuss the matter. Neither confirmation nor denial could be obtained at his office.

The financial editors of the newspapers fared no better. He was never too busy to see them; but all news about his work came from his bankers.

On the same day that Tom went to Boston, a young man went to the Merriwether offices in the Transcontinental Trust Company Building. A stout, rather high railing fenced off the bookkeepers' room from the general and unwelcome public.

At a small, flat desk near the gate sat, not a freckle-faced boy, but a man, powerful of build, keen-eyed and quick-muscled. He was writing a letter on a very good quality of note-paper. He said: "Well?" —but kept on writing. He did not look up. This always discouraged strangers, by making them feel their utter insignificance. The effect on millionaire magnates, who similarly found themselves ignored, also was salutary.

"I wish to see Mr. E. H. Merriwether," said the young man, pleasantly and unimpressed.

The gate-keeper wrote two paragraphs and then, still writing, asked, wearily:

"Got an appointment?"

"No; but—"

The over-mature office-boy, in one breath and in a voice that dripped insolence, said, still without looking up:

"What do you want to see him about? He is very busy. Cannot possibly see any one to-day. Good day!"

There was a laugh, not at all ironical, or in the nature of an exaggerated and audible sneer, but full of amusement; and then the stranger without the gate said:

"When I tell you what I am you will bring Mr. E. H. Merriwether to me."

The voice was not menacing at all or cold, but there was an assurance about it that made the Merriwether hireling look up. He saw a young man, of about thirty, with very intelligent, gray-blue eyes, a straight, well-modeled nose, and a determined chin. His square shoulders and general air of muscular strength made him look as if he could give as good an account of himself in a rough-and-tumble fight as in a battle of wits.

The Merriwether gateman felt his entire being permeated by a feeling of hostility. This was neither a crank to turn over to a complaisant police nor an alms-seeker to be shooed away; nor yet a millionaire in good standing. He must be, therefore, a reporter of the new school made possible by the eccentricities of the Administration in Washington.

"My good James," said the new-school reporter, with a mocking superciliousness, "I would see your boss. Be expeditious."

The gate-keeper, whose name was not James but Doyle, flushed dangerously; but his wages were high, and he forced himself to keep his temper under control. For all that, his voice shook as he said:

"If you have no appointment, you ought to know it's no use. No stranger from a newspaper ever sees Mr. Merriwether. I—I'm sorry!" Here Doyle gulped. Then he finished: "Good day!"—and resumed his writing.

The reporter said, "Look at me!" so sharply that Doyle in a flash pushed back his chair, jumped to his feet, and looked pugnaciously at the man who dared to give commands in E. H. Merriwether's office.

"My Celtic friend," pursued the reporter, in a voice of such cold-blooded vindictiveness that Doyle listened with both astonishment and respect, "for years the domestics of this office have been rude and impolite to my profession. Mr. Merriwether never cared how angry reporters might feel or what they said about him; but to-day I am the one who does not care, and E. H. Merriwether is the man who is vitally concerned. *I* don't give a damn whether he sees me or not. And as for you, in order to avenge the poor chaps to whom you have been intelligently rude, I, to whom you have been unintelligently impolite, shall have you fired. I've got E. H. Merriwether where I want him. If I can end your boss I can end your job—can't I? Oh no, Alexander! I am not crazy. I simply have the power. It was bound to happen, for Waterloo comes to all great men who are not clever enough to die at the right time. Now you go and get McWayne—and be quick about it!"

Doyle at times saw things through the top of his head, which was red. He said, a bit thickly:

"When you tell me in plain English, so I can understand—"

"You are not paid to understand; you are paid to use common sense and discrimination. You go to McWayne and say to him a reporter is here and wishes to speak to him about a sad Merriwether family matter."

Doyle knew from the office gossip that something was supposed to be wrong with Tom Merriwether; so, his heart overflowing with anger because chance had put the one weapon in the hands of an insolent newspaper man, Doyle went off to tell the boss's private secretary. Presently McWayne, walking quickly, came from an inner office, and asked:

"You wish to see me?"

"No!" answered the reporter, flatly.

"Then—" began McWayne.

"I don't wish to see you. I wish to see if you have the sense to understand that I wish to do Mr. E. H. Merriwether the favor of letting him talk to me. Do you want me to tell you what I want you to tell Mr. E. H. Merriwether?"

The reporter looked as though he hoped McWayne would say no. Reporters did not usually look that way; therefore McWayne was perturbed. He replied, with a polite anxiety:

CHEAP AT A MILLION

"If you please—"

"Tell Mr. Merriwether that I wish to see him about his son's marriage. Tell him that if he does not wish to talk about it, he needn't. You might add that there is absolutely no use in his trying to keep it out of the newspapers. Make that plain to him, McWayne."

McWayne did not dare deny the marriage. Tom was, alas! capable of even worse things. He did the only thing possible while there was still a chance to suppress the news; he said:

"And you represent which paper, please?"

Reporters do not always know why or how news is suppressed, nor the price; but this reporter laughed good-naturedly, and replied:

" McWayne, the trouble with you Irish is that you are so infernally clever that plain jackasses like myself are prepared for you. I represent myself and I don't want to be paid to suppress. No blackmail here; no threats; nothing except amiability and good-will. Have you begun to accumulate a few suspicions that your taciturn boss is going to talk to me?"

"I'll see!" promised McWayne, non-committally; but he was so perturbed that he could not help showing it.

Doyle, who had made a pretense of resuming his letter-writing, noticed it, and felt uncomfortable.

"And—say, McWayne," pursued the reporter, "could you let a fellow have a photograph or two? You know we've got some, but we'd prefer to publish those you think the family consider the best. Some people are queer that way."

McWayne shook his head and went away, convinced of the worst. He returned and beckoned to the reporter, who thereupon said, sharply, to Doyle:

"Open the door—you! Quick!" And Doyle, who saw McWayne beckoning, had to do it.

Four hundred and seventeen reporters were avenged!

Doyle was so angry that he was full of aches. He was tempted to throw up his job. Then he hoped E. H. Merriwether, who was a very great man, would order him to throw the insolent dog out of the office. Doyle would earn a bonus.

E. H. Merriwether, autocrat of fifteen thousand miles of railroad, fearless fighter, iron-nerved stock gambler, but, alas! also a father, was seated at his desk. He turned to the reporter the inscrutable poker-face of his class:

"You wished to see me?"

"Yes, sir," said the reporter, and waited; two could play at that game. The great financier was compelled to ask:

"About what?"

"About what McWayne told you." The reporter spoke unemotionally.

"About some rumor concerning my son?"

"No, sir."

"No?" E. H. Merriwether looked surprised.

"No. I wished to know what statement you desire to make about your son's engagement and marriage. If you do not care to say anything we shall not publish any fake interview, no matter what opinion I personally may form as to the real state of your feelings."

"I take it you are from one of the yellow papers,

young man?" E. H. Merriwether spoke coldly; but, within, his heart-tragedy was being enacted.

"You usually take what you wish if it isn't nailed down, I have heard; but that, doubtless, is one of the slanders that automatically grow up about a great man, sir," said the reporter, without the shadow of a smile or frown.

"If I am mistaken about the newspaper you represent—" Here Mr. Merriwether paused, as if to allow the young man to introduce himself; but the young man said:

"If I told you the name of the newspaper that honors itself by playing fair with you, I suspect you would set in motion the machinery that you—er—men of large affairs use to suppress news. You couldn't reach my city editor, who is a poor man with a family of eight, or the reporter, who is penniless; but you could reach the owner, who is a millionaire. This is my first big story in New York and it will make me professionally. It means a lot to me!"

"About how much does it mean to you, young man?" asked E. H. Merriwether, with a particularly polite curiosity.

"Speaking in language that should be intelligible to you and using the terms by which you measure all things down here—" He paused, and then said, bluntly, "You mean in cash, don't you?"

"Yes."

"Well, I should say, Mr. Merriwether, that this story is worth to me— Let me see!" And he began to count on his fingers, like a woman. This habit inexpressibly angers men who find no trouble in remembering numbers of dollars. "I should say, Mr.

Merriwether, that it is worth about three thousand two hundred and eighty-six—millions of dollars. If I am to stop being a decent newspaper man to become a blackmailer and general damned fool I'd want to make enough to endow all my pet charities and carry out a series of rather expensive experiments in philanthropy."

"But—" began the magnate.

"No, sir," interrupted the reporter, "no money, please. Just assume that I am a damned fool and, therefore, refuse to consider a bribe."

"I have not bribed you," suggested E. H. Merriwether, calmly. His eyes never left the reporter's face.

"Then I misjudged you, and I apologize abjectly; but permit me to continue to be an ass and blind to money. What about Thomas Thorne Merriwether, only son and heir of the railroad king of the Southwest?"

"Well, what about him?" The face of E. H. Merriwether showed only what you might call a perfunctory curiosity. The reporter looked at him admiringly. After a pause, he asked:

"Do you know her?"

"Do you?"

"Then you don't!" exclaimed the reporter, triumphantly. "This is better than I had hoped."

"Better?"

"Certainly; it means a better introductory article. The first of the series will be: 'To whom is Tom Merriwether engaged?' Think of it, sir," he said, with the enthusiasm of the true artist, "the heir of the Merriwether millions! By the way, could you tell offhand how many millions I might safely say?"

CHEAP AT A MILLION

Whatever Mr. Merriwether may have thought, he merely said, with the cold finality that often imposes on young reporters:

"Young man, if you begin your career by being vulgar your ruin will be of your own doing."

"My dear sir, vulgarity never ruined any career. All the great men of history were at the beginning accused of hopeless vulgarity—by those on whom they trod. I tell you it is not vulgarity that prompts me, but mastery of the technic of my trade. Do you care to have me tell you about my article?"

What Mr. E. H. Merriwether really wished to hear was that Tom was not in love—that he was not on the verge of brutally assassinating all the hopes and dreams of a fond father. What he said to the unspeakable reporter was:

"Yes."

"Well, I start with this basis—my knowledge of your son's engagement."

"Where did you get that knowledge?"

"One of the few things a reporter is incapable of doing is betraying a confidence. To tell you the source of my information would be that. Starting with that one fact, my problem is to make that one fact so important as to enable me to write several thousand words. To justify this I must make your son very important. He is not really very important, but you are. I shall slightly over-accentuate here and there"—he waved his hand in the air, and repeated, dreamily—"here and there! You will be the Napoleon of railroads, the Von Moltke of the ticker, doer of deeds and upbuilder, indisputably the greatest captain of industry that America has yet produced!"

"Heavens!" burst from the lips of the imperturbable little magnate.

"You are a stunning study for a novelist. Yours is the great romance of the American business man! Having made you romantic, I wave my magician's wand and quadruple your millions. Yours, my dear sir—if you don't happen to know it—is one of the great fortunes of the world! You've got Crœsus skinned to death and John D. whining over his lost pre-eminence!"

"Now look here—" interjected E. H. Merriwether, sternly; but the reporter retorted, earnestly:

"Hold your horses!" And the great millionaire did. The young man continued in his enthusiastic way: "It is much to have the hundreds of Merriwether millions, but it is infinitely more to have all the Merriwether millions and such a father and youth. I thus make Tom, who is really of no importance, of even greater importance than the great E. H. Merriwether. Do I know my business?" And he bowed in the general direction of the elder Merriwether.

"I begin to suspect," replied the elder Merriwether, "that you do."

He was watching the reporter closely. He always had found it profitable to let men talk on. A man who talks is apt to show you what he is; and that furnishes to you the best available weapon. You also may learn when it is better not to fight.

"When it comes to picturesque writing about people I do not know, I can assure you, Mr. Merriwether," the young man said, modestly, "that I haven't an equal in the United States. In your case I shall not be handicapped by either facts or knowledge, which are always fatal to the creative faculty. I shall be free—absolutely free to write!"

Mr. Merriwether permitted himself a frown in order to conceal his uneasiness. This young man was talking like a humorist. The eyes were intelligent and fearless. The combination was formidable.

"Your theory has doubtless many supporters among your colleagues."

"There are," admitted the reporter, cheerfully, "other bright young creative artists on our staff. Well, I proceed to make your son a paragon—a clean-minded, decent, manly young millionaire."

"Which he is!" interjected Mr. Merriwether, sternly.

"Of course! I know it. Have no fear on that score. I'd make him all that even if he wasn't. I proceed to draw attention—with a cleverness I'd call devilish if it wasn't my own—to the strange and, on the whole, agreeable vein of romanticism in the Merriwether nature. There you are, a hard-headed man of affairs, whose name the world associates with great engineering deeds and great high-finance misdeeds! You are—do you know what?—a poet!— a wonderful poet whose lines are of steel, whose numbers are of tonnage, whose song is chanted by the ten thousand purring wheels of your tireless cars."

"My car-wheels are lubricated. They don't purr," mildly objected the railroad poet.

"They do in my story," said the reporter, firmly. "And to prove it I'll quote some striking lines from one of those unknown books we great writers always have on tap. Your romantic nature expresses itself in the creation of an empire in the alkali desert.

You have written an epic on the map of America—in green!"

"That sounds good to me," said Mr. E. H. Merriwether, with the detached air of a critic of literature.

He did not know just how to win this young man's silence—perhaps by letting him talk himself out of creative literature; perhaps by the inauguration of a molasses diet at once!

"Thank you! Your son Tom's romance is in his unusual love-affair! This young man, the most eligible bachelor in the world—handsome, rich, a fastidious artist in feminine beauty, with a heart that has kept itself inviolate—pretty swell word that?—in-vi-o-late—all these years, opens at her sweet voice. We alone are able to announce the engagement. High society is more than interested—more than startled. As thinks society, so thinks the shop-girl; and there are fifty million of her. What society is incinerating itself with desire to find out is: To whom is Tom Merriwether engaged? Will our fair readers devour the article? I leave it to you, Mr. Merriwether!" The young man looked inquiringly at Mr. Merriwether.

"I'd read it myself," said Mr. Merriwether, very impressively. "I couldn't help it!" You could see that literature had triumphed over the stock-ticker. A great diplomatist was lost in a great money-maker.

"Thank you! And what do you find at the end of the article? What? Why, a nice psychological little paragraph to the effect that we propose to print the name of the one woman who, of all the tens of thousands who have tried, has won the heart of Thomas Thorne Merriwether, whose father you have the honor to be. We refrain, in order to have the parents of the young people formally announce the engagement. By doing this we get the full value of the to-be-continued-in-our-next suspense, for the first time utilized in a news story; and we also increase our reputation for gentlemanly conservatism, which prevents the refined reporter of the—of my paper from intruding into a family affair."

"Will your paper be damned fool enough to—" began E. H. Merriwether, intentionally skeptical.

"It is not damned folly to extract all the juice contained in the scoop of the century—it is technical skill of a very high order. Now what happens? My esteemed contemporaries, morning and evening, chuck a fit and bounce their society editors. They then rush for the telephone and despatch their strongest photographers, sharpest sleuths, and entire dictagraph corps to the scene. They can't find Tom—because, as you know, he is in—he is out of town. And they can't find her—because I haven't said who she is. There remains you!"

"That won't do them any good," said Mr. E. H. Merriwether, decisively; but he shuddered.

"Pre-cisely! I banked on that. But, even if you did see them, what could you tell them? Deny what is bound to be confirmed in the next issue of my paper? You know better than to acquire a reputation for lying in the newspapers. No, siree! Your game is to deny yourself to all inquirers and say nothing. My esteemed contemporaries have now but one desire—to wit: to print the name and publish the portrait of your son's fiancée. Of course you see what happens then, don't you?"

The reporter looked at the iron-hearted E. H. Merriwether, with such pity in his eyes that the great little czar of the Southwestern Railroad for the first time in his life realized he was merely a man —a human being; an ordinary, every-day father; one drop in the vast ocean; one of the crowd temporarily aboveground and therefore exposed to the same sorrows and troubles and sore vexations as all mankind. His millions, his position in the world, his great work, his undoubted genius—could not avail even to rid him of annoyance. Can you imagine John D. Rockefeller living on Staten Island in June and unable to buy mosquito-netting — price, five cents a yard?

"What will happen?" asked the great millionaire, who was also a father.

"My intelligent colleagues, of course, will look for the lady. Where there is a strong demand the supply automatically offers itself for consumption. And what will the seven hundred and fifty alert young men, with great capacities for fictional art, who are temporarily assisting actress-ladies and self-paying authoresses and unprinted poetesses and fertilizer-manufacturers' unmarried daughters, do? What will those estimable young artists, miscalled press agents, do when they encounter the demand for Tom's fiancée's photograph? What except 'Here she is!'—six thousand words, thirty-two poses, and a facsimile of a love-letter or two, to prove it! And then—chorus-ladies, poetesses, fair divorcées about to honor the vaudeville—" The reporter stopped—he had seen the look on E. H. Merriwether's face. He felt sorry. "But it is true," he said, defensively.

"Yes!" Tom's poor rich father felt cold all over. The reporter pursued, more quietly: "You know the ingenuity of my colleagues, the great American respect for a millionaire's privacy, and the national sense of humor. Will your son's love-affair be discussed. Will it be discussed with the gentlemanly reticence and innate delicacy of feeling of *my* story?"

Mr. E. H. Merriwether never before realized that the law against homicide was even more absurd than an Interstate Commerce Commission order; but he had to bow to the inevitable. He was beginning to understand how Napoleon felt on the deck of the *Bellerophon* when on the way to St. Helena. Do you remember the picture? He nodded—not dejectedly, but also not far from it.

"Well, in a day or two or three, according to conditions; we come out with it. We print the lady's name and her portrait—possibly not the best of all her photographs, but the only one I could—"

"Who is she?" burst from the lips of the reporter's victim.

Instantly the reporter's face became very serious. "I feared so, Mr. Merriwether," he said, very quietly.

"Look here, my boy!" interrupted Mr. Merriwether, with an earnestness that had in it a threat. "I don't know what your game is and I don't care. I'll admit right now that you are a very clever young man and probably not a crook; but I tell you calmly, quietly, without any threats, that you are not going to publish any damned-fool article about my family in any paper in New York."

The reporter rose and looked straight into the unblinking eyes of the great financier. Then he said, slowly, and, the old fellow admitted, distinctly impressively:

"And I tell you, twice as quietly and ten times as

calmly, without any fool threats, that all the daily newspapers in New York and Philadelphia, Chicago, San Francisco, Boston, and ten thousand other towns in the United States, Canada, Mexico, the Canal Zone, and countries in the Postal Union, are going to publish articles about your son Tom's engagement, and later on about his marriage. Understand once for all, that there are some things all your millions and all your will-power cannot do. This is one of them. It is the penalty of being a public character— or, if you prefer, of being an exceptionally great man. Do I understand that you have nothing to say about your son's coming marriage?"

E. H. Merriwether in less than five seconds thought of more than five thousand possibilities, all in connection with his son's marriage. Then he said, very slowly, fighting for time and a chance to escape:

"My son will marry whenever he and the young lady chiefly interested judge fit to do so. He and I are in perfect accord, as always." Mr. Merriwether was looking into the too-fearless and too-intelligent gray-blue eyes of the reporter. Then he did what he did not often do in his Wall Street affrays—he capitulated. "Will you give me your word that you will not use for publication what I am about to tell you?"

"No, sir, I won't!" emphatically replied the reporter. "You might tell me something I already know and then you'd always think I had broken my word. I will not pledge myself not to print the name of your daughter-in-law-to-be; but anything that concerns you personally or your attitude toward your son's finacée, or hints of a family quarrel—or those things that offend a sensitive man

—I promise not to print. You have some rights; but I also owe certain things to myself and my paper. I've been frank with you. You can be frank with me if you wish. I put it up to you."

Mr. Merriwether, after a thoughtful pause, said: "Look here! I don't know anything about my son's engagement. I cannot swear he is not engaged, but I don't know that he is. It follows that I do not know the young lady. You don't have to print that, do you?"

The reporter gazed on the financier meditatively. Presently, instead of answering the question, he asked:

"Have you had no suspicion of any romance?"

"Well"—and it was plain that E. H. Merriwether was telling the truth, having made up his mind to that policy as being the wisest—"well, I have of late suspected that such a thing might be possible. It is, I will confess to you, a terrible predicament, because a man naturally cherishes certain hopes for his only son." On Mr. Merriwether's face there was a quite human look of suffering.

"Of course," said the reporter, apologetically, as though offering an excuse for a friend's misdeed— "of course a man in love is not always wise."

"No. And though I have no intention or desire to bribe you, and though I would not presume to interfere with you in your professional activities or influence you by pecuniary considerations, you will pardon me for suggesting—"

The reporter did not let him go on. He rose and said, with real dignity:

"Mr. Merriwether, suppose we drop the matter right here?"

"You mean?"

"I will not print any story yet—on one condition."

"Name it. I think likely I can meet it."

"Give me your promise that you will give me an interview the next time I come to see you. It may be in a day or two, or a week. I don't promise not to print the story, you understand, but it will give you time to—well, to see your son."

E. H. Merriwether held out his hand and said: "I will see you any time you come. But let me say, as an older man, that if you should suffer any loss by not printing—"

"Oh no—I shall not suffer. I propose to print my story. I am simply deferring publication; but I thank you for the offer you were going to make. It shows more consideration and, therefore, far greater common sense than most men in your position habitually display before a reporter. I'll do even more—I'll give you a friendly tip." He stopped talking and looked doubtfully at E. H. Merriwether.

"Thank you," said Mr. Merriwether, with a remarkable mixture of gratitude, dignity, and anxiety. "I am listening."

"Find out why he goes to 777 Fifth Avenue. There are some things a really intelligent father, poor or rich, should—" He caught himself.

"Please finish, my boy!" cried the great little man, almost entreatingly.

"There are just a few things"—the reporter was speaking very slowly and his voice was lowered— "which an intelligent father does not trust to others —not even to the most loyal confidential men— things that should be done by the father himself. The number is 777 Fifth Avenue!"

CHEAP AT A MILLION

"I thank you, Mr.—"

"William Tully," said the reporter.

"Mr. Tully, I thank you. I think you are throwing away time and brains in your present position, and if you should ever—"

"Thank you, sir. Don't be afraid. I shall not bother you by—"

"But I mean it," said E. H. Merriwether.

The reporter smiled and said, "If you knew how often my fortune has been made by men whose story I have not printed you'd be deaf, too."

"Young man, I sometimes forget favors, but not the possession of brains. I need them in my business."

"Well, then, suppose you show your appreciation by telling the red-headed person in the outer office that he is to take in my card to you when I call again?"

"Certainly!" And the czar of the great Pacific & Southwestern system nearly slew Doyle by accompanying the reporter to the outer door and saying:

"Doyle, any time Mr. Tully comes to see me let me know instantly, no matter what I may be doing or who is with me. Understand?"

"Yes, sir!" gasped Doyle, looking terrifiedly at the sorcerer.

Tully! Irish! That was the reason, of course; but he was a wonder, all the same.

"Good day, Mr. Tully. I thank you. And don't forget my offer."

Mr. Merriwether bowed as the door closed on Mr. William Tully and then, walking like a man in a trance, returned to his private office. He rang the push-button marked No. 1, and when McWayne appeared turned a haggard face to his private secretary.

"McWayne, that reporter has a story of Tom's engagement, but he wouldn't tell me who the girl is."

"I don't believe it!" cried McWayne, with a not very intelligent intention of comforting his chief. At times the male Irish mind works femininely.

"Neither do I—and yet I do. It confirms Dr. Frauenthal's diagnosis. I guess he knows his business, after all. Well, the story will not be published yet. He acted pretty decently."

McWayne wondered how much it had cost the old man, but he said, "Didn't he intimate—"

"That reporter knows his business," cut in E. H. Merriwether. "He ought to be a dramatist. Have you heard from your men?"

"Yes, sir. Tom has gone to Boston. Two of them are with him. He suspects nothing."

"What else?"

"They will let me know by long distance if anything happens."

"If anything! Great Scott! isn't it enough that— Let me hear what they report—on the instant!"

"Yes, sir."

"And, McWayne—" He hesitated.

McWayne, his face full of sincere solicitude, prompted, gently:

"Yes, chief?"

It was the first time he had ever used that word. It made his speech so friendly, so affectionately personal, that E. H. Merriwether said:

"Thank you, McWayne. I wish you would find out for me at once who lives in 777 Fifth Avenue."

CHEAP AT A MILLION

"Yes, sir," said McWayne. "That's where—"
He caught himself.

"I am afraid so!" acquiesced the railroad czar,
listlessly.

VIII

Within an hour McWayne walked into the private
office. His chief closed his jaws—a weaker man
would have clenched his fists—in anticipation.

"Breese & Silliman, the real-estate men, say they
rented 777 Fifth Avenue, furnished, to a Madam
Calderon—an American woman, widow of a Peruvian
nitrate king. She came up here and asked Breese
about a suitable location. She has a daughter she
wishes to marry in America. She talked quite
freely about her affairs. The house was for sale, but
she leased it, furnished, with privilege of purchase.
Belongs to the Martin-Schwenk Construction Company. The daughter is about thirty, dark, Spanish-
looking, and fleshy; rather—er—inclined to make
googoo eyes, as Breese says, in a kind of foreign
way."

"Go on," commanded E. H. Merriwether.

"Mrs. Calderon said point-blank that she wished
her daughter to marry a nice young man of wealth
and position, preferably a blond. I gather that the
agents were rather anxious to let the house and probably encouraged her. She has paid quarterly in
advance, and her banking references are O. K.; but
nothing about her personally is known to any one.
That's all I could get."

"Very well. Thank you, McWayne."

The private secretary stood beside the desk, hesitated, and presently walked out. Shortly afterward,

the great and ruthless E. H. Merriwether, full of perplexity and regret—and some remorse over his neg-
lect of his only son for so many years—went up-
town. He desired to know what to expect, in order
to be able to think intelligently, and, therefore, to
fight efficiently. How could he fight—not knowing
what or whom to fight?

He told the chauffeur to wait, and then rang the
bell of 777.

One of the four footmen whose faces had impressed
Tom as being distinctly too intelligent for menials,
opened the door.

"I wish to see Madam Calderon."

"I beg pardon, sir. Have you an appointment?"

"No. Say it is Mr. Merriwether."

"Mr. who, sir?"

Mr. Merriwether took out a card. The footman
received it on a very elaborate silver-gilt card-tray
and, pointing to a particularly uncomfortable, high-
backed Circassian-walnut chair in the foyer, left the
great little multimillionaire under the watchful eye
of footman Number Two. This annoyed Mr. Merriwether. Nobody is altogether invulnerable.

The footman returned, with the card and the tray.

"Madam is not at home, sir; but her brother
would be glad to see you, if you wish, sir. He is
madam's man of affairs."

"Very well."

"If you please, sir, this way." And the footman
led the way to the door of the library, where Tom
had been received so often.

"Mr. Edward H. Merriwether!" The emphasis on
the first name made the little czar of the Southwestern roads think it was done in order to differentiate

him from Mr. Thomas Merriwether. Even great men are not above thinking themselves clever.

He entered the room and took in its character at one glance, just as Tom had done. He became cool, watchful, alert, and observing, as he always did when he went into a fight. He looked at the man who was said to be the brother of the woman who had leased the house—the woman who had a daughter she wished to marry to a blond with money and position.

The man had a square chin and, even in repose, suggested power and self-control. Mr. Merriwether met the remarkably steady, unblinking gaze of two extremely sharp eyes, and recognized without any particulare motion that he confronted a man of strength and resource, who, moreover, had the double strategical advantage of being in his own house and of not having sought this interview.

"Be seated, sir," said the man, in the calm voice of one who is accustomed to obedience, even in trifles.

Mr. E. H. Merriwether sat down. He noticed little things, as well as big. He noted, for instance, that he had begun by doing exactly what this man told him to do. The man intelligently waited for Mr. E. H. Merriwether to speak. Mr. E. H. Merriwether did so. He said:

"I called to see Madam Calderon."

"About?" The man spoke coldly.

Mr. E. H. Merriwether raised his eyebrows. He did it in order not to frown. There is no wisdom in needless antagonisms. His only son was concerned.

"About my son," he said.

"Tommy?"

THE PLUNDERERS

The great railroad magnate, accustomed to the deference even of the self-appointed owners of the United States, flushed with anger. Had things gone so far that such intimacy existed?

"I understand," he said, trying to speak emotionlessly, "that my son visits this house."

"Of his own volition, sir."

"I did not think there was physical coercion; but, of course, as his father—" He stopped in the middle of the sentence.

This never before had happened to this man, who always knew what to do and what to say, and always did it and said it with the least expenditure of time and words; but, as a matter of fact, what could he say, and how?

"That relationship," the man said, calmly, "often interferes with the exercise of what people formerly called common sense. Will you please do me a very great favor, sir?"

"A favor?" Mr. Merriwether, skilful diplomatist though he could be at times, now frowned in advance.

"Yes, Mr. Merriwether—indeed, two favors; or rather, three. First: Will you please ask me no questions now? Second: Will you please return to this house at eleven o'clock to-morrow morning? And third: Will you promise not to speak to your son about your visit here until after you have paid your second call, to-morrow?"

It flashed through Mr. Merriwether's mind that to grant the favors might expedite Tom's appalling marriage. He said, decisively:

"I cannot promise any of the things you ask."

"Very well," said the man, composedly. "Then, I take it, there is nothing more to be said."

He rose politely, and as he did so pressed a button on the table. The footman appeared and held the door open for Mr. Merriwether to pass out.

The autocrat of fifteen thousand miles of railroad, with unlimited credit in the money-markets of the world, was not accustomed to being treated like this: but, precisely because he felt hot anger rising in tidal waves to his brow, he instantly became cool.

He remained sitting, and said, very politely:

"If you will allow me, sir, to tell you that my reasons—"

The man, who was still standing, held up a hand and broke in:

"And if you will allow me to tell you that I am neither a criminal nor a jackass I shall then proceed to say that nobody in this house has any intention of entering into any argument or controversy with you. I am actuated much less by personal considerations of my own than by a desire to avert from you eternal regrets and—er—unseemly displays of temper."

E. H. Merriwether knew exactly what he would like to do to this man. What he said—very mildly—was:

"You must admit, sir, that your requests might be interpreted—"

"Oh, I see!" And the man smiled very slightly. "Well, suppose you take Tom to your office with you to-morrow morning, and keep him there while you come here? Tell him to wait for you, because you wish to have luncheon with him. I do not care to discuss my reasons—for example—for not wishing you to speak to Tom about this visit. I do not wish to wound your feelings; but I am not sure that you know Tom as well as a father ought to know his only son. And there are times when a man must be more than a father, when he must be a tactful man of the world, and a psychologist."

Mr. Merriwether realized the force of this so clearly that he winced, but said nothing, since he could not admit such a thing aloud. The man proceeded coldly:

"If you are both an intelligent man and a loving father, you will promise what I ask—not for my sake, for yours. There are many things, Mr. E. H. Merriwether, that money does not cure, and that not even time can heal. Ask me nothing now; come here at eleven to-morrow morning, and in the mean time do not speak to Tom about himself—or your fears."

"If you were only not so—er—well, so damned mysterious—" And Mr. Merriwether forced himself to smile pleasantly.

"Ah—if!" exclaimed the man, nodding. "Do you promise?"

"Yes!" answered Mr. Merriwether.

He had made up his mind that Tom would not be abducted. As for worse things, if Tom had not already committed matrimony, he could not very well do it in his father's private office. It was wise to keep Tom virtually a prisoner without his knowledge. And parental opposition has so often served merely to add gasoline to the flame of love that one father would not even whisper his objections.

He bowed and left the room, angry that nothing had been accomplished, relieved that within twenty-four hours the matter would probably be settled, and not quite so confident of the power of money as he had been for many years.

CHEAP AT A MILLION

IX

Tom arrived at his home early enough to have his bath at the usual hour. Though he had never been asked to account for his movements, he nevertheless made it a point to breakfast with his father. He would do so to-day. There was no occasion to say he had been to Boston or that he had slept in a Pullman.

As a matter of fact, he had not slept well. The stateroom seemed full of those elusive flower-fragrances that always made him think of her, particularly sweet peas—a beautiful flower, and of such delicate colors, he now remembered, who had not thought of them for years. He really loved them, he now discovered. Their odor always tinged his thoughts with a vague spirit of romance; and this, in turn, in some subtle way, rendered him more susceptible to the lure of adventure. It almost made him feel like a boy.

For all the stimulating reaction of his cold plunge, Tom looked a trifle tired about the eyes at breakfast.

Mr. Merriwether looked at his son with eyes that also looked tired; said, "Good morning, Tom!" in his usual tone of voice, and hid behind his newspaper. Instead of reading about the absurd demands of the railroad workers all over the United States for higher wages, he was thinking that he had never allowed anybody to do his work for him, because he had always intended that Tom should succeed him. He had at one time fully intended to train Tom for the succession, to have him learn railroading from brakeman up.

Indeed, the boy after leaving college had seemed much taken with the idea and listened with interest to his father's talks about his plans and desires and hopes. But with the great boom, that wonderful era of amazing reorganizations and stupendous consolidations, the great little man had been swamped by the flood of gold that poured into Wall Street.

And gold, as usual, had been ruthless in its demands on the great little man's time. For years he had averaged a net personal profit of a million a month; but it was not that he wished to make more money. It was that his time no longer belonged to himself; it was not his family's, but his associates'—not his only son's, but his many syndicates'. And he had devoted himself to the welfare of his syndicates and had written a dazzling page in the annals of Wall Street.

But what about his son's present and the future of the Merriwether roads? If Tom died, the Merriwether dream would follow him, but that would be a natural death at the hands of God. If Tom lived and refused to be a Merriwether, the death of the Merriwether dreams would be by slow strangulation. In short, hell!

His promise to the brother of the woman who had a daughter that might prove to be the executioner of his dreams stared him in the face. The situation called for tact and skill and superhuman self-control. He liked to fight in the open; but this was not a battle for more millions; it involved more than the deglutition of a rival railroad.

McWayne had reported that Tom had acted like a lunatic when he could not secure the room in the Hotel Lorraine that had been engaged by Mrs. Calderon and daughter. The only ray of light was that Tom had not talked to the ladies.

"Tom," asked Mr. Merriwether, casually, "have you anything on special for this morning?"

Tom had in mind a visit to 777 Fifth Avenue, at which he promised himself to end the affair; but he answered:

"N-no."

"I mean," said the father, speaking even more casually, because he noted the hesitancy, "anything that could not be done just as well in the afternoon."

"Oh no, I have nothing special; in fact, nothing at all," said Tom.

Mr. Merriwether saw in his reply merely Tom's way of not declaring his intention to see the girl.

"Then I wish you would come down-town with me. I have some papers I want you to look over, and we'll have luncheon together. What do you say?"

A prisoner accused of murder in the first degree does not listen to the jury's verdict with more interest than E. H. Merriwether waited for Tom's reply, for at this crisis he realized that he had not been in his son's confidence in those other important little crises of boyhood that breed in sons the habit of confiding in fathers.

"Sure thing!" said Tom, cheerfully.

Though thus relieved of some of his fears, there remained with E. H. Merriwether the determination that Tom had not volunteered any information. The little czar of the Pacific & Southwestern was so intelligent that in general he was fundamentally just. He did not exactly blame Tom for not confiding in him, but, also, he did not blame himself. And this was because he had habituated himself to paying for his mistakes in dollars. What could not be paid off in dollars was never a mistake, though it might well be a misfortune.

They went down-town together. Mr. Merriwether took Tom into one of his half-dozen private offices, made him sit down in one of those over-comfortable arm-chairs that you paradoxically find in busy Wall Street offices, and said to him very seriously:

"My son, here is the history of the Pacific & Southwestern system from its very start. It goes back to the early stage-line days and is brought up to to-day. I had it prepared in anticipation of an ill-advised Congressional investigation. I have thus far succeeded in staving off the investigation, not because I was afraid of it or because it might hurt me, but because the market was in bad shape to stand the alarmist rumors and canards and threats that always go with such affairs. Other people would have quite unnecessarily lost money. As soon as the investigation cannot be used as a bear club I'll let up opposing it. I'll even help it." He paused and gave to Tom a book bound in limp black morroco. "I want you to read this book because it is written with complete frankness in order to spike certain political guns. You will get in it the full story of what has been done and what we hope still to be allowed to accomplish. When you get through with it you'll know as much about the system as I do!"

The old man had spoken quietly and impressively. Tom was so pleased at having something to occupy his mind and keep it from dwelling on the girl he had never seen and the exasperating scoundrel at 777 Fifth Avenue that his face lighted up with joy.

"You could not have given me anything to do that I'd like better, dad!" he said, with such obviously sincere enthusiasm that Mr. Merriwether felt profoundly grateful for this blessing.

Then came the inevitable reaction and with it the thought: "Have I gained a successor only to lose him to some—"

He shook his head, clenched his jaws, and looked at his watch. It was not yet time to go to fight for the possession of his son. He had much to do before he left his office to go to 777 Fifth Avenue.

"Tom," he said, "you stay here until I return—will you?"

"You bet!" smiled Tom, looking at the thickness of the system's history.

"I have a meeting or two before luncheon, but I'll try not to let them interfere."

"Any time before three, boss," said his son, cheerfully.

His heir and successor, but, above all and everything, his son! There was no sacrifice he would not make for this boy to keep him from blighting his own career—and his father's hopes, he added, with the selfishness of real love.

Knowing that Tom was safely imprisoned and could not marry at least for a few hours, he was able to concentrate his mind on his railroad's affairs. He disposed of the more urgent matters. At ten-forty he sent for McWayne.

"I'm going to 777 Fifth Avenue."

"Again?" inadvertently said the private secretary.

Mr. Merriwether looked at him.

McWayne went on to explain: "I've had a man

watching it since we found Tom called there, just before going to Boston."

"Right! I expect to be back in time to lunch with Tom; but if I should be delayed—" He paused.

"Yes, sir?"

"—delayed beyond one o'clock have luncheon brought from the Meridian Club and tell Tom I wish him to stay until I return. This is important."

"Yes, sir."

"I think that is all."

"If no word is received from you by—" McWayne paused.

Mr. Merriwether finished. "By two o'clock, come after me. But always remember the newspapers!"

"Yes, sir."

"I'll telephone before two in case I expect to stay beyond that hour."

"Very well, sir."

E. H. Merriwether put on his hat, familiar to the world through the newspaper caricaturists—and walked toward the door. Then he did what he never before had done—he repeated an order! He said to McWayne, "Look after Tom!"

"Yes, sir."

Then he went to 777 Fifth Avenue to learn whether Tom was to be his pride and successor or his sorrow and dream-slayer.

X

E. H. Merriwether drove to the house of mystery in his motor, told the chauffeur to wait, and rang the bell. One of the over-intelligent-looking footmen opened the door.

CHEAP AT A MILLION

"I wish to see Mr.—whoever is master in this house."

"Yes, sir!"

The footman led the way. At the door of the library he knocked twice, sharply, then, after a pause, once, and then twice again. He waited; and presently, having evidently heard some answer not audible to the financier, he opened the door and announced:

"Mr. E. H. Merriwether!"

Why had there been any necessity for signals? Why such cheap theatrical claptrap? To make him think things? These questions in Mr. Merriwether's mind showed that the mysterious master of the house knew the advantage of suggesting the important sense of difference.

"Good morning, sir."

"Good morning," answered E. H. Merriwether, and looked about the room.

No girl!

It began to irritate him. The man intensified the feeling by speaking very deliberately, as one to whom time is no object:

"Will you not be seated, Mr. Merriwether?"

"I am a very busy man," began the autocrat of fifteen thousand miles of railroad.

"Sit down, anyhow," imperturbably suggested the man.

The autocrat sat down. He said, "But please understand that."

"I won't keep you any longer because you are sitting. Shall we get down to business?"

"Yes."

" Mr. Merriwether" — the man spoke almost

dreamily —"do you know why I asked you to call to-day at eleven?"

"No."

"Because when you were here yesterday it was after banking hours."

"And?" The little czar was in a hurry to finish.

"You, Mr. Merriwether, are one of those fortunate mortals about whom the newspapers do not lie."

"Oh, am I? I take it you haven't seen a newspaper in twelve years." Mr. Merriwether, after all, was an American. His sense of humor helped to make him great.

"I've read every line that has ever been printed about you—I had to, in order to study you exhaustively. I find that you are acknowledged by both friends and foes to be an intelligent man."

"Oh yes!"

"A very intelligent man," continued the man.

"And therefore?" said the very intelligent man.

"And, therefore, I now ask you to give me one million dollars."

Mr. E. H. Merriwether never so much as batted an eyelid. He kept his eyes fixed on the stranger's eyes. He repeated, a trifle impatiently:

"And?"

"A certified check will do."

"Come to the point. I am a busy man," said Mr. Merriwether.

The man looked at the little financier admiringly. Then he said, "You mean you wish to know why you should give the million, or what you will get for it?"

"Either! Both!"

"You should give it because it is I who ask it.

CHEAP AT A MILLION

You will get for it what is very, very cheap at a million."

"My dear sir, we'd do business quicker if you'd play show-down."

Now that it was a matter of money, of paying, of trading, Tom's father felt a great sense of relief. Still, there was Tom's unhappiness to consider. Poor boy!

"I want you to give me a million so that in return I may give you a daughter-in-law."

"You mean you will not give me a daughter-in-law if I give you a million, don't you?"

"I am in the habit of meaning what I say. The sooner you learn that, the quicker we'll close the deal. I mean that for a million dollars I'll give you a daughter-in-law."

Mr. Merriwether shook his head. It was plainly to be seen on his face that every moment spent in this room was a sad waste of time.

"Isn't it worth a million to you?" asked the man, as if he knew it was.

Mr. Merriwether proceeded to look as though it were worth even less than a Santo Domingo mining concession. Then he said, with finality:

"No."

The man rose.

"Then," he spoke indifferently, "come back when it is. I'll ask you to excuse me. I, also, am a busy man. Good day, sir."

Mr. Merriwether rose and bowed. He looked straight into the man's very shrewd eyes, smiled very slightly—and sat down again.

"Do you mean," he asked, very pleasantly, for his bluff had been called, "Miss Calderon?"

The man sat down.

"Oh no!" he answered, unsmilingly.

"No? Then?" Mr. Merriwether was so surprised that he forgot not to show it.

"I am sorry you are a busy man, because what I have to say can not be hurried. First, you must chase from your mind all thoughts of Wall Street, high finance, railroad systems — and fill it with love!"

Mr. Merriwether looked alarmed. Would it all end with a Biblical text and an exhortation to endow some sort of a Home?

"You can do this," pursued the man, imperturbably, "by thinking of your son Tom. He is your only son. You should love him. Once your mind is attuned to thoughts of love, you will be able to understand me more easily. Concentrate on love!"

The man leaned back in his chair as though he were certain the attuning process would consume an hour, this being, alas! a Wall Street man; but Merriwether said, very promptly:

"I am ready for chapter two."

"I doubt it. Love! The love of father for son, of son for mother, of son for wife, of son for father!"

"I understand. My mind works quickly. Go on!"

"Do you by any chance happen to know that your son is in love?"

"Yes. Where is the girl?"

"It isn't the girl. It's just girl."

"Oh, hell! Quit vaudevilling!"

"There is no girl who is the girl. There never was. There doesn't have to be any!"

Quite obviously this man was a lunatic—with the eyes of a particularly sane person. If there was no girl Tom was in no danger of marriage. A million for not marrying an undesirable person, yes, but a million for a daughter-in-law, when Tom was not in love!

"Only," thought Mr. Merriwether, "in case I have the selecting of her! And if I pick her I don't have to pay."

"And yet," said the man, musingly, "Tom loves her!"

Mr. Merriwether's perplexity was fast rising to the dignity of anger.

"If there had been a girl of Tom's own class," the man went on, as if talking to himself, "why shouldn't he have been seen in public with her?" Mr. Merriwether was listening now with his soul. "And if this girl were of the other class—that financial geniuses, alas! sometimes have to accept for daughters-in-law—a nice, vivacious chorus-lady, or a refined Reno graduate, or worse—she would have insisted on being seen in public with Tom, to show her power and to raise the paternal bid-price for a trip to Europe—alone!"

The man ceased to speak and began to nod his head slowly, his gaze on the rug at his feet. Mr. Merriwether could stand it no longer.

"If there is no girl, what in blazes do I get for my million?"

"Your pick of eight."

"Eight what?"

"Eight perfect daughters-in-law!"

A thought shot through Mr. Merriwether's mind: Was any form of insanity contagious? He looked at the lunatic. The eyes were sane, cold, shrewd, mind-reading eyes full of a sardonic humor.

"They are all," added the man, as if he wished to dispel unworthy suspicion, "in love."

"With Tom?"

"With love—like Tom!"

"With love—like Tom!" helplessly repeated Mr. E. H. Merriwether.

"Your mind"—the man spoke very slowly and distinctly, as if he wished to deprive Mr. Merriwether of every excuse for not understanding him—"does not seem to be working this morning with its usual efficiency!"

"No!" admitted Mr. Merriwether, sadly. "If you'd only use words of one syllable I think I could follow you better."

"It isn't that. It is that your mind was not attuned in the beginning to the thought of love, and, therefore, could not follow my words. You compel me to spend time in explaining the obvious. Listen! If you wish Tom to become the heir to your name, to your railroad, to your work, and to all the dreams you have dreamed about your work and about your son; if you want him to be your successor, to continue your work, to perpetuate the name and influence of Merriwether in his country—I say, if you wish all this, he must do one thing, and you must see that he does it. And that one thing, Mr. Merriwether, is for him to marry wisely. Do you get that?"

"Yes," answered Mr. Merriwether, very simply.

"If he doesn't, it will be death to your hopes, a tragic break in the Merriwether succession. No, don't shake your head. Admit it. Face it frankly. I know it. I know that you also know it. Can you expect me to believe that you want Tom to be the fool husband of a fool girl whose influence on him—"

"Tom isn't that kind," interrupted E. H. Merriwether.

"All men are that kind. Does history record the case of a man, greater even than E. H. Merriwether, who, when it came to women, was an utter ass? Yes, of a thousand; in fact, the stronger the man, the weaker she makes him—the better his brain, the worse his folly. And the cure? When an intelligent man realizes that he is a hopeless ass over one woman he realizes that his only escape is by the suicide route. No! It's much cheaper for you to pay the million. Oblige me by thinking. Isn't it cheaper to pay a million?"

He held up a silencing hand, as though he wished Mr. Merriwether to spend a full hour thinking of the bargain he was getting. Mr. Merriwether thought— quickly and accurately as was his wont. And he admitted to himself that it was indeed cheap at a million. But there must be value received. Promises, however plausible, are no more to be capitalized blindly than threats. It depends on who promises, and why; and also on what is promised. He thought of offering a smaller sum and of going through the usual preliminaries of a trade, but decided to be frank.

"If you can deliver the goods, I'll pay the million." And, after a pause, he added, "Gladly!"

"I banked on that when I decided you ought to contribute a million to our fund," said the man, simply. "I studied you and your fortune and your vulnerability, and I decided to attack *via* Tom. This was easier and cheaper than a stock-market campaign."

The man somehow looked as though he had said all that was necessary; but Mr. Merriwether reminded him:

"You must prove your ability to deliver the goods."

"I thought"—the man seemed mildly surprised—"we had."

"Certainly not. The million hasn't stirred."

"You are a brave man, Mr. Merriwether."

Mr. Merriwether laughed, and said:

"What should I fear? People don't murder a man like me and get away with it—not when the motive is money. Political assassination, perhaps; but not for a few dollars—especially when my heirs would spend millions to see that justice did not miscarry." He shook his head, smilingly.

"My dear sir, when we decided to go into the gold-mining business—"

"Gold-mining business!"

"Exactly! We thought to save time and effort by getting our gold already coined. Our general staff studied various methods—the ticker, for instance, and legislative attacks on your roads; but we went back to Tom. It is, of course, nearly as stupid to overestimate as to underestimate one's opponent; so, while we provided against every contingency arising from your undoubted possession of a resourceful and fearless mind, we also thought—please take note—that you might display stupidity; and we prepared for it. Such as, for instance, in case you point-blank said No! We have also provided ways of preventing you and your uncaptured millions from hurting us. Of course we could make the stock-market pay us for the trouble of kidnapping you or of murdering you. Don't you see clearly what you would do if you were in my place?"

"Oh yes—I see it clearly; but I don't believe you could do what I could in your place?"

"Nobody is free from vanity, for everybody seems to be a natural monopolist when it comes to brains. You are kidnapped at this very moment, aren't you?"

"People know I am here—"

"Oh yes! We expect to have you telephone McWayne presently not to expect you to lunch, and that we have extended every facility to his detectives for having this house under surveillance. We kidnapped the great Garrettson and kept him out of reach of the great world of finance long enough to enable us to cash in. Not only that, but he never told how we did it. You remember when Steel broke to—"

"You didn't do that!" exclaimed E. H. Merriwether.

"Oh yes, we did; and I'll tell you how." And the man briefly outlined the case for him.

E. H. Merriwether listened with much interest. When the man made an end of speaking, the financier shook his head skeptically, which made the man ask:

"You don't believe it?"

"No!" answered Mr. Merriwether.

"Nevertheless, it is so. We also might have engineered in your case some deal such as that by which we compelled Ashton Welles to disgorge some of the money he had no business to have." And he proceeded to enlighten the financier.

"Very clever!" said Mr. Merriwether.

"Rather neat!" modestly acquiesced the man. "Suppose we had decided to kidnap you? The first thing to do is to get you here. Well, you are here."

"How will you make money by that?" asked the financier, smiling.

"We don't expect to. We have not planned to make money by kidnapping you. Nevertheless, you must admit it can be made a very expensive matter for you. But please let me kidnap you without interruption!"

"I beg your pardon!" said Mr. Merriwether, gravely.

It struck him that the possession of a sense of humor makes a crook ten times more dangerous. It was what made the reporter, Tully, really formidable.

"We assume that you foresaw the danger to yourself in coming alone to this house. You'd employ private detectives to watch it at ten dollars a day a man, exactly as you have had your son watched the moment we decided it was time for you to begin the watching. McWayne, your efficient private secretary, is ready to move to your rescue. I don't see what else you could have done to protect yourself that we have not provided for."

"The police!" mildly suggested Mr. Merriwether.

"And the reporters!" mocked the man. "Pshaw! We know what we are doing. Why, we have rehearsed your kidnapping and even your death. Our ablest members have in turn impersonated you — put themselves in your place and fought us. I will not bore you with more details, and I admit that the human mind cannot foresee accidents; but we have studied how your mind would work. Suppose you assume that you are kidnapped and beyond the possibility of help from your friends. Shall I tell you what we have done to make Tom marry one of our eight desirable candidates?"

"If you still wish that million."

"Having decided to attack through Tom, we studied him and his ancestry on both sides. We easily learned that he had never had a serious love-affair, and that he was imaginative and adventurous, like yourself. There were many young women who would have liked to become your daughter-in-law—too many. That was Tom's trouble. But our problem was really ma⁻e easier by that. We simply had to turn his thoughts to love and to one girl. We therefore did."

"How?"

"We got him here. I piqued his curiosity and made the affair an extraordinary one by saying all we wished him to do was to answer one question. As we had rather expected, he would not come; but, of course, we had foreseen that, and so we got him here in one of our own taxicabs."

"How?"

"We telephoned him that the doctor said he should come instantly, and that you were not really in danger. We don't believe in lies; but we took pains that no other cab should be in front of the club when we telephoned him from the corner drug-store. Attention to details, my dear sir, always brings home the bacon. Having roused the spirit of adventure in a remarkable way, I then asked him the great question. What do you think it was?"

Tom's father shook his head.

"It was this: Where did you spend your summer at the end of your freshman year? He told me.

THE PLUNDERERS

Then I gave him a box made to order for me by a French expert, which would deceive other experts so long as we did not try to sell it. Anybody can imitate the goldwork of any period. In all the museums of the world you will find fakes. Attention to details! I was prepared to have him show that box to local experts. I assumed he would do so, being a Merriwether and, therefore, intelligently curious."

"Box with what?" asked Mr. Merriwether, also intelligently curious.

"Wait! When your son told me where he spent his summer at the end of his freshman year I knew he was then about nineteen—too young to think of marriage, but old enough to think of love. He had for the first time in his life been free from home influences and direct parental supervision. He was bound to regard himself as a man of the world and think of innocent flirtations as a manly art. Being in that frame of mind, and at the same time being a nice, rich, good-looking chap, all the girls would naturally make a dead set for him. Their numbers would keep him from having one love-affair. All love-affairs at twenty are much the same. A boy always begins by being in love with love. Indeed, I believe twenty-year love to be exclusively a literary passion—that is, boys get it from reading about it. Of course I studied time, period, locality, and manifold probabilities; and, therefore, I sent him on a mission that suggested love—love for the one girl that Fate intended him to love and to marry. In order to fix, accentuate, and accelerate his love-thinking I used the perfume of sweet peas."

"How does that work?"

CHEAP AT A MILLION

"I picked out sweet peas because they are found everywhere. Their odor is strong and characteristic. He must have inhaled that odor thousands of times when he was flirting with pretty girls the summer he spent at Oleander Point with Dr. Bonner."

"Yes; but about suggesting—"

"I advise you to read up on the psychology of odor associations. You will learn that there is a very close relation between the olfactory sense and the desire to love. Oliver Wendell Holmes declared that memory, imagination, old sentiments, and associations are more readily reached through the sense of smell than by almost any other channel; and, also, that 'olfactory impressions tend to be associated with a sum-total of feeling-tone.' This has been known for thousands of years. A very interesting paper was written by Mackenzie, of Johns Hopkins. If you read it you will know more than I can now take the time to tell you. The Orient understands the value of perfumes in lovemaking, and I could tell you amazing things; but I will refer you to Cabanis, Dadisett, Hobbes, Jaworski, Iwanicki, Schiff, Wolff, and Zwaardemaker. If you wish, my secretary will prepare an exhaustive bibliography of the subject for you."

"No, thanks," said Mr. Merriwether. "But I still don't understand—"

The man sighed. Then he said, "I'll tell you, of course." He then told Tom's father about the message in the dark that Tom had carried.

"But he couldn't believe it!" exclaimed Mr. Merriwether.

"No; he couldn't—but he did. Of course I have taken you behind the scenes—that is, I have opened your eyes and turned your head in the proper direction and held it firmly there and shouted, 'Look!' And of course you see the machinery standing still and you can't imagine it in motion. You are not as imaginative as I thought you were."

"Huh!" said E. H. Merriwether, thoughtfully. Then after a pause he said: "I see the wheels revolving. Ingenious!"

"More than that, practical! My object in having Tom fall in love with love, suggesting that there was one girl born to be his bride, accentuated by my use of the sweet-peas odor as a *leit-motif*, was to have something to offer you which would be cheap at a million. The next step was to make Tom do foolish things—for effect on you. First, to make you fear Tom was crazy. I had a girl who knew young Waters talk to him about Tom's new and alarming queerness and suggest that he telephone to Mr. E. H. Merriwether. Of course Waters wouldn't telephone—and of course I did. And, of course, if you had disbelieved or suspected you would have sent for young Mr. Waters and he would have denied the telephone, but admitted the queer actions of Tom and the fact that people were talking about them. That would have allayed any suspicion you might have entertained. So I stage-managed the opera scene and the Boston trip to make you fear the worst. In that frame of mind you could be induced to come here voluntarily. I sent Tully to you. You had to come!"

"Very clever!" said Mr. Merriwether, with a thoughtful absence of enthusiasm.

"Therefore," continued the man as if he had not heard the other's interpolation, "your son, being full of the thought of love and, even worse, of marrying the mate that Fate selected for him five million years ago, is now ready to marry any girl that smells of sweet peas. We thought that, instead of vulgarly extracting the million from you by torture or threats, we would place you in our debt by perpetuating the Merriwether dynasty. Hence the preparation of eight very nice girls—three of them in your own set, three others children of people you know, and the remaining two equally desirable but less historical, as it were."

"Who are they?" If Mr. Merriwether was to pay a million he might as well see the label.

"Cynthia, Agnes, and Isabel, daughters respectively of Gordon Hammersly, William Murray, and Vanderpoel Woodford. Any objections?"

"No; but you can't—"

"Yes, I can. Also, Louise Emlen, daughter of Marbury Emlen, the lawyer—"

"He's a crook!" interrupted Mr. Merriwether.

"He doubtless interfered with one of your deals; I see you respect him. He's a crank, but she is a brick. And a Miss Lythgoe, daughter of Professor Lythgoe, of Columbia, the most beautiful girl in New York. Ramona Ogden; her father is Dr. Ogden, the lung specialist; her mother was a Jewess. The remaining two are of humble birth. But all of them are healthy and beautiful, plenty of honesty, brains, and, above all, imagination. Any one of them will not only make Tom happy, but will make him a worthy successor of a great man. And such grandchildren as they will give you! I envy you!"

The man spoke with such fervent sincerity that E. H. Merriwether merely said:

"It is a risky business, even though the chances appear to be—"

"That's why we ask one million dollars—because we have eliminated the risk. Very cheap. Are you ready?"

"Yes," said Mr. Merriwether, grimly.

"Then, will you kindly—"

"Yes; I will kindly tell you that you are a damned fool! You've wasted my time. I'm going to my office, and if I don't have you put in jail it will be because I don't want the publicity. But don't push me too far or I'll do it anyhow!" And Mr. E. H. Merriwether rose.

"Sit down!" said the man, with a pleasant smile.

"Go to hell!" snarled the czar of the Pacific & Southwestern, and looked at the man with the eyes that Sam Sharpe once said reminded him of a mink's when it kills for the sheer love of killing.

For all reply the man clapped his hands sharply twice. Four men—the over-intelligent-looking footmen—came from behind the heavy plush portières. Also, the ascetic-looking man who had held the glass of acid in the taxicab and had brought Tom into the house the first time. The ascetic-looking man held a cornet to his lips, and his lungs were filled with still unblown blasts.

"Three weeks ago, Mr. Merriwether," explained the mysterious master of the house, "this worthy artist began to practise on his beautiful instrument at exactly this time every morning. This was in anticipation of the morning when you should be here—the idea being to drown your cries. The neighbors have complained and I have promised to play pianissimo; but a few loud blasts, which will do the trick, will be forgiven. Attention to details, Mr. Merriwether! Ready!"

The cornetist inflated his lungs and held the cornet to his lips in readiness. The footmen seized Mr. Merriwether by the arms and legs, one man to each limb.

"Doctor!" called the master.

A sixth man came from behind the portières. He had some tin cans in his hand—plainly labeled ether —and also a cylinder of compressed laughing-gas and an inhaler.

"Expert! Anesthetics!" said the man, curtly, to Mr. Merriwether. "We propose to take you out of this house if we kidnap you. If we decide to kill you we have arranged to do it right here at home. I think we'll kidnap you. A week or two will make you amenable to reason. We realize, of course, that every day you spend under our hospitable roof will make it a little bit more difficult to get the million into our clutches. Would you like to know how we propose to kidnap you and get away with it?"

"Yes," replied Mr. E. H. Merriwether, with a pleasant smile.

"Tell our Mr. E. H. Merriwether to come in," said the man to the cornetist, who thereupon disappeared and presently returned, followed by a man made up to resemble the great financier.

The task was rendered easy by the famous flat-brimmed hat, with the crown like a truncated cone, so familiar to newspaper-readers through the cartoonists' efforts. The resemblance was not striking enough to deceive at close range, but it probably would work at a distance.

"Walk like him!" commanded the master.

The fake Mr. Merriwether walked up and down

the room with the curious swaggering, jockey-like jauntiness of the little railroad man. From time to time he snapped his fingers impatiently in the same characteristic way Mr. E. H. Merriwether almost always used when giving an order to subordinates.

"That will do!" said the man, with a broad grin at the impersonator of the little financial giant. The double left the room—still walking à la E. H. M.

"I have had that man—an actor of about your build with a gift of mimicry—coached for weeks to imitate you. We told him it was a joke and guaranteed him an appearance before the most select audience in New York at one of Mrs. Garrettson's world-famous functions. We pledged him to a secrecy so natural, under the circumstances, as to rouse no suspicions. A few minutes ago we sent a footman to tell your chauffeur to go away and return at one. He wouldn't do it. The footman said the boss said so. Your man retorted that he took orders from only the boss himself—especially when countermanding previous orders.

"So our Mr. Merriwether went out to the front door, yelled 'One!' in your voice, and snapped his finger at the intelligent chauffeur, who thereupon beat it. But the sleuth remains. It makes us laugh! But, after all, since we have provided for him, it would be a pity not to go through the entire program. Does this bore you?"

"Must I tell the truth?" asked Mr. Merriwether, anxiously.

"Yes."

"I can stand more." In point of fact, Mr. Merriwether was sure the situation was serious for him. That is why he joked about it.

CHEAP AT A MILLION

"Over six months ago we opened an antique-shop on Fourth Avenue. We had the usual truck. Also we have had this antique-dealer—who is your humble servant—go from house to house on the Avenue offering to buy or exchange those antiques of which people have grown tired. We even asked you. We have offered such good prices and such excellent swaps that we have taken antiques from some of the wealthiest houses on the Avenue. Also we have made a practice of importing antiques from Europe, which we auction off every two weeks. The money we get we deposit in various banks, and then we buy bills on Paris. The banks now know us. Remember that—it is important. Well, we also have an exact copy of your motor, even to the initials in the door panels. Pretty soon we send for our Merriwether motor and our E. H. Merriwether emerges from this house and gets into his car and off he goes—and the watching sleuth with him."

"But if there should be two, and one stay?"

"Then number two will see not long afterward an elaborately carved Gothic chest taken from here into the antique-dealer's wagon—a wagon now known to the traffic squad. We carry you away and lock you in a small sound-proof room, to get to which people would have to move out of the way a lot of heavy pieces of furniture. There is no question of our ability to kidnap you and to keep you a prisoner. I tell you we have paid attention to details persistently and intelligently. Meantime what does Sam Sharpe do to the stock-market? And Northrup Ashe? How much will a month's absence from your office cost you?"

"Not half as much as it will cost you when I get out."

"And if you don't get out?"

For reply Mr. E. H. Merriwether grinned broadly.

"My dear Mr. Merriwether"—the man spoke very seriously now—"we had not really expected such unintelligent skepticism from you; but, as we prepared for everything, we, of course, prepared for even crass stupidity on your part. In demonstrating our power to do what I say some painful moments will be your portion. This I regret more than I can say. Just now our problem is to prove our complete physical control of you and also our utter indifference to your feelings. I am going to do what will make you hate me to the murder point. In deliberately making a violent enemy of a man like you we pay ourselves the compliment of thinking ourselves absolutely fearless. I propose to have you spanked—to whip you as if you were a bad little boy. We shall at first use a shingle on you—undraped. You may begin when ready, James."

"Sir," said one of the footmen, very respectfully, to Mr. E. H. Merriwether, "will you kindly take off your coat and waistcoat, preliminary to the removal of your trousers?"

Mr. E. H. Merriwether tried to smile, but desisted when he saw that the men's faces had taken on a grim look—as if they knew that after the whipping it would be a fight to the death. They somehow conveyed an impression that, though they would not stop at murder, they nevertheless appreciated the gravity of the offense.

"We know," said the master, solemnly, "that for every blister we raise you will gladly spend a million to clap us into jail. Do you really wish to be spanked and to hate us for it for the rest of your life?"

"No."

"The alternative is the million—or death."

"You can't kill me and get away with it."

"Oh yes—even easier than kidnapping. I'll show you how we'll do it." He rose and took from one of the drawers of the table a small, morocco-covered medicine-case, opened it, and showed Mr. Merriwether a lot of small tubes tightly stoppered. "Cultures!" explained the man — "typhoid; bubonic plague; anthrax; *Bacillus mallei*—that's glanders—meningitis; Asiatic cholera; and others. This, for instance—number thirteen—is the virus of tetanus. Inoculation with an ordinary culture would take days; but with this virus it will take hours. What a wonderful thing science is! You know what tetanus is?"

"Yes," answered Mr. Merriwether, calmly, "lock-jaw."

"Exactly! Well, this will lock your jaws, and all your millions won't be able to pry them open for you, and all the antitoxin injections won't help you. You will have your consciousness almost to the last—and you will not make yourself understood. The *risus sardonicus*, which is a most unpleasant sort of grin resulting from your inability to smile naturally, will linger in the memory of Tom to his death. You really ought to have a moving-picture film of your last hours taken as a warning to those stupid millionaires whose plunder we would recover. And, of course, I have here seven poisons, of which prussic acid is the mildest and slowest. Will you please assume the fact of your death?"

THE PLUNDERERS

"I'll do that much to please you," said Mr. Merriwether. He still believed that murder would not be profitable to these men and hence did not believe they would go that far.

"Would you like to know how we propose to dispose of the body?"

"I might as well see everything," he answered, in a resigned tone of voice. The man looked at him admiringly, and said:

"Come on!"

They led the great E. H. Merriwether to the cellar. There he saw that the furnace coal had been taken out of its bin and put in the adjoining compartment. The plank floor had been taken up, and what looked like a short trench—or a grave—had been dug. Outside stood a pile of crushed stone, some bags of cement, some bundles of steel rods, a section of five-inch iron soilpipe with a mushroom-head trap at one end, and concrete-workers' tools.

"After we make absolutely sure that you are dead we throw a lot of soft mortar into the grave, deposit the corpse, and then pour in more cement—so that you will be completely surrounded by it. It will make it very difficult indeed to recognize you when they try to chip away the hard cement—if they ever try! Then we fill the grave up to the top with concrete, using plenty of steel rods—not to re-enforce the concrete at all, but to make it very hard digging with a pick.

"We also stick the soilpipe into the—er—cavity in order to account for the disturbed pavement. Intelligent searchers—your son and his detectives—will assume it is plumbing—and seek no further. We replace the plank flooring in the bin and fill it

up with coal, thereby further obliterating all traces
of your grave.

"We have provided for that part, you see. Why,
my dear Mr. Merriwether, what we really do to you
is confer immortality on you. We elevate you to
the rank of one of the mysteries. Charlie Ross and
E. H. Merriwether! Just assume that we'll do what
I say. Very well! Now, visualize the search made
for you. Endow your people with superhuman ingenuity. Useless!"

The man waved a hand toward Mr. Merriwether;
but Mr. Merriwether said:

"You assume that the search will be exclusively
for me—but they will also search for you!"

"My dear sir, that is unkind of you!" The man
spoke reproachfully. "We know that when we go
into the plunder-recovery business we must guard
against the chief contributory cause of the vast ma-
jority of all business failures, according to the statistics of Dun and Bradstreet—to wit, insufficient
capital. Murderers are caught when their faces and
habits and families are known. Usually their lack
of means forces them to betray themselves. But nobody knows how the men who will kill E. H. Merriwether look, simply because we have enough money
to go anywhere. We will become tourists—like
thousands of others. Some of us will stay in New
York; others will go on round-the-world tours.
See this?"

The man pulled from his pocket some packages of
well-worn bills, with the bank-wrappers round them,
though a finger hid the bank name. Also the man
showed to Mr. Merriwether several books of travelers' checks of the fifty-dollar denomination—the

specimen signature also being covered by the man's finger.

"Enough for all," said the man. "Kindly oblige me by thinking of what you would do in my place; and, in all frankness, acknowledge that nothing would be easier than to get away. Ordinary crime is so largely accidental that the average criminal is at the mercy of even the unintelligent police. Professionals do the same thing over and over and acquire telltale mannerisms. Also, they lack culture, and find the class attraction too strong to resist—besides always being hard up and therefore defenseless. Whenever you find a crook who is thrifty, you will find him always out of jail—like any other business man of equal thrift. We have gone about this case systematically. We wanted your million—but, more, we wanted the sport of taking it from a man who had no moral right to the particular million we desired. If you had been a really conscienceless financier we'd have made it five millions; in fact, it is because we are not sure that even this million is tainted that we ask you to pay it to us for giving you a fine daughter-in-law. Shall we go up-stairs?"

The master of the house led the way up-stairs and Mr. E. H. Merriwether, escorted by the stalwart footmen with the intelligent faces, followed, his own intelligent face impassive. That he was thinking meant only that he was doing what he always did.

The man sat down in his chair, with his back to the stained-glass window. He asked, pleasantly:

"What do you say now, Mr. Merriwether?"

"I say," the little czar answered, with a frown of impatience, or anger, or both, "that when you are

CHEAP AT A MILLION

tired of playing the damned fool I'd like to return to my business."

The man rose to his feet quickly, his face pale with anger. He took a step toward the financier, his fists clenched—and then suddenly controlled himself.

"You jackass!" he said. "You idiot! Have you no brains whatever? Must I lash common sense into you? Take 'em off!" It was a command to the footmen.

"Will you disrobe, sir?" very politely asked the oldest of them.

Mr. Merriwether, six inches shorter than the speaker, and a hundred pounds lighter, drew back his fist, but the four men seized him and began to take his clothes off. Mr. Merriwether, recognizing the uselessness of resistance and the folly of having garments torn so far from home, helped by unbuttoning here and there. Presently he stood *in puris naturalibus*. His face was pale and his jaw set tight.

"Tie him!" commanded the master.

They tied him to the library table, face down.

"Music!" cried the man; whereupon the cornetist began to play the Meditation from "Thaïs" softly, but obviously ready to play fortissimo at a signal from the chief.

"I am going to lick you with a whip; and, for every lash I give you, you will have to pay me one hundred thousand dollars in addition to the original million. Theatrical, is it?" And his voice was hoarse with anger. "Yes? Well, look at this melodramatic whip. Your tragedy will be my comedy, you —— —— jackass!"

He showed to Mr. E. H. Merriwether a quirt—a veritable miniature blacksnake of plaited leather.

"You can stand twenty; that will make three million in all. I'll draw blood after the fifth. I'll stop when you've got enough. Remember the price!"

He snapped the whip viciously and walked round the table until he stood behind Mr. Merriwether. He lifted his arm and then the great Merriwether, autocrat of fifteen thousand miles of railroad, iron-nerved, fearless, imaginative, and intelligent, yelled:

"Wait!"

"The million?"

"Yes!"

"Help him!" said the man; and the intelligent-looking footmen respectfully served as valets.

"I don't believe you would kill me—but I never liked spankings." Mr. Merriwether spoke jocularly —almost!

The man confronted Mr. Merriwether and said, very seriously:

"Mr. Merriwether, we should certainly have killed you if you had persisted in your stubbornness to the end. We knew we had to convince you."

The man looked inquiringly at the financier to see whether any doubt remained; but Mr. Merriwether asked, quizzically:

"Honest, now, would you—"

"We would!" interrupted the man, looking straight into Mr. Merriwether's eyes. And what Mr. Merriwether saw there made him ask:

"How will you have the million?"

"In cash. I'm glad you will make the payment. But really, sir, I wish to impress on you that Tom is ripe to be taken for better—or for worse."

Mr. E. H. Merriwether looked long and earnestly

into the eyes of the mysterious man who was despoiling him of a million dollars. It began to seep into his understanding that if Tom could be married to a nice girl the resulting peace of mind would indeed be cheap at a million.

"Now, if you please," pursued the man, pleasantly, "telephone to McWayne that you wish him to come here with certified checks on your different banks, aggregating one million dollars, made payable to Michael P. Mahaffy."

Mr. Merriwether started. The name was that of the world-famous political Boss of New York City. Explanations as to the million might be embarrassing to any political boss; but for a million dollars in cash any political boss would be glad to explain—or even not to explain.

"From this house Mr. McWayne will go to the banks, accompanied by the studious gentleman who had the honor of holding your left leg. You will indorse each check by writing 'indorsement correct' and signing your name. McWayne will go with our Mr. Michael P. Mahaffy and get the money in fives, tens, and twenties, in handy wads—old bills preferred and so requested from the paying tellers, who will intelligently understand that Mr. Mahaffy is not signing his name in person, so he can swear in any court of justice that he never saw the checks. Asking for old bills is to make them impossible to trace. This will also allay the banks' suspicions. The worst that can happen will be that a few tellers will wonder what Mr. Merriwether has to do with city politics that he needs Mahaffy's aid."

"I see!" said Mr. Merriwether, thoughtfully. Then, after a pause: "Where is the telephone?"

"There!"

In plain sight and hearing of the master of the house the master of the Pacific & Southwestern called up his own office. He spoke to McWayne:

"Make out checks on all banks according to my balances in them, so that the checks will aggregate one million dollars, payable to Michael P. Mahaffy. ...What? Yes?...Have the checks certified....Of course, if there isn't enough!...We shall want bills that have been used—fives, tens, and twenties...Yes, all cash. Come up to 777 Fifth Avenue. You will go to the banks with a man—"

"With Mr. Mahaffy," prompted the man.

"With Mr. Mahaffy," repeated Mr. Merriwether.

"And tell Tom to have luncheon and wait for me," again prompted the man.

"And tell Tom I can't go to luncheon with him, but to wait for me."

Mr. Merriwether hung up the receiver and turned to the man, saying:

"The idea of using Mahaffy's name—"

"Rather good, isn't it?" smiled the man. "Of course you wondered how we were going to cash the checks, didn't you? Well, that's the way. The bank officials will be surprised to see the checks and they will watch McWayne and my man to the last. They will thus be able to hear my man say loudly to the chauffeur, 'Tammany Hall, Charlie!' Attention to details, my dear sir!"

"I still am not quite convinced that—"

"My dear Mr. Merriwether, there are so many ways of safely getting money from you Wall Street magnates that the only thing that really protects you is the sad fact that the professional crooks are even more stupid than you. Men like you are compelled to bet your entire fortune, your very life, on averages. The average man is both stupid and honest; so you and your like are fairly safe for fairly long periods of time. Of course if we had been obliged to kill you we should have done so and buried you, and we should have been wise enough to utilize your death in as many ways as possible in the stock-market—and out of it. For instance, I should have instantly telephoned to all the men in your class and told them we had eliminated you— as an example—and to remember that in case we ever had occasion to ask anything from them. We should also give them a countersign, so that they would be able to recognize us when the proper time came. I can kidnap or permanently suppress any millionaire in New York, with neatness, despatch, and safety."

"But killing a well-known man—" began Mr. Merriwether.

"If Big Tim Sullivan could be killed and lie in the Morgue for days unrecognized, what chance do relatively unknown people like you great millionaires stand to be found, once dead? A dead capitalist, remember, is no more impressive than a dead street-car conductor. If I got you into this house on the strength of Tom, as I got Tom to come in on the strength of you, what millionaire would refuse, for example, to go, in answer to a telephone message that his child had been run over and was now, let us say, at 128 East Seventy-ninth Street? Or that his wife, acting more or less as if she were intoxicated, was scattering money at the corner of Seventh Avenue and Twenty-ninth Street? And suppose the million-

aire is bound and chloroformed, and taken to the top
floor of a tenement hired by a humpback with red
beard and one leg shorter than the other—same
humpback not being really a humpback or red-
bearded or a cripple, but a fake, to furnish false
clues in advance—and this humpback has previously
given fire-extinguishing hand-grenades to all the
other tenants, as advertisements! Then we have a
charge of dynamite inserted in the thoroughly prepared corpse of the millionaire—his face burned off in
advance—and he is also soaked in inflammable
material and set on fire. And the deed is done at
11 A.M.; so that all the children will be in school
and all the adults awake and able to get out. Find
you? Bits of flesh and sympathy for the poor humpback is all the police would find in that tenement.
Oh, sir, you were wise to pay—very wise indeed!"

Mr. Merriwether looked at the man a long time.
He could not deny that to really desperate men such
deeds offered no particular difficulty. The average
crook is not dangerous to a millionaire; but a man
like this is more than dangerous. He thought
quickly and formed his conclusions accurately.

"How are you going to make Tom marry one of
the girls whose names you mentioned?" he asked, in
the tone of voice one uses toward physicians.

The man smiled slightly and said: "Oh, I am not
going to do it. I don't care whether he marries or
not. You must do that. But I'll tell you how, if
you wish,—after McWayne gets here. Just think
over the affair. It will put you in a more intelligently receptive frame of mind." And with a
pleasant smile the man took a little book bound in
green leather and began to read.

CHEAP AT A MILLION

Mr. E. H. Merriwether, as was his wont when thinking, began at the beginning and reviewed the entire affair quickly but carefully. He did this again—it did not take him long—and then he began to co-ordinate his ideas and study the case. Within ten minutes he had forgotten his animosity. In fifteen he felt respect for this man. In twenty he was thinking how helpless any one man is against his ten billion trillion natural foes—microbes, seismic disturbances, floods, and the chemical reaction of hostile brains. This man, whose very name was unknown to him, had vanquished the victor—had looted the tent of the victorious general!

This was incredible when spoken in a conversational tone of voice. Perhaps this same remarkable man might tell how to make Tom choose a desirable wife. It was worth while making the experiment. It was in the nature of a gamble in which E. H. Merriwether stood to win a happiness worth all the money in the world and stood to lose nothing!

A knock at the door roused him from his reverie. One of the footmen arrived from the threshold.

"Mr. McWayne!"

Mr. Merriwether's private secretary entered. E. H. Merriwether held out his right hand.

Mr. McWayne took four slips of paper and gave them to his chief, who quickly looked at them and passed them over to the master of the house. The man looked at them, indorsed them, and handed a pen to Mr. Merriwether. The czar of the Pacific & Southwestern wrote on each of the checks:

> Indorsement correct.
>
> E. H. MERRIWETHER.

He returned the checks to the man, who thereupon pushed a button a number of times.

One of the footmen with the non-menial faces appeared dressed for the street. He looked Irish. He wore a big solitaire scarf-pin. His hat inclined to one side noticeably. He carried a square valise in each hand. They looked as if they had seen service. On each was printed, "Treasurer Tammany Hall."

"Go with Mr. McWayne to the banks and cash the checks. Mr. McWayne will identify you," said the master of the house.

"Yis, sor!" said the footman.

The brogue was unnecessary, but E. H. Merriwether smiled slightly. McWayne and the footman in mufti left together.

"Think some more!" said the man to E. H. Merriwether, and resumed his reading of the little green-leather book.

Mr. Merriwether leaned back and thought some more. To him the million-dollar loss was already ancient history. The only virtue that the Wall Street life gives to a professional is the ability to take a loss of money with more or less philosophy. That philosophy is also met on the race-track, and among experts in faro as well as among real Christians.

McWayne and the man were gone an hour and eighteen minutes. Mr. Merriwether had time to think of Tom and of himself and of the relation that had existed between himself and his son, and of the relations that would exist between them in the future —God willing.

"Mr. McWayne!" announced the servant.

CHEAP AT A MILLION

The private secretary entered; also the Irishman with the two valises.

"Tell the others! At five o'clock!" said the master of the house, and the footman left the room—with the valises!

"Mr. McWayne, will you kindly wait in the other room?" The man rose and parted the portières for the secretary to pass through.

"Certainly," said McWayne, frowning politely.

"Now, Mr. Merriwether," said the man, "as I told you, Tom's mind and soul are prepared for love. The romantic vein in him has been worked to the limit. He can be laughed out of it very easily, for he is not entirely convinced; but it is too valuable a frame of mind for a really intelligent father to destroy. The young ladies, also, are ripe for the coming of the one man in all the world. They will respond readily—and, I may add, respond with relief if they see he is a man like your son, against whom nothing can be said. It will clinch the affair. My advice is for you to call on the young ladies I have mentioned and judge for yourself, and then you be your own stage-manager!"

"Have you any choice yourself?"

"You know Woodford?"

"Very well."

"And his daughter Isabel?"

"No."

"Well, she has the complementary qualities. She will, as it were, complete Tom. She is bright, healthy, very handsome, utterly unspoiled by the knowledge of her good looks—that is, she is highly intelligent. Her mind functionates quickly and is regulated and made to work safely by her keen sense

331

of humor. You will love her for herself, as well as for Tom's sake and for Tom's children's sake. Arrange two things and you can do it. One is prepare her to meet Tom. Tell her you don't know why you want her to know him, but you do. Tell her you wanted this before you ever saw her. And tell her you know she must think you must be going crazy—but will she meet Tom in her father's home? —in some room with the lights turned out? She will ask you why you ask such things. And you will rub your hand across your eyes and say, dazed-like: 'I don't know! I don't know! Will—will you do it?' And when you take Tom to her, take advantage of the dark, and open this little bottle and touch Tom's lapel with this. It is essence of sweet peas. He will associate Isabel with the mysterious girl to whom he took a message in the dark, and by the same token she will know he is the man who destiny decrees shall be her husband. Then leave the rest to nature. They won't struggle. They couldn't if they wished; but they won't wish to fight. My parting words to you are: the man who was smart enough to get a million dollars out of you finds it even easier to make a young man who wants to love fall in love in the springtime with a handsome, healthy girl who wants to be loved. You and McWayne will now use one of my prisoner-carrying motors. This way, sir!"

He led the way into the next room, picked up McWayne, and escorted the financier and his private secretary to the curb. A neat little motor stood there.

Mr. Merriwether climbed in. McWayne followed. And then the man said:

CHEAP AT A MILLION

"You will find that the doors cannot be opened from the inside. The chauffeur was told this queer feature was due to the fact that his master expects to use this car for his two very active and very mischievous children. He will drive you anywhere. You can arrest him if you wish; but it will be useless. We have spent a good many thousands of dollars in accessories that will be thrown away to-day." And the man sighed.

"Who do you mean by we?" asked E. H. Merriwether, politely.

"The Plunder Recovery Syndicate, which, having completed its operations, will now dissolve. Good day, sir."

In the issue of the *World* of June 9th two advertisements appeared. One, under "Marriages," read:

MERRIWETHER–WOODFORD.—On June 8th, at the Church of St. Lawrence, by the Rev. Stephen Vincent Rood, Isabel Woodford to Thomas Thorne Merriwether.

The other, under "Personals," read:

P. R. SYNDICATE,—It was cheap at a million!

E. H. M.

On June 10th the great railroad financier received a typewritten letter. It read:

In the course of our operations, having for an object the recovery of plunder taken from unidentified individuals by malefactors of great wealth, it has happened that we have grown fond of some of our contributors. We thus are able most sincerely to extend to you our hearty congratulations. It was indeed cheap at a million, and we shall remember your good fortune if ever we need advice or additional funds. What we took from you and from some of your fellow New-Yorkers

THE PLUNDERERS

we propose to return to the public at large. Mr. Amos F. Kidder will tell you his suspicions, if you ask him. In return you might tell him that we propose to capitalize time. We shall make a present of fifty years to the world by transmuting the recovered plunder into unspent time. Don't forget that we who were the Plunder Recoverers are now

THE TIME GIVERS.

THE END